Eat More Bloody Meat Y'Bastards!

By

Mial Pagan

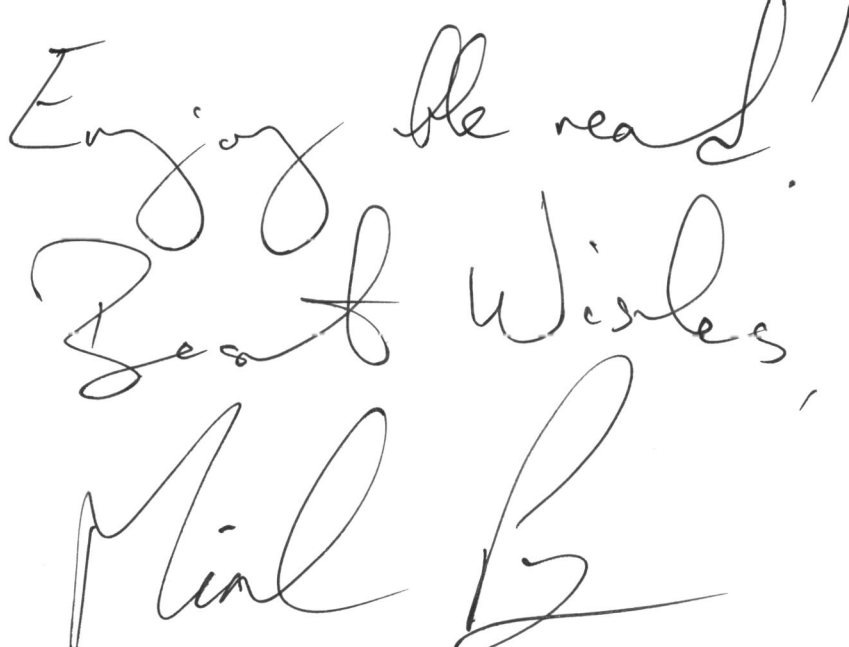

"Advertising is the rattling of a stick inside a swill bucket."
George Orwell

Dedication:

To Ali for her support and encouragement.

Chapter One.

Telephone Manners

This story starts probably in 2012, possibly in May but definitely after lunch because I, Denis Mahoney, am drunk. At the same time as being drunk I am also trying to have a phone conversation with my girlfriend Rach or, when her parents are around, Rachel. Despite a liberal attitude to everything else in life she has some moral objection to me drinking three pints at lunchtime. As far as I can remember, the call goes like this. Phone rings. I pick up and say, 'Denis Mahoney speaking.'

There is a pause at the other end. I say,

'Hi Rach! How are you? Angry? What about? Three pints, as usual. OK, three and a half. Yes, I found the sandwiches. That's the fourth time this week I've had tuna and sweetcorn. No I hate tuna and sweetcorn but the ducks love it. Yes, I cannot lie, I am drunk. No, I haven't got a drink problem it's just that it's the only way I can cope with this place. OK we'll talk later but I cannot guarantee I'll be any more sober. In fact I'm going out with the Freak and Bob for a couple of pints after work. I told you this morning. Of course you weren't listening – it's not a skill you possess. Yes, and you. OK, bye!'

I know that's only my side of the conversation but you've probably got the impression from it that our relationship was not in the best of health and you'd be right. In fact if our relationship were a person there would by now have been discreet calls to Dignitas or at least a move to intensive care. But there we are.

I am in an office, in that part of West London where the town planners gave up on creating something of lasting beauty long ago and resorted to architectural cretinism. I am lolling in a chair, in front of a computer screen, working off the effects of my three and a half pints of bitter consumed in The Ferret and Mattress. This was something we did quite a lot of at Buy-O-Soft Retail Systems, drinking beer then letting the effects gently wear off over the course of an afternoon although it wasn't in our job description. Indeed the company had the expectation that I would spend a reasonable amount of my time writing computer programs for them to keep the wheels of industry whizzing along as smoothly and effortlessly as possible. But the gap between what Buy-O-Soft wanted to pay and what Buy-O-Soft needed to pay to get someone who would embrace the job with enthusiasm was a wide one. Into this gap I had fallen and was now contentedly breathing beer fumes into the warm, soothing atmosphere of the open plan office.

I lay back for a moment in my chair to have a think about the stock control system on which I was supposed to be working and its many problems. In my mind I could see the lines of code whirling through the system's wires like I'd seen in an advert on television. Lines of whirling code suddenly disappeared and I sat bolt upright in astonishment as the door to my left opened and the attractive form of Sue Grant, senior programmer, appeared. It's not as though Sue wasn't allowed to appear through the door of her office or that it was particularly unusual. But this time I stared, almost unable to believe what I was seeing. I stared some more. Then a lot more, for Sue was completely naked and smiling at me. I looked round. There was no one else in the office. She came over and sat on the edge of my desk and began to stroke my leg with her long fingers. At one point in my life I had been predominantly Catholic and for Catholics guilt about sex and the desire for sex are found in more or less equal and conflicting measure. Paralysed with lust I gazed at her, tentatively stretching out my left hand to return her advances and fulfil a long held fantasy by cradling her right breast. As I moved forward to touch her, my knee crashed into the tray beneath the desk. The jangling sound of my phone and a vicious, searing pain in my left leg confirmed that I was fully awake again. Agony, frustrated sexual expectation and hatred of the caller coursed through me in more or less that order, although, if I'm honest, frustrated sexual expectation was way out in the lead.

There was a noise from the other side of the partition as my closest colleague, known to all as 'the Freak', noticed my encounter with the under desk tray and sudden return to the waking world. He raised his gaze from a magazine about extra-terrestrials. The Freak's face had the colour, shape and texture of an elderly aunt who had let herself go. He had a serious junk food habit and beneath a stained woollen tank-top and polyester shirt smelling of week old sweat and grease, his flabby body was a living warning about saturated fats. Velour pastry features rearranged themselves into a deathly, pallid leer.

'Ah!' he said, mumbling through a mouthful of food, 'I know what you were thinking. I bet you've just noticed that bug on line 13,175 as well! Nasty one. Dunno how that got through quality control? Must have been Neil programming that bit. He's shit. Would have caused an error 41. Corrupted indexes!'

I glared at the little weirdo who, it was rumoured, hid a copy of 'Java Programming – the Ultimate Resource' inside a porn mag. Summoning up as much sarcasm as I could muster, I replied,

'Really? No exciting as that bug is Freak, I was dreaming of Sue with no clothes on.'

He stared, open mouthed, revealing a half-chewed burger, (double cheese with gherkin and ketchup for those of a curious nature), an expression that did nothing to enhance his complete lack of charm. A few seconds passed as he compiled this information into something he could process. His universe had just crashed into planet lust. He vaguely recognized that there were things called emotions somewhere but walking out onto the terra incognita of human feeling was not a comfortable place for the Freak. Querying, through half chewed meat, 'Why would you want to do that?' he finally gulped, swallowed the wreckage of the burger and nodded towards my desk.

'Better answer your phone,' adding needlessly, 'It's ringing.'

Sighing deeply I picked up the ghastly beige handset on the other end of which I knew there would be a tale of misery, loathing and abandoned hope. But instead of a customer, the voice of a stranger greeted me. The voice whispered,

'Can you listen?'

Interesting philosophical question I thought. And one with a wider number of answers than you might first assume. Of course it could be someone conducting a Zen questionnaire. Or maybe it was a conceptual artist such as Yoko Ono randomly accessing numbers in the London telephone directory? Not being deaf or in any other way hearing impaired, it seemed churlish, if not downright dishonest, to say anything but 'Yes' to the question.

'Yes,' I said, wondering perhaps if it was MI5, the CIA or whatever the KGB was called these days. It seemed unlikely but I suppose that even security services occasionally dial a wrong number.

'OK listen,' the voice said.

Listening seemed to be of great importance to the caller so I did so.

'Are you listening?'

I assured him I was.

'Do you mind swearing?' he went on.

I looked round. There were no humans worthy of the name near by so I saw no difficulty in complying with the request.

'What would you like me to say?' I asked. 'I'm in an open plan office so I'd better keep it fairly mild.'

'No, no, I mean, would you be offended by swearing?'

I deliberated for a few seconds.

'Well it depends what you were thinking of saying.'

By now I had the distinct impression that this was an obscene call but thought it considerate of the caller to check my level of sensitivity before coming out with a stream of expletives. He interrupted me impatiently.

'Listen. My name's Tony Leon - I'm a recruitment agent. I may have a job for you at a well known company but it's quite a, well, shall we say a 'robust' environment. There's a fair bit of swearing and it may not suit everyone.'

'Oh, I see,' I replied, although I didn't really. Pausing for a moment I searched my mind for all the intelligent salient and insightful questions that might impress him. Picking one, not entirely at random, I asked.

'What's the salary?'

After all there was no point being sworn at for a pittance. The recruitment agent replied. I thought I'd misheard. He repeated it. I swore.

'Yep,' the agent said, 'sounds like you'd be perfect for the role. The interview's on Thursday 15th. By the way do you drink?'

I looked round to see if there was either:

A.) A TV crew filming a set up of me accepting some completely improbable, wildly fabulous and of course fictitious job.

B.) Angels flapping elegant wings to show I'd died and gone to work heaven where swearing, drinking and a large salary were all part of the package.

As far as I could see the office contained:

A.) No TV crew.

B.) No angels.

'Martin Fitch, their IT Manager – he's the guy who'll be interviewing you, is very hot about drinking on the job.'

'Oh I see.'

My voice couldn't hide my disappointment. I thought of my lunchtime intake and conceded,

'Ah well, it'll be good for me to drink less I suppose.'

The agent laughed. For a long time. Hard. When he stopped he said,

'Great sense of humour! Love it! Mind you, you'll need it if you get this job. Excellent! Oh by the way, at the interview best not to ask what happened to the previous guy. I'll email you the details immediately. Bye.'

I stared at the phone as I put it down. Weird. Picking up a piece of paper with the lurid details of a client's problem scrawled on it, I balanced it on the top of my monitor.

I called out, 'Freak!'

The pasty face reappeared over the partition. A doughnut was now disappearing into his mouth like a lifebelt being sucked into a whirlpool.

'Yeah?'

'Bob was saying you're the employee who knows most about the stock control system – could you have a look at this bug for him. Cheers.'

I sat back and returned to fantasizing about Sue but was barely into the first part of my reverie when a door opened behind me and the nauseatingly jolly voice of Bob Scott, our euphemistically titled 'Customer Care Director,' bellowed out. Bob was from Sutton Coldfield but in his head he was in Silicon Valley. He usually dressed in what he thought made him look like Steve Jobs but perfectly captured his essential well meaning twattishness. His Brummie tones rang out.

'Hey everybody! Listen up! One big Bob announcement coming up for y'all!'

I turned round and was startled to see that today Bob was sporting a vivid jumper consisting of yellow hoops with purple edging.

'Why do you think someone's vomited over Bob?' I asked the Freak.

'Huh? Oh it's another of his charity things – did you not read the email? We all sponsored him to wear it. It's for colour blindness.'

'It'll certainly cause that.'

Bob cleared his throat in an unpleasant manner and announced,

'OK everybody, as you all know we're possessed by Americans'.

There was a silence as he waited for hysterical laughter. He waited a bit longer.

'As you know we're possessed by an American company....' This time there was a response as the clipped tones of our Financial Controller corrected him.

'I think, being strictly accurate Bob, we're owned by an American company. 'Possessed' suggests some sort of quasi-occult taking over of the spirit or soul as those of a religious bent would have it.'

'Thanks Andrea I knew I could rely on an accountant to appreciate my joke!'

Bob huffed briefly, staring into the faces registering a peculiar mix of boredom and expectation gathered before him.

'Actually it's quite appropriate you should bring that up as it directly affects you. Our American owners...'

'Or possessors!' said the Freak out loud, demonstrating the comic timing of Robespierre. I nudged him, and felt my elbow sinking into several inches of rolling flab.

'Good one Freak!' beamed Bob. 'Our American owners want to find out what's happening on the ground here in the UK and have decided to pay us the compliment of sending their Finance

Director or Vice President of Finance as they call it, to spend six months with us.'

Andrea paled and reached for the back of a chair to support herself.

'Randy J. Feckenburger is coming over here?'

'Yes Andrea. Randy J. Feckenburger the Third is indeed coming here. I hope we'll make him as welcome as our transatlantic cousins make us feel.'

I couldn't resist.

'What? You mean we'll site a few missiles in his garden making him a target for any nuclear armed nutter?'

Bob glared at me.

'That, Denis, is exactly the sort of thing I don't want to hear! And what are you laughing at Freak?'

The Freak's facial flesh was vibrating seismically and his piggy eyes had all but disappeared.

'It's his name Bob. I can't call him 'Randy' every time I see him. I mean,' he sniggered, 'the first time I meet him, do I go up and say, 'Are you Randy?'

'It might be the only time in your life you'll get the chance to say those words without being beaten to a pulp so I'd give it a go.' I whispered.

Bob bristled, 'Until he indicates otherwise we will all address him as Mr. Feckenburger.'

'The Third.' Andrea added helpfully.

'What?'

'He's Randy J. Feckenburger the Third.'

Bob thought about this.

'But it's the Randy J. that's the Third not the Mr. Feckenburger surely?'

'How do you know? He might be very sensitive about it.'

'How can any one called Randy J. Feckenburger the Third be sensitive about his name?' retorted Clive, the office manager.

'Good point Clive!' I agreed. 'He'll be used to people taking the piss out of his name so he'll be fine with it. Probably have a sharp sense of humour.'

Clive nodded approval while Bob frowned at me again.

'He also happens to be an evangelical Christian. Vice President of Finance and born again Christian is not a combination that does humour Denis.'

'Better get on the right side of him then,' muttered Clive.

'When's he arriving?' Andrea nervously ventured.

'Tomorrow,' sighed Bob and turned back into his office disappointed and not for the first time, at his work colleagues' lack of respect for him.

'Thank fuck I've got an interview,' I thought as I sat down again to resume my reveries about Sue.

Chapter Two

Here Be Dragons - The Arrival of Randy J. Feckenburger
(The Third)

And lo, on a fine Tuesday morning Randy J. Feckenburger
(the Third) arrived on the premises. The first sign of this was
Bob emerging from his office like a hermit crab and coughing
gently behind me. I'd learnt to ignore this as it usually meant
either a bollocking or an unwelcome addition to my workload,
interrupting my well planned day of indolence. The Freak,
facing in Bob's direction, looked up from his breakfast and
stared open mouthed (bacon sandwich, tomato sauce,
something yellowish, possibly mustard in the mix there as
well). If it shocked the Freak it must be extraordinary and
worth seeing, so I turned round with anticipation. Bob exceeded
all my expectations and by a fair margin. He was wearing a
denim shirt, bootlace tie, denim jeans and this confection was
topped with a Stetson flying a confederate flag on top. Beneath
the Stetson Bob's eyes goggled through his thick glasses,
somewhat diluting the intended effect. If Billy the Kid had
chosen accountancy instead of gun-slinging as his day job this
is pretty much what he'd have looked like. Shifty and self-
conscious, as well he might be, Bob whispered, 'Randy's just
arrived I thought I'd try to make him feel at home.'

I alerted Bob to an alternative interpretation of his welcoming costume.

'He'll think you're taking the piss.'

Bob, pondered and with a worried frown said, 'Why do you think that Denis? I can't see a problem.'

There was no way of telling if Bob was as insensitive as he appeared but his lack of empathy was legendary. I vividly recalled the day he'd taken a phone call, and in a misunderstanding, told the Freak his mother was dead. As you can imagine the Freak took this quite badly. Eventually discovering the truth and with a very live and very angry Freak mother on the other end of the phone, Bob felt he was giving the Freak good news by reversing the dead / not dead decision and was piqued at the Freak's lack of gratitude. So on that scale, dressing like something out of a Wild West Show to greet our new American colleague was junior league insensitivity.

'Imagine if you went to the States Bob and your hosts thought they'd greet you by dressing like a' (I was cautious here not to say "fuckwit") 'a Beefeater? What would you think?'

Our ruminations were disturbed as a tall, sinister shadow appeared outside the glass walls of our office.

'I think we're about to find out,' said the Freak and without doubt the gangly stranger who had flung open the door, nearly crushing Carol the Receptionist, could be none other than Randy J. Feckenburger (the Third). The first object in his line

of sight was Billy the Kid / Bob the Git and it threw him.
Randy eyed Bob up and down as a python might weigh up a
tasty looking goat.

'Is this Buy-O-Soft Retail Systems?' he asked in a hesitant
fashion.

'It surely is! Howdy friend!' Bob gushed enthusiastically in
peculiar Brummie-American. For one awful moment I thought
he was going to slap his thigh and shout out 'Yes sireee!' As it
was my toes curled in embarrassment and for the first and
almost last time, I felt sympathy for Randy J. Feckenburger (the
Third).

'Right! You must be Bob Scott?' Feckenburger ventured.

'That's correct and you must be Randy.' Bob confirmed,
stretching a hand out in greeting. I shot a warning glance at the
Freak but it was too late. A weird sucking noise informed me
that he'd breathed in the remnants of his sandwich. His face
turned the colour of a sunburst lobster and I prayed I wouldn't
have to perform the Heimlich Maneuver on him thus bringing
me into inhumanely close contact with the notorious tank top,
something no one, to my knowledge, had ever survived.
Mercifully the Freak was again breathing normally but
sniggering in an unpleasant, sandwich remnant spraying sort of
way. Feckenburger glared at him in a manner that did not bode
well for their working relationship.

'Hey Bud! Are you laughing at my name sir?'

This apparent respect for him confused the Freak. He stopped sniggering and stared back at Feckenburger.

'Er, no I just felt sorry for you. And my name's not Bud it's the Freak.'

I don't know what he was feeling but I could see the Freak's career flashing before my eyes. Randy scrutinized him closely then he smiled broadly.

'That's a truly Christian attitude you have Mr. Freak! Stand up so I can see you properly!'

The Freak stood and Randy appraised him.

'You have a great future here if you can relate to clients in that way y'know.' Swivelling to face the escapee from the Wild West who was still standing behind him, witnessing the exchange, Randy commented.

'Excellent Mr. Scott – good hire! Now I've been tasked to reach out to all the staff and decide on key resource levels on an ongoing basis. If we can just use your office I'll go outline my thinking about the future of Buy-O-Soft with you.'

It wasn't long before it became clear that Randy's thinking about the future of Buy-O-Soft and that of the people who worked there were totally at odds with each other. Take this as an example. With the help of the Freak I'd sorted out a thorny problem for our most difficult and unpleasant client Mrs. Rhodes or Rhoda the Rhino as she was known. She had come as near to thanking us as was likely in this life (I think she mentioned something about not suing us this time) and I'd taken the Freak to our local for a celebration pint and a pie. Or, in the interests of strict accuracy, three pints and a pie for me, three pies and a pint of coke for the Freak. We got back to the office just after two but my usual post-lunch reverie was broken by the voice of Randy J. Feckenburger (the Third). It was difficult to believe that there had been two before him who thought Randy J. Feckenburger a name worth perpetuating but there he was large as life and twice as mad. Since his arrival we'd discovered that he hailed from South Carolina, he believed in Jesus Christ, Creationism and I think he saw himself as America's revenge on the British for the Pilgrim Fathers. He also considered George W. Bush to have been the US's finest President and spoke English from a parallel language universe. Anyway on that afternoon I was woken from my afternoon siesta when he sat himself on the corner of my desk.

'Denis,' he drawled, 'Almighty God put us all on His good dear earth for a purposefulness only He can see and understand in His wisdom and foresightitude. He gave us the eagle to soar and make us think of the wonders of heaven, the great beasts of the field to provide for our nutritional needs and the cougar to show grace, speed and muscularity.'

I stared at him with apprehension. The wide big skied plains of South Carolina or wherever this guy hailed from, were a long way from Brentford and the only place likely to house cougars, eagles and the rest was 'Pete's Pets' in the High Street where the front of the shop purveyed run of the mill fauna such as cats, dogs and hamsters (three for two offer this week) while at the back you could furtively order snakes, alligators and other exotica. Possibly even cougars, who knows?

'What about rats Randy?' I ventured. 'If God is so keen on a purpose for His creations why do we have rats?'

As we all know, the rat argument has baffled theologians for centuries and I could sense the rational, finance side of his brain was grappling with the illogical, God bothering bit thus heating up the frontal lobe.

'God moves in mysterious ways and maybe rats are the most mysterious of His creatures. Anyways, speaking of rats, does it ever occur to you that the computer keyboard in front of you is attached to your bank account in much the same way that a lab rat's wheel is attached to a supply of peanuts? The idea is that if you perform certain actions at the keyboard then every month we place a meagre amount in your checking account. It is perhaps more accurate to say that to you the amount seems meagre but to us, as your employers, it feels extortionate. It is not what we Americans call a 'win - win' situation, in fact it's closer to 'lose - lose'. Now if you are awake enough and it's not too much trouble, there's a client needs a fix for his stock control system.'

He dropped the details of the client's problem in a note on the desk and ambled off to his office in much the same way a cowboy might amble towards a convenient sunset, the sound of his habitual gum chewing giving the impression that we kept a cow in the office. The Freak had been listening to this encounter.

'He's full of shit. Rats don't eat peanuts.' was his perceptive contribution. He nodded towards the direction of the wild blue yonder behind me.

'Bob's gonna make an announcement.'

He was right in every respect. Bob Scott had emerged from his office and was clearing his throat like a mongoose trying to dislodge a chunk of eggshell from its larynx.

'Right all if you'll just listen for a mo. We've had a very good year and as a thank you we're going to take everyone to the Skypath next Thursday. We've hired a room there so we can all get together. I'll be announcing the Employee of the Month as well so be there and be square! Er.. be not there and not be square. I think. Anyway it should be a good piss up.'

Randy came out of his lair like a disgruntled bear after winter and tutted at Bob's language. The Freak stared, masticating in his customary open mouthed style and we all set our various expectation levels for next Thursday. Not high seemed to be the average.

Chapter Three

Zero to Hero. And Back Again

The Heathrow Skypath Hotel, a low-rise mid 1970s
construction, squatted on the A4 between Colnbrook
Immigration Removal Centre and "Hair by Amnesia".
Internationally named meeting rooms twinned with a
threadbare air and dull brown décor combined to suggest exotic
travel and career failure in equal measure. Buy-O-Soft had
hired a fleet of mini buses from a local firm (Sam's Travel -
"Most of Our Passengers Get Home OK"). Our vehicle pulled
up at the front of the Skypath and out we climbed. Twelve
minutes in a cab with the Freak had left most of us short of
oxygen so breathing lungfuls of air thick with aviation fuel
outside the hotel was like champagne. Beyond a pair of smoked
glass doors the reception area beckoned. In one corner was a
board covered in stick on letters detailing events taking place in
this centre for lost souls. Halfway down, just below, "Hounslow
Accountancy Annual Dinner Dance - The Maldives Bar," were
the words, "Buy-O-Soft Reception - The Stockholm Suite."
On arrival we were handed complementary cocktails
consisting of watered down spirits blended with watered down
fruit juice. A waitress in a dress giving off enough static to
affect aircraft communications, passed through our throng
offering stale crisps and cocktail sausages skillfully crafted

solely from gristle. Once the formality of cocktails was dispensed with, Bob got our attention.

'Before we get on to the presentation of the Employee of the Month, Randy J. Feckenburger our Finance Director, all the way from the U.S. of A would like to say a few words.'

Bob waved his hand to the side and announced.

'Randy J. Feckenburger.'

There was a pause.

'The Third.'

And on bounded Randy J. Feckenburger (the Third). Like Bob, Randy had delusions of grandeur and in his mind possibly believed he was in the Grand Ballroom of the Waldorf Astoria New York. In reality he was standing on a small slightly raised plinth at the far end of the Stockholm Suite of the Skypath Hotel at Heathrow. As he raised his arms in a sort of Messianic greeting a voice announced over the tannoy.

'Would the owner of a green Ford Focus, registration number HN06 GFC please move it as you are restricting access to the laundry room. Thank you.'

Randy hesitated briefly then flung his arms wide again.

'HEEEEEYYYYY HOW YA DOING BRENTFORD? YOU ARE AWESOME! HEEEEEYYYY BUY-O-SOFT, WE ARE THE DUDES! WHAT ARE WE GONNA DO??? WE'RE GONNA KICK ASS!!'

He pumped the air violently with a clenched fist, as fifty people stood before him, their mouths slightly open, witnessing this horror. Somewhere behind my neck a horrible prickly feeling began squeezing a sweat of embarrassment from every pore of my being. The Freak stood, openmouthed, mid chew of an innocent vol-au-vent.

'Holy fuck…' he whimpered. The tannoy burst into life again.

'If restaurant manager Gareth Thompson is in the hotel could he make his way to the Rainforest Sky Garden where Baz from pest control has got the rat cages. That's Gareth Thompson to the Rainforest Sky Garden. Thank you.'

Randy scowled at the tannoy and raised his voice to drown out the occasional announcement. The tannoy kicked in once more.

'This is a message for Gareth Thompson again. Further to my last announcement Baz just wants to know what you want him to do with the rats. Now, for all our customers, The Ronaldo restaurant will be open in five minutes serving a wide range of tasty tapas and drinks including San Miguel beer and Tequila Slammers at half price. Thank you.'

Feckenburger upped the volume another notch.

'OOOOKKKKAAAY. LET ME HEAR YOU ALL BIG IT UP FOR BUY-O-SOFT! WHAT ARE WE GONNA DO?'

There was silence.

'WHAT ARE WE GONNA DO?' came the rallying cry once more.

More silence. An older programmer at the back politely raised a hand.

'Er, write better code,' he ventured.

'YEESSSS SIR THAT'S AWESOME! BUT WE'RE
GONNNNA KICK ASS AND HAVE A BALL WHILE WE
DO IT. SOOOO WHAT WE GONNA DO?'

This was exactly the kind of situation most of the people in the
room had become software programmers to avoid. A collective
sweat broke out. I prayed I was in one of those weird dreams
that cause night terrors and then you wake up to the massive
relief of knowing reality isn't like that. But it was. And anyway
what sort of dream would feature the Freak? Or Randy J
Feckenburger (the Third) who was now waving his arms,
exhorting us all to stand?

'OOOOOKKKK WHEN I ASK YA THIS TIME YOU'LL
ALL SHOUT " WE'RE GONNA KICK ASS!"
OOOKKKAAAAY - WHAT WE GONNA DO?'

A polite whisper came back. 'Er, kick arse?'

'LOUDER!' Randy screamed.

A slightly higher volume of 'Kick Arse' resulted. Randy
stopped, perhaps sensing the crowd wasn't warmed up enough
yet for his brand of encouragement.

'Phew,' said the Freak. 'I think he's finished.'

But Randy J. Feckenburger (the Third) had other ideas.

'OOOOKKKAAYY. LET ME REACH OUT TO A
COLLEAGUE – TO COME UP AND SAY A PRAYER
WITH ME TO JESUS TO LET HIS SPIRIT ENTER THIS
GREAT COMPANY OF OURS!'

I am convinced if you'd offered anyone in the room a bullet through the head at that moment they'd have jumped at the chance. I know I would.

'Please don't let him pick me…' the Freak snivelled. Randy put a hand up to shield his eyes from the light and hunted round the Stockholm Suite with a psychotic look. His gaze swept like the searchlight of a POW camp across our trembling ranks. It finally stopped on the Freak.

'HEEEY! YEAH YOU! COME ON UP HERE AND JOIN ME FRIEND!' Randy bawled at the unfortunate Freak, gesturing lavishly for him to stand beside him on the stage / plinth. The Freak went a translucent shade of jelly fish but set out towards Randy like a compliant zombie heading for the guillotine. When the Freak reached the low plinth, Randy put an avuncular, if overly enthusiastic, arm round his shoulder. He rapidly withdrew it as the slick of grease on the Freak's tank top repelled his affectionate grip. Randy made an expansive movement with his arm as if showing the Freak the wonders of the world and as he did so, quizzed our unlucky colleague.

'NOW WHAT ARE YOU THINKING MY FRIEND? ARE YOU THINKING JESUS IS WITH US TONIGHT? TELL EVERYONE HERE WHAT IS IN YOUR MIND RIGHT THIS MINUTE!'

Randy gestured again like a torch song singer to his audience. I could see that the Freak, though his eyes were open, was in some kind of terror induced trance-like state or maybe even unconscious. Randy cajoled him.

'COME ON FRIEND! JESUS KNOWS WHAT'S IN YOUR HEART SO DON'T YOU BE SCARED TO TELL US! WHAT ARE YOU THINKING ABOUT – WHAT CAN YOU SEE IN YOUR MIND AT THIS VERY MOMENT? CALL IT OUT TO ALL THE GOOD FOLKS OF BUY-O-SOFT AND LET 'EM KNOW WHAT'S ON YOUR MIND!'

The Freak's eyes goggled and from some strange space deep within he shouted loudly,

'BRITNEY SPEARS' CUNT!'

Even the tannoy paused in the midst of an announcement that the barbecue in the Jamaica Grill would be commencing in five minutes. Randy went a startling shade of white then red, like an octopus climbing a stick of rock. Bob, standing next to me, stroked his beard thoughtfully and whispered, 'You know it's the Freak's appraisal this week, well, I was wondering just this morning whether to give the little sod a pay rise or not. God bless him! I'm going to double his bloody salary!'

I'm not sure who started the applause but it spread rapidly throughout the room and within a minute the Freak had turned from sweaty nerd in woolly tank top into heroic, foul-mouthed knight in shining armour. Randy strode from the stage mopping his brow and muttering something about possession and the devil appearing in strange guises, though if he'd thought about it for a moment he'd have realized that even Satan would have baulked at a tank top. The Freak rejoined us and stared around, dazed, as people shook his hand. He was clearly enjoying his new found popularity. I looked at him with admiration.

'Did someone dare you to say that?'

'Say what?'

I could see he wasn't joking. I gave him the edited highlights of his moment of fame on the stage with Randy J. Feckenburger. There was a blank look in his eyes.

'Who's Britney Spears?' he asked in wonderment.

I caught up with Randy J. in the bar where he was downing an orange juice and still in shock from the Freak's psychotherapeutic moment. Something more than orange juice was required as I tried to pour oil on troubled waters. Randy stared into space somewhere just above the optics as the tannoy, equilibrium restored, announced, 'The Donna Smith Quartet's next demonstration will be taking place in ten minutes in the Laguna. Would the owner of a dark blue Peugeot 307 registration number HV04LKJ please move it from the disabled parking bay as security have reported seeing you dancing in the Astaire Room.'

Putting my case for the defence of the Freak was no easy task.

'He didn't mean to be rude, its just he's very... awkward and shy. I think he was overwhelmed by the moment. He does have a tendency to just blurt stuff out...'

'What he said was an affront to all decency Denis!'

'Well, I see your point but I'm sure we've all...'

Randy skewered me with the sort of look that a particularly zealous member of the Inquisition might have given a heretic who was arguing for a bit of give and take. About to launch into a poorly rehearsed argument that the Freak was only young and we're all a bit wild at that age (although frankly the only sign of wildness in the Freak was on Fridays when he had two pasties and chips rather than his usual one) it dawned on me that Feckenburger really had no idea about this sort of thing. His was a world of certainty where purity of thought was the norm. I spoke to Randy in that well meaning but patronizing way people talk to elderly relatives who are going through a bad time.

'Come on. We'd better get back to the rest of them. Bob's about to announce the Employee of the Month.'

Our path to the Stockholm Suite took us past the Laguna Lagoon from whence loud music with a heavy beat was issuing. Randy was deep in thought and I was looking forward to leaving his company once we were ensconced among our colleagues again. The lagoon curved round in an arc and the water was rippling more than might be expected for an indoor pool. As we passed it I nearly jumped out of my skin as a pair of legs suddenly broke the surface and began thrashing in a peculiar scissor action. Randy, being a man of action did more than jump. Without hesitation he ripped off his jacket, dived in and within a second had a young woman round the waist and was dragging her to the safety of the pool steps.

'I've got you maam' he exclaimed in loud voice. 'Don't struggle - just relax! I'm Randy by the way.'

I inwardly applauded his courage. Outwardly I noticed there was a lot of noise as the other members of the synchronized swimming team had scrambled out of the pool and were advancing on him in menacing fashion. I could already hear the tannoy requesting the hotel manager and security to attend the Laguna Lagoon as a matter of urgency. My first instinct was to get offside as quickly as possible and it was a sound one. The words 'pervert,' 'police,' 'sex offender' and some that might even have shocked the Freak, were being freely bandied about as the manager, accompanied by a posse of stocky, shaven-headed security men dashed past me in the opposite direction heading for a showdown with the hapless Feckenburger. Reaching the sanctuary of the Stockholm Suite I made a beeline for Bob.

'So has Randy got over the Freak's little outburst?' he asked as we watched Louise, one of our software gurus, accepting her Employee of the Month award.

'Yeah… I'm pretty sure he's forgotten about it by now,' I said, glancing nervously over my shoulder for stray synchronized swimmers who might have associated me with the lifeguard turned sex pest or vice versa.

'That's very forgiving. Maybe I've misjudged him,' Bob mused.

'Mmm.'

Chapter Four

Appraisal

By some terrible accident or in one of those weird moments
when the Gods of management are in a particularly
mischievous mood, I had become the Freak's line manager. I
don't think the Freak saw it quite like that but Bob had long
realized the Freak was unmanageable and shirked responsibility
or as he said, delegated the task to me. Of course it might have
been that the prospect of talking to the Freak in a small office
with inadequate ventilation didn't appeal to him. On a dull
Wednesday morning I dutifully trekked over to Sheila in HR
and picked up an 'Employee's Skills and Performance
Assessment Form'. A minute or so later I was sitting in a small
office with inadequate ventilation staring across a grimy desk at
the Freak. There was a tangible odour of something deep fried
emanating from him, even though it was eleven in the morning
and food wise, the Freak was unarmed. I picked up my pen and
fiddled with the clip as I scanned the battery of questions
designed to mystically tease out the Freak's hidden strengths
and weaknesses.

'You're a psychopath.' The Freak casually offered.

'What?'

'You're playing with your pen clip. Did you see that film with
Humphrey Bogart where he plays with metal balls and that

shows the jury he's a psychopath so they execute him or whatever?'

I felt the interview wasn't getting off to a great start so I'd better exert control over my supposed underling.

'Really? No I didn't see it. Anyway. How long have we worked together?'

The Freak's eyes wandered to that place in the room where inspiration might be found.

'Is this a trick question?' he asked.

'No!' I shouted, then moderating my tone with some difficulty, assured him, 'No, don't worry, there are no trick questions.'

'OK well I think it's about two years, seven months twelve days and,' here he checked his watch, 'three hours and twenty nine minutes.'

I laughed, pleased that he was relaxing and able to make a joke.

'What's so funny?' he said.

'Well, that was a good joke.'

I didn't say "for you" but I'm sure he could sense it.

'So we're quite long standing colleagues and I want you to know that I respect your work and value our relationship.' I said, not entirely truthfully. Or indeed truthfully at all.

'That wasn't a joke – you asked me how long we'd worked together and I told you.' the Freak said peevishly. This wasn't going to be as easy as Sheila in HR had suggested. The air had grown a bit more soupy than at the beginning so I got up to open one of the metal windows which turned our building into a furnace in summer and rendered it sub-Arctic in winter. It was welded shut for some bizarre reason. I glanced at the first part of the sheet. It said 'Employee Name.' It suddenly dawned in me that I had no idea what the Freak's real name was. It would be embarrassing to ask him directly and have to admit that I, as his line manager and closest colleague, didn't know his name. Worse, I couldn't think of anyone who might know it as he was universally referred to by his nickname. I had to call him something apart from 'the Freak' or 'Freak'. Inspiration struck.

'So are you called after your Dad?'

'I don't think so.'

'Right… why's that?'

'He died about two years before I was born.'

I pondered this information briefly then decided not to pursue that line. The fug in the room was nearly visible, I was beginning to lose the will to live and just as I was about to say, 'well that all seems fine' so I could fill in the details in my own time, there was a knocking and what I saw as rescue arrived in the unlikely guise of Randy J. Feckenburger (the Third). He opened the door with a flourish but stopped abruptly on the threshold.

'What's that smell?'

'What smell?' the Freak replied looking puzzled.

'I think someone was eating lunch in here.' I suggested.

'It's only eleven twenty,' Randy pointed out, reasonably enough.

'From yesterday. Anyway, can I help you?'

'Jeez, they must have been eating a dead raccoon or something. Yeah, anyway,' Randy beamed, 'Bob told me you're doing an appraisal so I thought I'd sit in.'

He jabbed a finger at the Freak. 'I want to see a three hundred sixty degree appraisal, like we do in the States.'

The Freak stood up and started turning slowly round. Of the three people in the room two were perplexed. I was first to the obvious question.

'What are you doing?'

My main concern was that the Freak would throw off a further miasma of poly-saturated fat, rendering the room unable to sustain life. He pointed accusingly at Randy.

'He said we're doing a three hundred and sixty degree appraisal,' the Freak explained. I cradled my head in my hands.

'Hey! Wicked sense of humour man!' Randy gushed, grinning at the Freak who was still gyrating. Feeling it was better not to let Feckenburger know that the Freak was serious and didn't do 'sense of humour' wicked or otherwise, I gave a wan smile and picked up the form again with heavy heart. Mercifully Randy appeared to have forgotten their previous encounter on the plinth / stage at the Skypath Hotel and just stretched his lanky frame out in the third chair. The Freak had come to a standstill and resumed his seat. As I was about to wade back into deep appraisal water, Randy chipped in,

'OK, yeah, sorry to interrupt again Denis – but you'd better introduce me to this dude. Then I'll just sit back and watch your Brit management style in action.'

Taking a breath, I was about to say 'this is…' but I still couldn't remember anyone addressing him as anything other than 'the Freak' I racked my brains for a possible name. It crossed my mind that perhaps he didn't have one. Or maybe he'd been named the Freak after that seventies song. It seemed unlikely though.

'Yeah, OK.'

Nodding at the Freak who sat placidly examining a small avalanche of dandruff which had drifted from his head during his slow spinning activity and settled on his tank top shoulder, I turned to our new arrival.

'Er… This is Randy J. Feckenburger… The Third,' I said drawing out the syllables as slowly as possible, 'he's Finance Director of Buy-O-Soft in the US, Europe, Australia and....'

Randy stopped me again.

'OK, wait, wait! That's part of Europe - there's no need to waste my time repeating it.'

'What is?'

'Australia!'

Even the Freak was goggling at him in a puzzled way and had interrupted the loving tending of his dandruff drift. I could see no tactful way of correcting our American colleague.

'Australia is about as far from Europe as you can get.'

'Yeah, kind of if you're gonna be all like, distancey, about it. But they're European like you guys.'

'Have you been there yet?'

'Yeah, sure! Well, not like boots on ground stuff - I had a video conference with them. But I'm flying out in a couple of weeks.'

'OK, well good luck with that. Anyway can we get back to the appraisal?'

I was beginning to lose patience and indeed consciousness through the combination of the Freak's personal odours and Randy's surreal take on world geography.

'Sure thing Denis, it's your gig!' Randy enthused, peering over at the questionnaire before me. 'So what's his name?'

'Whose?' I asked, more in hope than expectation that he'd forgotten the whole 'tell me his name and I'll tell you mine' malarkey. He pointed unhelpfully and unambiguously at the Freak.

'His! I know your name Denis, and you know mine so there's no one else really is there? So what's our mystery man's name?'

It must have appeared as if I'd only noticed the Freak because I'm sure I flinched when I saw him.

'What? Oh *his* name?'

The Freak of course wasn't helping me at all by venturing any clue as to what he was called. Or perhaps he didn't know either. Randy however was insistent.

'Yeah, him, the guy in the bra top or whatever it's called!'

'Tank top!' corrected the Freak, like Yves St Laurent addressing a particularly stupid fashion editor. We didn't have time to sit all day trying to guess our malodorous colleague's name. I picked up the paper from the desk again and a light bulb flickered in my brain.

'Damn, I've got the wrong form – back in a min.'

Bob's office was next door. Taking a huge gulp of relatively Alpine fresh air in his office as I went in, I hissed at him.

'Bob. What's the Freak's real name?'

Bob, nonplussed sat back in his chair and gawped at me for a few seconds .

'It's just, 'the Freak' as far as I know…' Then the penny dropped.

'Oh, I see. He must have another name but… Why do you need it? Just call him the Freak like you always do.'

'I'm doing his appraisal in front of Feckenburger who wants to know the guy's real name.'

'I see. He is a bit of a stickler for detail is old Randy. Hang on a mo.'

Opening a filing cabinet Bob rooted through several folders.

'Here we go, yeah I thought it was a bit off the wall when I interviewed him. 'His name's Ryman Boxfile'.

'Ryman Boxfile? That seems odd and yet familiar. Let me see. For God's sake! That's the name of the stationery Bob!'

'Is it? OK let me check again. Ah here we are, this is it, 'Sharon Gadfield'.'

'What? Sharon? Sharon's not a bloke's name. I can't go back in there and introduce him as Sharon.'

'Randy won't know, he's American and they have pretty weird names themselves,' Bob argued with searing logic.

My response was I'm afraid, terse.

'But the fucking Freak will!'

'That's a point. I don't think it would worry him though do you? No, you may well be right, Sharon's probably not his name either. The personnel records got in a bit of a mess during the Christmas party. I keep meaning to sort them out but y'know how these things get put back. Hold on! There's another file here. I think this might be it – matches the photo as well! Yeah, this is it. Maximilian Epworth.'

'Maximilian Epworth....? Are you sure?'

'No, not really but it's what it says on his contract.'

I was beginning to think that 'Ryman Boxfile' or even 'Sharon Gadfield' were more plausible. I took a huge breath of fresh air and armed with what might or might not be the Freak's real name, re-entered Fug Central. The Freak and Randy appeared to be having an amicably violent conversation. Our VP Finance was enthusiastically pointing a finger close to the Freak's head and saying,

'Yeah, say I wanted to blow you away and make sure your head's just like ten pounds of hamburger meat. Well I'd use a FN Scar, y'know the special forces' weapon?'

For the first time ever the Freak's podgy features were animated.

'Awesome! What about an AK47 though, would that not do the job just as well?'

'Sorry to disturb the psychopaths' support group but you're supposed to be having your appraisal Fr... er,' I glanced down at the personnel form, 'Maximilian.'

The Freak goggled at me like a blowfish. As the sinking feeling that I had the wrong name grew, I was just about to venture 'Sharon,' on him when he said, 'Wow, you know my real name! No one's ever called me that before!'

I could see he was quite moved and his eyes had become moist. Unfortunately Randy interjected, ruining our moment of employee – line manager bonding.

'Jesus! Y'mean even your folks called you "the Freak"?'

The Freak (or Maximilian) bristled a bit.

'No! I meant since I've been here.'

He turned to me.

'Thanks Denise.'

'It's Denis actually but don't mention it. OK can we get on?'

I looked at the next category on the sheet. After the minefield of trying to get the little bastard's name right I was now venturing onto the thin ice of a section alarmingly entitled,

"Peer Communication and Working Relationships"

The first item was **"Does the Subject Maintain a Professional Dress Code?"**

I almost wept. I looked up from the sheet at the Freak and analysed his get up. What profession the Freak was dressed for would have mystified the best psychologists money could buy. A small group of like minded, discerning flies was hovering around him savouring the pungent aroma of his tank top. I must have gurgled or something because Randy asked if I was OK and poured me a glass of water. Skipping over dress code and several other areas of potential difficulty I got on to what I considered to be the fairly safe ground of "Technical Competence." The Freak was an average programmer but at least I could stretch the truth a bit to make him sound better than he was.

'Well Fr, er Maximilian. How would you rate your technical skills?'

I expected a bit of a delay while he mulled this one over. Instead he wobbled with glee and announced with the misplaced confidence of the truly deluded.

'Awesome!'

'That's what I like to see! This dude has self belief!'

It was becoming clear that Randy J. Feckenburger (the Third) and the Freak (the First and hopefully Last) were forming a peculiar and implausible bond. Interrupting this developing bromance, and in an attempt to sound professional and appraising I asked him,

'Could you be a bit more specific and give me an example?'

'I get on really well with our customers! Remember that problem Mrs. Rhodes had?'

'Vividly.'

The contract for Mrs. Rhodes' large chain of DIY shops paid a major proportion of all our salaries. The Freak gushed on.

'I fixed it – no one else could do it?'

'Yes indeed, you are correct in saying you fixed the problem but no one else would have addressed her as 'Rhoda the Rhino' as you did, nearly losing us the business.'

Randy's eye brows shot up at this but the Freak was ready with his answer.

'Everyone calls her Rhoda the Rhino!'

'Everyone calls her that when they're not on the other end of a phone to her,' I pointed out.

Feckenburger rallied to the Freak's defence.

'We all have bad days and when you get a difficult customer....'

'And I was empathising with her...' continued the Freak

'How do you work that out?'

'Well I told her my name was "the Freak" and she said she was glad she didn't have a nickname and I said but yes you do, we call you "Rhoda the Rhino". I thought she'd see the funny side and feel part of the sort of, team.'

I had a moment of despair.

'Holy fuck!'

Randy scowled, 'There's no need for language like that Denis. It's one of the things I've noticed with you guys. There's a lot of swearing round here.'

I thought I'd better give some perspective on what Rhoda the Rhino meant to the company.

'Rhodes DIY's contract is worth four million pounds. A year.'

'Holy fu... mololey. Yeah OK, I see the problem. Swear away!'

Randy gazed at the Freak with a steelier glint in his eye and fired a question at our paragon of customer service.

'Any other examples of your "technical ability"?'

'My Mum reckons I've got asparagus syndrome like Bill Gates – that's why I'm brilliant with computers!'

Possibly the balance of oxygen to greasy sweat odour in the room had reached a critical level or maybe it was just having to go through this charade but I had an out of body experience where I saw myself from above shouting at the Freak while a startled Randy J. F. III looked on.

'Are you completely deluded? You're not like Bill Gates, because A) you're not a billionaire B) you're not brilliant with computers, C) it's Asperger's Syndrome and you don't have it and D) your Mum said you were a talentless nerd.'

Randy clasped me by the shoulder.

'Hey, why don't we take time out and have a bit of a break?' he suggested.

Drawing in deep draughts of fresh air as we exited the room I noticed Randy was at my side.

'OK I know the guy's a bit off the wall but so was Steve Jobs or....'

'Charles Manson?' I said, maybe a touch bitterly. 'Sorry it's just the Fre... er Maximilian's company, can be a bit wearing day in day out.'

The American checked round the office.

'Yeah, I can understand that. I see why he's called the Freak as well. Smells like one! Anyway between you and me Denis he's not going to be around much longer. I'm drawing up a list of resources we need to de-allocate and that guy's probably one of them. Don't give him any cause to y'know get all, legally, with us. You understand?'

In that second I realized Randy's camaraderie with the Freak wasn't genuine.

'I take it 'de-allocate' means 'fire'?'

'I see it as rebalancing the skills within the company. And his don't really fit. Especially when he's calling a major client a rhinoceros!

'You can't just get rid of the Freak like that! He's been here for...' I tried to remember the exact length of time but gave up at two years.

'Are you telling me who I can and can't get rid of Denis? Of course your Freak friend may not be the only one to go... Anyway I'm not his boss so I'm not going to get rid of him. You are!'

At this, Feckenburger lurched off towards Bob's office, presumably to start talking about the 'de-allocation' of the Freak. Stunned, I opened the door of the Freak's interrogation room and indicated for him to come out.

'I'm sorry for shouting at you. It's been a... difficult day. Why don't we do the rest of your appraisal over a pint at the Ferret and Mattress?'

'Is Randy coming as well?' the Freak asked.

'No he's... he's got to speak to Bob about something.'

I was touched by the Freak's welcoming of our transatlantic chum but it changed to something like admiration when he said, 'Good, I don't trust that big fucker one inch.'

As the Freak and I chatted and I sipped my pint and he his lemonade, I suddenly remembered that my interview was the next day. In a spirit of diligent preparation I limited my intake to two pints. And a half. Very abstemious I thought.

Chapter Five

Interview

Just after nine the next morning I pushed open a glass door in a building on a narrow street in Soho and found myself in what appeared to be a very expensive bathroom. A sheet of water cascaded down a deep grey granite slab erupting from a steel tray that filled the centre of the floor. Engraved in silver on the granite were the letters JDFT Media. To the right there lay a sleek and ostentatiously expensive slab of black marble on which stood a massive display of alien looking and probably poisonous flowers. A glass atrium soared all the way up some six floors so that people in their offices looked down into reception and across at each other on three sides. The lifts were fashioned from curved glass so that occupants looked like specimens in a futuristic laboratory being delivered to their relevant destinations. A disembodied sing-song female voice that I thought I recognized from a sat-nav system said,

'JDFT Media, good morning. One moment I'll put you through.'

I looked for the source of the voice but there was no one in sight. As I approached the black marble excrescence, Prozac voice spoke again. From the first syllable the false gaiety in the voice had grated on me and the feeling grew as it said,

'Hi, welcome to JDFT Media how can I help you?'

Stifling a natural urge to say, 'You could shut up for a start,' I leaned over the front of the reception desk and saw a woman sitting about three feet below and behind the monolith. I say 'woman' but I wasn't sure she was real. In fact I suspected she was some sort of animated doll or maybe even a hologram. Never had I seen such an artificial looking human being. Her hair should have had a sign saying 'this is an extremely expensive hairdo - do not touch the exhibit'. Likewise her skin was slightly translucent and seemed to glow with an unnatural inner light. Yet all this was as natural as water compared with her smile. It chilled the blood.

'How can I help you?' she repeated in the tone an executioner might use when checking how many volts you wanted.

'I'm here for an interview with your IT Manager, Martin Robot, sorry Fitch, Martin Fitch.'

Curiosity finally forced me to ask,

'Why are you so far down behind this thing?' I queried, gesturing at the marble.

'It were made wrong were'nit?' she said swapping effortlessly from robo-speak into fluent estuary English. Picking up the phone the automaton stared to one side as she said,

'Martin there's a geezer here for ya.'

She paused as she digested the information coming from the other end, finally looking up at me with undisguised boredom.

'What'sha name?'

I stared back with undisguised contempt.

'Denis Mahoney.'

Returning to the receiver she intoned,

'Denis Mooney. Says he's got an innerview wiv ya.'

Pausing again she looked blankly at her side of the desk.

'Alright.'

Conversation over, she informed me,

'He's coming dahn to get ya. Take a seat.'

Sitting on a grey and red striped sofa I glanced past the waterfall feature and studied the reception area. It was self-consciously trendy with jagged black and fluorescent orange zigzags on mirrored walls. Here and there pieces of artwork hung on the wall. On closer inspection they appeared to be projectile vomit on a background painted by users of Class A drugs. If Van Gogh had risen from the dead and consumed a bottle of absinthe he could not have created anything more psychotic. Possibly this explained why the receptionist was so vapid and rude. I picked up a magazine and buried my face in it to avoid the loathsome walls and art. The writing was pink on a red background and I immediately developed a splitting headache. A woman walked in and as she went past I noticed that her main distinguishing feature was that she had managed to tuck her skirt into her knickers. After working in Brentford for so long I wasn't sure if maybe this was a Central London style statement. She crossed the floor, got into the lift and with her rear still exposed, started her journey. As the lift rose floor by floor her dressing faux pas brought crowds of people to the windows to watch her progress in a sort of vertical Mexican wave. When she finally alighted somewhere around the sixth floor, her public were hammering on the glass and whooping like animals. While I'd been watching this spectacle the second lift had reached the ground floor. I was still staring up into the atrium when a voice mumbled something. A stocky figure with fair hair through which I could see pink scalp, was standing next to me regarding me with some curiosity. Then he turned his head to look up into the atrium, speaking as he did so.

'I'm Martin Fitch, you must be Denis Mahoney.'

Suddenly I remembered why I was there.

'Yes, I am. Pleased to meet you Martin.'

As we shook hands I gazed again up into the atrium.

'I... er.'

I wasn't quite sure of the etiquette of the situation. Maybe Debretts has an entire section on explaining to someone who is about to interview you that you have just witnessed a woman with her skirt tucked into her underwear being barracked by yobs. Martin had seen the whole incident as well.

'Patricia! She's brilliant but so absent minded sometimes. Bunch of bloody animals.'

I warmed to him immediately.

'Right, well, let's go,' he said, indicating the left hand lift.

In the lift the conversation was as stilted as lift conversations go. Alighting at the sixth floor we stepped out and immediately I felt like I was up to my knees in the deepest pile carpet I've ever known. The corridor was hushed and wood panelled. Although my knowledge of wood is limited, being on the lines of, 'that's a tree, that's not a tree,' I could tell that this wood was at the very expensive end of the scale. The hush was extraordinary as well. It seemed three dimensional, as though someone was playing absolute silence through a perfect audio system. Martin was unimpressed by our surroundings.

'This is the executive suite where all the tossers reside!' he boomed. Ushering me into a long room with the same costly wood mostly covered by framed commendations and awards, Fitch slumped into a chair and opened a file in front of him. On the centre of the wall behind his head was a photograph of a large chunk of raw meat seeping blood onto a white plate. Above it a caption spelled out in sausages, liver, chops and other pieces of dismembered animal, 'Eat More Bloody Meat Y'Bastards!' Underneath was an overly ornate certificate with a commendation and a graphic depicting seven yellow pencils bundled together like Roman fasces. The image and the words certainly drew my eye. So did something else. Martin was waving a hand to attract my attention.

'Sorry', I said. 'It's just that the photo of the meat and the caption are, well, very striking.'

Martin swivelled round and looked at the picture.

'Yes it is isn't it? Can you tell what it's for?'

Considering the options I hazarded a guess.

'An anti-meat ad for The Vegetarian Society?'

'What? Bloody hell, no!'

I shook my head to indicate a complete lack of ideas. Fitch waved again in the general direction of the picture.

'The Australian Meat Marketing Board. Our Sydney agency created it. It was the most successful Aussie press ad last year.'

I was impressed. 'Wow, they must have seen their sales rocket?'

Martin looked at me as if I'd spoken in Swahili.

'Fuck that! It won more awards than any press ad in history including a Gold Lion at Cannes!'

I had no idea what this meant, Gold Lion sounded vaguely like a chocolate bar but that seemed meagre compensation for such a feat. I replied with a catch all, 'Wow!'

He grinned approvingly and I settled down, ready to answer any number of questions about swearing and technology. Scanning my CV he said,

'OK. So are you any good at cooking? For instance, what's your favourite dish?'

An uneasy feeling came over me. Presumably there was a staff restaurant somewhere but why the head of IT should be interviewing for a chef I couldn't fathom. Perhaps staff had to take it in turns to cook lunch. It seemed improbable though.

'Well, er. Sorry, can I just check; I'm not sure I'm in the right interview.'

'What?'

'I'm here for the IT job.'

'Yes I know that. I've looked at your CV – that's all fine. I'm trying to find out if you'll fit in here. It's not just another office you know.'

Thinking through all the crap I'd heard about interviews I sifted for some shred of advice that would help me. There was nothing in the memory banks to assist with an inquisitor asking about culinary skills. My mind turned to the cod lying on the draining board in my flat, our cat attached to one end and me to the other. Not haute cuisine. I was high and dry. Then my eye caught the lurid meat and 'Eat More Bloody Meat' flashed like a neon sign. Taking my cue from the Aussies' direct approach I decided to take a flyer.

'Tell you what, why don't we go to the pub and have a chat there over a pint or two?' I suggested. Martin beamed; he was out of his chair in a moment and at the door.

'Brilliant idea! You're going to fit in here perfectly. Now, when can you start?'

There and then Fitch produced a contract and after a brief perusal lasting all of ten seconds, I signed it.

Laying the pen down on the desk I glanced up at the gruesome ad and said a prayer of thanks to the patron saint of dodgy advertising. Randy J Feckenburger (the Third), The Freak and Buy-O-Soft were soon to be things of the past.

Chapter Six

Firing and Not Firing the Freak

Walking into Buy-O-Soft early next morning I felt free, liberated, almost giddy with the sense of change in my life. Passing the opaque glass of our offices on the first floor and about to reach for the door handle I saw a figure dart down behind the desk. Opening the door I saw the top of Bob's head behind the Freak's desk. Then Bob's eyes began to reveal themselves, the rest of Bob coming into view as he stood up.

There is no other word for what he was doing and that word is 'lurking.' I mean he was perfectly entitled to lurk on his own premises if he so wished but you have to admit it was strange behaviour. I was about to ask, not surprisingly, 'What are you doing Bob?' but he pre-empted me with exactly the same question, although of course he substituted 'Denis' for 'Bob' at the end of the sentence. Otherwise it would have been disturbing on a whole other level.

'I'm coming in to work Bob! I do this day in day out, it shouldn't be a surprise any more.'

'You startled me that's all,' he admitted.

'What were you doing? Are you looking for something?' I enquired.

'Me? No I was just… checking your desk,' he answered with a guilty aspect to his face, 'for… risks.'

'Risks? But you were at the Freak's desk,' I pointed out.

'I'm thinking of rearranging the office.' Bob said and I immediately knew he was lying. Bob cannot lie. Keeping surprise parties for people's birthdays secret was beyond him. He was a decent, straightforward sort of character and in fact far too honest for his own good, even once going so far as to admit to Mrs. Rhode that our software was often unreliable and we used our clients to test it without telling them. As if anyone had to tell her. I knew what was behind this and that Bob was measuring the Freak up for firing.

'Look Bob. I know Randy wants to get rid of the Freak.'

Bob seemed downcast.

'Sorry to be so devious Denis. I'm not sure he doesn't want to get rid of all of us.'

'You're probably not far off the truth. I can see other people getting jobs but the Freak… well.'

Bob agreed.

'Yeah, I know – I mean he can be a pain but he's actually good at his job, not brilliant but reasonable. I've tried telling Randy that.'

'Maybe Randy just wants brilliance.'

'I think you're right; well he's out of luck round here.'

'Thanks Bob!'

'You know what I mean - Randy thinks everyone should be Bill Gates – he seems to have a bee in his bonnet about Bill Gates in fact. Funny that.'

'You don't think he's got the Freak in his sights because of the Britney Spears incident?'

Bob grimaced and laughed.

'Well it probably didn't help! I'd feel really bad if we had to get rid of the Freak. He's like the office pet. What's his real name again?'

'Maximilian Epworth. I may have an idea,' I said. 'Leave it with me.'

Bob went off to his office muttering "Maximilian Epworth" and shaking his head.

The Freak arrived shortly afterwards. Oblivious to his impending doom he followed his normal morning procedure of a loud fart followed by some mumbling on his mobile as he called his mum to inform her he'd got to work safely having survived the perilous twelve minute journey on the local train. After firing up his computer he exited only to return ten minutes later with a bacon butty, a doughnut and a coke. This was the Freak's breakfast, the first of his five-a-day cholesterol based snacks.

At around nine thirty Mr. Feckenburger (the Third) arrived. The usual gum chewing, bovine noise preceded him and in he ambled. He'd commandeered Andrea's office, a move which had not endeared him to anyone. I got up from my desk and knocked on the partially open door. Randy was unpacking a briefcase and placing papers on the desk in front of him. He looked round as I closed the door behind me.

'Hi Denis. Do we have a meeting?'

I saw no point keeping him in suspense.

'No we don't. I just wanted to tell you I'm not going to fire the Freak. He's a valuable member of staff.'

I must say I wasn't absolutely convincing myself at this point but thought I'd better lay it on thick.

'He gets on well with clients, he's a good programmer...'

'What? Like Bill Gates?' sneered Randy. 'You're better than he is and you're better with clients – we don't really need him as well.'

'Fair point. I suggest you give Bill Gates a call and see if you can recruit him to do the Freak's job for twenty five thousand a year. I'm sure he'll jump at the chance. I think you're acting out of malice because of the Freak's outburst at your first company meeting.'

Randy looked blank. I had to jog his memory.

'Britney Spears? Remember? Just before you molested the woman in the swimming pool.'

'I rescued her!' Randy shouted before subsiding back into his chair. 'OK,' he went on in an unpleasant, pseudo-amicable tone, 'So you're not going to do your job and fire him. That's fine. Now we know where we stand. Anything else?'

'No that's all. Have a nice day!' I quipped and went back to my desk.

From where I sat I could see Randy opening up a spreadsheet and it didn't take a genius to work out he was looking at salaries. An hour and a half later he came out of his office and went into Bob's. I was reading a letter of complaint from Rhoda the Rhino. If you took out the words "solicitors," "incompetent," "sue" and all the swearing it was quite mild for her. I became aware, over the Freak's frenetic mid-morning doughnut chewing and coffee slurping, a heated discussion evolving in Bob's office. After a lengthy, quieter interlude the door opened. Bob emerged and in contrast to his normal, placid self he was clearly very angry.

'Denis, could we have a word in my office please.' he said struggling with his emotions. The Freak, mouth open (crushed doughnut, coffee mixed in, not pretty) sensed something was in the air. I winked at him, stood up and followed Bob into the office. Bob sat down and I took my place next to Feckenburger who was still there, seemingly not at all perturbed by their disagreement.

'Hi Denis,' Randy greeted me, 'I've had a change of mind on the Freak. Your argument this morning was very convincing. And talking to Bob here I recognize that we need someone to support that product. So we're keeping him.'

'Good. I think that's a wise decision.' I commented.

'But it means of course there's no place for you,' Feckenburger added, a degree of satisfaction showing in his voice. Bob must have been surprised at my lack of response. He jumped in, 'I realize this is a shock Denis and you haven't had time to take it in. I'd like to add that I didn't want to do this.'

Randy smiled, 'But since I'm the bad guy round here, I did. I know how it works Denis. We're making your position redundant.'

'We're offering you fifteen thousand as a severance payment.' Bob hastily explained and must have noticed the fleeting look of triumph on my face. Sitting next to me Feckenburger hadn't.

'I didn't want to give you anything but apparently there are laws and Bob has been more than generous. And you don't have to work a notice period.'

'It's not Bob's money or indeed yours to give,' I pointed out to them, 'make it eighteen and I won't contest this.'

Feckenburger laughed, 'Eighteen grand! Jesus, yeah right…'

Bob interrupted him. 'OK that's fair enough Denis.'

'After tax,' I added, thinking this was really pushing it.

Feckenburger was fuming as Bob considered my request.

'Yeah we can do that. I'm sorry about this Denis.'

Randy rolled his eyes.

'What? Are you out of your mind? Do you want to give him a gold watch as well!'

I stood up to make it clear the meeting was over and I was happy with the arrangements. I shook Bob's hand and said,

'Well, that seems fine – can you put all this in writing and sign it, not that I don't trust *you* to be honest Bob but…'

I gave Randy what could only be described as a scornful glance.

An hour later Bob dropped an envelope on my desk. In it was the redundancy agreement, a letter of reference and a touchingly personal letter from him. How he'd done it I do not know but he'd also persuaded Randy to pay for a leaving party at the Ferret and Mattress on a date of my choosing. Having checked that the redundancy agreement was all correct and signed I walked into Bob's office.

'I think we should get Randy in for a minute Bob,' I said. 'I've got something else to tell you.'

Bob picked up his phone called an internal number and Feckenburger came in; Bob ushered him to sit down. Randy, with a jaundiced glance said,

'Mr. Mahoney we are not going to give you any more money, buy you a car or go back on our decision.'

'You don't have to. I'm happy with the payment. And the fact that I can leave immediately is a bonus so I can start my new job after a couple of week's holiday. They will be pleased about that.'

I could see Feckenburger was confused.

'Who is "they"? Sorry "new job"?'

'I think you mean who are they. They are JDFT Media. I was about to bring you my letter of resignation when Bob called me in.'

I could feel a storm rising from the chair to my right. Randy was searching the desk either for clues as to how this could have happened or something to strangle me with.

'For Christ's sake you just got eighteen grand out of us for nothing!' he shouted. There was a strange sound and I noticed that Bob was laughing as Randy got angrier.

'Denis that is brilliant!'

'We're going to tear up the redundancy agreement!' Randy bellowed.

'No we're not!' Bob said, through his laughter and wiping tears from his eyes. 'God Almighty that's the best thing I've heard in a long time!'

'Fuck's sake Bob! This is extortion!' Feckenburger shouted.

I was now concerned for Randy's well being.

'I thought you said there was too much swearing in this office?' I asked innocently as the American got up and exited, slamming the door. Bob sat back and contemplated me for a moment. He frowned.

'I'm not sure we can pay for the leaving do now though – we didn't put that in the agreement. Shame...'

'That's OK Bob – you win some, you lose some. I'm happy with what I got and the Freak's keeping his job. I think next Friday for my leaving drink?'

'Are you going to invite Randy?'

'Of course! I have a lot to thank him for!'

Chapter Seven

Leaving Do.

If you ever happen to find yourself in the farthest reaches of
West London and are at a loose end you could do worse than
drop into one of the many fine local pubs in that neck of the
woods. Unless of course that pub is the Ferret and Mattress, a
watering hole about quarter of a mile from the offices of Buy-
O-Soft. Known to one and all as "the Ferret" it was a low
ceilinged, tobacco coloured, tobacco stained dive of a place.
Unfortunately it was also the only pub within staggering
distance of our workplace. So when I sent out an email
informing my workmates that this would be the scene of my
leave taking of Buy-O-Soft several people doubted the ability
of the Ferret to host anything other than a brawl. Len the
barman and owner of the Ferret had assured me that he could
supply food while drink was a given. Eventually everyone
conceded that as the only other pub in the area had ambulances
permanently parked outside and was strongly rumoured to host
dogfights, the Ferret it was.

Len had done us proud. On Friday at about four I left my desk
for the final time and the Freak and I wended our way down to
the Ferret. As I'd been a fairly regular customer Len had put up
a cheap plastic banner inside the pub which read, "Piss Off
Denis You Bastard! We'll Miss Ya!"

'It's like witty isn't it?' Len explained when I cast doubt on the wording but it seemed ungrateful to complain too much. He'd also provided a mountain of sausage rolls, chicken goujons for the more sophisticated consumers and mini-burgers for those in between. I had to steer the Freak away from the food until everyone else arrived. Since I'd shared a desk with him for two odd years, I thought the least I could do was buy him a pint. Of course the Freak, living up to his name, didn't drink much, his annual intake being a couple of halves of shandy at the Christmas party.

'Fre... er Maximilian,' I said, 'can I buy you a beer – this is the last time we'll get a chance to celebrate working together?'

The Freak looked at me suspiciously as he sat down at a table by the window next to the fruit machine.

'My Mum told me not to accept sweets, drink or drugs from strangers.'

After trying to work out whether this indicated smothering authoritarianism or great liberal values in his mother and giving up, I argued, 'I'm not a stranger – we've worked together for two years.'

'Two years, seven months, nineteen days, eight hours and nine minutes,' came the precise reply.

'Well there you are! And I've bought you drinks in the past.'

'Might have a pint later then,' he begrudgingly agreed, 'and don't call me Maximilian... it just seems weird.'

If you avoided the subjects of sci-fi, fast food, lethal weapons, war games, C++ programming, Java programming or in fact any sort of programming, the Freak could occasionally be reasonable company. This wasn't one of those occasions. He was telling me a long and rather convoluted, OK, tedious, story about his uncle at a family get together which had gone dramatically wrong when Len interrupted us with a worried look on his face.

'Denis,' he beckoned me over to where he was laying out more food on a side table, 'do you think these burgers are OK mate?'

'People like burgers Len – they're fine thanks.'

'No, I mean, they smell a bit funny to me; greasy or something.'

We sampled the air around the food table, following the aroma until we identified its source by the window.

'Ah… don't worry, it's not the burgers Len, it's my colleague's tank top.'

Len looked across the bar at the Freak who was happily flicking at a pool of beer.

'I see. Good that's a relief. I mean, not good he, um, y'know… I'm glad it's not the burgers - I got them special. Yeah, you couldn't ask him to sit a bit closer to the door? It's just he might put people off coming in.'

'Well we're this side of the pub and everyone coming to the leaving do is used to him so it'll be OK.'

As I reassured Len, Bob arrived and waving a tenner at the barman bought a round. He whispered, 'You won't believe this but Randy's coming along a bit later.'

'You're joking? What for?'

'Well I think he secretly admired how you got your redundancy payment *and* a new job. He won't say that of course but he seemed to have mellowed a bit when I saw him yesterday.'

Len had put three pints in front of us.

'Who's the other pint for?' I asked Bob.

He indicated to the Freak.

'I can't leave the Freak out – I'll be asking him to take some of your workload so I've got to keep him sweet.'

'He doesn't drink!'

'Doesn't he? Is there something wrong with him?'

'Sorry Freak!' Bob called over to our deep fried chum. 'I'll get you something else.'

But the Freak took the pint quite happily – I presumed he'd decided his 'one of the evening' would come at the start to make the rest of the time a bit more bearable for him and the rest of us. Bob and I joined him as The Ferret began to fill up with my erstwhile colleagues. I would like to be able to say this was an indication of my popularity and that they'd come to say a teary eyed farewell but you get the picture when Ann, who I think worked in admin of some sort, raised her glass of white wine in my direction and said, 'So, you're getting married

Dave! Congratulations! Hope it goes well. Better than mine anyway… the bastard…'

Then she burst into tears and dashed for the Ladies.

'Better keep an eye on Ann tonight – she gets a bit emotional after a few. Punched me at the Christmas lunch. It's surprising who turns up when there's free food and drink.' Bob observed.

'Indeed – and mentioning turning up, look who it is,' I said in a low voice as Randy stooped through the doorway. Spotting Bob, the Freak and me he came over,

'Hi guys – let me get you a beer.'

'A bit later Randy thanks – Bob's just got me one.'

Then we started going through the whole, at what point should someone coming in be inducted into your round or should they maintain splendid isolation and get their own, bolt it down and then join the now synchronized drinking system. Bob got up and we initiated Randy into our round.

'What are you drinking Randy?' Bob called out.

This was unfortunate timing as Ann was passing Bob at that moment, returning to the solace of her wine.

'You dirty bastard! I'm only just single!' she exclaimed before producing another salty outburst from her eyes and retreating to the Ladies.

'I'll have an orange juice please Bob – on the rocks!' our head honcho of Finance bellowed.

The prospect of an evening spent with one teetotaler, a reluctant occasional drinker and Bob, did not fill me with glee.

There was an awkward silence while we waited for Bob to bring Feckenburger's drink. The Freak, socially adept as a cobra, stepped into the breach with an unexpected question.

'Do you ever get dandruff Randy?'

I'd noticed the Freak had been fishing something out of his pint but didn't look too closely until I realized his beer was becoming like of those little glass things with liquid in them that you see in the shops at Christmas time. The idea is that you shake them and it turns into a facsimile of a snowstorm falling on some sort of Nativity scene or maybe Father Christmas and a robin or two. Anyway the Christmas scene in the Freak's pint wasn't quite up to that standard as yet but a few flakes had settled on top and absorbing the liquid, began their long journey to the bottom. Randy J. Feckenburger (the Third), to his credit, didn't flinch at this. He thought for a moment and said, 'I tend to use a shampoo that treats dandruff as well as washing and conditioning.'

Frankly the repartee wasn't scintillating. Worse was to come. The Freak, looking at Randy's head thoughtfully said, 'You have very lustrous hair.'

I'm not sure why but I was getting really uncomfortable with this whole conversation and was on the verge of calling to Bob to hurry up but fortunately he'd made his purchase and was heading back towards us. Randy however proved unembarrassable.

'Thank you,' he said simply.

I thought he might respond with something along the lines of 'And you have very fine dandruff sir,' but mercifully he kept his silence. Bob gave Randy the orange juice, raised his pint and said, 'Well Denis, good luck in the new job! We'll miss you.'

Trying not to look at either the Freak's pint or Randy's hair I said, 'Thanks Bob – I'll miss...' but stalled after that as I tried to think what I'd miss. The Freak? Randy? Mrs. Rhodes? So I carried on with a generic, 'you all!' Randy thankfully moved us away from hair admiring, colleague missing territory.

'Hey, I really enjoyed firing you!' he uttered. I think it was his attempt at a joke.

'I really enjoyed taking your money!' I shot back.

Now it was Bob's turn for unease.

'Er, let's leave on good terms shall we?' he said.

'No hard feelings,' I said.

'No hard feelings!' answered Randy and we clinked glasses

The Freak, in an attempt to join in this mildly threatening banter said,

'Well, I think you were right to get rid of Denis!' to which Randy responded, possibly without thinking it through.

'Hey if it hadn't been Denis, it would have been you!' he chuckled.

At this point there should have been a rueful answering laugh from the Freak and perhaps some slightly barbed bantering response. Instead there was silence. Glancing at him I could see he was on the verge of tears. I glared at Randy then turned back to the be-dandruffed one.

'That was a joke Freak – don't take it seriously!'

'Was it?' his podgy face lit up with hope. Or it might have been confusion. Randy finally took the cue which Bob and I were trying to send him and consoled the Freak.

'Yeah. Y'know I was saying to Bob how valuable you are to the company. Sorry buddy! I need the spirit of the Lord to make me a bit more charitable.'

I was concerned the evangelical, sermony side of him might be about to come out and my sense of discomfort wasn't getting any less. The Freak stood up and said, 'OK, I'll get the drinks in.'

Bob collared Randy, 'Randy you have to be gentle with the Freak, he's very sensitive.'

'Sorry guys I was just like not thinking really.'

'We noticed,' I couldn't resist saying. The conversation became a bit stilted and there was a palpable sense of relief when Ann, on a break from weeping duty, patted Bob on the shoulder.

'Bob, I'm really sorry – I thought you were being personal earlier. I'd forgotten Mr. Feckenburger's first name.'

Bob accepted Ann's apology with good grace and offered her a seat. At least now that we have some intelligent, civilized company, maybe Randy won't be quite so abrasive I thought. The Freak had supplied us with drinks and though I can't honestly say it was rip-roaring fun we listened with patience firstly to Ann's account of what passed for an amusing incident in the admin department. Something involving a misfiled document apparently. Then we tolerated the Freak telling us about the five most hilarious bugs in our software. I went to the bar and Len asked 'Same again?' I nodded and took my liquid booty back to the table. Bob was now reminiscing about the old days and the history of the company, as he always did after a couple of beers. Randy suddenly said, 'C'mon Bob don't be so boring! You haven't told me who's fucking who round here? I want to hear all the gossip.'

Taken aback I stared at our new colleague. He seemed to have a gleam in his eye which hadn't been present before.

'Well, er...' Bob replied and understandably so. Randy brushed aside his protests. 'Y'know in head office last month, just before I came over here to you guys, John Serino's PA Ellen emailed her boyfriend telling him what she was going to do with him that night! It was only supposed to go to him - his name was Al something or other but she hit All Staff by accident. Boy, that guy was going to get the ride of his life I can tell you!' Randy furrowed his brow, 'Y'know there was one thing she said she was gonna do I didn't even know was physically possible... maybe you could help me out on this Anne?'

Ann coughed like an alarmed sheep. Bob jumped in.

'Randy, how about a game of darts?'

'Hey Bob I'm telling a story here!' our American chum snapped, a tad aggressively, 'Yeah, she was going to fuck his brains inside out man!'

'Yes, er, I'll just go to the bar and get us all a nice drink.' said Anne. 'What's everyone having?'

'Len knows – just say the same as last time,' the Freak told her.

Bob and I exchanged a glance and he stood up.

'Denis we'd better check the food out,' jerking his head in a backward fashion towards the rear of the pub. I joined him in the room behind.

'What's got into him? I'd just got used to the prudish born again evangelist type. Now he's gone all frat boy on us.'

'I don't know. I think I'll start drinking orange juice though.'

Bob's phone was ringing, he turned away to answer it.

'Bob Scott speaking. Oh, hi! Yes. He's here with us at the moment.'

There was a lengthy pause and I could see by Bob's face that he was assimilating information from the caller.

'No. We'll make sure he's fine. He's what? That's fine, you can rest assured… yes don't worry he's in our capable hands.'

I was pretty sure who was on the other end of the conversation. As Bob hung up I guessed,

'The Freak's Mum?'

Bob, thoughtful now, said, 'Er no. That was John Serino.'

'The man with the sexually flexible PA?'

'The very one Denis and he also just happens to be CEO of Buy-O-Soft US.'

'I take it he wasn't calling to wish me a bon voyage?'

Bob steered me to a corner as far from our table as possible.

'No... he was checking to see if Mr. Feckenburger had arrived and was settling in OK. Apparently Randy's a recovering alcoholic! Used to be a really wild man but since he gave up drink and found Jesus he's been OK. They had to move him because of a sexual harassment charge after he got pissed at a company do. He was saying we must make sure Randy doesn't get tempted into drinking. He holds me personally responsible for him staying sober.'

'You've made a good start Bob, taking him to a pub...'

'Yes... That's a point... I suppose if you look at it that way...!'

Then Bob beamed, 'But at least we've only been buying him orange juice and he seems quite happy just drinking that!'

As he said this a thought struck me.

'Hold on a sec Bob.'

I went to the bar where Ann had just been served and had taken the drinks back to our table. Len was drying a glass while eavesdropping on the conversation floating up from our table though you'd have had to be stone deaf not to hear Randy saying, 'Ann, you got a real cute ass, anyone ever tell you that?'

I said to Len, 'Len, you know our round - what is it?'

Without missing a beat Len reeled off the order, 'Pinot Grigio, two pints of Pride, pint of Broadside and a vodka and orange. Sorry, double vodka and orange.'

'Double vodka and orange! Who's drinking that?'

'I think it's for your American colleague.'

'Who ordered it?'

'The little gingery guy who smells of chips.'

'What the fuck's he up to?'

I went over and not so gently guided the Freak up by the arm.

Randy said, 'Hey Denis I was just saying to the Freak here you dudes need to lighten up and enjoy yourselves a bit more. It's like a fucking convent in here! Isn't that right Ann?' and he winked at her in a horrendously leery way. Alarm was spreading across Ann's face. Having dragged him out of Feckenburger's earshot I said to the Freak, 'We've all been buying Randy double vodka and orange without realizing it – I make it four so far - that's eight shots. He's a raging alcoholic and we've got him off his face! Len said you ordered the first one. Why?'

'He asked for a spirit!' the Freak protested.

'Oh? Did he? Are you sure? Well he shouldn't have. According to his boss he's given up drink.'

This seemed puzzling. Then I remembered Randy calling on the spirit of the Lord or some such thing.

'Freak, you are a fucking idiot! Sorry, don't take that personally.'

I have to admit though that Randy was much better, if slightly unhinged, company with a few drinks inside him. I surreptitiously bought him an unadulterated orange juice and told the Freak to take it over to our US guest to try and dilute the vodka in his system. He took a slurp and there was an immediate bellow from the table, making Ann spill her wine.

'Hey barman! Yeah you!' Randy shouted at Len, 'there's something wrong with this orange juice buddy – it's not like the ones you were serving earlier!'

Len shrugged, poured vodka into a glass and added a shot of orange.

Randy cheered up as he swigged his new found nectar.

'That's better! Anyone see Miley Cyrus – wow awesome! Hey Freak, she makes your Britney Spears look like a fuckin' nun!'

Bob, now fully up to speed with the situation gave the problem his full attention.

'I think he needs something to eat,' he suggested. It only took the mere mention of food to get Feckenburger lurching across the pub into the back room. The Freak, sensing pastry and fat in reasonable quantities, joined him. Surveying the table like Great Whites spotting a tray of snack sized seals, they were off. With the hunger of a man who had consumed nine vodkas, Randy started wolfing Len's food. He and the Freak were as one as they stripped food, locust like, from the table. Relieved that Randy was soaking up the alcohol with sausage rolls and the like, I wandered over to talk to various bods from around the company and was having a pleasant time when Ann suddenly grabbed me by the arm an hour or so later. It was an ominous sign and I felt a momentary fear at what Randy might have said or done to her.

'It's Mr. Feckenburger Denis. I don't think he's very well.'

I wasn't really surprised at this but when I saw Bob heading my way I was even more worried.

'Denis, Randy's foaming at the mouth!'

'What?'

'He's in the men's bog. Just sitting there saying he's had a vision and foaming at the mouth.'

Sure enough the reports were accurate. Randy J. Feckenburger (the Third) was slumped in a stall with flecks of foam round his lips and bubbling like a malfunctioning dishwasher. By this time he was completely comatose. We managed to lift him up and brought him into a back room which also served as Len's crisp store. We propped Randy on a chair in between boxes of cheese n' onion and salt n' vinegar. Bob started shouting at him, 'Come on Randy, come back to life! You can do it!'

'He's not dead Bob,' I pointed out. 'Just shitfaced.'

Len supplied copious black coffees and eventually our Finance Director's eyes began to open. The Freak had arrived on the scene.

'It'll be rabies I reckon,' he opined. Bob seemed to consider this possibility.

'Do you think it could be?'

'For God's sake Bob he hasn't been bitten by anything.'

'But he's foreign,' the Freak said, adding, 'my Mum says all foreigners have rabies.'

'Thanks for your xenophobic input Freak but it's not rabies!'

Randy suddenly opened his eyes and gave us a searching look.

'Pineapple!' he said, surprising me at least.

'He wants pineapple,' Bob said. 'That's strange.'

'I told you – it's cause he's foreign,' offered the Freak.

'More pineapple!' Randy muttered.

I thought of all the food on the table and couldn't remember seeing pineapple unless it had been part of a dessert I hadn't tried.

'Can people have an allergic reaction to pineapple? Anyone else have pineapple?' I asked the Freak, Bob and Ann who had now arrived and burst into tears at Randy's alarming appearance. They all shook their heads.

'Pineapple' he repeated, more foam welling from his mouth as he spoke.

'Or he could be possessed,' the Freak surmised.

Len came in with a face like thunder.

'How is he?'

'Don't know but he's opened his eyes and is speaking.'

'Well one of your guys has done something really weird.'

'Oh God, what now?' asked Bob.

'Someone's stolen all my Zesty lemon cistern blocks.'

'Len, I think this is more serious…' I started saying then paused, 'what do they look like Len. I mean are they a bit like say, pineapple?'

'Now you mention it Denis, I suppose they are quite like pineapple rings when they've worn down a bit. They're super foaming ones - I'm really not happy.'

Bob and I looked at each other then at our super foaming friend.

'At least he's going to have very clean insides…' Bob mused.

Chapter Eight

Gorillas With Calculators.

Another three weeks of my life passed. I pushed open the same glass door in the same building on the same narrow Soho street but this time I entered a cross between a McDonalds and the set of a pantomime. A curved translucent red plastic barrier split the reception area in two, palm trees, festooned with small cakes hanging from silver threads, lined both sides. The robotic receptionist had now been elevated and was perched on a stool two feet above the desk, requiring her to stretch down to her computer. The phone rang. She was doing sugary, grating voice today.

'JDFT Media good morning.'

As a fully fledged member of the company I thought I'd foster better relations with her. After she put the phone down and before she could get her nail file out, I approached the desk with what I thought was a warm tone of camaraderie.

'Good to see you again, how's the new desk?'

'It were made wrong werenit?'

'Well better than being hidden behind that big rock last time I saw you.'

Ignoring my attempt at camaraderie she stared from her lofty height.

'How can I help you?'

'I'm starting today – working for Martin Fitch.'

'What's your name?'

'Denis Mahoney.'

She lifted the phone and dropped back into grumpy grating voice.

'Martin, Dan Moloney ere for ya. Yeah OK.'

Without looking up she said.

'He'll be dahn in a minute, take a seat.'

Her complete lack of grace spoke volumes. Of course she'd probably seen this a thousand times before. As gatekeeper she'd watched legions of young hopefuls, pumped with enthusiasm bound through these doors only to be broken, all spirit crushed, by the monstrous wheels of the advertising machine. But at this point I was still towards the bounding enthusiasm end of the scale. Ten minutes later Martin arrived in the foyer.

'Good to see you! Welcome on board as the dick-brains upstairs say! How was the leaving do?'

I thought of Randy J. Feckenburger foaming at the mouth and decided that it was a little early to start telling that particular story.

'Well… most of those attending were software developers but it wasn't too bad.'

He laughed, 'We're probably a bit livelier here than you're used to. Don't worry, you'll fit in fine.'

Our office was a fairly cramped space down a short flight of stairs at the back of the fifth floor.

'OK. Well let me introduce you to the team.'

There was one other person in the room, a woman who was looking at a sheet of paper covered in scribble and transferring it to the computer in front of her. She was stunningly pretty, with long brown hair and freckles. Martin introduced us.

'Denis, this is Karen Ellison. She's our presentation manager.'

She looked up and extended a hand which I shook as I stared at her open mouthed. Realizing this was not a good first impression I shut it and followed Fitch. He headed out down a short corridor then stopped at a lift. Inside the lift was a poster which said, "The Only Way Is Up!" advertising a financial product of some sort. The doors hissed open as Martin spoke,

'OK we'll break you in gently – on this floor are the creatives.'

Up until that point in my life I'd never seen so many Apple computers in my life. In one corner was a white grand piano where a guy with very long hair and a goatee, wearing torn jeans and a scruffy t-shirt, sat playing a simple, haunting phrase over and over. As we approached he stopped and sighed.

'Hi Martin. Can't seem to get this right. How the fuck do you write music that makes oil sound romantic?'

'I thought it was amazing. Really moving,' I commented.

The long haired guy perused me.

'Thank you! You've obviously got good taste!' he smiled. 'I happen to agree but it's not really what we want. Sorry, who are you?'

Martin introduced us.

'Denis, this is Trevor Hutchins, our Creative Director. Trevor, this is Denis Mahoney our new IT Executive.'

Hutchins stood up and shook hands.

'Good to meet you – hope you enjoy yourself here. Maybe you can give me a lesson on using a Mac! My guys are brilliant but I'm a bit old school – give me a pen and a graphic pad any day! Have you taken him into the lions' den yet Martin? That's our media buyers – gorillas with calculators - the necessary evil of advertising. Don't let them scare you!'

'Thanks Trevor – we want to keep Denis,' Martin scowled. As we left I heard the few notes starting up again. Martin held the door open for me.

'Old school! Trevor has the best creative mind in the industry. Last year we had a softball competition – he made a film and wrote a stunning score to it – it was a work of art! I hate softball but I watched it three times! Once sober! If I'm honest he's wasted here.'

We took the lift back down and stopped at the top of a short flight of stairs.

'Right, well, let me feed you to the lions' den!' he muttered.

'These are the television buyers – they're the ones who buy the airtime for the ads which adorn our screens every evening and indeed daytime but we try not to mention daytime.'

In front and below was a pit with some forty to fifty people, mostly male, in it. They were all standing in front of computer screens and seemingly having tantrums into their phones. One stocky, thuggish looking guy in the middle was shouting into a handset. His face was stroke red, his whole demeanour that of a man just on or slightly over the edge of psychosis.

'Stevie my old son, listen to me. No, no *you* fucking listen! To me! Now! If you don't get me the fucking centre break of Coronation Street I will tell your fucking boss about you and that slag you was with at the Capital party last month. D'you understand? Yeah, *I* know it's bollocks and *you* know it's bollocks but Gav's a gullible dickhead; he likes me and he doesn't like you. Am I right? Am I? Yeah, so get me that fucking break NOW!'

His blood pressure was probably not measurable on any normal scale. Slamming the phone down so hard that it shattered, he turned to the general melee and shouted to no one in particular, 'Fucking useless bastard phone! Oi! Get me another phone you wankers!'

One of his team opened a drawer and handed him a virgin phone which the mad bastard plugged in. It rang immediately. He snatched up the new and probably nervous receiver.

'What? You got me it! Good fucking man! Steve, you are a fucking gem y'know that! Must go out and get shitfaced soon. Say hi to that tosser Gav for me. Cheers!'

Martin ambled over to him.

'Mark, this is Denis he's our new IT man.'

The thuggy looking guy turned and with eyes that bulged threateningly, sized me up.

'Good to see you mate! Welcome to JDFT. Hope you're better than the last twat,' he beamed amicably, turned, picked up the phone and began another foul mouthed rant.

Martin raised an eyebrow.

'That is the legendary Mark, our second most feral buyer.'

'Second most?

'You wait till you meet Nick the Bastard. He's off at the moment on a hangover day.'

I laughed. Martin shook his head.

'I'm not joking – he negotiated twelve hangover days a year in addition to his holidays when he joined. He sometimes goes off the rails a bit. During his medical the company doctor, who you will meet next week, asked how much he drank. He needed a pen and pad first, then a calculator before she told him not to bother.

'At least he's not a born again Christian', I said.

I made a mental note to check his PC before he got in each morning. Martin guided me through the rest of the floor. The TV buyers communicated with each other via constant pisstaking and obscenities but at the other end of the floor was a row of four offices which seemed like havens of tranquility.

Martin scowled, 'You don't really have a problem with born again Christians do you?

I thought of Randy J Feckenburger.

'Not in general, just one in particular.'

'Good. Well let me introduce you to Katriona and Parky. She's a very smart German woman, head of research. These two spot trends before the trends know they're happening. They're JDFT's secret weapon… Parky's a brilliant mathematician but a tad odd sometimes.'

Nothing surprised me about this place any more so if he'd had horns and scales I don't think I would have flinched. Fitch knocked on one of the doors and a gentle, reassuring voice said 'Come in.'

Behind a desk, surrounded by a dangerously teetering stack of papers sat a bespectacled, curly haired man in his mid to late thirties. To his left was a blonde woman, of a similar age, working on a computer.

'Katriona and Andy, I'd like you to meet Denis Mahoney who's just joined us as IT Executive. Keep him happy and he'll keep your beloved databases running.' There was an air of academic serenity in the room in stark contrast to the barbarian bedlam just outside. Katriona smiled at Martin and me, gave a brief wave and returned to her screen. Andy was a quietly spoken Welshman who shook hands politely and seemed to be completely not odd. In fact I wondered how he could survive in such a place. We exchanged pleasantries but it was obvious the two of them were absorbed in their work so we left them to it. The building was a labyrinth and I thought it would take me weeks to find my way round the different levels so I was relieved that Martin led the way back. Returning to our unhomely office I found a smallish box on my desk. In the box was a new mobile phone and of course, being in IT, I was keen to see how quickly I could break it. Martin watched as I set up the phone and started charging it.

'We keep our work mobiles on until seven pm – unless there's a pitch when we keep them on permanently. And occasionally Eric will call you at some odd time.'

'And Eric's wife,' added Karen. 'And Eric's wife's friend from her golf club. Steph her name is.'

I laughed at her wit.

'That's not a joke,' Martin sighed, 'she called me at midnight once – she was having problems with her Amazon account. Once you get a corporate mobile phone it's just a short step to being electronically tagged. Anyway hopefully you won't get too many nuisance calls…'

'Yeah right,' Karen added to the conversation.

Chapter Nine

Canteen Pete's Gastro Bistro

On the way down the stairs leading to our little IT lair, Martin had commented, 'We have a few odd bods round the place but hopefully you can see we're a fairly normal crowd. As normal as humans get anyway…'

I was thinking about this, comparing the Freak with Mark the psychotic thug. If I had any lingering illusions that this was a 'normal' company they were shattered when I glanced at my screen. I had to read the first email several times to take in the words and arrange them into something sensible.

```
From: Matt Griffiths
To: All Staff
Subject: Ariadne Insurance shoot_
Importance: Normal
Hi,
Has anyone got a leopard I could borrow
for a shoot next Wednesday or know where I
could get one? It will be a full day
starting around 9:00 a.m. finishing about
7.00p.m. - cheers in advance!

Matt
```

I asked the obvious (to me) question.

'What's a leopard?'

Karen raised her head and tutted. Martin made a gruff, disbelieving sort of noise.

'What? You don't know what a leopard is?'

'Well, I know about the spotty scratchy cat type but this guy must mean something else – like an Apple operating system maybe?'

'I'll ask him.' said Karen, picking up the phone.

There was a brief conversation at the end of which she said,

'It's the spotty, scratchy cat type. He says it doesn't have to be a snow leopard or anything like that, just an ordinary one will do. Preferably trained.'

'Why didn't he say?' I asked, mustering as much sarcasm as I could in a feeble attempt to win back some respect after my idiotic question earlier, 'There must be loads of trained leopards roaming London just waiting for a chance to be in an ad! Good luck to him with that one!'

I was silenced by the next email which had popped up in front of me as I was delivering my withering verdict.

From: Matt Griffiths
To: All Staff
Subject: Re: Ariadne shoot_
Importance: Normal

```
Thanks for all the replies guys - got
one,
 Ta
 Matt
```

Curiosity got the better of me.

'Ask him where he got it.'

Karen made reluctant noises but called the freshly leoparded Matt. Another brief chat before she reported back to us.

'He got three offers but one of them's done other films and stuff – Dan in Press has a sister who works for an animal casting agency.'

'Very useful to know in case I feel the need for an Italian speaking kangaroo.'

'He got his leopard didn't he?' Karen replied ill-temperedly. 'And you were the one who asked.'

'OK OK. Sorry I'm just not used to people asking for wildlife before lunch.'

'Mentioning lunch and wildlife…' Martin said.

It was now getting on for one o'clock and as Martin guided me down a concrete staircase at the back of the building he paused.

'OK there's no easy way to do this Denis I'm afraid. I'll have to introduce you to the delights of Canteen Pete. Best you know what you're letting yourself in for. Have you any food allergies, coeliac, peanuts, gluten, arsenic…?'

'Arsenic makes me come out in death but no allergies apart from that.'

'You will have by the time you've visited Canteen Pete's a few times. Of course you might be the rare soul who survives unscathed.'

'I'm pretty much omnivorous.'

'Good! As our in house caterer, if that's the word for it, he leaves something to be desired. Cooking skills mainly. But he has his moments. Eric got him on the cheap when he came out of prison.'

'What was Eric in prison for?'

Martin laughed again.

'No, Pete was in prison. Mind you the idea of Eric in prison is an appealing one.'

'Decent of him to give Pete a job though.'

'Huh, definitely out of character. I'm sure it was just because he knew Pete'd work for bugger all.'

'So, what was Pete in prison for?'

'Poisoning his first wife… and one of her lovers.'

'And he runs the restaurant?'

'Calling it a restaurant is pushing it. No, it's OK, they survived. Long time in hospital though. Most of her organs failed at one time or another. And she was in a coma for month.'

'Great, I'm reassured! That's not so bad – we're only risking major organ failure.'

Martin ushered me down a long corridor at the back of the building into a gloomy room with a massive television at one end, a bar at the other and a food counter running along one wall. A few people sat round red plastic tables dotted about the room. Behind the counter a lugubrious man, possibly in his early sixties, stood watching twenty four hour news on the vast TV. This was Canteen Pete. Behind him a chalkboard announced, "TODAY'S SPECIAL" and below it in smaller script, "NOTHING." It didn't look promising. Pete greeted us over the metal counter where steaming containers of food bubbled beneath.

'Afternoon Martin,' he said in a low, depressed tone. 'We're a bit limited today on the old ad-hoc stuff mate, hence the lack of specials I'm afraid but tomorrow looks a bit more promising.'

'Oh, how's that?' Martin asked gruffly.

'Badger I found last weekend should be ready. Very similar to venison if you hang them right. Probably only just been killed when I got to it. Still warm in fact – bit gutty but OK if you know what I mean. But as I say that's for tomorrow, what can I get you gentlemen today?'

Avoiding the hot food, panic set in as I glanced at the range of sandwiches. They looked innocent enough. But who knows. Can you make sandwiches from rat or other feral animals?

'He's joking of course? About the badger?' I asked Martin as I sat down with the most boring but hopefully safe cheese sandwich I'd ever seen.

'Probably not,' said Martin, 'last year we won the account of an environmental charity who believe in recycling all sorts of stuff. One of their campaigns was about 'wild food.' They meant berries, fungi, maybe rabbit, that sort of stuff but Pete really took it to heart. I mean it's good in one way that he's very conscious of CO2 emissions etc but…'

From our vantage point at the other side of the room I could now see a hand painted sign that read, 'Pete's Gastro-Bistro.'

'That's a new idea – 'gastro bistro' – what does it mean exactly?'

'The 'gastro' is there only because he couldn't spell 'enteritis' and the bistro is also a mistake – he means Bisto - Pete uses it in everything he cooks.'

Pete assumed our interest in his sign marked us out as connoisseurs of adventurous cuisine. He called across, 'Sorry lads I forgot to mention; I'm doing my 'all in one' special tomorrow – it's very 'andy if you're in a bit of an 'urry. It's main and dessert all in a single package. You'll probably never guess what it is but I'm very proud of it – I sort of created it; a bit like the way that geezer Heston Bloomingdale does his stuff at his place the Fat Fuck.'

For some reason I felt queasy. Fitch, rashly encouraging him said, 'Really? By the way it's Heston Blumenthal and the Fat Duck. So what is it Pete, this 'all in one' of yours?'

'Baked beans and Ambrosia creamed rice. Mixed together. Marvellous! Surprisingly different! You'll have to try it.'

My queasiness didn't get any less but mercifully Karen arrived to take my mind off it.

'You don't think it's a bit early to introduce him to this place?' she interrogated Martin.

'It's lunchtime,' he protested, fairly enough.

'I mean in career terms. We want this one to last. Remember?'

Feeling a bit out of the conversation I got their attention.

'I'm not sure why but I've gone from queasy to uneasy. What do you mean "you want this one to last"? What happened last time?' I asked, remembering just too late, the warning of the recruitment agent not to ask this very question.

'Ah, well…' Martin stalled.

Karen raised a carefully pencilled eyebrow.

'We'll tell you sometime.'

'He is still alive isn't he?' I queried in alarm.

'Yeah…' Karen reassured me, in a not reassuring way.

'Probably,' added Martin. 'I think. Yes, no reason for him not to be. Anyway was the cheese sandwich to your liking?' he asked, as if inquiring about a gourmet extravaganza.

'Edible,' I replied feeling that I should maybe have asked more questions at the interview.

Chapter Ten

The Post Room

When I got back to my desk there was an envelope lying on it. Something bulged within so I lifted and shook it gently. No sound. Opening the envelope a sleek grey pen dropped out. It had a snug grip and as I discovered on giving it a test drive, a smooth writing style. Karen stared, then looked round and attracted Martin's attention from the screen he was swearing at in customary fashion.

'He's been given a good pen.' she said, in hushed tones.

Martin, electrified at this news, jumped up.

'What?!'

''It's a black gel roller ball,' Karen enunciated in a reverential tone.

'It's a black gel roller ball,' I said like a somewhat defensive parrot, though I wasn't sure why I felt defensive about a pen.

'Black!' Karen interjected.

'A gel rollerball!' Martin said, coming over to verify this outrage. 'What the fuck's going on?'

Clearly the foundations of hell had been shaken and I sat there, proudly but I have to admit, slightly sheepishly, holding the controversial writing instrument. It said 'Uni-ball Signo' on the clip and the barrel informed me that it was made by the Mitsubishi Pencil Company. Apparently it also had a gel grip and, judging by my colleagues' reactions, I wouldn't have been surprised if it also possessed some sort of mystical powers.

'Can no one else write or something?' I asked. 'I mean if it's embarrassing you I'll send it back.'

'Send it back!' screeched Karen. 'Are you mad?'

'Is it just me or is everyone over-reacting to this pen?' I wondered aloud.

I thought for a second Martin was going to stroke the pen or grab it from me.

'Over-reacting! You don't understand – it's a symbol.' He affirmed in a reverential tone.

'Is it?' I asked, clasping it tightly for some unknown reason.

Martin assured me it was indeed a symbol. I'd also found an A4 sheet within the envelope and extracted it, in a surreptitious way in case it was something so exciting it would be construed as witchcraft. It was in fact a very dull request for information about stuff like bank accounts so they could pay me, one section asking for name of next of kin in case I managed to sustain fatal injuries in my day to day activities, another requesting a convenient date for a medical, plus a request for what I would like to be called on my ID badge. I was tempted to put 'Zorg the Mighty, Gel Rollerball Pen Bearer' but restrained myself. Finally, in this envelope of dull delights, there was a request to come down to the post room at my earliest convenience to be photographed for my badge.

'Well if you don't mind I'm just going to use this symbol to fill in that sheet then I'll nip down to the post room.'

But Martin hadn't finished.

'Y'see, Greg doesn't just give out rollerball gel pens to any old person. You have been chosen! Most people get a blue biro. If you get a black biro it means Greg quite likes you.'

Karen pondered wonderingly. 'But a black gel rollerball…'

'Greg?'

She enlightened me.

'He's head of post and interdepartmental memos.

'But that really doesn't do justice to him.'

'Oh?' I said in the absence of anything else to add.

'Put it this way, his information gathering would put MI6 to shame.' Martin explained.

'Right. Anyway I've got to go down and see him.' Then I paused as something odd struck me and I asked Karen, 'Sorry did you say "interdepartmental memos"?

'What?'

'You said this guy, Greg, is head of "post and interdepartmental memos."

'Yeah…'

'You still use memos here? As well as email?'

Martin looked up.

'Not any more we don't. Haven't seen a memo in years.'

'So why's he head of memos then?'

'It's a… kind of old, out of date honorary title. Like being a freeman of the city of London – you're allowed to drive sheep across London Bridge but no one does it. And no one sends memos any more.'

I stared at Martin.

'Good, I'm glad we cleared that up. I'll be off then.'

And off I went, frankly bewildered, to visit the Master of the Worshipful and Ancient Order of Post and Memo Non-Senders. I almost expected Greg to be dressed in frock coat and breeches with buckles on velvet shoes so I was disappointed to find a normal looking individual sorting through a stack of mail in a cramped room on the next floor down. He peered over a pair of reading glasses as I introduced myself and remarked, 'Ah, you're the lucky man who got the roller ball gel pen!'

I wondered if everyone in the company was talking about my pen and why they didn't have better things to do with their time as he went on, 'Gavin didn't have any biros left so you got the expensive pen! Mind you he got them for the same price as the biros – special offer this week.'

Some pathetic part of my ego felt deflated at this news.

'Good. Thank you for that. I've got the doo da here for my ID card.'

He showed little interest in this.

'Oh yeah, right – just stay there for a minute, I'll get the camera and do your photo. Once you've settled in come back down and I'll run you through who's shagging who.'

I thought I'd misheard him.

'Sorry?'

Greg glanced at me conspiratorially. I thought he was going to tap his nose like in a bad spy movie but he just smiled.

'It's helpful to know what's going on especially if you're in one of the service departments as you are. Never know when a bit of information will come in useful. Have you had your medical?'

'Not yet – I've put tomorrow morning down – I think I said 10:30.'

Greg pursed his lips and frowned.

'Oooh... I wouldn't advise tomorrow morning.'

'Why not? It's the best time for me.'

'How can I put this?' he went on, 'Dr. G. may not be at the height of his powers.'

It sounded as if I was making an appointment with the Oracle of Delphi.

'He's just the company doctor isn't he? And a medical's just a formality. Hopefully no open heart surgery!' I joked.

'Yes and yes to the first two points but he can mix things up a bit if he's... well... Between you and me Denis, he's no stranger to the dragon!'

'I have no idea what you're on about.'

'He's a smackhead! And as for whiskey... drinks like a fish! Mind you always good stuff – last Tuesday's bottle was Lagavulin 16 Year Old. If he doesn't want you to know he's drinking then it's Grey Goose in his desk drawer. Can't smell it!'

And this time he did tap his nose.

'Well, if he drinks and does smack all the time, does it matter when I go to see him?'

'It's Tuesday tonight…' Greg said meaningfully.

'I'm aware of that Greg…'

'Tuesday night is Binge Night at the company bar!'

'OK so I get a hung over doctor? I'll take the risk.'

Greg peered at me again and slowly shook his head.

'Well, don't say I didn't warn you. Anyway I shouldn't be keeping you – you've a meeting with someone from IBM at 14:30.'

'Yep.' I said then stopped. 'How do you know that?'

He beckoned me over to his work station in the corner. Flicking through a few screens he typed in my name and pulled up my diary.

'I have viewing rights to everyone's diary. Wait till you see Eric's!'

Another quick tap on the keyboard and I could see our esteemed chairman's working week. I use the term 'working' loosely as it consisted mostly of lunches and meetings with various people, a couple with the letter 'K' beside them.

'What does 'K' mean?'

Greg seemed miffed I'd asked the question.

'Not sure. We're missing information on that – it's only just appeared in the last couple of weeks. If you hear anything let me know. Useful for my dossier on Eric.'

Astonishment is the only way I can describe my reaction to this news.

'You're keeping a dossier on the chairman!'

'Of course! You need to know where the bodies are buried in case of career glitches. And I record his extra-curricular activities as well.'

'Such as?'

But Greg had shown enough of his underground service for the day.

'Some secrets have to remain that way I'm afraid. By the way welcome to JDFT – good to meet you.'

We shook hands and I went off to my meeting. After about twelve slides I realized I was facing a death by PowerPoint presentation. I'm not good in post lunch meetings at the best of times and as the supplier droned on about cost benefit analysis and resilient supply chain permeation (I think, though I might be wrong on that last bit) my eyes began to lose focus. Then came that stage when you're not asleep but not awake either and bits of reality begin to morph into dreams in a pleasantly drifty sort of mini-coma state. Soon real deep sleep threatens to take over. It was just at this point that movement through the glass panel in the door caught my eye and woke me fully. Greg was peering in. He seemed interested in the end of the room where the presenter stood pointing out a particularly fascinating feature which would (from what I remember) increase productivity by 80 % or it might have been 8%. Something like that. My attention had slipped a bit. The corridor side of the room was a wall lined with windows which sported an opaque bottom section but clear upper, allowing light to come in while retaining privacy for the occupants of the room. Suddenly, half along this wall, Greg's head popped into view through the upper transparent section. He wasn't tall so could only have achieved this by leaping some two feet off the floor. I presumed he was out on another none too subtle fact finding mission. Then he appeared again this time further along and looking back towards the presenter. I was thinking of going out and inviting him in if he was so interested in the apparently limitless benefits offered us by this company's product. There was then one more incidence of Greg leaping like a moustachioed salmon heading upstream to breed – this time at that part of the wall near where the guy was pointing to a graphic which seemed meaningless but of which he was ludicrously proud. I hadn't really been paying attention to the latter part of his pitch so I was caught out a bit when he asked, 'Is there anything you'd like to ask me about this slide?'

'What the fuck does it mean?' might have been interpreted as rude and given away the fact I hadn't been entirely in the room with them mentally during the previous forty five minutes. Nodding sagely I put my fingertips together and rested them just under my lower lip in a 'well that's quite possibly the most profound thing I've seen in my life,' kind of way, while actually thinking, A) 'I've just lost an hour of my life that I will never see again,' B)'does this guy get paid to do this?' and C) 'what the hell is Greg doing?'

Finally after a bit more of the sage nodding / fingertip action I said,

'Thank you. That has been really informative. I think it might be useful if you'd send me a copy of the presentation so I can show it to our Finance Director,' knowing full well that, given the FD's understanding of IT, I might as well show him a translation of the Bible in Aramaic.

My visitors left and as I was tidying up the room ready for the next poor bastard to waste precious minutes of his or her short existence in some inconsequential meeting, it occurred to me that Greg's salmon impersonation might indicate that he wanted to see me. I guessed it would probably be about my ID so I was about to revisit the post room when the man himself pitched up.

His initial salvo was, 'I suppose you were wondering why I was trying to look into your meeting?'

I admitted that it had crossed my mind but also thanked him for stopping my brain dying from excruciating boredom.

'His name's Tom Manning isn't it?' he asked.

A glance at the business card in the folder before me confirmed this fact.

'You know him?'

'I had him one night on the Northern Line!' Greg asserted.

'Right – you mean…'

'Yeah coming home from a party and we just did it there and then!'

'What did the other passengers do? I mean were they…'

'Oh no - nothing like that! There was no one else in the carriage – well no one conscious.'

Difficult to know what to say to this so I thought I'd change the subject.

'Will my ID be ready soon do you reckon?'

'Yeah, drop in tomorrow morning.'

He shot a suspicious glance round the meeting room then relaxed.

'It's OK we haven't bugged this one yet. You ought to ask Karen out you know.'

'What?'

'She ditched her boyfriend a few months ago so she's in the market as it were.'

'I hardly know her!'

'So you're not against the idea in principle?

'Well, no, she's very attractive, smart, funny...'

'Oh dear you've got it bad,' he said.

'But it's not a good idea going out with someone you work closely with,' I argued feebly. Greg reeled off a long list of people in the company who, according to his intelligence, had been, were, or would shortly be, in relationships with each other. It seemed to be all the staff.

Chapter Eleven

Medical

I'm pretty laid back about matters medical, especially an undemanding once over by a company doctor. Usually it's just a matter of counting limbs and other useful bits and there you go. Done and dusted. But I have to say I did feel a slight concern as at 10:30 the following morning I made my way to keep the appointment with the drink and drug crazed medic. From an office beyond the post room I could hear a voice gently humming a tune. On the door was the sign, 'Dr. M. Graham. M.D. I knocked on the door and a brighter voice than I was expecting called out, 'Come in!'

I approached the doctor's desk, my eyes scanning for single malts, syringes or other tell tale signs of the doctor's habits. On the desk were a stethoscope, monitor and keyboard but, more disturbing than drug paraphernalia, a prominent calendar advertising "McCallan's Funeral Service". It didn't strike me as a sign of confidence in his abilities. Worse, what if he had some cosy arrangement with McCallan's Funeral Service to deliver a certain amount of business every year; targets to be met, that kind of thing, in exchange for money to feed his addictions? The doctor lifted his gaze from the form he'd been filling in and smiled.

'You're studying me with some degree of astonishment, possibly trying to work out how much whiskey and heroin I've consumed and why I seem so alert for an opiate addicted dipsomaniac?'

Briefly I wondered if he was telepathic, an unexpected side effect of his drug consumption perhaps.

'Er,' I said uninspiringly.

'It's OK Mr. Mahoney. For the record, I drink a little and the last time I had a narcotic of any kind was during a clinical trial when I was a medical student. Greg, who will have given you a different impression, has a lurid imagination and alas he and I had a disagreement some four years ago which has led him to attempt character assassination on me. Anyway you're here for a medical not a synopsis of old feuds. I won't ask you if you drink – everyone in JDFT does – in fact you certainly wouldn't have got the job in Mr. Fitch's team if you didn't. I won't ask how much either since everyone lies about that, even me. OK if you would just take your shirt off please.'

As he approached me with his stethoscope I was still sampling the air for traces of single malts but there were none at all. He carried on with his questioning.

'Do you currently have any health problems, including psychological problems, or are you awaiting surgery?'

As he asked this he was checking blood pressure, heart rate and all the other metrics doctors are supposed to examine.

'No.'

'Do you smoke?'

'No I don't. Should I?'

'Wouldn't blame you if you did but probably best not to. You can put your shirt back on.'

Resuming his seat behind the desk he started ticking boxes and making notes on a fairly lengthy questionnaire.

'Ever had any sexually transmitted diseases?'

'No.'

He was scribbling while quizzing me. At this he stopped and looked up at me.

'Really?'

'Yes really!'

'Quite sure?'

'Yes!'

He checked my details again.

'Ah! Sorry! Of course you're not a media buyer. You're I.T. '

'Yes.'

'Any history of OCD in your family?'

I straightened the pen and mouse mat in front of me so they were equidistant from each other and the edge of the desk.

'No.'

'Hmmm. Do you have any health condition that might be damaged by work?'

'Sanity possibly?'

Ignoring my levity he ploughed on.

'How many days off sick have you had over the past two years?'

'None as far as I can remember.'

'Have you ever suffered from depression, stress, anxiety or other mental health

problems such as panic attacks, sleep deprivation which have caused you to see a medical practitioner?'

'Nope.'

He looked up and surveyed me sympathetically.

'Hmm. You haven't met Eric the Chairman yet have you?'

'No not yet.'

'Hmmm. All I'll say is he'd make an interesting study in how a manipulative, psychopathic personality can be very successful given the right environment. Do you bite your nails?'

'Is there a sort of range of answers on that one; yes / no / sometimes / don't know?'

'I'll put you down as a "sometimes". Anyway you appear to be in good health and reasonably sane. Which leads me neatly to my final question, why do you want to work here?'

I thought about this and how we choose jobs. Rarely is there a clear path set out from the very beginning. I'm sure there are some who have a plan, possibly even written down, laying out how they are going to climb the greasy pole from day one to retirement but I didn't fall into that camp.

'The money's good and it sounded… interesting.'

'Fair enough. As valid reasons as any I can think of. Now have you any questions for me?'

'Yes. Why have you got a funeral director's calendar on your desk?'

'You're the first person to have asked me that! They started sending me them a few years ago – I must have been on a database somewhere. I was going to just bin them. Thought they were a bit morbid or might cast doubt on my ability, something along those lines. Then after a few medicals and consultations it became clear that people here don't take their health very seriously so I brought back the death dealers' calendar to make them think about their own mortality. And if anyone happens to perish on my watch I have the details close to hand.'

'Is that likely?'

'Statistically it's bound to occur at some point.'

Little did he know how prescient his words were to prove. Standing up he stretched out a hand in farewell.

'If you have any problems I'm here on Tuesdays and Thursdays. Welcome to JDFT Media Mr. Mahoney and good luck!'

Chapter Twelve

Pub One, Hoover Nil

After a month I had settled into my new routine. I was usually, make that always, first into the office – a fact I put down to a combination of insomnia, a good train service and laidback colleagues. But on this particular morning Fitch had arrived before me, was already at his desk and looking dangerously efficient. He even appeared to be sober. I eyed him with suspicion.

'Morning Martin. Anything happening?'

'One of the servers had a bit of a glitch. Not sure what's wrong with the bloody thing. Had a look at it – won't come on.'

'Bugger. Sounds like a power supply problem.'

I knew that Martin's idea of 'having a look' wouldn't have involved getting up and journeying the fifty feet or so to the server room so I went off and checked for myself. Where the server should have been plugged in, there was a Hoover. The curse of the cleaners had struck for the third time in a month. I unplugged the Hoover and reattached the computer to its power supply. While I waited for the machine to get back up and running I took the Hoover's cover off, vandalised the interior thoroughly, put the cover back on and binned the critical parts. For good measure I cut the plug off as well. That would teach them. At the top of the short flight of stairs leading down to our office I stopped as I heard Martin's voice on the phone to someone. There was a more contrite tone than normal for him.

'No Eric, I saw Olivia this morning. She seemed fine with the last campaign? What? No she loves the work. Yes, really! Sorry I've got to go, I've another call coming in.' Once I heard him put the phone down I carried on into the office. Looking round he muttered.

'Oh, ah, yes, all OK then?'

'Yep, it was the power supply – it's OK now.'

'Excellent.'

He looked briefly at his watch.

'Got a meeting. Better dash. If Eric calls again tell him I've got a meeting with a couple of hardware suppliers.'

Karen had arrived during this exchange and was checking emails. She looked at me, rolling her eyes and shaking her head as Martin left the room. I wasn't sure what was wrong so I said,

'What's up with Martin going to a meeting?'

Although she was some five years younger than me, in terms of wisdom there were light years between us and I was not ahead.

'How long have you been here now?' she interrogated me.

'A few weeks.'

'Haven't you noticed that Martin is always out at meetings.'

'That's what management's all about Karen. Networking, making new contacts all the time.'

'Have you also noticed that his meetings tend to start at 11.00 promptly every morning and finish just after 3.00? Where do you think he spends his time?'

Thinking about this, he did seem to have a very regular schedule of meetings. By eleven he would have left for his first one and at 3.30 in the afternoon, regular as clockwork, he returned.

'What are you suggesting?'

'Martin spends most of his day and all of his evenings in the pub.'

I could testify to the latter being correct.

'He wouldn't be working here if that was the case – Eric would have fired him ages ago.'

'Eric can't fire him!'

'He's chairman! He can fire anyone he likes.'

'You do know why Martin is still working here don't you?'

'I take it this is a rhetorical question?'

'You what?'

She waited for more information.

'I mean I'm not supposed to know the answer to this.'

'I suppose not.'

'So since you know the answer are you going to tell me?'

It would have been easier negotiating with a stone.

She turned back to her screen to check an email then began typing a reply. My curiosity got the better of me.

'Are you going to tell me or not?'

'Tell you what?' she said peering at me then back at the screen.

'Your theory as to why Martin is still working here at JDFT.'

She giggled, 'Oh sorry I forgot. Yeah, anyway, you see his girlfriend is Olivia Lloyd?'

I could feel that my face was blank. Not a muscle stirred to give even the slightest hint of intelligence. Karen shrugged impatiently.

'Who is our biggest client?' she asked.

I thought for a moment. The moment extended into seconds then a minute or so. Why is it that the mind always goes blank when you want to impress with your knowledge and expertise? From somewhere a phrase from the company induction presentation surfaced.

'Oroco Oil.'

'Jesus, very quick! Exactly! Martin's girlfriend is marketing director of Oroco Oil. Advertising budget last year ninety six point five million dollars.'

A shaft of light pierced my ignorance. Oroco Oil was our biggest client and paid most of our salaries. Little escaped Chairman Eric, and he would have calculated that firing Martin was not a commercially clever move.

'Ah,' I said.

'Of course Eric wants to get rid of him. They hate each other but Eric can't risk losing a client that size so Martin stays until she ditches him, he ditches her or they ditch us.'

'They?'

'Oroco Oil – keep up! If they move the account somewhere else then Eric can get rid of Martin, no probs.'

I saw an opportunity here.

'Who'd take his place?'

'Before you think you've a chance, think again. For a start if we lose that account most of our jobs are toast. Second, Eric's son Gordon wants a job here and Eric wants him working here. The moment Martin's out Gordon's in.'

'Thanks for the moral support!'

'I'm only telling you what's going on. Jesus! Don't be so sensitive!'

'I'll try not to be. So what's this Gordon like.'

'He was here last year for two months on work experience and I can honestly say he's the most repulsive twat I've ever met.'

'I sense an air of antagonism towards him.'

'You what? Are you taking the piss again?'

'No, sorry. So he wasn't popular then?'

'He was punched three times while he was here which is a record.'

'That sounds a bit rough on the guy.'

'Wait till you meet him. It wasn't nearly enough'

Karen was bashing furiously on her keyboard as she told me this tale of nepotism and hatred. For the sake of the keyboard I thought I'd better change the subject.

'I think I might go and have a word with Martin. You reckon he'll be in the Prince of Wales?'

'Well if he's not there he's been kidnapped on the way or he's dead.'

Of course I knew the Prince of Wales, a local which opened its doors early to receive postal workers who felt they were falling behind in the race to contract cirrhosis. I'd just got to the pub when a coach pulled up outside. It disgorged a stream of what, judging by their accents seemed to be Japanese, Dutch and American tourists. Their guide stopped them as they entered the low 1960s standard issue boozer. Without turning a hair he said,

'You will note that some parts of the bar clearly date back to the 17th century when the Prince of Wales who later became Edward the Tenth, built it to accommodate friends who may have visited his hunting lodge nearby, alas now lost to history.'

'Might Shakespeare have been a visitor?' a keen Dutch student of faux history asked wonderingly.

'Excellent question! There is very little doubt that when he was performing in this area this pub or tavern as it was then, is where the King's Men would have dined and even lodged.'

The guide continued shamelessly, 'the stained glass window which you see now was etched by the artist Timothy Taylor as you see from the name. It replaced one depicting scenes from the life of St Warren, the patron saint of snake baiting. In fact there was a snake baiting pit behind the pub, now replaced with a patio built by the previous landlord to get over his irreconcilable grief at the sudden death of his third wife.'

I tore myself away and took my pint over to the trio standing at the far corner of the long bar counter, just before it turned into the final straight where the diehard alcoholics sat.

Martin had a brace of habitual drinking buddies, Ken Holden and Alex Norman. Holden was large, round, loud and punctuated his speech with robust exclamations of 'well quite'! Norman was small, round, loud and red-faced, resembling a sun burnt hedgehog. He would get agitated and snuffle heavily when talking, interspersing incomprehensible stories which always seemed to end in a bizarre punch line, with a cry of what sounded like 'woight?' delivered with a look that was part bewilderment, part challenge to question his authority and part seeking approval from his audience. I had just got to our usual place at the far end of the bar next to where the landlord had seen fit to place a large python (dead and badly stuffed) in a glass case that had never seen a duster in its life. Norman was regaling the others with a story that finished with, 'and in the end you see it was Henry VIII who invented scampi! Woight?'

Holden goggled at him through thick glasses, 'Well, quite,' he bellowed, swaying slightly.

Martin supported him with a well timed, 'Exactly, exactly! Pint Denis?'

I doubt if they had ever held a conversation where all of them completely understood what the others were on about. After twenty minutes of trying to understand three people speaking fluent drunk, I gave up and went back to JDFT, planning to tackle Martin on the subject of his impending career demise at a later date. Catching him sober was going to be a problem. I would have to bide my time. Sometime after three thirty Martin returned to the office. Sitting down with a degree of vagueness, his chair gently castored across the floor. A strong smell of, at a guess, six pints of bitter and several whiskies washed down with a Cornish pasty, wafted across from his direction. After a minute or two perusing emails and muttering darkly about, 'Fucking Eric, no idea what he's up to,' he turned to us and said,

'Anon green a brook on enochs.'

This might have been exactly what he meant to say but it seemed unlikely. I weighed up the possibilities, decided I'd misheard him and tried a wild guess.

'A book on Unix?'

A nano-syllabic grunt suggested the guess was right. I pointed to the top shelf, wondering why Martin was showing an interest in a technical subject about which he knew little or nothing. Such ignorance kept the world safe. Without further ado and with the supreme and misplaced confidence of the very drunk, he wheeled his unstable chair over to a position more or less under the book. He then glided up onto the chair with agility unsuspected in one who, if not overweight, had certainly left the underweight division a long time ago. His entire bulk was now over the centre point of the chair. All good, nothing bad so far; phase one successful and base camp reached. Karen and I watched, rapt with amazement, yet also with a certain foreboding. Strong as our foreboding was it didn't quite run to telling him not to do this as ghoulish curiosity took over. Phase two began to unfold when Martin reached up and out to grasp the desired title. Somewhere in the laws of physics there must be an equation dealing with angles of lean, leverage, mass, drag factors and the like, that describes what happened next (although there probably isn't a variable for the effects of shedloads of beer and whiskey combined, not to mention a Cornish pasty wildcard). In layman's terms the chair, feeling a large weight pushing on it, obeyed the laws of physics and accelerated off to the left in a manner that would have done credit to a Ferrari. Martin's bulk was therefore left unassisted to fight the law of gravity. The law of gravity won. For us open-mouthed witnesses, time went into slow motion as the following events unfolded. The chair headed right; Martin, book clutched in one hand, began a mid-air ballet during which he pirouetted, spinning gracefully, a look of horror passing swiftly across his face. Somehow he kept more or less upright as he touched down like a jumbo jet in a strong crosswind before staggering sideways and executing a soft landing on the chair which, after bouncing off the wall had oddly enough self-parked exactly in its normal place before his desk. Briefly dusting himself down he nodded at the book and slurred,

'That's the one,' and began reading. It struck me that perhaps Martin had been operating in one universe where he had nimbly leapt onto the chair, taken his book and alighted with no mishap whatsoever, while Karen and I, in a neighbouring but parallel cosmos, witnessed a gravity-defying near disaster. She and I looked at one another, shrugged and carried on working until interrupted by Martin, who unexpectedly said,

'I've ordered a safe,' adding, not unexpectedly, 'anyone coming for a pint?'

Karen glanced at me again and winked.

'Now that's not a rhetorical question!'

Chapter Thirteen

Chairman Eric.

Sandra was Eric's PA. That's to say she did all the things for him that a normal adult should reasonably be expected to have mastered by the age of say, twenty and Eric was roughly three times that age. The list of things he couldn't do was long. Among that list were: find his way to work unaided, buy a sandwich, write an email, write a letter, use a computer, use a mobile phone with any degree of reliability, buy, write and send a birthday card to his nearest and dearest, book a restaurant, go to the restaurant at the correct time, master the basics of a window blind, leave dry cleaning at a drycleaners, make a small purchase at a shop, use a lift, book a haircut, collect dry cleaning from a drycleaners. I often wondered how he managed to get himself ready before his driver collected him in the morning; even doing up his shoe laces must have been outside his narrow range of abilities but I presumed Mrs. Eric was tasked with this complex operation. I didn't even want to think about the remote chance of him being toilet trained. It was as though his development had been arrested at the age of about two and a half. Yet, even with this extensive catalogue of incompetence and inability, he was deemed fit to run a major company. Granted there are those who are not good at practical day to day stuff but can inspire their staff to great things with their sparkling, perhaps occasionally irritating but inspirational personalities. Eric was as charismatic as a snail and his attitude to staff was cold / borderline psychopathic. His face had two emotional modes; mask-like was the norm but if something good had happened then he had a faint flicker of the last death throes of a slight smile, reminiscent of a piranha that's just had a particularly succulent horse drop into its bit of the stream. Of course with Canteen Pete around, any piranha would have had to be quick off the mark to get to the succulent horse first. So when Eric (or rather Sandra) called me up it was with a sense of doom that I walked the green mile to his office. Sandra was engaged in some critical work on her Facebook page but having sorted out her social life she eventually noticed my presence, rang Eric who was sitting all of eight feet away in his office, had a conversation with him and finally said, 'Go on in he's free.'

I entered the inner sanctum where Eric sat in his chair staring out through penetrating glasses at nothing in particular. I thought for a moment he was in a catatonic state when he suddenly moved his head.

'You're...' he looked at a piece of paper on which Sandra must have written my name and put in front of him, 'Denis.'

'That's right. I'm Martin's new IT Executive.'

He said nothing but somewhere deep within there had been a flinch at Martin's name.

'I'd like a new computer. How much will that cost?' he demanded.

He had an Apple Mac which looked fairly new, on his desk.

'Is there a problem with this one?' I asked.

He surveyed me with a frosty glance.

'I'm the Chairman. I want a new computer. Get me a price.'

That morning I'd been looking at these things so I knew the price. I imparted this information to him. There was a further, longer silence. Deeper frost. Possibly a danger of ice developing later.

'I'm sure I could find it cheaper.' he intoned

'They don't tend to discount them.'

'I bet you fifty pounds I can get it cheaper.'

It was the first almost human thing he'd said.

'OK I'll bet you can't,' I replied, imagining he'd smile at this, maybe shake hands and we'd part as buddies bonding over the pricing of computers. Instead he said,

'Get me a price by lunchtime. Close the door behind you.'

By twelve o clock I'd managed to shave a further twenty quid off the price and glowing with business acumen, I called Sandra.

'Is Eric free?'

'Think so – ya, reading a paper. Pop over.'

He was in his lair, perusing the Telegraph. Frosty stare with slight piranha hints should have warned me.

'You owe me fifty pounds,' he said. If he'd gloated I almost wouldn't have minded so much but he said it in a tone that suggested no other outcome could ever have been likely. To rub salt into the financial wound he'd undercut my price by fifty pounds.

I told my colleagues my tale of woe.

Karen said, 'Dickhead!'

'Me or Eric?' I enquired. She paused just slightly too long for my liking.

'Eric of course… though… '

Martin gave me a more sympathetic hearing.

'Ah…' he finally uttered.

'Ah?'

'Eric is as tight as the proverbial gnat's proverbial chuff.'

'How much is he paid?' I asked, knowing this would just provide more pain for me.

'Around half a million plus bonus which is three or four times that,' Martin casually informed me.

'Do you realise he's just spent two hours looking for a cheaper computer. What a waste of time and money! We didn't save anything!'

'No but you've had a valuable and early lesson into what a complete shit Eric is. By the way our safe should be here tomorrow.'

'Yipppee.' I said morosely.

Chapter Fourteen

Safe

And so on a clear spring day the safe arrived. The first I heard of it was when Mike Abbott phoned me. Abbott was our office manager, a grumpy South Londoner who should have been kept as far away from other human beings as possible. Once a week or so he called to complain about some minor infringement of health and safety or a free training course which he imagined was free because he'd negotiated brilliantly but in fact was free because it was useless. So when I saw his number displayed on my desk phone I tried to get Karen to take the call. She refused. Apparently he had leered at her during the previous Christmas party. So, despite all evidence to the contrary, he was human after all. I dutifully answered the phone.

'Ere Denis,' was his opening salvo.

'Mike, what can I do for you?'

'Safe.'

'Glad to hear it. When you're in danger call me again or better still try 999.'

I put the phone down but kept my hand just above it. It rang. I picked up.

'Nah. Martin's safe.'

'Great. You're safe, Martin's safe. You've been on that free customer service course HR found haven't you?'

'Nah. Martin's bought yous a safe. For yer cassettes and like… information, valuables n' shit.'

Mike's grasp of the modern world was not strong but still way ahead of his communication skills.

'Ah right. Has it arrived?'

'Yeah that's what I been telling ya. Problem is, it's been like kinda, installed.'

'Good. Isn't it?'

'Well yeah and no.'

I've always noticed when people say 'Yes and No' they always mean no.

'It's been put in the old storage room.'

The old storage room was in a twilight zone at the very furthest reaches of the building from my office. It attracted all the stuff that inhabits that limbo where it isn't needed but you're just not quite sure it might not be of use at some indeterminate point in the future. Which is usually the day after it's been thrown out or sent to the Victoria and Albert Museum. I tried to cheer the miserable bugger up.

'That's fine then – it's out of the way.'

'Well yes, you might think that. Now, and this is the interesting bit …'

I've also noticed that if someone prefaces a story with 'and this is the interesting bit' you know you are about to be subjected to a balls-achingly dull tale usually featuring an obscure way of getting to Basingstoke via Galashiels.

'… y'know this building was once a warehouse.'

I sighed wearily, 'Really?'

'Well you see the floors in this place can take several times the load of a normal floor. It's down to the use of more RSJs than normal. Reinforced steel er, what-d'ya-ma-call -its beginning with J. Did you know that this building could withstand…'

Sometime around this point the world went all swimmy and my eyelids grew heavy. I was dreaming that I was eating freshly poured concrete from a large safe when I heard a voice calling me back from my near-life experience.

'Ello! Denis? Are you still there mate?'

'Yeah, that's fascinating Mike. I've always been interested in shit post war industrial architecture.'

His complete stupidity made him invulnerable to sarcasm. He carried on.

'Anyway of course the whole building weren't warehouse like – they needed offices, canteens, broom cupboards, washing facilities, all that shit. So not all the floor had to be built to the same strength – would have been a waste of money.'

'I can see that. How fascinating! Sorry Mike where's this going?'

'Well the floors in the main warehouse can take up to three tons per square foot stress but in the other bit – the admin side if you like, that's only a quarter of a ton stress.'

I suddenly saw the light.

'And the safe is in a room on which bit?'

'Well that's just it. The old storage room is on the admin side.'

'How much does the safe weigh.'

'Well, and this is the interesting bit...'

This time I hung on his every word.

'The specifications and all that shit, as it were, say, let me see.'

There was a pause: down the line I could hear paper rustling, lips moving, maybe even a little light slobbering and dribbling.

'Looks like it's a touch over half a ton.'

'Fucking hell! I'll come and have a look. Meet me there.'

We both reached the storage room in record time. The safe had been crammed in blocking access to the stuff behind, not that anyone would want access to it ever again. The delivery guys had pushed the safe right back to the wall rucking up the rotting carpet below it. I saw that the floor was made of narrow concrete slabs which were decaying and crumbling so you could actually see through to the ground some thirty feet below. Or rather you could have seen the ground if there hadn't been a grey shape on top of it. The lithe, beautiful grey shape of an Aston Martin DB9. 'Tungsten Silver', Mike corrected me pedantically. Eric's brand new car which he'd got the week before was parked directly below the safe.

'It'll probably be alright won't it?' I said to Mike with what can only be described as a wheedling tone in my voice.

'Well, it might be I suppose. You never know. On the other hand…'

I started to race back to our office to call Eric but got detained by Nick the Bastard who had lost some critical data. After one of the fastest support calls in history I picked up Nick's phone then thought the privacy of our IT office might be a better place to explain that we were about to put Eric's new Aston through our home made car crusher. I got to my desk and dialled Eric's office.

His PA answered.

'Eric Bateman's PA Sandra speaking, hi.'

At that moment far away in the building something moved. It was almost imperceptible. I would imagine it was similar to that moment on the Titanic when passengers in the first class dining room heard the chandelier tinkle slightly and their sugar tongs made a tiny noise as the mighty ship received her death wound. Had we had a chandelier in our office I'm sure at that moment it would have tinkled and if in an even wilder flight of fantasy, we had had sugar tongs, they would have made a tiny noise. All I knew with terrible certainty was that sitting in the middle of Eric's brand new Aston Martin, lay a half ton safe. I could not see any circumstances under which Eric would be pleased at this turn of events. I would have given anything to be on the Titanic. A voice on the phone was trying to get my attention.

'Hello Eric Bateman's office. Helllooo!'

'Sandra, it's Denis here from IT. Is Eric about?'

'Hi Denis! No he just nipped out a few minutes ago.'

My mouth went dry and I gulped. Trying to sound casual I asked

'Oh. Where to?'

'Well between you and me I think he just wanted a drive in his new car. Although he doesn't drive - he just sits in it and plays with the buttons. You know what he's like - not great with techie stuff. It takes him forever to even start the engine it's so complicated. He really bored me this morning with something about its valves. You men are weird if you ask me.'

She had a high pitched laugh like a hyena that had been watching too much Downton Abbey.

I felt a chill run through me as if someone had filled my entire body with liquid nitrogen.

'So a few minutes ago Eric would have been sitting in his car?'

'Oh yah for sure! Why? Do you want him to take you for a spin?'

She laughed again in her lunatic way, little knowing that her boss was now effectively the filling in a very expensive can of Spam.

'Anyway Denis would you like to leave him a message?'

I briefly contemplated a joke about Ouija boards then thought better of it.

'No, nothing important. It can wait.'

A very long time in fact. During this conversation the world had gone all swimmy again. I turned to Martin.

'Er…

He looked up expectantly.

'Is it that time already? he beamed.

'What time?'

'Prince of Wales time?

'No, no it's not… mind you I think I might need… No, no, listen! Could you just give Blodwyn a call.

'Blodwyn, the HR Director?'

'How many Blodwyns are there in the company? Yes, Blodwyn the HR Director!' Although I thought Blodwyn the Funeral Director might be more useful.

Martin huffed a bit.

'Anything important I should know about?'

'It's – well, the good news is your safe's arrived.'

'Excellent! Oh I see! You're thinking of offering Blodwyn space for personnel records – well if there's room why not? Good thinking Denis.'

'Er, no it's not that, it's… no you see.' I breathed slowly and said, in what I meant to be a calm, measured tone, 'I think we may… have just… killed Eric.'

Martin stared in an unnerving fashion. Karen swivelled round rapidly on her chair to face me. They both chorused the same word at me.

'What?'

Martin got up slowly.

'What do you mean 'killed Eric'?'

I gave them a brief run through of the situation. Martin stared again then suddenly leapt up and punched the air.

'Yes!! Happy, happy day! You fucking genius Denis! I love you! Oh joyous day! Flat Eric!! Rejoice, rejoice!'

It was Karen who, as always, injected a note of restraint into the celebrations.

'Yeah, you don't think, well, it's probably against some rule or other or maybe it's in your contract not to kill the chairman of the company.'

She paused and did the sort of pseudo sympathetic clucky tone of voice that says, 'Thank fuck it's you and not me in this situation.'

'We know you didn't do it deliberately Denis...'

'I didn't do it at all!' I protested to her.

'Yeah. Well, it is partly Mike's fault as well I suppose,' she said doubtfully.

'Firstly, I didn't order the safe and secondly I didn't put it in the dodgy bit of the building! OK y'know we should really go down and see if there's anything we can do for Eric,' I suggested in a vain attempt to retrieve some good from what looked like a difficult, not to say dire, situation.

'Anyone got first aid experience?'

'First aid! It's a half ton safe! Eric's now seeping out of the gaps! Mop and bucket should do for first aid kit!' Martin observed with a great deal of glee in his voice, 'I'll get a pint glass from Canteen Pete - we can pour him into that. He could be one of Pete's specials – real road kill! Or I could keep the fucker on the window ledge!'

Martin was now laughing out loud, verging on the hysterical. Then, gathering his composure, he phoned Blodwyn.

'Blodwyn hi, Martin Fitch here. I was just wondering what the company policy is on a death on the premises – just out of curiosity, research… sort of thing. If say one member of staff, accidentally killed another?'

Martin's eyebrows waggled as he took in her considered reply. Blodwyn had a first rate legal brain and was not one to show emotion or give anything other than bone dry, accurate advice.

'I see. Actually yes we may need your detailed opinion - just in case. In fact it's Eric – um, he may have been crushed by a safe landing on his car.'

Karen and I heard Blodwyn's whoop of delight from where we were sitting.

'I think there was some distortion on the line Blodwyn. Almost sounded like you were laughing at our terrible mishap. Shock I expect. Yes. A tragic loss indeed.'

He listened to Blodwyn's advice for a minute or so, thanked her and put the phone down.

'It's OK we're covered by building and key person insurance apparently.'

Something told me that it wouldn't be so simple.

'Great,' I said, 'I'll just fill out the form so I can stop worrying about killing Eric the Chairman and carry on with my day!'

I brooded gloomily. Martin was already putting his coat on and humming as he got ready to leave for the Prince of Wales and celebratory drinks.

'Yep. All good, nothing bad!'

As he swung an arm joyously into the sleeve of his venerable waxed jacket the door to our office opened slowly and Eric appeared. Eric, or at this stage with the information we had, Eric's ghost, surveyed the scene. As always, behind his back he had a smouldering cigarette cupped in his hand. I don't claim to be up with laws in the afterlife about smoking in public places or indeed if it would matter much as health shouldn't really be an issue if you're immortal / dead. What I did know was that in the here and now at JDFT Media they took a dim view of smoking (legal substances anyway). On my arrival office manager Mike had given me a long and characteristically tedious lecture about the perils of smoking in our building, every surface of which, according to him, was potentially and violently combustible in some way or another. I interrupted Abbott at regular intervals to tell him I didn't smoke but he was in 'tell him about not smoking' programme mode and couldn't be stopped. Eric of course was a law unto himself and thought that holding lit cigarettes behind his back gave him immunity from this rule. Karen stared at the undead Eric, Martin, arm halfway down a sleeve stopped and stared at the apparition,

129

muttered something about 'too fucking good to be true.' I felt a strange blend of relief and disappointment but mainly relief. Eric spoke, proving he was alive, kicking and as unpleasant as ever. He had a curious, inhuman diction which slightly elongated even short words, conveying the impression that he was extremely displeased and probably on the verge of issuing your P45 or stealing your soul.

'Martin,' he said, pronouncing it "Ma-hart-in." 'Someone has dropped a safe through the floor into the car park. Had my new car been there it would have been damaged.'

Understatement of the year, I thought, as Eric glared at Martin through glasses that though they weren't thick, gave you the uneasy feeling they might have an X-Ray function, seemingly concentrating his pupil-less eyes into evil points of interrogation.

'After speaking to Mr. Abbott, I find that the safe was for your department. And you asked for it to be placed in that part of the building. So I put this down to your usual incompetence. I'll have payroll deduct the cost of the safe and repairs to the floor and car park from your salary. Had my car been damaged you would of course have been paying for that as well so count yourself fortunate. Good day.'

'Fuckwit!' Martin growled as Eric left. The air warmed as the evil one departed. Martin stormed out. Karen stopped what she was doing, or pretending to do.

'Eric is such a twat!' she said.

'And Mike,' I added, 'He let the guys install it there. Dickbrain!'

I thought that as Eric had nearly been turned into pâté perhaps it wasn't a surprising response for him to want to exact revenge on someone and we should cut him some slack. I put this argument to her.

'As you said, it was Mike's fault,' she fulminated, 'not Martin's.'

'It *was* Martin's safe though.' I pointed out. This just elicited a scowl from Karen. 'Are you sticking up for Eric?' she asked.

'No, but maybe he's still in shock following the… incident.'

'But there was no incident! Nothing actually happened to Eric- he just got back and found a safe on the ground.'

She had a point and I knew that Eric possessed a calculator implant where his imagination should have resided and probably couldn't be traumatized. Feeling brave and adventurous I headed for Canteen Pete's. Picking up a tray I noticed that his board was announcing;

'TODAY'S SPECIAL'

'LEGAL (ISH)'

Once again a cheese sandwich seemed the wise choice.

By the end of that day I was emotionally exhausted by the stress of almost killing the chairman of the company, which, although positive in one way as no one liked him, had the downside that health and safety would have frowned on us for negligence. Around 5.30 Martin looked up and said, 'A chap could die of thirst round here; who's going to buy me a pint?'

Karen gave me a questioning glance. I sighed, closed down my laptop and accepted the offer.

'Yeah I'll go for a quick pint. The Prince of Wales?' I offered. After all I wasn't on cooking duty that evening and provided I was home by 7.30 would possibly be fed.

'No, we'll just go over the road,' Martin muttered.

'I'll be finished in a minute – see you over there.' Karen said.

Fitch rose and like the Pied Piper of Alcoholism, led the way to 'The Red Lion.'

Chapter Fifteen

It's Only Love

As we went down in the lift I casually said to Martin,
'How's Olivia?'

'Ah. So Karen's told you I'm fucked if we split up! Mind you
so's this company!' he guffawed. I felt guilty at asking about
his personal life and embarrassed by the gauche transparency of
my question. He seemed quite happy to talk.

'Between you and me, she keeps complaining about me
working late. Stuff like that. She works until all hours but
that's fine apparently! If I stay here on the odd occasion for a
pint that's not fine!'

'Ah...' I replied, 'tricky one that.'

The Red Lion had been a dingy, backstreet boozer stranded on
a tiny patch of wasteland left over from the Second World War.
In the eighties it was bought by a chain who turned it into a
dingy theme pub. Internally it was a marketing man's idea of a
medieval baronial feasting hall. There were nooks, crannies and
rooms on the first floor leaning out at odd angles surrounded by
black plastic 'aged' beams and the toilets were marked "Henry"
and "Anne". Martin told me that the decor, like the food, was
designed in a small high-tech building just outside Reading. Its
style could best be described as moronic eclectic. Because of
the eccentrically angled architecture you felt drunk even before

you'd had any alcohol. I thought I'd have a couple of beers then scoot off but Martin offered to introduce me to some of the other inmates of JDFT which seemed like a good idea. Bearing in mind that this was July, hearing Wham's 'Last Christmas' on the sound system provided a suitably disorientating soundtrack to the evening. Sometime after seven Karen arrived. Martin's two chums Holden and Norman were with him. Norman had been telling us about, I think, a postal service drawn by horses that still ran beneath the streets of modern London. 'And that's why they call it Horseguards Parade, woight!' he was saying as Karen pushed through to the bar where we were standing. She steered me away from the Fitch, Holden, Norman triangle and out to the far reaches of the pub.

'Sorry to drag you away from the conversation,' she apologised, 'but I've just had Olivia on the phone.'

'Yeah, Martin was saying on the way here she gets a bit annoyed about him working late.'

'Bollocks working late! She's really fucked off with him coming in hammered at three in the morning.'

'Three? He leaves here at 11.00 – where does he live?'

'Tooting,' said Karen, 'but he and those two go off to clubs and places. She is not happy at all; I mean I wouldn't be either but she's about to pull the plug.'

'How come she phoned you?'

'She and I had a heart to heart at a party last year. She wasn't all that happy then.'

'Doesn't sound good – anyway I'd better go – shit look at the time.' At that moment Martin appeared, handed me a pint and shot back to his place at the bar.'

'I'll just have this one, then bugger off,' I said.

Karen raised her eyebrows.

'Great willpower! Just don't end up like Martin…'

'No chance,' I asserted.

At that moment Holden arrived.

'Is there a romance developing here we should know about?' he asked.

Karen glared at him. I'd noticed glaring was something she was very good at.

'Fuck off Keith,' she hissed.

'Charming as ever my dear. I was just coming over to ask you two to join us, to revive our flagging conversation.'

'Provided Alex isn't talking nonsense - what was he saying about horse drawn post under London?'

Holden goggled at me.

'Not the faintest idea – I haven't understood a thing he's said since 1998. And I think then I may have misheard him. Now let me get you two a drink.'

At 11.35 I staggered from the Red Lion, hopelessly pissed. Finding a taxi rank nearby, I fell into one of their vehicles and slurred my address to the driver.

'You must be a mate of Martin Fitch.' he observed and Charon the Taxi-driver pushed out on to the Styx of Oxford

Street. I staggered out of the taxi and up the short path to our flats. Pressing the buzzer there was a long pause. Nothing. I tried again then thought OK so Rach has gone to bed in a huff. And now she's not going to be happy I've woken her. I waited for a stroppy voice but there was just silence. Eventually I found my keys, fiddled with the front door until it opened and went into the hallway. The automatic light came on. There were seven cardboard boxes with post; ours was second from last and the day's haul of post was a letter from Visa and a handwritten envelope. Picking them up I stumbled up the stairs to our first floor flat. The moment I opened the door I knew she was gone. I know that sounds weird. I can't explain it but there was a vacuum, a silence that hung in the air like mist. The fridge hummed into the void. From outside on the stairwell of our flats I heard footsteps. I stopped, waiting for her key in the door but the footsteps carried on up to the next floor. Chucking the Visa letter into a drawer I ripped open the envelope with my name scrawled on it. I tried to focus on the scruffy bit of paper announcing the inevitable. The note was terse but didn't leave too much room for doubt.

'I'M AT SARAH'S. IT'S OVER.'

This was it, there was nothing left. One part of me felt a surge of relief that it was over, while another, the bruised ego, a wish to have instigated it myself, was shattered. Rach and my relationship had been like a planet circling a sun in a concentric orbit. Sometimes there was warmth but more and more the orbit took us off into the dark, cold expanses of sullen silence and decaying affection. And that's how it happens. Someone who seems to be a permanent fixture suddenly slips out of your life and off into a different stream.

Chapter Sixteen

Board Meeting (I)

When I woke in the morning I was pretty sure my heart had stopped, my brain was lying in a pool of broken pieces of razor blade and all vital signs were closing down. A strong feeling of dread accompanied the physical disaster assailing my head. Deep in my stomach a small lizard, possibly one of those little thorny chaps you find in Australia, was lashing its tail causing waves of pain and nausea to travel the length and breadth of my digestive system. I managed to down four Berocca and two Paracetamol before making my way on autopilot to the train station. By the time I reached JDFT Media, something was taking effect and somewhere ahead lay the slim possibility of life. I thought "I will get over this. One day. Maybe not today, maybe not tomorrow but…" then I forgot what I was thinking. Sometime around eleven o'clock I felt the feeling of dread reduced and I had a first tiny glimmer of genuine hope. Nothing tangible, just a vague notion that perhaps I wasn't going to die at any second. But I couldn't see it in any physical change. Karen spoke and I nearly jumped out of my skin. My head felt like it was deconstructing into its constituent parts. I groaned.

'What's up with you?' she said critically but sizing up the situation ventured her remedy . 'Right it's Canteen Pete's for you - he'll have a cure!'

'No! No! Please just let me die quietly here. Don't be cruel!'

Canteen Pete made a rapid diagnosis.

'It's either Ebola or a hangover mate.'

'Can you do anything for me?' I moaned pathetically.

'If it's Ebola yeah, maybe.'

'It's a hangover for fuck's sake Pete!' I said tetchily.

'OK OK no need to bite my head off! My Granny had a cure for hangovers.'

My feeling of dread increased substantially. If it had been a government warning about the threat of terrorism it would be a code red.

'Really?'

'Yeah, simple like all them old remedies. She swore by crushed nettles and hedgehog saliva. Mix them thoroughly and rub it into your chest. Worked every time.'

'Rub it into your chest? How would that cure a hangover?' Karen asked as a wave of nausea swept through me like a cavalry charge. Pete pondered this, while I wondered what she was doing not questioning the hedgehog spit part.

'Y'know that might have been for colds,' he said after giving it lengthy consideration, 'In fact now I think about it she probably didn't have a cure for hangovers - she was in the Sally Army and they're not all that enthusiastic about drinking.'

'Where can I join?' I asked. 'I'll have a cheese sandwich Pete. Hold the hedgehog saliva.'

Martin, seeing my plight took advantage of it. Ever since I'd joined JDFT I'd listened to Martin grumbling about the onerous nature of his job and the leaden responsibility that was crushing his spirit. I noticed that the grumbling was on a cyclical basis, like an old semi-dormant volcano; minor rumbles and tremors at the end of one month with a crescendo of complaining and general gurning at the start of the next, building to expletive filled eruptions during the middle fortnight. Then relative peace again. The reason for this was the board meeting or rather, 'The Board Meeting' which happened every Monday of the final week of the month. As a perk of the job Martin was invited to Board meetings which took place once a month. Naturally he didn't see them as a perk but rather as a cross to bear, taking him away from the delights of the Prince of Wales.

As I sat recovering from my hangover he slouched into the office, threw his briefcase into the corner and muttered, 'Fucking board. Tossers' meeting.' A few minutes more general muttering and complaining followed. Karen looked at me and we shrugged simultaneously. Then I noticed a change in the weather from my left. Martin was beaming in an alarming manner at me round the corner of his laptop.

'Denis!' he said brightly. 'I have an idea!'

I won't say that I looked over at him with unbridled joy. When Martin said your name in that tone, coupled with the word 'idea', it meant that an unpleasant or onerous task, if not downright trouble, lay ahead.

'Yes?' I retorted curtly.

'No, this is good!' he attempted to reassure.

Karen huffed and went back to doing whatever presentation designers do at three in the afternoon.

'Go on', I urged him cautiously.

'You know the board meeting I have to go to every month.'

'Yeees?'

'Well, I thought you could go instead. It's just a bit of reporting and that sort of crap.'

I think I heard Karen's jaw hit her desk at this point.

'You're really selling it to me Martin,' I scowled at him.

'OK why don't you do one month and I'll do the next? Could be useful for you if that fucker Eric decides to get rid of me. Or I fall under a bus.'

'We can only hope,' said Karen leaning forward to examine a peculiar graphic on her screen. As a director Martin was supposed to attend but in my interview he had let me know that he might, at some indeterminate point in the future, maybe, although of course it was unlikely, delegate the brief IT report to me, as his deputy. Presumably this would be on one of those occasions when the Prince of Wales couldn't wait or a genuine reason kept him away.

Seemingly one of those occasions had now come. On a gloomy Monday afternoon I navigated a corridor on the same floor where Martin had pointed out the 'tossers' as he always called senior management. Here lay the boardroom. Mostly used for presentations, team-building sessions and firings it hosted the board meeting once a month. As I sat down in the empty room I still had some sort of misguided expectation that the meeting would be a rarified, philosophical exchange of brilliant business concepts. Doubts began to enter my mind when our Finance Director, Gary, an unpleasant, short, gingery chap, with a personal hygiene problem that made me think nostalgically of the Freak, shambled in and sat next to Phil, our Operations Director, a scruffy, foul-mouthed man. There were four women on the board, by some way the brightest people in the agency, a fact which patently rankled with my Gary and Pete, who, as two of the women came in, started singing, 'Who Let the Dogs Out,' at them. I stared at the bozos in disbelief then looked away in case they thought I was giving approval to this. Phil was scared of Gary and followed everything he did like a slavish disciple. Debbie, the New Business Director flicked a pitying glance at them.

'Knuckles sore?'

Gary, in his boorish way, laughed and said, 'What ya mean?'

'From dragging on the ground.'

This took time to filter down through their dimness and a no doubt witty response was forming in their reptilian brains when our esteemed chairman Eric arrived, followed by Caroline Miller, the CEO. Eric, wearing a purple suit and green shirt took his place at the head of the table without acknowledging anyone else in the room. It seemed that these meetings were no more than rubber stamp affairs. Under company law they had to be held but in fact all major decisions were made within the capacious confines of Eric's office by Caroline the CEO, Eric and maybe Eric's cactus plant. Then the board would sit back and listen to Eric's wisdom and put their hands up when told, to agree with what Eric said. Eric fixed me with a gaze about a quarter of a degree above absolute contempt and said, 'I take it Martin's shitfaced again?'

'No, he's at a meeting over in Liverpool Street.'

Eric sighed, 'I'm sure your loyalty to Fitch is commendable but maybe you should think of your own career.'

This was not an argument I was going to win. Gary of course had to get a word in,

'IT put in their place yet again! Result!' he sniggered. Eric slowly swung the death-ray round towards him.

'Gary, when you learn how to use a spreadsheet or manage to pass even a basic accountancy exam you may criticize others. Until then just read out the quarter's billings – you know the ones that your more able assistants compile for you?'

I had to admit that Eric was unpleasant in an evenhanded sort of way. Gary turned white as a sheet and Phil smiled in a creepy way at Eric.

'Is there something you want to say Mr. Sprote?' Eric asked.

'No Eric, I was just thinking how much I enjoy being here,' Phil said slimily.

'Really? Don't get too used to it. OK can we get on? I have more important things to do. Let's leave billings for the moment. First item, "Operation K".'

"Operation K" sounded mysterious and I guessed it was probably a pitch for a major new client. One notable feature of the agency was the obsession with secrecy but the absolutely dire level of security. Only the previous week an account manager I'd been chatting to in the pub had looked round him and said, 'So... some big news!'

'What's that?' I'd asked.

'We're pitching for the B.A. account.'

'British Airways?' I'd added for clarification.

'Sssshh! Fuck's sake Denis! I'm the only one who knows!' he'd said, panic writ large in his eyes.

'Apart from Martin. And Nick the Bastard who has a bet on us getting it. Oh, and Griff the barman at the Prince of Wales, Karen... all the finance guys; need I go on? Everyone knows about it.'

'Fucking hell! That's the problem with this place no one can keep a fucking secret!'

I pointed out that everyone in the company drank so much they'd forget everything they'd been told within minutes so it was safe to say what he wanted. I wasn't really interested anyway. So as I sat listening to Eric I was quite surprised that Operation K hadn't been in open discussion at the Red Lion for the last few weeks. Maybe I'd check with the barman there afterwards to get the real story. In the meantime Eric was in full flow.

'As you know over the last year we've been looking at a number of ways of raising the agency's profile. One of those was engaging with a charity promoting, social cohesion, racial equality and multi-culturalism in deprived areas. These are issues close to my heart and...'

At this, Neil, the company lawyer, a genial, humane sort of creature, nudged me.

'Close your mouth!' he whispered.

It was no wonder my mouth was open. I wasn't sure if I'd fallen asleep again and was daydreaming that Eric had morphed into the lovechild of Mother Theresa of Calcutta and Kofi Annan. Our esteemed chairman beamed in a sinister way.

'And as you also know I've been going down to the East End and spending time there with these people to help them rebuild their lives; or should I say to build their lives in the first place.'

I was utterly confused. Maybe I'd got him completely wrong and the cynical, ruthless bastard was in fact a paragon flowing with the milk of human kindness. Eric sat down and there was a murmuring of support around the table although I noticed Debbie rolling her eyes and shaking her head slightly. Next it was my turn to give my report which seemed shallow, slight and irreverent compared with the humanity of what had gone before, to the extent that I nearly blessed myself as I addressed the newly minted Saint Eric. Something at the back of my mind was bugging me and I noticed that Eric wasn't taking the blindest bit of notice of what I was saying. As I outlined a new training schedule he interrupted.

'My iPhone isn't working properly - come up after this and fix it,' he barked, turning back and scribbling on a pad in front of him.

'You probably haven't charged it again you dickhead,' said Caroline calmly. It's not often one has a ringside seat at a CEO on Chairman brawl but this was promising.

'Of course I fucking charged it! It's just shit!' Eric commented in his understated impatient infant style.

'It'll be like the time you got your first PC and you were pointing the mouse at the screen from two feet above your desk!' Caroline laughed and turned to me. 'Thank you for your report Denis.'

Eric glowered round the table. 'Anything else?'

Our doughty office manager Mike piped up.

'Bogs.'

There was a silence round the table. Mike sat and brooded. Eric glanced up from his notes.

'What the fuck are you on about?'

'Bogs,' repeated Mike in his monosyllabic way. Forthcoming information was going to be slow at this rate. Another thought was going through a lengthy gestation period.

'Dahnstairs. Blocked. Bogs.'

'Are you, in your own inimitable way trying to tell us that there's a problem with the ground floor lavatories?'

'Yeah that's what I been telling ya. Bogs. Dahnstairs. Blocked.'

'Well that's your department.'

'Yeah. Need a spend a bit a money on em,' Mike said in a rare burst of near eloquence. Eric pondered briefly as he scrawled something else on the paper before him.

'Well get a couple of ethnics in to do it! Just make sure you don't pay them too much - in fact get illegals they'll be happy with half the minimum wage. What's next?'

Neil next to me inhaled sharply, 'Jesus!'

Eric doodled as other board members gave their reports. During Gary's account of the finances he gathered his papers got up and without reference to the rest of us left the room. Caroline said, 'Carry on Gary, the rest of us are listening', which was polite of her if not strictly accurate. As the meeting broke up I asked Neil what was going on with Eric who had gone from Mother Theresa to Adolf Hitler in one easy bound. Neil grinned.

'It's Operation K. It's not about raising the company's profile at all. Eric wants a knighthood and he reckons that there's more chance the government will chuck him a gong if he can be seen doing good works. Only one problem.'

'What's that?'

'Well, the man himself of course. He wouldn't know a good work if it bit him.'

'But he said he goes to the East End and helps disadvantaged families?'

'Strictly speaking, yes. He goes down to the East End with his driver who goes to a couple of charities there under the banner of Eric's charitable actions.'

'And Eric just sits all cosy and warm in his car.'

'Nope, he visits a massage parlour where he's well known! So he is bringing business of a sort to the East End...'

Neil checked the time – the previous hour and a half of my life had seemed to last for a day. It was just after five.

'Fancy a pint?' he asked.

We went over to the Red Lion. CEO Caroline had beaten us to it and was tackling a large white wine. She saw us come in and turned back to the bar.

'Melvyn, whatever these two shell shocked survivors of Eric's rudeness want, put it on my tab. So, Denis, how did you enjoy standing in for the invisible man? Are you getting used to Eric's abrasive style yet?'

I didn't give away what I felt about him. Caroline Miller was as hard as nails. She'd come up through the media buying side of the company but had managed to retain some sense of humour and humanity.

'Eric's a very effective Chairman in many ways,' she mused. 'but what you have to understand is that he's a complete cunt.'

I was stunned. I couldn't imagine Bob at Buy-O-Soft calling anyone that, never mind the Chairman. Neil tutted but in a way that suggested he'd heard this before, 'Caroline!' he reproached her. She batted away his concern.

'It's OK! I suspect Denis is big enough and ugly enough to have heard that word before and he's probably worked out that Eric and I hate each other. Eric *is* a cunt. Would you disagree with that character analysis?'

Neil had to concede defeat on this point.

'I mightn't have put it quite so bluntly.'

Caroline smiled at him and patted his shoulder.

'Of course not, you're a lawyer. You're here to make sure we don't behave too ferally. But you have to admit there are cuntish elements about him?'

Neil put his drink on the bar and groaned in mock desperation.

'You see Denis? This is what I have to deal with! I'm not here to comment on the finer points of law – my job is to stop Caroline and Eric embroiling the agency in scandal.'

'Good luck with that one!' I said.

After her character assassination of the Chairman she smiled at me and I had to admit when Caroline smiled at you, you felt good about the world.

'Anyway Denis. Are you enjoying yourself?'

'Yes, I am actually. It's a bit different from my previous place but, yeah, it's a lot of fun. And hard work of course.'

Caroline was still brooding about something and I was stuck for a reply when she raised her glass and said, 'By the way I heard about the safe episode; shame it didn't flatten the bastard! Better luck next time!'

Chapter Seventeen

Nick the Bastard's Secret

The phone rang. It was Nick the Bastard. I had learnt to be careful about striking up a conversation with him. Especially if I'd eaten recently. The most innocent remark or question would elicit a stream of filth and sexual depravity describing what passed for his love life. He had an encyclopaedic knowledge of the drinking holes of London and a girlfriend who, if his stories were even half true, had the flexibility of a gymnast and a carnal appetite that would have embarrassed Caligula. This time he seemed harmless enough. It was a Monday, about 10.30 a.m. and by the time I got to his desk he was sound asleep, face stuck to a porn mag open in front of him. Presumably doing a spot of research for the evening's lewd festivities. Needing to check a problem on his computer I had to wake him up or try and prise mouse and keyboard out from under his face. From the side of his mouth a stream of alcoholic dribble attached him to his keyboard. As he woke a volley of obscenity erupted. Automatically I asked, 'How was your weekend?' and instantly regretted it. Eyes red as a dog's balls stared at me. Then brightening, as he came to an upright position he warmed to his task, launching into a blow by blow account of his activities. Edited highlights, with the most intimate gynaecological details removed, follow.

'Faaacking brilliant! Went down the Dog and Duck Saturday morning, got faaacking shitfaced, went to the Emirates, saw the Arsenal thrash faacking Fulham, went dahn the faacking Swan, came home, gave the faacking bird one on the kitchen table, had something to faacking eat then went out for a piss up with the faacking lads.'

And so it went on unceasingly. In between bouts of vigorous sexual deviancy and drinking that would have had a Norse warrior heading for the health farm, he somehow found the occasional free moment to do a bit of work. So it was odd to find that one of his bosom buddies in the agency was the born again Christian Researcher, Andy Parkinson, with a set of morals that made Oliver Cromwell seem a bit of a lad. Rather like the bacteria that thrive in highly toxic environments, Parkinson existed among the media buyers, seeing it as his mission to save the souls of those misguided creatures who inhabited the company. On my second day I watched him walk down into the pit where the buyers lurked. I could almost hear the hiss of foul breath and the slither of scales as they eyed him up. A sensitive, well meaning guy, it was clear they were about to devour him limb from limb. He wandered down and passed a brief pleasantry with Nick the Bastard.

'Wotcha Andy, how you doin' mate?' Nick quipped. Good weekend?'

'Excellent – we have a new preacher at the chapel. Very good indeed. How was yours? I trust you avoided the temptations of the flesh?'

I feared for him. Then I stood dumbstruck as Nick the Bastard replied.

'Yeah not bad Andy. Rather quiet but there you go.'

'Good, glad to hear it. God bless you all in your work. You might like to know I'm presenting a research paper on the 18 to 25 market, Thursday at five in the boardroom.'

To my surprise everyone on the floor stopped and looked up. There were various calls of 'Take care mate! See you then Andy, cheers,' other noises of approval and a noticeable lack of swearing. I waited for a bout of vicious piss-taking as Parky left the floor after chatting to a couple of others. None. Not a word.

Then, a few days later, I discovered the first of Nick the Bastard's little secrets. Trying to coax a sorely abused laptop into life early one morning down in the pit I heard his raucous cough and a splat of spit into a bin. I looked up and there he was larger than life. I say 'larger' because this was literally true. He had a huge lump on the right side of his forehead from which a red welt trailed across his brow. His left cheek was swollen with extensive yellow and purple bruising that stretched all the way across it. I greeted him.

'Morning Nick! Good weekend?'

'Yeah not bad; what about Arsenal then? Six nil.'

'What happened to your face?'

'What? Oh this? Nothing really. Fucking Roundheads again. Battle of Stow on the Wold – what a fucking balls up.'

It was as though I'd time travelled and was eavesdropping on Charles the First chatting informally to his generals. The unlikely Royalist made a swift check round the TV buying area and seeing it was clear of others, explained,

'I'm in the Sealed Knot. We were doing a re-enactment for a medieval festival. You'd have enjoyed it – great fun.'

'I thought it was all choreographed so you didn't get hurt.'

'Oh yeah, no, like, the battle was fine but we were in the pub afterwards, had a few beers, getting a bit shitfaced like, and a Roundhead put his hand on the bird's arse. I gave him a slap and it all got a bit out of hand. By the way if anyone asks, tell them I was in a bit of a ruck after the match.'

Who knows? Perhaps it wasn't Charles the First's policies and his attempts to force religious reforms upon Scotland but some bloke putting his hand on Henrietta Maria's arse that pitched England into a bloody civil war? Of such stuff is history made. It certainly gave me a new insight into Nick the Bastard, now nobly recast as 'Lord Protector of the Girlfriend's Arse'.

Unfortunately the laptop wasn't so resilient. I went back to my desk to email our supplier for a new one but got distracted by the following.

From: Caroline Miller
To: All Staff

Subject: Good News.

Importance: Must Read!!

Dear All,

Very good news! I'd like to see everyone in the bar at 6:00 this evening. We have won a major new piece of business and will be celebrating this win with our usual joie de vivre! And free beer of course… Thanks to all the pitch team who worked so hard, especially Sarah J. Debbi R. and Charlie P. Thought I'd get that in before someone else – Eric - tries to take the credit. Special thanks to Karen Ellison for a fantastic job with the presentation. See you in the bar at 6. Please be there!

Caroline

The one thing that really excited everybody was a major pitch. This saw JDFT Media at its finest, everyone working together to win a contract worth a small, or indeed large, fortune. Eric gathered us together beforehand and ever the romantic, likened it to courtship and wooing.

'When we're pitching we try to keep our worst features hidden and impress with our best. We tempt with gentle blandishments until our beloved is clasped in our arms and is blissfully happy.'

I thought this was very eloquent until he said,

'Of course once the contract's signed, just as in marriage, you can do whatever you want and fuck around. And by the way if anyone screws this one up you'll be out the door faster than you can say "Bollocks." '

Uncharacteristically the pitch had been kept secret which meant that either a) it was for a tiny bit of business or b) it was for a client no one was interested in working with. But, as Martin sagely noted, free beer is free beer so we trooped down to the bar just before six to make sure we had pole position. Caroline was already there, as was Karen who was readying the presentation kit. Leaning against the brushed aluminium counter I noticed Canteen Pete's sign.

'**TODAY'S SPECIAL**' and below it in his familiar scrawl.

'**IT COULD BE YOUR LAST**'

No matter how busy people were, the siren song of free beer always ensured a good turnout and the place was filling rapidly. Trevor Hutchins, the Creative Director arrived in with two of his creative team.

'Any idea who the unlucky client is?' asked Martin. Trevor bridled, 'They didn't ask for my input on this one. So no idea matey. Sorry.'

The younger of the two creatives whispered, 'I've heard it's Microsoft!'

The other one fired a scornful glance at her.

'Bollocks! Simon said it's Apple. And he's usually right.'

'Well either of those would move us up the pitch league. Might even get to keep our jobs,' Trevor muttered sardonically. Matt, he of the leopard borrowing activity, joined us. I had to look twice to see if I was really seeing what I thought I was seeing. Trevor said, 'OK Matt I'll have a line of Billy hoke if you don't mind.'

Matt, who seemed fidgety and agitated said, 'What makes you think I have any?'

Martin grinned, 'You've got a rolled up twenty quid note sticking out of your nose!'

'Fucking hell!' Matt exclaimed, removing the note. He unrolled it and shaking remnants of white powder from it into his palm he licked it. Trevor laughed.

'He even called his kid Charlie!'

Karen had finished her set up and joined us. Martin, leant over to her.

'OK, c'mon, who is it?'

She was ordering a beer and in a fine example of evasive multi-tasking said, 'Who's what?'

It's difficult to mumble impatiently but Martin managed it.

'The new client!'

'Yeah right! I've had to keep it quiet for eight weeks so I'm not going to tell you lot with eight minutes to go am I?' Karen said, outdoing Martin in the acerbic stakes.

'OK, OK…. Just a hint?'

'Piss off!'

Martin looked at her.

'Is that a hint? Is it Ryanair? Or a beer brand?'

'No it just means, "piss off".'

Trevor had momentarily deserted us but returned with the air of a man in the know. He beckoned us together conspiratorially.

'Leanne from Finance told Paul in the post room who mentioned it to Nick the Bastard that she saw a load of pitch stuff on Caroline's desk last week. Guess who it is?'

Karen scowled at Trevor. Trevor beamed at Martin. Martin, the beer beginning to work its magic, half focused on Trevor.

'No fucking idea. C'mon Trevor, just tell us.'

Exuding smugness, Trevor whispered, 'Oracle!'

Karen scowled so hard I thought her eyes would cross.

'Wazzock! Caroline's ready to tell us and you spoil it for everyone.'

I pointed out that it was only me, Martin and the two creatives. And frankly, it wasn't so exciting that I would have been overwrought if I was told three minutes early. At the rostrum Caroline tapped a glass loudly to attract our attention to the main event. Beginning with another fulsome tribute to the pitch teams who had probably not seen their families or pets in a few weeks, she warmed to her theme.

'This is the first hi-tech account we've won and we did it against tough competition!' Then she went all Oscary on us and started listing every last one of the people whom she had to thank. Trevor rolled his eyes and tapped his empty bottle against his lip.

'She hasn't mentioned her "Mum and Dad" yet. Think she'll do a Paltrow in a min and start blubbing?'

Martin huffed.

'I think you'll find Caroline had a tear duct bypass several years ago. Fuck this. I'll get a beer – tell me when she thanks Eric - that'll be the final one on the list.'

'Not a bloody chance of her doing that! Get me a Sol while you're at it,' Trevor addressed Martin's back as he headed for the now crowded bar. Karen seemed very relaxed and was smiling in the same enigmatic way as the Mona Lisa, although as far as I know the Mona Lisa didn't work in an ad agency. Or drink beer. Nick the Bastard had materialized at my side. He did shifty or very shifty and tonight he was in very shifty guise. And very pissed. He whispered to me and I think what he said was this.

'Y'know the Sealed Knot thing I mentioned earlier? Well I'd really fuckin' appreciate it mate if y'didn't, y'know say anything about it to… y'know. I mean there's something else I do that's even more like, well, hush hush but anyway, y'know… well you don't need to know about that either…'

'You did say earlier Nick - don't worry I won't tell anyone.'

'You're a fucking diamond mate. Yeah…'

After this enigmatic, inarticulate and repetitive flourish, he lurched off into the throng. I turned back to other events in the room. Having vented her gratitude to all and sundry, Caroline was explaining how closely we'd be working with this new client. Martin handed me my pint, Trevor his bottle and we stood in a half circle, sipping as we listened. Then Caroline turned to the screen behind her and said, 'I'm sure you've all been waiting for this moment. The company I'm very proud to welcome as our latest client is…' at this she clicked the remote and the words on screen appeared.

'Buy-O-Soft Systems.'

I think my glass hit the floor before she'd started speaking again but I can't be sure.

'Fuck my old boots!' I said.

'Fucking idiot!' said Karen. 'There's beer on my shoes!'

Trevor stared at me.

'You seem very excited about this win Denis! Never seen anyone waste drink just on the announcement.'

'God's giblets! That's the company I came from,' I explained in hushed tones as I scraped the glass together with my foot.

'You remember from my references Martin?' I asked my boss.

Fitch looked completely baffled.

'References?'

'Didn't you get a reference from them?'

'No I can't be arsed following up references. It might put me off - I'd already made the decision!'

'Fine. Anyway – that's my old company.'

'What are they like?' asked Trevor.

Tricky one. How do you describe the Freak and his tank top, Bob and his garish sweaters and Randy J Feckenburger (the Third) and his, well, just Randy J Feckenburger (the Third)ishness…

'Yeah…. They're mmm. Yes, "different" I suppose is the word that comes to mind. Definitely very… different.'

Martin drifted off and was speaking to Caroline. I stood, staring at the words, 'Buy-O-Soft' still searing their way into my consciousness from the screen.

'I think you might need this…' a voice at my side said. Karen was offering me a new pint, 'I've put it in a plastic glass for you.'

'Thanks… I'm really sorry about your shoes I'll get them cleaned or get you a new pair… Obviously you'd choose them…'

'Don't worry. Sorry for swearing at you.'

Then I remembered her brilliant double bluff.

'So now I know why you were smiling at the four of us – you kept that secret!'

'Yep, Caroline and I knew someone would wander by and see the pitch document so I mocked one up with the Oracle logo on it!'

'You are a lot more devious than I thought.'

I was also thinking how attractive she was but at that moment she said, 'I think Martin and Caroline are trying to attract your attention.'

Sure enough, the main customer of the Prince of Wales and our Chief Executive were waving me over. Caroline nodded towards Martin.

'I've just given him a bollocking for not telling me you worked for Buy-O-Soft before coming here. That might have been useful to know for the pitch. Inside information.

'I pleaded ignorance but it didn't wash with her.' Martin protested.

'If you're going to be so secretive that's what happens.' I replied.

She nodded, 'It was actually their Finance guy, an American, who insisted on all this secrecy. At one point we were over there for a meeting - there was an alert about possible terrorist activity in Europe and he ordered all the company signs to be covered up with plastic bin bags! Bit paranoid maybe...'

'Randy J. Feckenburger the Third,' I sighed.

'You know him?'

'Oh yes! Not a close buddy but, yes I know him alright.'

'What's he like?'

'Fine, if you're not a synchronized swimmer. Or a pineapple ring'.

'I won't even ask what you mean. Yet. Anyway you won't have to deal with him.'

I breathed a huge sigh of relief as she carried on, 'Our poor accounts department can cross that bridge. I was saying to Martin though that in the pitch we promised robust and close communications between us and Buy-O-Soft. I want IT and Research to work closely with this client. I'd like you to liaise with their infrastructure manager, he's called Epworth. In effect he'll be running that side of things. Do you know *him*?'

For a moment I went blank, 'Epworth. Epworth?' It rang a bell somewhere. The bell was replaced by a red flashing warning light that began to flicker in my brain. From a dark recess I had a terrible, horrible flashback to when I was standing in Bob Scott's office and he was saying the words,

"Hold on! I think this might be it – matches the photo as well! Yeah, this is it. Maximilian Epworth."

Alarm bells and red lights exploded into a major, 'civilization about to end' alert and back in the present, the world had become a darker and potentially more evil smelling place. I looked from Caroline to Martin and back again.

'Fucking Ada! It's the Freak!'

'Well, whatever he's called, you've a meeting with him at the offices of Buy-O-Soft next week. You're taking Andy Parkinson with you. Introduce him to these guys. Make sure it goes well...'

The joy of winning was outweighed by the certainty of having to meet the Freak again in circumstances that meant he was practically my boss. Karen was at the bar and I may have been a bit morose as I greeted her again.

'What's up? You're getting as grumpy as Martin and you've only been here a few weeks.'

I gave her the lowdown on the unfragrant Freak, Randy J. and she made some non-committal sympathetic noises.

'What are you doing on Saturday?' she asked, in a sort of consumer survey way.

'Oh, I suppose being a sad bastard and sitting round on my own watching TV in the flat before going to the pub,' would have been the truthful answer.

'Might catch up with some friends and er, that sort of thing.'

Then, inspirationally I asked, 'why?'

'It's just I have a spare ticket for a... show. At the Excel.'

'OK. Yeah, sounds good.'

At this point I was expecting a run down on the lineup of artists and I waited for more information but there was a tense silence during which we sipped respective beers and watched the rest of our work colleagues celebrating. Karen was staring around in the way people do when there's something hanging between them. I'm not good on picking stuff up like that so I thought a practical question might be appropriate.

'So... who's playing?'

An innocent enough question you might think.

'Did I say anyone was playing?' she snapped.

'Right. I just assumed if there's a show there has to be at least an element of someone doing something and everyone else watching them do it, otherwise it's just going to the Excel Centre and coming back. Fine as a journey but not great as a show.'

'You can be really sarcastic d'y'know that?' she said.

'Look, am I missing something here? You invited me to a show which is maybe not a show and I'm just trying to find out what it might or might not be. That's all!'

'OK I'll tell you!'

Silence. It extended to the point where, like in an avant-garde play, you're not sure whether an actor's forgotten his or her line or he or she's just trying to stretch the silence to create dramatic tension. The dramatic tension was beginning to get spaghetti like when she looked up and said,

'You won't laugh?'

'What at?'

In fact I'd forgotten what we'd been talking about.

'What I'm about to tell you!'

'I don't know. Give it a go.'

She was weighing me up for my likelihood to laugh.

'I know you'll take the piss.'

More saggy, spaghetti like dramatic tension.

'It's a Star Wars convention,' she finally divulged.

I didn't laugh for the simple reason I didn't really know much about Star Wars, or Star Wars conventions. Making a shruggy, "so what?" gesture, I answered,

'So what? That's fine – sounds… interesting.'

'You'll like it.'

'I'm convinced - really.' I assured her, though I wasn't. Another worry had risen to the surface as we talked.

'Are you meeting anyone else there? I mean, anyone from the company?'

'Why? Bad for your credibility?' she asked.

'Yeah, something like that,' thinking of the piss taking I'd receive at the hands of Nick the Bastard and the rest of the media buyers.

'Don't worry no one else will be there – from here I mean. Anyway you work in IT; being a Star Wars fan is a given.'

'That's where I've been going wrong. OK how do we get there?'

'The Excel centre's in Docklands – dead easy to get there. Outside the West Entrance at ten.'

'OK see you then.'

Chapter Eighteen

Star Wars

At nine o' clock on Saturday I was somewhere in central London and completely lost. Deep in the bowels of the Circle Line I was about to give up and head home when a tube pulled in and I noticed seven people weird, rather threatening looking characters in futuristic white armour. Either Earth had been invaded and our local radio station had missed the story (not impossible or indeed unlikely) or these fine citizens of fantasy land were going to the Star Wars convention. I had nothing to lose but my self respect or if it was a real invasion, my life, so I got on and sat down in a vacant seat next to one of them. Unsurprisingly the rest of our carriage was empty with tourists crammed into the next one peering through the doors in a nervous manner. The direct approach was, I felt, the best one.

'So… are you going to the convention at the Excel centre as well?' I asked. The stormtrooper looked at me threateningly and given how idiotic the question was, I couldn't blame him.

'Yes we are,' an incredibly shy young woman's voice answered from inside the costume. 'Are you?'

'I'm supposed to be but I'm not sure how to get there. South London's more my patch.'

'Oh well come with us –we've been to Excel before. If you lose us in the crowd just change at Tower Hill for the DLR.

Get off at Custom House – it'll say Excel on the signs anyway. You can't miss it.'

I couldn't imagine how I'd miss seven storm troopers in any crowd but when we got to Blackfriars the platform was swarming with storm troopers and other assorted alien beings including several tall hairy creatures. The atmosphere on the tube was much more agreeable than the usual brutality of the rush hour and I was rapidly discovering that Star Wars fans were very polite and considerate folk. Never having seen the films I hadn't a clue about the names of most of the characters were but I did recognise the intimidating figure of Darth Vader sweeping into the carriage and apologizing to a Japanese tourist for treading on his foot. 'It's the helmet', the Dark Lord explained to the cowering man, 'it's a real sod for trying to see downwards.'

The Japanese man bowed politely, grateful his life had been spared.

Assisted by my seven strong storm trooper escort I made it to the Excel centre with a few minutes to spare and looked for Karen. We'd arranged to meet at the West Entrance so I stood at the West Entrance and watched the flow of bizarre visitors. There seemed to be a lot of the tall hairy blokes and trying to see past them was proving difficult. One woman was standing there, just in front of me in a long white dress with a dangerous looking metal belt round it. She had a hairstyle which looked as though someone had stuck two Danish pastries to the side of her head.

'Excuse me,' I said, 'I'm looking for someone and I can't see past your… pastry, er, curls things.'

'Yes, I know, you're looking for me.'

I sighed, thinking that there were bound to be a few nutters in a crowd of this size and demographic make up and was about to walk away, when I realized that out of the white dress, metal belt, Danish pastry confection, Karen's voice had spoken to me as if possessed. A moment's further investigation confirmed that this was indeed my work colleague. She was looking up at me with an amused expression in her grey eyes. Returning her gaze I said without thinking,

'You look… beautiful…'

There was no other word for it either. I'd noticed of course at work that she was pretty but now she was transformed into an elegant, statuesque woman. I still didn't like the Danish pastry effect much, though this wasn't the time to quibble about details like that. She blushed slightly.

'Thank you. That's the idea.'

'I'm guessing you're an inter-galactic Queen?'

'Princess Leia actually. Let's get a coffee and I'll give you a run down of who's who in Star Wars.'

Accoutered in jeans and t-shirt I felt distinctly under dressed for the occasion. I knew she'd noticed this.

'Who've you come as? Jar Jar Binks?' she asked as we bought our tickets and went up a level to a restaurant.

'I've no idea who you're talking about but I guess it isn't flattering?' I said as another of the hairy blokes ambled by.

'Who are they?' I asked, 'there were loads on the tube. By the way the white armoured chaps are very helpful.'

'Don't be fooled - they're the evil foot-soldiers of the Empire.'

'Well I have to warn you, they know their way round the Circle Line.'

'The hairy ones are Chewbacca, he's a Wookiee.'

'Of course! Glad I asked.'

'See, over there you can buy a Chewbacca costume.'

In one of the side booths there was a company with several costumes on dummies and one of them was indeed that of my hairy Tube companions. For a second I considered entering fully into the spirit of the day and getting myself a costume, until approaching the stand I saw a price tag of £374.99 attached to it with another card warning, (NOT INCLUDING WEAPONS) . As we went towards the source of coffee we were assailed by stalls selling everything from light sabers (£20 to £924!) to original props which were guarded by a couple of large beefy men and had apparently cost $60,000 at auction. Everywhere there was merchandise.

'Wow! It's a massive industry.' I whispered to her in awe.

As we sipped our coffee Karen gave me an intensive briefing by the end of which my head was swimming and I could barely remember where I was. Phrases such as "internal chronology not the film sequence", "Jedi", "Sith Lord", "Clone Wars", names of planets and people (not sure which were which) spun round my brain. It made history at school seem a breeze and I was rubbish at history. So, filled with a shallow level of knowledge and fortified with caffeine I set off to accompany Princess Leia on a punishing schedule of talks by actors (interesting), demonstrations of weaponry (so so) and fan discussions about who was best in what role (vitriolic and dull).

After lunch we sat with a Chewbacca and a storm trooper. The storm trooper took off his helmet and was uncovered as a her, while Chewbacca was a supply teacher from Guildford. Karen and the other two devotees chatted about favourite scenes, characters and swapped notes on which events were worth attending. I was getting bored and my gaze strayed to the far side of the hall where I noticed a bar with several screens all, naturally, showing Star Wars footage. Surreally three Darth Vaders were standing round a table, presumably discussing the annihilation of Earth or some other unfortunate planet. Nudging Princess Leia, I said, 'I'm just going for a pint – are you coming?' I think by this stage Chewbacca's level of detail (his assertion that the 'TIE' in TIE fighters stood for Twin Ion Engines may have been the straw that broke the camel's back) was getting to her so we made our fond farewells and trekked across to the bar. Surprisingly, as we got closer I heard one of the Darth Vaders say, 'They should play him up front, he's wasted in midfield.'

'They must be having a break from world domination planning,' I commented to Karen, 'Of course they might be talking about Tatooine United's recent run of poor results.'

'Hey – you're learning – so you were listening to me!'

'Of course – I may not have taken it all in but you're a good teacher.'

The bar was thronged so we got our drinks, went out into the main hall and found a table near a stand advertising Tunisia where apparently some of the films were shot, as a holiday venue.

'Hard work isn't it?' I said to her.

'Yep – I'd no idea there'd be so many people here.'

This was a curious thing to say as our immediate horizon was full of either metal, hairy, white armoured or scaly creatures, none of whom looked vaguely like people.

'They take it seriously don't they?' I nearly blurted out 'sad gits' but remembered that my companion was pretending to be a princess from a galaxy far, far away and not from Bromley. Surveying the crowds I saw people enjoying themselves, gathered together in a common interest and not doing anyone else any harm. I reflected on what I'd have been doing if I hadn't come along and thought I should reserve judgement on who was the sad git.

'It's a hobby,' she said but I detected a tinge of regret or dissatisfaction in her voice.

'So, do they have many of these conventions?'

'Yeah, loads. There's one in Manchester next month.'

'Are you going?'

'No. A couple a year is enough. You should have a look at the films – you might even like them.'

'I might do that. Have you got them on DVD?'

'Of course! You could come round some time and see them.'

'OK – I'll be a Wookiee before you know it.'

'Yeah right - don't get carried away…'

'Did your boyfriend used to come to these things with you?' I asked.

I don't know if Princess Leia was scary in the films but the one next to me shot a look that would have felled Darth Vader. There was a pause leaving enough time for me to regret asking my clumsy question.

'How the fuck did you know about my boyfriend? It's none of your business!'

'I'm sorry Karen. Greg said something. I didn't mean to… I guess it's painful. Sorry. If it's any consolation I've just split up from someone as well.'

She was looking away as she drank and I saw her take a tissue from a sleeve and wipe her eyes. When she turned back to me she said, 'Yeah he got me into Star Wars.' Then I realized how stupid I'd been and what was going on.

'You're here to see if you can meet him again aren't you?' I sighed.

'Yes. I'm sorry I shouldn't have invited you, but I needed…. I didn't want to be on my own. I don't know what I want… I really like your company though. If that helps at all.'

'It's OK – but you should have just said. I don't mind. Anyway Rach and I weren't getting on - it was a relief for me to be honest.'

Karen smiled.

'Yeah so I heard.'

'What?'

'Greg told me!'

'Fucking hell! Does that guy know everything?'

'Well if we're dumb enough to tell him...'

I couldn't help smiling at the way in which Greg gained and distributed information. In some attempt at revenge on the mine of all information I told her about Greg's admitting to late night sex on the Central Line. She feigned shock at this then said, 'Greg's antics are legendary!'

I raised my glass to hers.

'Let's just enjoy ourselves for today and not worry about past lives. To past lives being past!'

'Yeah! Exactly! To past lives being past,' Karen replied, her eyes now sparkling again. Our attention was caught by what could only be described as a commotion from the direction of the bar.

'It'll be Darth Vader and Luke Skywalker having a staged light saber fight!' she surmised adding, 'Nope I was wrong! Now that's definitely not in any episode I've seen.'

In the centre of the bar area a Chewbacca was grappling with an Obi-Wan Kenobi. Obi-Wan had a lethal right hook and delivered a couple of crunching blows to the hairy one's head. By far the most exciting thing to have happened yet, the scrap was attracting audiences from far and wide across the hall. As the battle swung this way and that, Chewbacca got the upper hand, gripping Obi round the lower leg and tipping him backwards into a table, which upset the Stormtroopers who had been chatting to another Leia and a Luke Skywalker. Suddenly there was an unexpected intervention as a tiny Yoda appeared and sank his teeth into the fur of Chewbacca's ankle.

'That's a dog! There's a real dog dressed up!' I said disbelievingly to Karen who was helpless with laughter. And I was right. I could now see that, bizarrely, a dog in a Yoda costume decided a ruck with a Wookiee was just what it needed to make its day and had its jaws firmly locked on Chewbacca's calf. During Karen's briefing she had informed me that Chewbacca only communicated in a series of weird noises so his first foray into English was remarkably fluent.

'Owww eeeoowww oooowww!' he called out, still plausibly in character as Chewbacca,' but then shouted, 'Fucked you are if my ankle you bite, fucking Yoda bastard!' He kicked out a

175

leg a few times and Yoda was flicked, spinning, towards a light saber stand.

'You are fucking out of order Kenobi you arsehole!' he carried on, rapidly developing a fine grasp of the English language, 'I'm going to break your fucking neck you shithead!' the Wookiee yelled at Obi who was picking up his dog, checking it for injury (none, its fall broken by the light sabers) and returning to the fray.

'He's making good progress on the language front,' I said

'Very quick learners Wookiees,' observed Karen. 'Especially since he's completely off his face and Obi's not exactly behaving like a Jedi Knight.'

As she said this Obi-Wan Kenobi, clearly upset at the Wookiee's treatment of Yoda, gripped Chewbacca by the ear and rather unsportingly, kicked him in the groin. Chewbacca, clutching his injured genitals, reverted to sounds more in keeping with his on-screen persona, staggered and fell backwards towards us. Alarmingly Obi-Wan, with a firm grip of Chewbacca's ears, was left holding the Wookiee's head while the body collapsed at our feet. We looked down and were amazed to see that there, above the hairy Wookiee body, were the scarlet flushed face and red bloodshot eyes of Nick the Bastard. His bewildered glance went from Karen to me and back again.

'Hi Karen hi Denis. How you doing? Er, you won't mention this to any of the fuckers back at work will ya guys?' he implored as he sprawled on the floor.

'Do you mean the brawling with Obi-Wan Kenobi bit, being bitten by Yoda part, the falling backwards headless fiasco or the whole general Star Wars stuff?'

Nick gazed at us pleadingly.

'Yeah. All that.'

I turned to Karen, 'What do you reckon? Maybe we could just mention it to Greg and leave it there?'

'Fucking hell! Not Greg! No please! C'mon Denis mate!' Nick the Bastard begged.

'I think we should pretend we didn't see anything,' Karen answered. 'We can just store it away for the future...'

'Fair enough,' I added.

'You are fucking diamonds!'

We helped Nick to his feet and as he was picking bits of peanuts, glass and crisps out of his fur, he noticed he was only Wookiee from the neck down.

'Where's me head?' he asked, in a panic stricken voice. Obi-Wan Kenobi threw him the head which was timely as the venue's security staff were arriving on the scene. Yoda uttered a low, threatening growl.

'OK who's been fighting?' they shouted at the crowd.

'Chewbacca!' came the general call.

'And Obi-Wan Kenobi.'

'Yoda bit Chewbacca.'

'Which one's that?' asked the security bloke and was immediately subjected to a wall of derision at his ignorance of fictitious film characters. Another of the guards was stupid enough to demand,

'Mr. Chewbacca please step forward and make yourself known to us.'

Karen and I slipped back to our table leaving the force to face The Force.

'I've learnt something today', she said.

'Oh, what's that?'

'The Jedi code includes effing, blinding and kicking people or rather Wookiees in the gonads.'

A group of Stormtroopers had now gathered round the security men and were having a pointed discussion about the rights of people to dress up and enjoy themselves. Watching the proceedings with a sense of admiration I said, 'Star Wars conventions are a lot livelier than I expected. I've really enjoyed it! But I'm exhausted.'

'Enough Star Wars for one day?'

'More than enough!'

Chapter Nineteen

Eric the Evil

One Monday morning a couple of months later when I got into work a surprise awaited me. I say 'surprise' but it was more a sense of fear and dread. There, in Martin's chair, sat Eric. Even Darth Vader at his most Dark Lordish couldn't match Eric for sending out a chilling aura of incalculable evil. Sensing a human being entering his presence he raised his dead eyes and stared at me as I came in. I could smell burning, which with any ordinary human being you would put down to smoking but in Eric's case might well have been the sulphurous fumes of the underworld still clinging to his person. He was shamelessly rooting through Martin's drawer.

'Can I help you Eric?' I asked as he put several pieces of paper to one side.

'Where's Martin?' the Evil One asked in a tone that told me he did not have Martin's welfare at heart.

'It's only half eight – he'll be here by nine,' I said, praying that this would be one of those mornings, becoming increasingly rare, when Martin pitched up on time.

'Very well. When he gets in tell him to come to my office,' Eric commanded, stuffing some of the papers into an envelope and leaving the room.

A few minutes later Karen arrived and my pleasure at seeing her was diluted by Eric's threatening behaviour. I told her what he'd been doing at Martin's desk and we both agreed that whatever he'd taken probably wasn't work related as Martin had a healthy paranoia about not printing things out. So the moment Martin arrived, two hours later, we brought him up to speed on the morning's events so far. Martin opened his drawer and went through it for a moment.

'Shit! The bastard's taken Olivia's letters to me. I'm going to get the fucker for this!'

He was incandescent with rage and I blocked his path before he could get to the door.

'Hold on a second Martin – if you go over there now you'll do something you'll regret.'

Karen tutted or made some similar noise.

'As Humphrey Bogart said.'

'What?'

'Isn't that what he said in Casablanca – "you mightn't regret this today, or tomorrow but some day you will", something like that.'

'What's that got to do with it?'

'I dunno, just saying,' she said, leaving Martin and I looking blankly at one other. He sighed and sat down again.

'Probably right - I was going to punch him.'

Karen's patience with both Martin and Eric was running thin.

'That's exactly what he wants – you behave like a pillock then he can sack you and get his twat of a son in.'

'Why's he taken them today though?' Martin mused.

'Uh oh,' Karen said, 'have a look at your email guys!'

I went to my desk and the first item in my inbox was this little beauty.

From: Eric West
To: All Staff
Re: Oroco Oil_
Importance: High

All staff,

I have just heard from our biggest client, Oroco Oil, that we are to be asked to re-pitch for their account which we have held for the last four years. As you may be aware Oroco Oil had a major disaster last year in the Gulf of Mexico and in an attempt to move on from the reputational damage they incurred, wish to re-focus their marketing on ethics and green issues. We must therefore reinforce our ethical image and this should be at the forefront of all our thinking for this pitch.

The pitch is in six weeks and all your efforts will be required to retain this client. I'm sure you are aware that if we lose the account many of you will be fired on a last in, first out basis although there will be some exceptions to this. On the plus side it may provide a timely opportunity to get rid of the dead wood in the company. Remember the ethical angle in all that we do!

Your Chairman.

Eric

'Did Olivia say anything to you about this?' Karen asked Martin.

'Olivia?'

'Yes. Any sort of, pillow talk?'

'Karen!' I said.

'No, it's OK Denis.' Martin answered looking defeated. 'I haven't seen her in about a month.'

'What?'

'We split up ages ago.'

'You didn't mention that!'

'It's not something I could broadcast to the world – old Eric would have had me out of here in a second.'

'So, what do we do?' I asked.

'Depends on whether we win this pitch or not.'

To cheer ourselves up we went through the pros and cons of working at JDFT Media for a while. Karen had just listed frequent free beer as a pro and Canteen Pete's burgers (meat unknown) as a con when Martin's phone rang.

'Ah, the summons! I think I can hear a blade being sharpened…'

'I'm sure it won't come to that…' I reassured him and followed with, maybe an ill judged attempt at lightening the mood, quipped.

'Now you know what Marie Antoinette felt like!'

Karen, ever quick to point out the obvious, commented.

'Marie Antoinette didn't have a beer gut. And she was into cake not Cornish pasties.'

I couldn't accept the unscientific nature of her approach.

'Strictly speaking, history doesn't say she didn't like pasties. Or beer for that matter. You'll be fine Martin.'

Karen still didn't seem so convinced.

'Good luck,' she said. 'Let's know how it goes.'

'Don't worry I will,' he assured us. 'If the fucker fires me I'll call you from the Lion. Or even if he doesn't.'

On this ominous note our portly beer and pasty consuming version of Marie Antoinette left the office to face his fate.

'So, what do you think'll happen?'

Karen had returned to working at making a truly terrible presentation look halfway presentable.

'He's fucked,' she said bluntly.

'That's what I was thinking. Eric doesn't seem the sort to invite you over for tea and a chat about last night's telly.'

'Stupid bastard should've told us about Olivia.'

'He couldn't – if it got out that would be it!'

'That's it anyway! He didn't trust us.'

My mobile rang. It was the presumably now beheaded Marie Antoinette stand in. I put him on speaker so Karen and I could both hear and make sympathetic noises (me) or tut unsympathetically (her).

'Where are you?' I asked pointlessly.

'The Lion.'

Possibly the least surprising answer I'd ever heard. Karen rolled her eyes. I asked the obvious question.

'What happened?'

'I've been promoted.'

If a document outlining Hitler's plan for a multi-cultural Germany had come to light, it could not have astonished me more than this. Like a well rehearsed backing band. Karen and I chorused 'PROMOTED!'

'Your drinks are waiting lowly employees,' Martin informed us. I was already getting my jacket on and checking my wallet, though since the Harry Houdini of the corporate world was awaiting us, he could pay.

Apart from Fitch there was no one else in the Red Lion when we entered its sacred portals three minutes later. Just as well because his grin, though understandable, verged on the manic and might have disturbed more sensitive folk. He handed Karen a large white wine and me a pint.

'Here's to crawling up the greasy pole!' he announced triumphantly. 'You see before you the new IT Director of JDFT Media!'

If at that moment a feather had floated through the window and struck me I'm not saying it would have knocked me down but it would definitely have made me stagger.

Displaying deep cynicism Karen opened the discussion.

'OK so you go into Eric's office. He says "I expect you think I'm going to sack you but instead I have to tell you I've admired you as a colleague for longer than I can remember and you are promoted!" Then you kissed hands and left ennobled and happy.'

Martin grinned in an alarming way again.

'Sort of but not quite as much admiration as that on Eric's part. Or indeed mine. He said "You should have been here at nine this morning. And I said "Why what happened?"

Karen groaned but I laughed.

'That's very good!'

Karen made another groany noise.

'Do you two ever take anything seriously? I bet Eric didn't think it was funny!' she seethed.

'No, well, he was a bit sniffy about it but you can't please all the people all the time.'

'So what else did you say?'

'I just told him that I had it in my power to persuade Olivia that we were the best agency for Oroco Oil and she should advise the board to keep us on. Then I mentioned that Olivia had recently said that I hadn't had a pay rise in a long time nor been promoted and that she felt JDFT Media weren't treating me properly. Some sort of gesture of goodwill on Eric's sort would go a long way to helping my argument about keeping them onside.'

'Which parts of that aren't true?' I asked.

'Which parts of it are?' Karen butted in.

'What do you mean?'

'You told us earlier that you and Olivia were no more,' she went on.

'Not strictly true. We're sort of taking a break from our relationship... a trial separation.'

'How's it going?' I heard myself say.

'OK – I'm enjoying the single life, staying out late, all that stuff.'

Karen sniffed.

'How does that differ from your attached life?'

'You're very lippy today Ms. Ellison. I thought you'd be happy for me!'

The same thing that had struck me must have occurred to Karen but not Martin.

'Eric's going to find out; what about the letters he nicked?'

'Oh, they're just bollocks - a lot of old ones – all the recent ones - the threatening ones are at home. It was funny though, as I was about to leave he said, "Don't forget – if you don't deliver on this and we lose Oroco you'll be out of here so quick you won't believe it!'

'Oh great! Hilarious! So it didn't go quite as well as you're making out.'

'Don't worry! It'll be fine. Another drink?'

Karen shook her head.

'That twat Gary sent me a presentation – it's yellow writing on a purple background again and he can't spell. I'd better get back and finish it off. See you here after though? Sixish?'

'I think I'll bugger off to the Prince if Wales see if Holden and Norman are about – drop in there! Denis are you coming with?'

Much as I was tempted, I was recruiting a new support guy and had to get back to read through a stack of CVs and prepare for my meeting with my old friends at Buy-O-Soft. Walking back across the road I enquired.

'We're fucked aren't we? Eric's bound to find out.'

Karen mulled this over.

'Not necessarily. Eric doesn't have much to do with Oroco Oil these days.'

'Hmm. We need a plan.'

'Yep that's for sure.'

Chapter Twenty

Customer Care: The Freak Revisited.

On the following Wednesday, Parky and I took what was for me a familiar journey out to west London passing landmarks I thought had long since become part of my history. The reception area was a lot less grand than JDFT consisting of a small desk where Ted the security guard sat reading the Sun, or if he was feeling particularly intellectual, the Mirror. He called up to the office and gave me a surly look. Ted talked in the manner of a sci-fi B movie robot that you knew would come to a sticky end before the start of Act Three.

'Mr. Epworth's asked me to inform you sir that you must proceed directly to conference room three where he awaits you. You may take the stairs or avail yourself of the lift to the second floor.'

I was irritated by the sure knowledge I was going to have to call the little twerp "Mr. Epworth" and Ted seemed to have forgotten that he'd ever met me before.

'I worked here for three years Ted - I know my way.'

'Health and safety sir. I have to inform visitors of their transport options to the various levels.'

I was about to ask Ted how two floors constituted 'various levels' and what other transport options there might be but at that moment Bob bustled down the stairs into Reception.

'Hi Denis mate, how are ya?' he enthused pumping my hand vigorously.

Of all my former colleagues Bob was the only one I missed, a fact I put down to him being relatively normal and not smelling like a Big Mac. I introduced him to Parky and we chatted for a minute.

'It's great you're doing our advertising Denis. Mind you,' Bob whispered conspiratorially, ' between you and me, Randy hasn't settled in at all well. Not at all well. He's a bit odd. You might not have noticed but he's quite the religious type. To the point of fanaticism I'd say. I mean, don't get me wrong, I'm not against religion per se - I'm quite religious myself but I don't go as far as Randy, y'know actually believing in God and all that stuff.'

Parky was diplomatic and kept silent during this exchange. Bob's interesting take on theology and belief systems had to wait as Ted attracted my attention.

'Mr. Epworth is enquiring as to your whereabouts and attempting to ascertain your location.'

I sighed, said my goodbyes to religious atheist Bob, tramped up the stairs with heavy heart and entered conference room three. There, once again, I found myself sitting in a small office with inadequate ventilation staring across a grimy desk at the Freak just the scenario I'd left six months before. A profound sense of doom filled my mind, as though maybe I'd never left and was damned for all eternity to keep thinking I'd escaped only to be dragged back. But what was before me wasn't the Freak as I'd known him. This was an upgraded Freak; Freak 2.0 if you like. He was wearing a black baseball cap backwards with the words 'Born To Die' emblazoned in Gothic script on it. As he turned to take his seat I was hoping to see the word, 'Soon' on the other side but disappointingly and mystifyingly it said, "Trapped Under Ice."

Well, that would do for a start. Assessing the changes to him in a north-south direction, on his chin there was a suspiciously pubic looking goatee, while concealing the fleshy contours of his podgy body lay a black t-shirt with just the top of a couple of words on display. The reason I couldn't see the rest was because surreally, unfashionably, possibly in a retro nod to his former persona, the Freak was still sporting a tank top. Plus, the aroma was still that of Freak 1.0. The familiar waft of burgers, chips and other lardy items, enveloped the room. He'd noticed my examination of his sartorial change.

'What do you think? Cool isn't it?'

Probably not the word I'd have used and our conversation would in the past have taken a different course but now the little fucker was in the driving seat.

'Mmm… yeah, cool. And the 'Trapped Under Ice' bit…?

'It's a band. Hardcore.'

I nodded but was no wiser. This was all very curious. Last time I'd checked the Freak's iPod it seemed to be wall to wall Michael Bublé; listening to it was like having warm snot

191

poured into your ears. He passed his iPod to me. The buds were tinged with greenish ear wax and I was about to refuse the offer but the Freak nodded to me encouragingly, 'Have a listen - it's brilliant you'll love it!'

The buds resisted as I tried to push them in.

'I always spit on them to lubricate them', the Freak added helpfully. I shuddered but as he was the client, I was in no position to argue. Gingerly pushing the buds in as little as possible I pressed play and the world exploded in a riot of agonizing metallic noise. Freak saliva became the least of my worries. The volume of frenetic sound was shatteringly high. It was akin to having red hot rivets fired straight through the front of the skull while a psychotic dentist drilled in via the rear. After twelve seconds I was pretty sure my hearing was destroyed forever and I'd probably suffered brain damage. I removed the waxy / spitty buds from my bleeding ears and sat staring at the Freak whose mouth was forming words which I could not hear and would possibly never be able to hear again. So at least there was an upside. I also had to admit it was better than Bublé but still seemed quite a leap in taste. I offered the iPod to Parky who was assessing the Freak in a critical manner. Inexplicably he declined the opportunity to have his eardrums blown into the centre of his brain. Handing the iPod back to its owner and trying to restore my splintered equilibrium, I noticed the tattoo. There, on the outside of his right forearm the Freak had a tattoo. It was in a similar Gothic script to the T shirt logo but in black, blue and red ink which, against his red blotchy skin, gave the impression that someone had scrawled a message on a sausage. I was trying to read it as the Freak settled himself in to his chair. When he moved a sheet of a paper I turned my head to keep his arm parallel to my eye. I'd worked out the capital at the beginning was probably a 'B' but a mole obscured the bottom bit so I wasn't sure if it was an 'R' plus mole equalling 'B' or just a 'B' plus mole equalling 'B.' The rest of the word, reading it upside down in that weird script, I thought said 'Rucksack' or possibly (depending on your view of the mole / script relationship) might have said 'Bucksack.'

Then I noticed he was watching me. Intently.

'You OK Denis?'

'Yeah, fine. Er, I just sort of noticed you've had a tattoo done. Does it say... 'Rucksack' or 'Bucksack?'

The Freak / Mr. Epworth harrumphed in scorn. He turned his plump forearm towards me and I could now see the letters spelt out the word, if it was a word, "Buakaew". Which didn't really help me much. I said "Buakaew" pronouncing it like 'boo a queue.'

More scornful muttering and glances were followed by the Freak exclaiming 'Oh a cow!'

I glanced round at the door but then remembering my experience when Feckenburger had just arrived, I had a light bulb moment and realised what he was getting at.

'Ah! You're talking about Randy chewing gum – you're right it sounds exactly like a cow.'

He kept on repeating it, each time in a more aggressive fashion and I started getting worried. The smell I could cope with. Even the vision of the Freak and his new thrash death metal, hardcore, tank top wearing, fusion persona was just about tolerable. But the Freak becoming seriously deranged and repeating 'Oh a cow!' for all eternity in this close fitting room was beyond human endurance. I couldn't begin to imagine what Parky, sitting quietly next to me, was thinking.

'It's her name!'

'Whose name?' I asked, nervously eyeing up my line of escape to the door.

'My wife's!' the Freak replied.

As I calculated that even a slow moving, podgy Freak, if crazed enough, might be able to stop me getting to the door I also took in the fact that sadly, the little bastard's mad music really had damaged my hearing. I thought he'd said, "My wife's."

I laughed.

'For a second there it sounded like you said "my wife's". Sorry what did you actually say?'

'That is what I said!'

'You said "my wife's."

'Yes!'

He seemed to be getting very agitated again. I thought some reality might help.

'But you don't have a wife.'

'Yes I do!'

You may have sensed by now that I was skeptical. I tried to create a mental photofit of a woman who might see the Freak as a suitable life partner. I gave up.

'You have a wife?'

 'Yeah!'

'And she's called 'Oh a cow?'

For some reason he seemed to get really quite angry and began shouting .

'Her name's not 'Oh a cow!'

'Why do you keep saying "oh a cow" then?' I asked reasonably.

'I didn't! I said "Boo a cow!" the Freak explained even more angrily.

'Ah that's fine! I see. She's called "Boo a cow".'

No! It's just pronounced "Boo a cow"!'

I didn't want to argue about the semantic difference between someone being called "Boo a cow" or their name being pronounced "Boo a cow." The conversation had strayed so far beyond the bounds of normality that I felt giddy.

'She's called, "Boo A Cow"? That's a pretty... strange name,' I commented.

'It's a Thai name – she's from Thailand. She's a death metal fan.'

Suddenly the mists of confusion cleared and all was clear as crystal.

'You bought a Thai bride!' I said, relieved at this simple explanation. The Freak rippled and looked sheepish, if you can imagine a sheep with a baseball cap, tank top and a tattoo.

'My mum got her for me as a birthday present.'

The moral ramifications of this were too disturbing to contemplate so I steered us back onto the straight and narrow.

'Right, well I think maybe we'd better get down to business.' Parky had been sitting quietly but nervously through the whole discussion about the Freak's Mum-bought-wife's odd name. I thought his influence might bring a breath of normality into the room. After introducing Parky to my old colleague we got on with the teeth grindingly frustrating task of getting information from the Freak; a task akin to opening a particularly stubborn oyster with a piece of jelly. Even Parky's saintly patience was tested. As our meeting of minds with the Freak closed, the door behind me opened and a familiar voice penetrated the miasma.

'Hey bud, how ya doing?'

There, large as life, was Randy J. Feckenburger (the Third). We shook hands and he was amicable enough in his own odd way. I was worried that he might have remembered me abandoning him during his molestation of the swimmer or blame me for his brief off piste foray into the demon drink.

Instead his opening gambit was, 'Last time I saw you was just before my visitation!'

I have to bring you up to speed here. Parky had not got on well with the Freak. When I said his patience was tested I should have added 'to breaking point.' Parky is ultra smart and the Freak's inability to grasp even the slightest idea of what we wanted had irked him. The Freak's insistence that we repeat everything at least twice caused him further vexation but when the Freak made a disparaging comment about the Welsh, fur, or rather tank top wool, flew. Parky's attitude strayed far from the ideals of Christianity. Doing good to those who hate you and turning the other cheek went out the window as he cast aspersions on the Freak's appearance, demeanour, character and lack of a base level of acceptable human qualities, including hygiene. If he didn't get on with Randy J. as well, our tenure with this client might be a short and unhappy one. But at the mention of Randy J's 'visitation' Parky perked up. Leaping to his feet, he seized Randy J. by the hand.

'I've had visitations as well – tell me about yours brother!'

The Freak was idly scratching a zit and staring out the window so he missed this momentous meeting of spiritual minds. Randy J. enthusiastically responded to Parky's encouragement to tell all.

'I was in a tavern,' (a tavern!), 'with my friends here and I saw a… a different world. I do still believe I died and was taken in rapture up to Heaven. Time stopped but then I heard

197

the Lord's voice exhorting me, "Come on Randy, come back to life! You can do it!" I knew then it was not my time and I returned to the blessed earth and my loved ones.'

Describing us as his "loved ones" was really pushing it. Nor do I think that whoever wrote the Bible had the Ferret and Mattress in mind when describing Heaven and it obviously hadn't struck Randy as odd that the Lord had exhorted him back in a Brummie accent. But Randy had certainly returned to the land of the living after his tangle with vodka. More importantly he and Parky seemed to be connecting so as far as I was concerned it was job done and mission accomplished.

Chapter Twenty One

Rumours

Over time offices become like religions. They develop their
own mythologies which the newcomer has to learn and there
are rites attached to everything. There are high priests (the
highest of which is he or she who controls stationery), there are
disciples and then there is the general crowd which goes along
with things because they can't be bothered to think up their
own religion. But above all, the thing that companies share with
religion is the seasonal timetable of events. And in the calendar
nothing ranks higher than the Christmas party. This is how
directors are judged and the mood and success of the company
is gauged. How much is spent per head, the quality of the hotel
/ restaurant / bar - all are analysed in acute detail and compared
to previous years. It was Greg, of course, who started raising
expectations in early November as the first rumours began to
hit his radar and like GCHQ listening to terrorist chatter, he
realized something different, possibly something big was in the
final stages of preparation. He'd dropped into our office on the
pretext of dropping off a package but we all knew he wanted to
impart highly confidential info without risking detection. His
opening gambit in these sorts of conversation was always, 'Do
you want to know something?'

Who could resist that?

On the day in question Greg dropped off a package and hovered in our office (pretending to check paper clip levels I think) then said, 'Do you want to know something?'

Karen pushed her glasses up her nose and gave him a sharp look.

'I'm really busy Greg - Caroline wants this stuff done by lunchtime.'

'Oh, don't worry. Some other time then. I'll go and tell Finance; they'll be interested. It was just about the Christmas party, that's all,' he said and turned to walk out.

'Go on then, I've got a minute,' Karen announced.

'It had better not be fucking karting again,' grumbled Martin, 'I'm still recovering from my injuries two years ago.'

'No, well it didn't help that you'd had a skinful of Old Shag Nasty beforehand did it?' Greg retorted somewhat waspishly. 'Anyway as I was saying you'll never guess what they've come up with this year!'

'No we won't so are you going to tell us or not?' I asked, trying to work out what Ralph in press meant in an email when he said an "untoward intimacy with a printer" had caused it to jam.

'He's getting very assertive isn't he?' said Greg, addressing Martin and Karen. 'I remember when he first arrived he was all quiet and meek.'

'Must have been a Tuesday, that's my quiet and meek day.' I answered, 'OK so what's the big secret?'

Greg approached us and motioned for us to huddle so he could divulge the information.

'The Christmas Party!'

He looked round at each of us in turn.

'Yes?' Karen said tersely.

'The Christmas Party… is going to be… in the Polish Club!'

'Not the Polish Club!' I pretended astonishment at this.

'Yes! 'The Polish Club!' Greg repeated, pleased at my reaction. 'Better go and leave you lovely people to whatever you do!'

And he was gone, like a spy in a novel.

'Does anyone know what the Polish Club is?' I asked.

Martin thought for a moment.

'No fucking idea. Of course we're relying on Greg being right…'

Karen, working at her screen again, said 'It'll be a club with loads of Polish people and vodka.'

'Excellent and perceptive analysis!' said Martin. 'That's we why we employ you!'

'Fuck off Martin!' she said amicably.

Before we could reach the sunny uplands and delights of the Christmas Party we had to endure the ritual of the Christmas lunch. This, for some unknown reason I.T. shared with Finance and Research. Research I was fine with, as Parky and Katriona were good company particularly if someone added the magic ingredients of Chimay and Chartreuse to Parky. But Finance…

I'm not saying there aren't many fine people in Finance; interesting witty, vivacious and the sort of characters you look forward to spending an entire afternoon of your life with. But they were working somewhere else at the time. In short I was not looking forward to the lunch. After Karen gave me a run down on what had happened in previous years I was looking forward to it even less. The gist was that two years before, Gary, the idiot FD, had got very drunk and verbally abused Martin and IT in general. Last year, in a spirit of fairness, Martin had got very drunk and verbally abused Gary and Finance in general. Then Gary tried to hit Martin, missed, tripped over a table and cut his head badly, resulting in a trip to the local A&E unit.

'Great! The lunch celebrating the season of peace and goodwill should be splendid.' I muttered and if you think that's whinging so be it. I was feeling very whingey, as Parky had come up with the bright idea of inviting Randy J. Feckenburger as our token client guest. I knocked this plan very firmly on the head at which Parky got quite irate, quoting the Good Samaritan and other Biblical worthies who had clasped their enemies to their bosoms, although even the Good Samaritan would surely have scurried by on the other side of the road if he'd seen Randy J. Feckenburger (the Third) in trouble.

'He could have given us a reading from the Book of Revelations,' Parky argued. I restrained myself from saying that I couldn't quite see how that sort of thing would turn lunch with Finance into an event of joyful ecstacy. Plus, the sight of Martin and Gary brawling requiring stitches and involving new heights of obscene vocabulary might not endear our new client to us. Parky reluctantly conceded this point and Randy's invitation was never posted.

'And we could have got him something meaningful as a secret Santa present!' Parky said ruefully.

'Tickets for a synchronised swimming competition maybe?'

Parky, fuming gently, went off to pray for me to see the light. But this had got me thinking and I'd come up with the perfect Secret Santa present for Parky. On the face of it Secret Santa was an innocent bit of fun. You pick someone for whom you wish to buy a present. Sometimes you select a name at random, other times you choose the subject of your (limited) generosity. The point is that it should be a lighthearted gesture, nothing too expensive or personal, a bit joky perhaps. But in every office it had assumed a deep symbolic importance and was often used as an opportunity to make your intentions known to a member of the opposite sex to whom you were attracted. In Finance this invariably resulted in the men buying dildos for their female colleagues, while the women bought the men porn magazines. Thus the sexual element was introduced so that future advances wouldn't be so much of a surprise or shock, reducing the chance of a sexual harassment charge or a knee in the groin. Other departments honed the Secret Santa give and take so that it became a web of intrigue and subtle suggestions as to who was in favour and who was beginning the slide down the slippery slope of preferment. However, IT was lumped in with the dildo and porn buyers so we just had to make the best of it. A fortnight before the Christmas lunch Sandra, FD Gary's PA, came round with a waste paper basket full of folded bits of paper.

'The limit's six quid this year – we thought we'd raise it to get better quality presents.'

I shuddered as I imagined how bad the previous years must have been.

Martin guffawed, 'How much dildo can you get for six quid?'

'You'd be surprised!' Sandra smiled enigmatically. 'Just choose a name Martin!'

Fitch rummaged in the bin and pulled out his bit of paper.

'Who did you get?' asked Karen.

'You're not supposed to tell – it's Secret Santa innit?' Sandra said.

'Greg will probably know by now,' I commented.

As with all rituals there was a strict pecking order, Martin first, then Karen and finally the newest member of staff, that being me on this occasion.

After we'd all chosen Sandra scooted off back to her lair in Finance.

'Who did you get?' asked Karen again.

'Sanjay,' said Martin. 'That's easy – he's into jazz – I'll get something online. Who've you two got?'

The idea of keeping secret the identity of the person for whom you were going to buy a cheap present seemed ridiculous. I nodded to Karen, 'Go on – you first.'

She shrugged.

'Gary – who's Gary?'

Martin answered her query, 'He's only the FD! God's teeth!'

Karen was unimpressed.

'I only know him as "the ginger wazzock". Any idea what he's into?'

Thinking of Gary's stupidity and boorishness I joked flippantly, 'Probably cross dressing. Apparently he looks stunning in his satin evening gown!'

Martin gurgled.

'Fucking hell! Gary in a dress - that's a scary thought. Like Eric in a thong!'

'Martin please!' I'm going to lunch soon,' Karen protested.

'Who did you get?' she directed this at me.

'Parky. From Research.'

'I'd forgotten they get roped in under the Finance umbrella as well.'

'What do you get a religiously fervent Welsh bloke? I suppose porn is out?'

'Probably – good luck with that one.'

'Try anything rugby related,' Martin pitched in.

'Ah! I've an idea,' I said and a couple of minutes later, courtesy of Amazon, Parky's pressie was ordered.

'What did you get him?' asked Karen

'I can't tell you that! It's Secret Santa!'

Chapter Twenty Two

Christmas Lunch

The venue chosen for our afternoon of degradation and torture was the Junction Arms. This fine establishment was renowned for bad beer and food that even the culinary adventurer Canteen Pete would have been nervous about serving. It also basked in a reputation for down market prostitutes during the later part of the day. When I say 'reputation' I mean the landlord had been prosecuted four times over the previous two years for keeping a brothel. The reason it was thought suitable to host lunch for IT and Finance was its cheapness and not the availability of cheap prostitutes. Probably. The other thing that gave the game away that all this jollity and generosity was being done on a budget was the date. We were in late November as Karen, Martin and I walked the half mile or so together to the Junction.

'Looking forward to it Karen?' I asked.

There was a surly silence.

'It's only one afternoon in the entire year! I protested. 'We can have a few beers – it'll be fun!'

'Abbott will be there.' she uttered in a doom laden voice.

'Ah.'

Our illustrious office manager was lumped in with all those who came under the banner of 'service' departments. Rumour had it that people bribed Charlotte, who organized the tables, so they wouldn't be put next to him.

'Well. He's probably OK when you get to know him.'

That didn't seem to be the response she required. Digging deeper for some shred of optimism I went on.

'There'll be what, thirty people there? Chances are you won't even be seated next to him,' I pointed out encouragingly.

'That's really tempting Fate.'

Fate, deciding to be a complete gobshite, seated me next to Mike Abbott. Summoning up all my powers of positive thinking, venturing into the territory of delusion, I thought, 'Right I'm going to make the best of this.'

My hopes were briefly raised when, shortly after sitting down, he said, 'I'm thinking of running for office y'know.'

'Really?'

I hoped I didn't sound too surprised at this but given that through the wonder of the Internet every idiot can express their uninformed views and get them read, why shouldn't they be allowed a crack at running things? I was genuinely interested in which political office he might have set his sights on. His next utterance firstly relieved my fears for the long term future of the country but meant that my own personal short term was going to be filled with several hours stretching endlessly until we could escape to the sanity of some other pub.

'I'm a member of the Potters Bar Allotment Association y'see.' Abbott informed me, 'n' I'm thinking of running for Secretary, cos of my management experience 'ere.'

It was as though someone had dropped a lead weight on my soul, crushing its very being. I did my best.

'Really. I admire your ambition. That must be… fascinating.' I really had tried to think of a wittier riposte but had to admit I just couldn't be bothered. Not thinking of the consequences I asked an open question.

'So… what sort of things do you grow?' I was expecting a reply along the lines of "oh apples and stuff". The answer came at one item per few seconds, drawn out like the ticking of the clock in the cell of someone doing life.

'Tomatoes, leeks, broccoli, spuds, cabbage, curly kale, carrots, peas, courgettes, marrows, onions, bok choy, chard, choi sum, turnip greens, endive, lettuce, mustard greens, watercress, sprouts…'

With heavy heart I quietly picked up the knife from my place setting to check for sharpness. Frustratingly it was no good for ending my own misery or, by assassinating the new leader of the Potters Bar Allotment Association, the world's. I was sure that none of my work colleagues would act as witness against me if I removed this menace from their midst. But it might put a dampener on the Secret Santa which Sandra had gone to so much trouble to arrange so I put the knife back down and accepted my fate.

'…Jerusalem artichokes, sweet potatoes, taro, yams, three varieties of cauliflower, chives, thyme, rosemary, sage… Then there's the flower side of things as well of course. Now what's interesting about that…' he intoned.

Inspiration struck. If he was going to bore me, surely I, as an IT person, had the wherewithal to strike back.

'Sorry to interrupt (!?) Mike but before I forget I must tell you this. You know the security system I'm looking at?'

His brain attempted the quantum leap from vegetation growing to technology. I could hear the faint crash and grind of cogs.

'Yeaah?'

I had his attention.

'Well I was thinking of rewriting it in Java so we could port it onto mobile devices and you could, for example, control it from home or anywhere.'

I was confident that a few more minutes of this would grind him onto submission and he'd amble off to report the doings of the Potters Bar Allotment Association to some other poor bastard? Big mistake. Not a chance. Not even close. Apparently next to growing green stuff, the fascinating ins and outs of security systems were this man's second passion. He started his next sentence with the fatal word that I knew would usher in a tedious tirade of trivia.

'Interestingly, I just been looking at a solution that helps protect a facility from unauthorised entry using a variety of sensors placed on outdoor windows, doors, and gates. Signals received from any sensor are sent as an alarm to a UK based Alarm Monitoring Centre where trained professionals will respond immediately with the appropriate actions.'

'Mike, did you get that from a brochure?'

'Yeah, how did you know?'

'Just a guess; it seemed very... detailed.'

'Yeah – I got a photographic memory.'

'Oh shit! I mean that must be... useful. At times.'

How cynical Nature can be. What a cruel combination. A photographic memory but virtually no brain power to process the information. Now the fucker was going to regurgitate the entire sales spiel of Acme Security or whatever they were called. And I was sitting next to him. Marvo the Memory Man kicked off again,

'It's interesting you talking about doing the thing with Jaffa so I can monitor it from home.'

'Mmmm. It's actually Java,' I said, finishing a pint in record time. It was getting to such a point that I seriously thought about dialing 999.

'Yeah well it's just I fixed up a webcam in the office a while back – you wouldn't believe the stuff you see! Did you know the building's haunted? By a monster... I saw it last week!'

'Really? What was it? Gary streaking through the corridors again?'

I was starting to weep at this point. Mike carried on remorselessly, his level of detail disconcerting.

'Nah. It was Friday – nearly nine o'clock - everyone had fucked off 'cept for one of the TV guys who was on their floor. He fucked off, probably for a slash. Maybe a dump I dunno. Anyway next second, well a few minutes after to be honest, this huge hairy creature like a Yeti lumbered across to his desk. Then it fucked off like and a few minutes later he came back. Lucky he didn't bump into that thing.'

There could only be one answer to this ghoulish mystery.

'Could you see who the TV buyer was?'

'I think it might have been Nick the Bastard. The webcam's not brilliant to be honest'

I felt a bit more human again as I imagined Chewbacca wandering the corridors of JDFT Media causing confusion to all those eavesdropping. It was also a good point to exit before Mike went back to his vegetable state.

'Sorry Mike – I think Martin wants a word with me.' I said, gesturing at Martin who sat with his back to us, engaged in intense debate with Sandra. I was beyond caring what the President Elect of the Potters Bar Allotment Association thought. Martin and Sandra were still talking so I left them to it and went up to the no man's land of the bar. There was a movement and Karen arrived at my side.

'How's it going with Mike?'

'How do you think? I am so sorry for doubting you. I see what you mean about him. He can list more vegetables than I've ever heard of.'

'Oh? Was he talking about his family? At least he doesn't try to feel your bum.'

'So far he's covered gardening and security systems, fascinating subjects both. I suspect he has a whole stock of riveting, photographically memorized topics to fill the long tedious days.'

I glanced behind me and saw there was still no let up in the Martin / Sandra conversation.

'Martin's very chummy with Sandra. She always seems a bit standoffish to me?' I commented.

'Shit! Not bloody standoffish enough. Better keep an eye on him. He's got a bit of history there.' Karen said, as we watched them, their heads suspiciously close together.

'What sort of history?'

'He snogged her at a leaving do last year.'

'Oh well.'

'Oh well? No, "oh well" doesn't work in this context Denis! If everyone took the attitude "Oh well" it means Martin carries on with Sandra and gets caught by Olivia which equals she definitely walks out on him, Martin gets the boot and we get Eric's idiot son as our fucking boss!'

'I came out to relax today – it's nothing to do with us - can we, sort of, just not worry about it?'

She gave me her "typical - you're a man – what do you know?" look, something which I'd noticed was becoming a frequent part of our non-verbal communication.

'OK we need to distract them.'

'Yeah, where's Chewbacca when you need him?' I quipped.

She sniggered but in a slightly malevolent way.

'Might be easier to distract her not him.'

I shrugged with indifference.

'One or other. Although I'm not sure we should be interfering at all.'

Karen ordered a pint and handed it to me.

'I just got one a minute ago - thanks anyway,' I said accepting her generosity.

'It's not to drink.'

'It's a pint; if it's not to drink what's it for?' I asked, confused.

'It's for throwing over Sandra. You're going to accidentally on purpose tip it over her.'

'What? No bloody way!'

'It'll get her off side for a few minutes while she goes to dry out – I'll have a quick word with Martin…'

'What? Oh I see. Simple. It goes like this: I mysteriously and implausibly chuck a pint over Sandra. She bolts for the Ladies. You approach Martin and say "Don't you go fucking Sandra OK?" He says "OK I won't and thank you for warning me of my possible impending slip from fidelity. Now in gratitude would you and Denis like a drink in celebration of my new found and probably temporary lapse into chastity?" Sandra comes back all forgiving and we have a laugh about my stupidity.'

There was a super huff this time as Karen leant on the bar next to me.

'I only asked you to do something to help us for fuck's sake!'

Then she went very silent. This indicated something sinister was going on, that much I knew. The silence carried on. She put her lips close to my ear.

'Would you like to kiss me?' she whispered.

My mind whirled through all sorts of possibilities. The first was that I'd misheard her.

'What did you say?' I asked.

'I said, "Would you like to kiss me"?' she repeated, now combining it with looking up at me with big grey eyes and pouting slightly. OK, I know you're thinking "shallow."

She pouted a bit more.

'It's an easy question – yes or no?'

'Of course I do!' I replied, perhaps a bit too enthusiastically.

'Right! All you've got to do is throw a pint over Sandra.'

And so I found myself in the position of being about to nip my boss's flirtation in the bud, while opening the door to a relationship myself. I could hear the word 'hypocrisy' being redefined as I deliberated. A couple of legal points, terms and conditions if you like, had to be cleared up first.

'Do we kiss before or after the beer throwing episode?'

Karen clearly was not born yesterday. She scanned the back of the bar and deliberated.

'That's your reward – you get the kiss afterwards.'

'Just the one kiss?'

'We'll see – depends how well it goes...' she said with a smile that lit her up from within.

'Sorry, can I just check again. When you say, how well it goes? How well what goes? Are you talking about the beer throwing or the kissing?'

'Both I suppose.'

Expectations were running high. As were the risks. On the one hand I might be about to kiss Karen, something which I have to admit had probably been lurking at the back of my mind since my first moment of arriving at JDFT Media and seeing her. On the other hand I was about to:

1) Ruin the Christmas lunch and afternoon of a member of staff against whom I had no grudge.

2) Thwart the romantic plans of my boss, the consequences of which were incalculable but probably not going to be great for our working relationship.

3) Appear a complete klutz to everyone at the lunch.

I weighed all this up and realized it was a no brainer. Commonsense won. I turned from the bar and pretending to trip, tipped the pint over Martin's lunch companion. It was a perfect drenching shot, pint accurately tipped over the head, rapidly working its way down thoroughly soaking the victim as if this was something I did every day. The only bit where it deviated from the original plan, the snag if you like, was that Sandra had inexplicably morphed into Mike Abbott, the power behind the Potters Bar Allotment Association. Obviously, unknown to me, Sandra had got up and our Office Manager, feeling he'd made my day with his vegetable related sagas, had gone over to bother Martin. I have no idea what was going through Mike's mind but I was suffering severely mixed emotions all crisscrossing each other resulting in severe confusion. Foremost was; would I still get a kiss from Karen? I was happy that I'd got revenge on Mike for boring me rigid. Would he be angry? Did I care?

'What's going on?' was Mike's delayed under-reaction.

'I am really sorry Mike!' I proclaimed. 'The carpet over there, I tripped over it,' I said, gesturing feebly at the pristine expanse of wood floor, the most noticeable characteristic of which was a complete absence of carpet.

'Er …' I floundered.

'Denis, sorry, it was my foot I just caught your ankle – are you OK?'

I had to give Karen full marks for quick thinking. Mike swallowed it hook, line and sinker.

'Don't worry Karen, these things happen. I'll just take everything off and use the hand drier in the bog. Tell the landlord he should fill in an AAW473 Part 2 accident form.'

Off he went, leaving a silvery, beery trail behind him.

Martin watched him go.

'Someone's in for a shock when Mike whips his kit off. Just as well Sandra wasn't sitting there,' he said, giving Karen and me a knowing glance. Then he said in a lower voice,

'Thank fuck you did that Denis – Mike was starting to tell me about some Potters Bar Arsehole Association or something. Jesus!'

I went back to the bar and sat beside Karen.

'Well, that didn't go too well,' I said, not knowing whether to feel relief or a sense of failure. She took my hand and squeezed it, moved closer, touched my cheek with her lips and then we kissed, for what felt like a very long time. Martin harrumphed and coughed at us from his vantage point at the table.

'Excuse me! What do you two think you're doing? Karen put Denis down - he's turning blue from lack of oxygen!'

Karen gave him a scathing glance.

'You told me to make him welcome. So I thought I'd go the extra mile.'

'Fucking hell. Anyone want a pint?' our perplexed boss asked.

'Please.' said Karen.

'Denis?'

'Provided it's for drinking.'

'How long has this been going on?' asked Martin. Karen checked her watch.

'About four minutes.'

This change in relationship status meant we were able to rearrange seating and the now returned, soggy Mike was positioned next to our finance controller who was slightly deaf and it happily transpired, had an allotment so was able to commune with Abbott and relate to his vegetable enthusiasms.

Chapter Twenty Three

Christmas Lunch (Part Two)

'So where's Sandra gone?' Karen quizzed Martin. With all the excitement of kissing Karen and dousing Mike in beer I'd forgotten my initial target.

'Oh, she's off getting the Secret Santa sorted.'

Now that the moment had arrived doubts began to creep into my mind.

'Yeah, on the Secret Santa thing - how's Parky's sense of humour? I mean does he take jokes well?'

'You've got him a porn mag haven't you?' said the desiccating Mike, who had joined us at the bar

'No, of course I haven't got him a porn mag!' I protested. Mike looked puzzled. 'What did you get him? A porn mag's traditional innit? Like lights n' cranberry sauce, n' sprouts, n' turkey n'....'

I sensed another list in the air.

'No! It's not. The Magi didn't arrive in the stable with gold, frankincense and porn mags!'

With exquisitely bad timing Parky arrived on the scene.

'Discussing the Nativity?'

'A version of it.' I told him.

'Ah yes, the four evangelists do differ slightly in their interpretation but of course…' our religious advisor enlightened us.

Mike, not to be deflected from his own interpretation interrupted.

'Does any of them mention a porn mag?'

Parky gave him a withering glare.

'No Mr. Abbott there is no mention of that sort of thing or any aids to weakness of the flesh in any of their accounts. And I think you should try to be more reverent and seek forgiveness for your sins.'

'Just wondering where the tradition started like,' mused the thick-skinned Mike.

Trying to take the heat out of the situation, or rather getting offside and attempting not to think about Parky's Secret Santa present, I turned to Karen and Martin.

'I guess we eat after Sandra's done her Secret Santa bit?'

'Yep,' Martin answered. 'Provided no one throws beer over her of course… I know what you two were up to. I appreciate your concern for me but…'

'It's actually concern for our jobs,' Karen replied bluntly.

'Thanks! Don't worry - I'm not going to do anything stupid!'

'There's a first time for everything, I suppose.' Karen muttered.

Sandra came back in followed by two of her team, each with a black bin bag presumably stuffed with dildos, porn and perhaps a maximum of three normal presents. Finance staff, fueled with a modicum of drink, started barracking her. She stopped and checking the numbers, asked, 'Where's Gary?'

'On his way,' someone shouted out.

'Where's he been? Never mind we'll start once he gets here.'

'Do we have to wait for the pillock?' Martin said.

'Now now Martin. It's the season of goodwill to all men. And Gary.' Sandra told him, adding, 'I can see the tosser crossing the road now.'

Our esteemed Finance Director arrived shortly afterwards with his little sidekick Phil and the ritual began. Martin greeted them in his own diplomatic way.

'The gruesome twosome are here at last!'

Gary sneered and said 'I hear you've got a marriage guidance course for your Secret Santa.'

Wittily and with childishness that would have embarrassed a twelve year old, Martin laughed at them and quipped,

'Well I see you've brought your rent boy along with you.'

Phil stared unsure if he should be flattered but took his cue from Gary.

'I'm not a rent boy!' he protested.

'Don't you charge him any more?' Martin mocked him. Sandra intervened.

'OK now we've had our testosterone filled managers' demonstration can we get on with Secret Santa? Please!'

There followed a depressingly predictable exchange of the usual. Karen, sitting next to me whispered, 'You look nervous – afraid you won't get 'Big Girls' Jugs' or whatever moronic mag someone's gone to all the trouble to buy for you?'

'It's what I got Parky that's worrying me.'

But my wait was at an end. Over on a table by the window Parky had torn through outer layers of reindeer infested wrapping and was plundering an Amazon package. A voice, like of that of a righteous Old Testament prophet finding out perhaps that there were more Jezebels around than he'd expected or more accurately a Welsh lay preacher discovering that some wag had bought him Richard Dawkin's 'The God Delusion,' boomed out across the room. At least it shut Mike up whose voice I could hear reciting to Charlotte, 'tomatoes, leeks, broccoli, spuds, cabbage, curly kale, carrots, peas, courgettes, marrows, onions, bok choy, chard, choi sum, turnip greens...'

Parky stood up. He seemed a lot more fierce than I remembered. Bigger as well. 'Who bought me this?' he thundered. There are some situations where you can't hide and one of those situations was the situation I found myself in.

'I did Parky. If you don't want...'

Suddenly and mysteriously, he grinned.

'No! It's brilliant thanks Denis! I've meant to get it for ages so I can learn the enemy's side of things and refute it but I felt as though I'd be letting the side down if I bought it myself. Must chat to you later!'

On balance it could have gone a lot worse. I thought that my penance in talking to Parky was probably going to be a case of out of the frying pan of allotments and into the fires of eternity. I couldn't have been more wrong. Parky was an engaging sort, able to talk on a wide range of subjects in an interesting way without mentioning vegetables or security systems once. We agreed to go out for a beer one evening and were checking diaries when Karen tapped me on the shoulder.

'We'd better watch Martin and Gary – they're starting to get shitfaced and a bit lary.'

She was, as always, dead accurate in her observation. Martin could shift enough alcohol to sink a barge without appearing particularly drunk. Gary's wasn't in the same league and now the afternoon was sliding away from him. His head was gently descending towards the horizontal. Unfortunately he wasn't losing consciousness quickly enough and had started an unpleasant tirade against Martin.

'You're just a fucker Fitch,' he slurred. 'Eric hates you, you know!'

'I know Gary. I'm very proud that Eric hates me. Y'see I don't care, whereas your problem, among many others, is that you care that he hates you!'

Gary tried to focus on where he thought Martin might be.

'Eric said I'm his right hand man!' he boasted in a seven pint slur.

'And we know what you do to him with your right hand!' Martin wittily riposted.

Karen leapt in.

'That's really homophobic Martin!'

'No it's not! Gary's not gay are you Gary?'

Most of the power to follow this argument had departed Gary's brain. He stared vaguely from Karen to Martin and back again via the rest of the pub. His head was lying on the table.

'I'm not a phomohobual no! Just pixolated.'

Martin put his face close to Gary's.

'Eric thinks you're an innumerate fucking idiot! Ha!'

If he'd had a big bushy moustache he'd probably have twirled the ends of it. But he hadn't so he didn't. Gary managed to raise his head up slightly and slurred, 'I hear Olivia's left you again you fucking loser.'

Not bonny at the best of times he had a particularly ugly and demonic glint as he started singing drunkenly,

"It's a hard oul life when you've got no wife

And the man next door's got three."

Karen and I looked at one another, I think partly in admiration that he was still able to sing.

'Do you think he just made that up?' I asked. 'That's very good for someone as pissed as he is.'

Trouble was brewing. Martin glowered at Gary. Gary squinted in a sort of grimacey way at Martin, then suddenly and unexpectedly accurately, reached out and gripped Martin's nose. Up until that moment I thought it was only in bad films that someone said 'Owwww' but Martin distinctly said 'Owwww,' sounding like a bad actor, with a bad cold in an even worse film. There was an indeterminate sort of gurgling, a sound that was the prelude to something sinister. Those of us who had not been working hard enough at getting completely off our faces had the presence of mind to draw back. Even those just this side of coma seemed wary. We didn't quite cower against the walls with our palms pressed to it but that's only because the walls were too far away. Suddenly Martin sneezed. Oddly enough the previous week Karen and I had been playing Trivial Pursuit and a question came up about the speed of a sneeze (the answer was 200 mph) and now a live demonstration was unveiling itself before my eyes. And ears. This was not a quiet, gentle Jane Austen exhalation style sneeze, but a vast percussive, nay, explosive, big bang eruption blowing Gary's hand away from its critical function of holding Martin's nose closed, which thus freed, hurled a nasal mass ejection of mucus directly over Gary. There was a 'shloop' sound as it enveloped the trapped F.D. who, Alien like, now stared wide-eyed through a web of ectoplasmic strands joining him to his table. Martin, surprised by the force of his sneeze, stared at him. Gary, whimpering, stared back, then collapsed to the floor.

'Bless me.' Martin added needlessly. Karen stretched out and gingerly handed him a tissue, though a mop, bucket, sterilizing fluids and major disaster kit might have been more suitable.

'Anyone want a pint?' Martin asked.

Chapter Twenty Four

Fitness First

One day, recovering from the worst hangover to have afflicted a human being since the last moments of Oliver Reed, I decided to live a healthier lifestyle. Working at JDFT Media this was akin to an inhabitant of Hell deciding to become virtuous but I was helped by two events. Just before lunch one day, Martin was cursing and grumbling through his way through his emails. Suddenly he started laughing. This normally meant Eric had come up with an "idea".

'Anyone want free gym membership?' he asked.

Karen tutted and I gave Martin a cynical glance.

'What's the catch?'

'No catch! Caroline's got us a deal with the local health place. It's because it's February - everyone's given up going after Christmas.

He rummaged electronically for a moment.

'It's called "The Third Era Fitness Centre".

'Sounds like a cult - Scientology, that sort of thing.'

I thought about the offer for a moment. 'It's completely free? No sudden three hundred quid charges?'

'Nope - apparently you just call personnel and they'll sign up anyone who wants to induce a heart attack in a convenient place. I'll stick to the Red Lion training regime.'

So I found myself calling Blodwyn and immediately felt virtuous and healthier. Amazing the placebo effect of gyms.

'You do have to actually go along and do some exercise you know.' said Karen, delivering a dose of reality to my new dream of an Adonis like body all brimming with health.

'I know - I can go every morning before pitching up here.'

Martin looked across and I could see disbelief writ large.

'I might join you.' he said. 'Do they have a bar?'

Karen muttered something sarcastic, her phone rang stopping her mid-sarcasm..

'Yes… Eric… yes. What? OK I'll be over in a minute.'

As she put on her coat she said, 'Do you want to come with me?'

I was still mid-fantasy about extensive gym use creating a new fab, fit me.

'Where are you going?'

'Eric wants me to take his phone for a walk.'

I stared at her. I was puzzled to the extent of being completely baffled. I thought it might be all the potential exercise I'd been taking. Maybe I'd overdone it already.

'I didn't know he had a dog.' I answered.

'He hasn't got a dog.'

'How are we going to take it for a walk then?' seemed a reasonable response.

'It's his phone for fuck's sake!'

'I thought I'd misheard you or maybe there's a rare dog breed called a "phone".'

'No. He says he's got a new phone - it tells him how many steps he's done each day against a target. He's too busy to go for a walk with it so he's asked me to do it so he hits the target.'

'Isn't that....?' I realised this was Eric we were talking about. 'Never mind. We can go down past Luigi's and get something there.'

'I think you'll end up just like Eric,' Karen commented as we left the building and headed off to give Eric some exercise. Or his phone at least.

'What? A ruthless, heartless bastard who becomes chairman of the company?'

'No. Shit at exercise. You'll last a week at the gym!'

'No I won't!' I protested, thinking, "a week! That's quite a long time".

'Look at this,' she said and showed me the screen of Eric's phone.

It showed Target: 12,000 steps and beside it: Achieved: 46 steps..

'How can he only have done forty six steps? Is he a Dalek?'

'Chauffeur driven into work.' Karen replied.

After visiting the Italian sandwich shop we walked round what seemed like half of Soho.

'How are we doing? Ten thousand yet?'

'Still only at six thousand steps...' Karen informed me.

'Christ, this is going to take weeks. Should we go back via John O'Groats?'

We tried taking smaller steps but the phone was far too smart for us.

'A dog would be easier you know. Why don't we encourage Eric to get one? At least then he could stick the phone onto the dog and just let it run.'

'I think that would be cheating.'

I considered the morality of this.

'And getting your employees to wander about aimlessly for ages isn't? I'm beginning to lose interest in all this health stuff. Seems like hard work.'

'You haven't even started yet. Just wait till your personal trainer gets hold of you...'

'Personal trainer...?'

A strange feeling of unease was kicking in and whatever hormone causes regret was now firing up and coursing through my veins, if that's where hormones course.

Three days later my gym membership came through. When they said it was free of course they hadn't mentioned the expense of getting kitted out for my new life of strenuous activity. Everything that normally should cost about twenty pounds, once associated with fitness rockets tenfold. On the evening before my first visit to the gym I gave Martin a baleful glare.

'I'm practically bankrupt with all this gym stuff!' I protested as I dumped several bags of account draining clothing and shoes beside my desk.

'No one said health comes cheap!' he answered.

'I think the shopping's been enough exercise for me.'

'Do you think you'll make it to the gym tomorrow morning?'

'Tomorrow?'

Not one to avoid having her say, Karen grinned.

'Yep. Tomorrow morning you will be doing your first hour at the gym!'

'An hour?'

Stark reality had just smashed through my idealized version of leisurely but effective gym.

'How long were you thinking of?' she sneered.

'Well, maybe… ten minutes. To start with.'

'Ten minutes!' and there's no other way to describe it but Martin sneered as well.

'Yes, I thought ten minutes, then if I felt I was overdoing it I could cut back a bit.'

There was considerably more sneering and tutting about my lack of backbone and commitment. That night, with heavy heart I set my clock for an hour earlier than usual as I climbed into the scratcher. What seemed like thirty four seconds later I was ripped prematurely from the womb of sleep by a clanging and general alarm. I leapt up and dashed round the room several times thinking there must be a fire. Finally coming to as much consciousness as I could muster at six thirty in the morning, I crawled off to see what the gym had to offer. Once there it wasn't too bad. They had a place where you could get coffee and toast and I thought maybe I could focus on that side of the fitness regime, at least to start with but a huge bloke in a tracksuit had other ideas. He gave me a guided tour of all the different exercise machines they had on offer. Of course they didn't call them anything as simple as 'machines'. There was one called (I think) a Life Fitness Cable Motion Dual Adjustable Pulley Solution. I broke out in a sweat and lost several pounds just seeing this device which looked incredibly dangerous and made a mental note to avoid it like the plague. Then we approached a series of racks with varying sizes of what appeared to be wheels on small axles. He handed me one of these things and it was as though he'd placed a large lorry disguised as a small wheelie axle in my hand as gravity suddenly accelerated and pulled me towards the centre of the earth. I'm sure I could hear all my tendons ripping and snapping. Mercifully the floor was there and with a loud thump the incredibly dense and heavy item and I met it at the same time.

'You're not very fit are you?' he commented which seemed blunt, even rude.

He was around three times my size so I didn't taunt him with his lack of IQ or other failings but just pointed out that fitness was the only reason for me being there. Next, once the searing pain in my arms had eased to medium agony, he pointed me at a row of what looked like circular saws but turned out to be rowing machines which, after a couple of entanglements, were fairly straightforward to use. The big bozo buzzed off to initiate some other poor sod into the ways of the gym. The rowing machine (sorry, 'Blade Fitness Air Rower' as it was known to the cognoscenti and indeed ignoramuses like me) made a lovely hissing sound like rowing on real water and I got into a rhythm which became quite mesmeric and twenty minutes passed in a blink. After a shower I felt invigorated, apart from the still intense burning sensation in my arm where I'd picked up the little dense axle device. There was even a zip to my step as I flung open our office door. I think Martin and Karen were as amazed as I was by my new found enthusiasm for fitness.

I continued for exactly one week and four days. Now before you rush to judgement, tutting and making "told you so" types of comments, let me unfold the full horror of what befell me. It would have turned the most committed fitness freak into a couch potato. I remember the moment I stopped with an intensity that will live with me to the day I die and if I'm reincarnated I dare say it will still be there haunting me like a big haunty thing.

I'd got into the gym at my usual time just before eight and was settling down to a sedate row, imagining I was on some calm, exotic river, possibly in the Amazon, though avoiding the realism of piranhas and irritable creatures like that. Just in front of the line of rowing machines there was a mirror along one entire wall and sets of small hand weights similar to the torture devices which had nearly destroyed my arm. Normally there was no one around this area in the early dawn but this particular morning I lifted my eyes. My brain was almost unable to process the information being fed to it. There before me, violating every code of decent behaviour was Eric. He was tightly, indeed clingingly, enrobed as they say in lurid green Lycra, every nuance and bulge of his bony body poking, sticking, thrusting and generally invading the innocent space around him. He had his back to me but now he bent over forwards, his two buttocks alarmingly and suddenly, accusingly even, jolting out towards me like the shoulders of a particularly undernourished chicken. I closed my eyes and tried to go back to exotic river rowing but it was too late. Just as when you stare at a bright light then close your eyes it's burnt onto your retina, so Eric's green buttocks, like those of a lewd lizard, were still visible to my traumatized brain. I opened my eyes, thinking maybe I'd been overdoing the exercise and this was a serious but temporary, if bizarre, side effect. Yet the scenario facing me had become so bad I almost prayed for sudden cardiac arrest or some other soothing event to get me out of the situation. Eric had turned to face in my direction and was doing a weird exercise which involved him vigorously thrusting his groin towards me while holding small weights up high behind his head. His genitals, as if shrink wrapped in acid green cling film, stared me in the face. Every wrinkly, bulbous, folding, slithery detail of his gonads was visible through the Lycra. I don't know if there's a word for anti-erotic but what Eric was doing defined it perfectly. Traumatised, I fell off the rowing machine and stumbled downstairs to the changing rooms feeling clammy, ill and swearing never to come near the place again. Finally reaching the sanctuary of our office I sat staring at my screen. Every so often between emails there would be a flash of Eric's buttocks or his groin thrusting at me and I would involuntarily call out in terror.

'Are you OK Denis?' Martin asked. I realised he'd been talking to me for a couple of minutes.

'Sorry… I think I'm suffering from Post Traumatic Stress Disorder.' I gibbered.

Karen had pitched up so I described my terrible experience to my unfortunate colleagues.

'I mean why couldn't he get someone else to go to the gym for him, like he did with his phone thing? That way no one would get hurt.'

'So is that it with you and the gym?' Karen asked. I gave her a sharp look.

'You bet it is - exercise is fucking dangerous!'

Chapter Twenty Five

In Which Parky Drinks To The Glory Of God (But Not Tourists).

The mystery of Parky's popularity was one I was determined to crack and an answer came sooner than expected. Early one morning before other staff arrived. I noticed Nick the Bastard tapping away at his keyboard and looking round with a furtive air. I didn't think it would be a porn site as he had no shame or qualms about publicly accessing the most lurid material on the web, even to the extent of claiming his membership fees for 'Asian Sluts' as a business expense. But today there was something distinctly shady about his behaviour. I was on the mezzanine floor looking down into the pit where he was entering data into his computer, after which a blue line appeared on screen as information was processed. I was familiar with all the software we used in the company but I didn't recognise this. Nick was so engrossed in his task that he didn't hear my not particularly stealthy footsteps. There were several bits of information in view and I could see the words "Towcester 3.30 , Pukka Minor." About to turn away thinking, "typical Nick", I noticed the blue band cross the screen again. Then the monitor showed "Pukka Minor - win probability 87.5%. Best odds given 6-1 online at PluckyPunters.com. Correct odds 5-4 FAV."

I was now at his shoulder and said,

'What's this software Nick?'

He leapt several inches from his seat, which given his size, probably registered on the Richter scale.

'Shit, what the fuck are you doing? Jesus Denis I nearly shat a chair!'

'I've never seen this before what is it?'

Nick the Bastard looked round him in what police might call a suspicious manner. He whispered at around 120 decibels.

'OK, you won't mention this to anyone else?'

'Go on then.'

'Well, y'know Parky's a researcher and planner, yeah?'

'Yes.'

'Y'know he writes all that software to work out the best place for an ad yeah? Well he's written this software see,' he jabbed a porky finger at the screen, 'it searches the internet for all the information on a horse, its form, then the going at the race course according to the latest weather reports, gets all the info and weighs it all up against the best odds given, and calculates what the odds should be.'

'Right. So occasionally he beats the bookies.'

'Occasionally! Fucking hell mate! What this does is it works out which bookies have got the odds wrong and are too generous! This beats the bookies just about every time! What he's done is written an algorithm that gets it right 94 percent of the time.'

Suddenly the reason for Parky's popularity became crystal clear.

'Jesus! How much have you made?'

He looked round and once again the only word that can describe his behaviour is "furtive".

'This is the bank account I keep for my betting activities.'

I looked at the figure several times. I looked at Nick the Bastard.

'Holy shit! How long did it take you to make that?'

'About six months. I've been doing so well three online bookies have shut my accounts, the bastards.'

'I can see why. This software is worth a fortune. Imagine what punters would pay for it!'

'I know but Parky says he's done it for the glory of God. You won't tell anyone though will you mate?'

'No, no. I'd better get myself a copy though.'

Nick smiled like a drug dealer with a new customer.

'That's it Denis my son, you make yourself some wonga like the rest of us. Luvly jubbly.'

At that moment I was thinking that there was more money to be made from selling the software than betting with it. A quiet word with Parky was needed.

And so it came to pass that one evening in late March I went out for a drink with the "Reverend Parky" as he was known to our colleagues. Walking down the winding streets of Covent

Garden to a pub I thought he'd like, I decided to broach the subject of his money making product.

'Parky, if you don't mind my saying, that horse race prediction software could make you a small fortune. No let me correct that; a rather huge fortune.'

'I suppose so. I'm not really interested in all that sort of thing it's not the Lord's work,' he replied as we negotiated an attempt by a black cab to mow us both down.

'But think of the good you could do – I mean the Lord wouldn't mind would he?'

Maybe somewhere in the bible there was a clause or indeed an entire sub-section about not ripping off bookies but I couldn't be sure. Parky airily answered,

'Ah, you see I believe the Lord moves in mysterious ways.'

'The Lord doesn't have to move at all if this is marketed properly. He just has to sit there put his feet up and let the loot roll in.'

We were just hitting the threshold of the pub so I stopped at this point, feeling it might be better to wait until he'd had a drink or two. Or more. The Coach & Horses was quiet for mid-week with just a small, melancholy elderly man sipping a half pint at the other end of the bar, occasionally passing odd comments to the barman. As we came in I could hear his mournful voice droning.

'In the end of course they found he was an alien. That's why he stopped coming in 'ere and it explained the old problems with 'is waterworks.'

The barman considered this for a few moments and countered the theory.

'No! I'm sure he died. Yes, of course he did - remember - we went to the funeral?'

Unfazed by this demolition of his argument the old bloke sighed,

'Oh yeah, you could be right on that. Always the way innit? Put another half in there will ya and I'll have a small Scotch.'

'What can I get you gentlemen?' the barman asked, turning to us.

'What would you like Parky?' I offered.

'I only drink the Lord's drink,' said Parky. With a sinking feeling I looked at the clock. It was only twenty to seven. The barman and I were clearly of one mind on this as I scanned the bottled waters, fruit juices and all the other extraneous garbage pubs have to supply to cater for those who are 'alcohol challenged'. The old guy looked sideways disapprovingly at Parky and muttered,

'kin 'ell.'

'Right, water or fruit juice, which is it to be?' I asked, somewhat testily.

'No, no. You misunderstand me. I only drink that which supports the work of the Lord.'

'Yeah, I know. You said. So you want…' Parky interrupted me.

'I see you have Chimay there.'

The barman looked with some surprise.

'Do we?'

Parky pointed. 'Down there on that shelf, next to the Duvel beer. That's OK as well by the way.'

'Oh yeah! So we do,' lifting up and blowing the dust off a bottle from a lower shelf.

Do you stock green Chartreuse?' he enquired.

'Certainly sir,' our host replied realizing he had a discerning customer on his hands.

'Great. I'll have a Chimay mixed with green Chartreuse in a pint pot.'

'OK,' I said while mentally scanning the Bible for references to any wedding where Jesus turned water into Chimay and Chartreuse, 'and how exactly is this the Lord's drink?'

Parky's theology kicked in,

'Chartreuse is produced by the Carthusian Fathers while Chimay is made by Trappist monks. Every time I drink it is to the glory of God - I put a couple of quid in the pockets of the monks and brothers.'

I turned back to the bar and there stood one of the most revolting drinks I've ever seen. If you can cast your mind back to primary school and the colour of the water jar in painting class after a hard day at the easel, you get a good idea of

242

Parky's potion. I ordered a deeply un-spiritual pint of bitter and we sat down.

The first of his unusual cocktails perked Parky up no end. He became expansive, or as expansive as anyone can be who believes the world is a swirling cesspool of sin and fit only to be tossed like a sausage into the barbecue of Hell, as he put it. As I came back from the bar with the fourth round Parky whispered loudly to me.

'Look all around you – we're in an occasion of sin!'

Surveying the Coach & Horses I wasn't convinced.

'Are we? You quite sure?'

The evening seemed to have brightened up at last. I looked around for the occasion of sin with a more optimistic air. I imagined an invite with 'An Occasion of Sin' emblazoned on it in lurid red letters. My optimism that the bar would suddenly and surprisingly break into a Bacchalian rout soon faded. It seemed more an outside chance for mild veniality. Parky was not to be put off by this clear lack of sinfulness. Warming to his theme he continued:

'Oh yes! We're in a sink of filth here alright boyo. I can feel the breath of the Evil One on my neck.'

He went on in this vein for several minutes.

'Can't you feel the horror? The feeling of what eternal fires burning your vitals and hell stretching out before you across millennia, after millennia, after millennia, after millennia might be like?'

'I'm getting an idea, yeah.'

'Millennia and millennia ah yes…' his voice tailed off. I think even he realized at that moment that the powers of evil had failed us miserably and gone home for cocoa and an early night. No, evil's just not what it used to be I thought to myself at the same time realizing that the prophet of impending doom had fallen silent. I sneaked a sideways glance. Parky was staring in a contemplative way, the sort of way in fact that only a man who has poured around five pints of Chimay and green Chartreuse into his system can stare. He suddenly broke off his contemplation, gripped me by the arm and gazing at me with mournful, though unfocused eyes, whispered,

'You know what I really want to be?'

Here we go, I thought. Of course I knew what was coming. Once full of liquor, every Welshman worth his salt is eventually going to lay bare the soul and say that he wants to be a poet, a singer or, if the beauty and art for which his nation is known are really suffused through his veins, prop-forward for Llanelli. I watched with expectation as he struggled inwardly, although that could have been the stale crisps he was eating.

'Archbishop of Canterbury,' he announced in a loud voice. I must say I wasn't expecting this. Nor clearly was the elderly bloke at the bar who raised his head from the counter and said, 'Where?'

Focusing on the back of a beer mat offering a competition to win 'Peanuts for Life', which seemed like a cruel comment on my career, I tried to hang on to reality.

'You won't tell anyone will you?' Parky whispered nervously. I tried to think who might be interested in this revelation but gave up after the Pope.

'No of course not but, well, don't you have to be a vicar or something to start with?'

'That's just it. I did some lay preaching last year and now I'm going to enrol in a course at college.'

'What? There's a course to train people to be Archbishop of Canterbury?'

I mean why not? If anyone can, in theory at least, become Prime Minister, why not Archbishop? I was going to ask how his betting software might go down with the interviewing panel of the General Synod but felt I was getting ahead of myself and that bridge could be crossed at a later date.

'No, not quite but there are theological courses on divinity that start you off. My belief is that the Lord works in mysterious ways.'

'So you've said, many times and it may well be true but there are mysterious ways and mysterious ways and even He would have to admit that JDFT Media is not a usual career route for bishops.'

Nodding sagely Parky gazed off into the middle distance, although I suspect he thought he was looking at me.

'I'm testing my soul you see. Putting it through its trial of fire and ice.'

I pondered this and could see only one reply.

'Let's have another drink.'

It may have been that Chimay and green Chartreuse that caused it or the next one, or even what proved to be the final one of the night but suddenly Parky leapt to his feet, cried out, 'I must get on with my mission,' and headed for the door. I threw back the last of my pint and sprinted after him. I heard the old guy shout after us, 'Fucking Archbishop! Don't come back ya git!'

We wended our way down to Waterloo Bridge. It was a clear night, fairly warm for the season and London was at its finest. Don't just take my word for it – the boatload of tourists who were on the river heading towards us were clearly in expansive mood, sitting in rows on the deck of the open topped craft. I thought for a second I was hallucinating. The passengers were all dressed in medieval costume and led by a chirpy cockney tour guide decked out in jester's clothes. He was one of those really jolly sorts who wants to make the entire human race happy and will keep people gingered up whether they want gingering up or not and who irritates the fuck out of everyone. As he manically commentated for his audience while they took in the landmarks on the river I don't think I've ever seen someone who deserved a good sound slapping.

'There on the left is the Tate Modern, full of crap art like piles of bricks and dead sharks,' he shouted with the natural confidence of the truly stupid. Glancing up he caught sight of our silhouettes above, looking at the ridiculous spectacle about to pass below.

'Hey look everyone!' he cried gleefully, 'Let's all wave to the nice local people on the bridge,' and started singing, "Maybe it's because I'm a Londoner."

One of the nice people on the bridge raised two fingers at him and a broad representation of the world's cultures got a clear view of my displeasure. The jester / tour guide inflamed the situation by shouting at us through the public address system,

'Oooohh. Well that's not very welcoming is it? Pillocks.'

At that moment an ominous gurgling sound from my right signaled that Parky and his evening's consumption were about to part ways. He lurched at the parapet and ejected the contents of his stomach in three major eruptions of a lurid, multi-coloured, liquid mass out over the tourists whose little upturned faces watched the approaching storm. Maybe some believed this to be for realism, representing the ancient habit of old London Town(e) when the contents of chamber pots were casually flung out of windows. Two things struck me. Firstly the Chimay and Chartreuse had separated during the digestion process and there were clear green and brown sections to the fall out. It was also interesting how evenly wind distributes vomit. I'm sure the people on the boat commented on it as well while they also had a brief opportunity to rue the fact it was a dry night and they had no umbrellas. It is safe to say there was a fair degree of noise coming from the faux medieval brigade below, echoing against the parapets and buttresses of the bridge. I turned to Parky who looked at me.

'Fucking great – I feel much better!' he announced. 'See you tomorrow!' and strode off in a zig-zag towards the tube station. I was left reflecting on why my colleagues didn't seem able to keep their bodily fluids to themselves. Looking on the bright side I imagined a day in the future when a tourist might tell of his experience of London and recount with pride how he was vomited over by the future Archbishop of Canterbury.

Chapter Twenty Six

Health and Safety

One afternoon we were all sitting at our various places not doing any one any harm, just minding our own business. Karen was working on the impending re-pitch to Oroco Oil and slaving over a hot computer showing slides with headlines such as "Target Audience", "Brand DNA", "Share of Voice" and "Viral Marketing".

The peace was abruptly broken.

'Anyone doing anything exciting this weekend?' Martin asked, in a rare and worrying show of interest in his staff.

'Why?' Karen asked suspiciously.

'No reason. Just y'know making small talk.'

Karen and I exchanged glances each wondering what was behind this sudden concern for our entertainment. My phone rang. A loud voice said,

'Denis! How are you?'

I was now getting worried that so many people, well two at least, were asking after my welfare.

'Caroline. I'm fine thanks. How are you?'

'I'm very well thank you Denis. I'm calling to tell you I've volunteered you and Mr. Parkinson to go to a presentation I think you'd be interested in. It's part of our building trust and empathy with Buy-O-Soft Systems.'

'What's it about?'

'Finance.'

After the tourist vomiting episode I'd given myself a break from Parky's company for a few weeks and here was Fate sticking its oar in again. Where would be the next venue for his Chimay / Green Chartreuse tourist bath I wondered. I thought too that Caroline might know my interests and that Finance wasn't top of the bill.

'Finance? It's not really my area of expertise I'm not sure it would build much trust Caroline.'

'The meeting's in Paris – Buy-O-Soft will put you up in a hotel for the weekend.'

And stranger still how you can develop a rapid fascination with something.

'On the other hand that's really interesting I've always thought I should learn more about Finance. Next weekend?'

'Yes – some of their people are coming over from the States so they want a few suppliers there to get a feel for the company.'

'Caroline I've just had a thought.'

'Yes?' she said, with suspicion in her voice.

'Well, I'll email you with an idea I've just had.'

'Why can you not just tell me on the phone?'

'It's not... fully formed as yet. More a concept.'

'OK but I've got my bullshit sensor on full alert!'

I tapped out an email and hit send. A few minutes later I got the answer I wanted.

At JDFT I'd divided the day into two parts: time before risk of food poisoning and time before risk of alcohol poisoning. It was getting close to risk of food poisoning time. Because I needed to talk to her alone I emailed Karen who was only four feet away.

'Lunch?' the terse email asked.

She looked at me as if I'd gone mad. I signaled for her to be quiet and we got up and moved towards the door. Martin, without looking up said, 'If I catch you two shagging in the stationery cupboard....'

'Martin!' Karen warned.

'Remember Mike Abbott's email from last year?' he said.

'I wasn't here.' I made my excuse.

'One of the press guys damaged a printer in a moment of carnal passion. I mean there was someone else involved of course. Abbott sent out one of his health and safety missives about not abusing office equipment. Anyway', Martin said picking up his coat, ' Canteen Pete's?'

This was an awkward moment.

'I need to speak to Karen alone. Sorry.' I told him apologetically.

Martin looked genuinely hurt.

'OK. I see. Right. See you later then.'

251

On our way down I said, 'We're not going to Canteen Pete's – I've had nothing there but cheese sandwiches, I'm turning into one.'

'Where are we going?'

'Silvio's.'

Silvio's was a little Italian place next to the Assembly of God Church. The reason we tended not to go there at lunchtimes was that we had to pass The Red Lion on our way. When I say 'pass' I mean Martin would insist on a pint on the way there and three on the way back. He would then break off and head for the Prince of Wales and an afternoon of "strategic planning" while we would try to work without falling asleep.

Silvio was a jovial Londoner who had never been closer to Italy than Dover. He greeted us warmly.

'Afternoon! Long time no see!'

Some way behind him an elderly woman was sitting on a small stool. She had one shoe off and was systematically harvesting whatever lay beneath her toenails and flicking it on the floor. Silvio said, 'What would you like?'

We scanned the cartons which had little plastic tags reliably informing me they contained tuna and sweetcorn, ham, deli turkey, deli chicken, deli roast beef, bacon, and chicken salad. Karen requested a BLT. As the toe-picking carried on in the background I felt less and less hungry.

'I'll have chicken please Silvio,' I said. He smiled and turned to the unhygienic creature behind.

252

'I've got to make up an order for a party – can you serve these lovely people Mama?'

She brushed some toe material from her hands and approached the counter to start making our sandwiches.

'I'm really sorry!' I exclaimed, 'I have a memory like a sieve. Martin's waiting for us. I completely forgot – sorry –we'll see you some other time Silvio.'

Like when hell freezes over I thought. Karen of course butted in.

'I thought...'

'No', I said steering her out, 'we have to see Martin. It's critical!'

No doubt firmly convinced that she'd managed to choose a complete lunatic as her new partner Karen barely noticed who was coming into Silvios. But it was Eric. Chairman Eric. Now this was not just unlikely but ultra extraordinary. If someone had put a bet with me on which human being I would see coming into Silvio's to buy a sandwich, Eric would have been behind the Dalai Lama and Lord Lucan. For a start I wasn't sure he was capable of doing anything as complex as ordering a sandwich without a PA somewhere in the vicinity. I was about to ask him if he was supposed to be out on his own but he ignored us so I thought better of it. As we left I stopped for a moment and watched through the window as Signora Toepicker picked up two slices of bread and a handful of something from one of the cartons and began to fill Eric's sandwich with it. Good luck with the filling / toe pickings mix I thought.

'Ah,' said Karen. 'He's lost another P.A. and has to fend for himself. Wanker.'

'Harsh but fair as always.'

'OK. Why did you drag me out of Silvio's? she demanded.

'I wasn't happy with their level of hygiene.'

'So where are we going?'

'You can't say I don't treat you well; we're going to The Red Lion.'

'And you were worried about hygiene in Silvios? Holy fuck!'

'It's all relative. But I am taking you to Paris next weekend...'

'What?'

I was now pushing open the door of The Red Lion and entering that palace of mirth, entertainment and cirrhosis.

'Sorry did you say you're....' her voice tailed off. There was good reason for her to be silent. I was dumbstruck as well. Across the right hand wall, where previously there had lived a cork notice board covered in small ads, notifications of local events such as "Charity Dogfight" and other valuable information, there was now a huge mural of a mermaid. What was immediately striking was that this mermaid had breasts so out of proportion to the rest of her body that she looked like a trout hiding behind a pair of false boobs.

Karen stared at the mural.

'I imagine swimming would be difficult. Floating fine but anything requiring streamlining out of the question. What bra size does she take?'

This last quip was addressed to Melvyn who ran the Red Lion and had come over to admire the mural with us.

'Some of the art students from the college down the road done it. Marvellous – could be worth a fortune one day if one of them becomes famous.'

'So you've decided to cover your walls in porn to bring in more punters Melvyn?' I asked.

Melvyn was shocked to the core of his being.

'Porn? Nah this is art mate! If Dave the decorator done it then that 'd be porn but as it's an artist's work it's erotica innit!'

We sat down in the far corner to avoid having Melvyn's 'erotica' as our background.

'Paris?' Karen prompted.

'Yes, would you like to go to Paris next weekend? Hotel and travel paid for by Buy-O-Soft.'

'Ah – it's business.'

'Sort of. I know Caroline only asked me to go because I know some of the guys going from the client. But I put it to her that because you'd worked so hard on the pitch you deserved to go as well. And she agreed. The bad news is we, sorry I, have to attend a couple of Finance conferences or seminars. But I can sneak out halfway through and we can be tourists.'

'So you have you got an ulterior motive for taking me to Paris?'

'Such as?'

'Well, this hotel… Have I got a room of my own?'

'You have indeed.'

'Paris is such a romantic city, that's a shame.'

'Of course we don't have to use all the rooms…'

'No we don't have to…' she replied and we kissed again.

There was a loud cough close by. Melvyn, the commissioner of soft porn / erotica, said in a stern voice.

'I won't warn you again! We have standards in this pub.'

Karen giggled at his prudishness and whispered to me.

'Very low ones. Thanks Denis. Top marks for blagging a weekend in Paris for us!'

Melvyn hovered.

'Now would you two young lovers like something to eat?

'What have you got?'

Melvyn considered the board listing his 'Fayre.'

'Lamb casserole – that's off. Beef Stroganoff – that's off. Fish and chips – let me check.'

He went out through a small door behind the bar and a brief, mysterious conversation ensued with a person or persons unseen. Someone shouted something and there came the percussive noise of a plate being smashed. The guardian of customer morality and purveyor of bare-breasted mermaids returned.

'Apparently that's off too. That's the problem with top notch chefs, temperamental bastards.'

He contemplated the mermaid for a few seconds. 'I could do you a tuna sandwich?'

I sighed but remembering our venture into Silvio's, saw the positives.

'That's fine Melvyn, two tuna sandwiches please!'

I said to Karen, 'So. Friday morning Eurostar to Paris it is then!'

Melvyn had returned to hover.

'Er. Tuna's gone I'm afraid. Cheese OK?'

'Yeah, a cheese sandwich will be fine.'

Karen gave me a hug and kissed me.

'In return for your romantic weekend I'm going to let you do something.'

'What's that?' I asked with a heightened sense of erotic promise.

'You can help me set up the boardroom for tomorrow's presentation!'

I heaved a sigh of disappointment.

'Right. The boardroom - brilliant!'

Chapter Twenty Seven

Oroco Oil and Water

Karen and I got in early on the day of the presentation to make sure the boardroom was in one piece, no one had 'borrowed' any bits of kit or generally buggered it up. Across the front of the building a banner read 'JDFT Media Welcomes Oroco Oil!' It was the reception area that really had the wow factor though. There, filling most of the space, was a scale model of an Oroco Oil super-tanker. It must have been thirty feet long. I looked at Karen, she looked at the tanker. We both looked at the double entrance door.

'How the...?'

The door to the corridor swung open and in came Jim Wilson, building supervisor. If you wanted a definition of exhaustion for a dictionary, Jim was the man this morning.

'Hi Jim - you OK?' Karen greeted him cheerily.

'I am bloody knackered!' he replied then pointed at the tanker in case we'd missed it, 'This thing arrived at two o'clock - the building team got here about half past and started on the glass. Finished half an hour ago.'

'You mean they took out the whole front of the building, put the ship in and put it all back?' I asked, suddenly realizing how important this presentation was to the company.

'Yep, exactly!'

'Where did you get the boat?' asked Karen.

'The boat as you call it weighs half a ton - there's a company in Liverpool makes them. Eric had it commissioned - I think it cost about forty grand.'

'It's brilliant!' I enthused. 'If I were Oroco Oil and saw that, I'd just hand the account back immediately! There's no danger of us losing it!'

'Doesn't work quite like that. I love your optimism but the presentation has to convince as well. This is just window dressing,' Karen explained, deflating my awe only slightly. Jim cast a critical eye over his and his team's handiwork.

'It's impressive isn't it? Well, I've done my bit - it's up to the guys upstairs now. OK, I'm off to get some sleep - have to be back at five to do it all in reverse. See you round - have fun!'

Everything worked in the boardroom and satisfied that, like Jim, we'd done our bit, we went out to a Starbucks round the corner. It was just before eight.

We sat at a window and as we sipped our coffee Karen was worrying about the presentation.

'I think they've got too many slides - I mean we've been working with them for years - they know what we do and how good we are! We're going to bore them to death!'

'Or into submission,' I added. 'we should have threatened them with a run down by Mike Abbott on the politics of the Potters Bar Allotment Association.'

'You can have too much of a good thing,' Karen quipped. 'I suppose we'd better get back - the client's in at eight thirty.'

'Early start!'

'Yep - eighty seven slides to get through.'

'Who's doing the presentation?'

'Eric, Caroline and Jeremy. Assorted other hangers on as well I expect. Caroline asked me to come up to meet the client.'

'You? Why?'

I hadn't meant it to sound so abrupt.

'Why shouldn't? I put together the fucking presentations!'

'Sorry - I didn't mean it like that.'

'Caroline always likes me to check the first slide - make sure it's OK then she introduces me to the client. Kind of to show the human behind the presentation I suppose. I reckon it's superstition actually.'

'How do you mean?'

'The first presentation I did was Oroco Oil - that's when we won it. I think she thinks I'm a lucky charm.'

'Hope it works this time.'

'Yep so do I…'

I suddenly thought of something.

'So Martin's girlfriend, Olivia, will be in this meeting?'

'Yeah, I suppose so.'

'Hmm. You don't think they'll mention that - it might come up or something?'

'Doubt it.'

By the time we got back Martin was in the office.

'Thought I'd better show willing!' he said. 'that ship thing in reception - it's amazing. How did they get it in?'

We gave him a quick lecture on the art of getting a supertanker into an office. Karen got up and said, 'Wish me luck - charm offensive here we go!'

She disappeared and Martin and I were left to our own devices.

'No word from Olivia?' I asked.

'Not as such... no.'

There was a heavy silence so I went back to my screen and left him to his thoughts. It was just coming up to half eight so I guessed tension was building as he realized the next few hours were going to be crucial to his future.

At that moment Karen reappeared. She came in briskly, sat at her desk and put her head in her hands, muttering, 'Holy fuck, holy fuck!' several times. Clearly something was up.

'What's up?' There was silence. 'Karen?' I asked.

Martin and I both got up and went over to her.

'What's happened? Are you OK?'

She looked up at us and she was as white as a sheet.

'We've just lost Oroco Oil!' she whispered.

'What? Didn't they like the ship?' I queried, finding the idiotic question at the right moment.

'It wasn't the fucking ship!' she said tersely.

'What happened?'

Karen was shaking as she told us.

'Caroline opened the boardroom door and showed the client in….'

'What? So…' Martin began. Karen looked up at us.

'The first thing the client saw was Nick the Bastard shagging Kelly from Accounts on the boardroom table!' she announced. I was still in idiotic mode.

'What did Caroline do?'

'She just said, "Ooops - we'll find another room" and closed the door.'

'Jesus!' Martin chipped in, 'what did the client do?'

'They just said "don't be too long shagging we need to get this meeting started",

'Really so what's the…?'

Martin had joined me in the idiot camp

'No of course they fucking didn't!' Karen shouted, furious now

'They told Eric their legal team would be in contact with him and no one from JDFT Media was to call them under any circumstances.'

'They seem to have taken it badly then…' Martin mused. Karen's anger flared again.

'Fucking hell Martin - remember our strategy for the pitch? Focusing on ethical reasons! It's difficult enough giving an oil company an ethical marketing strategy. Great! First thing they see as we go to unveil our ethical strategy is Nick's hairy arse pumping up and down on Kelly spread-eagled over the table.'

'Bit too graphic!' Martin said puritanically.

'You're lucky you didn't actually see it - not easy to forget!'

'So what's going to happen to them?'

Karen shrugged.

'Eric's called an emergency board meeting for this afternoon.'

'Nick and Kelly will be fired for sure but what happens about Oroco?'

The full implications were sinking in for Martin.

'Maybe I should call Olivia - pour oil on troubled waters…'

Karen glanced across at him. She thought about what Martin had said.

'Yesterday I would have said that was a ridiculous idea. But we've nothing to lose.'

Before he got a chance to call anyone, Martin's phone rang.

'Ah the Prince of Darkness himself…' he said picking up the call.

'Eric! Yes I heard. No Olivia hasn't been in touch yet but I'm sure she will be. Two o'clock? OK - I'll be there.'

Breathing a sigh of relief Martin hung up.

'Doesn't sound as though Olivia has informed on me yet. I've been summoned to the meeting. I don't think it's going to be a convivial one.'

'We heard! Do you want me to go instead?' I asked.

'Sorry - have to pull rank and disappoint you but Eric asked for me personally. I think he misses me when I don't go.'

Karen was still in a state of fury and admonished him.

'Just don't say anything to antagonize him - he's not in a good mood!'

'No shit! When is he ever?'

Karen stood and slung her bag over her shoulder.

'I'm going out. I need to do something to get the image of Nick the Bastard's buttocks out of my mind!'

Martin peered over his glasses at her.

'OK - are you alright?'

She grunted.

'I'm just pissed off at all the hard work that went into this. Poor old Jim - he was up all night getting that ship into reception. He'll kill Nick and Kelly when he hears about this.'

'Don't spend too much!' I warned and off she went leaving a void in our office life. It was difficult to concentrate knowing that Martin was facing possible firing this afternoon. At eleven he got up as normal.

'Where are you going?' I asked, feeling this was a not unreasonable question.

'Prince of Wales. Coming?'

'Martin! What about the meeting - do you not need to be kind of sober and sharp to cope with that?'

'I'll be fine! Better to have a pint or two before these things I find.

'I'll see you there about half twelve. I think I've got a good guy for the support role. Interviewed him yesterday - he seems disturbed enough to work here. I'll tell you about him in the pub. That's his CV.'

Martin gave it a cursory glance.

'Looks good. What happened to the one from last week?'

'He answered his mobile during the interview...'

'Ah! Right - OK - give him a call and offer him the job if you think he's alright. Ask Jemima to send him a contract. See you in the pub.'

I got on the phone and gave Dave Maxwell the news that in the great lottery of life the poor bastard had just drawn the short straw and was about to become an employee of JDFT Media. Karen got back a bit later, only a bit less angry and stressed.

'Where's Martin? she asked and before I could answer, she'd guessed.

'He really is such a twat. Eric's going to be looking for blood this afternoon and Martin's just behaving like a... a... I don't even know what's he behaving like it's so bad.'

'Do you want to come with me to the Prince of Wales? If we go down he's got to come back - I've a feeling he's not keen to go to the board meeting.'

'Did he call Olivia?'

'He hadn't when he left. Probably better he lets things calm down a bit.'

Shaking her head she said, 'There's no chance of them keeping us. We're fucked.'

'But we're going to Paris this weekend!'

'Yeah, so we are. Good. I need a break.'

After plucking Martin from the temptations of the Prince of Wales and restricting his intake to a light four pints we pointed him at the boardroom and hoped for the best. An hour or so later the reprobate returned beaming like the Cheshire Cat.

'They weren't still shagging on the table when you got there?' I asked.

'No! God almighty you two are going to love this!'

Karen flicked one of her dart-like jaundiced glances at him.

'Really? I take it Kelly and Nick have both been handed their P45s?'

'Nope!'

'What? Is shagging in front of clients acceptable behaviour now?'

'If you'll let me tell you - this is priceless!' Martin perched on the corner of his desk like a storyteller of old, albeit a slightly beery and unfocused one.

'Right - I went into the meeting. Pretty unpleasant atmosphere as you might imagine. Eric read out the charges and said "I want these two employees fired with immediate effect". Gareth was there and he pointed out that though Nick the Bastard might have some unsavoury qualities, he was the best TV buyer in the company and it wouldn't be a wise move to fire him. He'd have a job with TMH within a day - very cunning on Gareth's part - Eric hates TMH with a passion. All our deals and secrets would be theirs. So they all muttered for a while

266

about this and eventually Eric decided Nick could stay but that Kelly had to be sacked.'

'That's typical! The woman gets the blame - they're both guilty of this!' Karen protested. Martin held up a hand like the ancient orator again.

'There's more! Monica, the Financial Controller is Kelly's boss and she said that Kelly was brilliant and had saved the company a fortune last year in expenses. I remember that expenses crackdown - she's a tough cookie Kelly when she wants to be. So there was a load more waffle and stuff. Eventually they decided Kelly couldn't be fired either. Eric was raging - you should have seen him! He said someone had to pay for what had happened.'

'Well, if they couldn't fire Kelly or Nick what did they do?'
Martin laughed.

'They fired the boardroom table!'

'What?'

'I know! Mike Abbott of course said there was a hygiene issue with what had gone on. So the boardroom table is going. Seems a bit unfair but justice must be seen to be done.'

'What about Oroco?'

'Ah... not so funny there. Eric's asked each department head to draw up a list of people to chuck overboard. I fear I may not be long for this world.'

I voiced my concern.

'I'm being selfish here Martin but if it's last in first out surely I'll go, not you?'

'All things being equal that's true but Eric's looking for an excuse to fire me. If he does, it means there's enough in the budget for you and one support person and his cretin son heading up the department.'

'Fucking hell!' Karen slumped in a gloomy, slumpy way. 'OK I'll say it this time. Let's go to The Red Lion!'

Martin was first through the door of the Lion.

'C'mon Melvyn cheer us up!' he called out to our host who was lovingly dusting his mermaid mural.

'That's the secret to looking after great art,' Melvyn explained, 'keep it free from dust and grime. I'm thinking of having a Perspex cover made for her to stop people touching her and damaging the essential fabric of her being.'

'Do you mean her tits?' asked Martin.

'Well, primarily yeah.' Melvyn conceded. 'Some of the customers have been getting a bit touchy feely with her. On that subject, I hear there's been a spot of table ending going on over at your place!'

'Good news travels fast. May I have a white wine and two pints of Pride?'

'You may indeed Martin. Nick and Kelly I believe?'

'You're very well informed, who told you?'

'Kelly was in at lunchtime. She was complaining about being disturbed by someone just coming in without knocking. She was saying she and Nick use that table every Thursday morning - never had a problem till today. There's your wine. Pride did you say?'

Once we'd sat down with our drinks Martin raised a toast to the unfortunate piece of furniture.

'Here's to the poor old boardroom table! Not that I'm connecting the two events but you two are off to Paris tomorrow morning for a dirty weekend!'

'Martin!' Karen warned.

'Good luck to you - why not?'

'It's not a dirty weekend it's a finance conference.' I corrected him.

'I'd sooner admit to a dirty weekend than a finance conference.' Martin commented. 'By the way I spoke to Olivia. Things don't look too good. GNB are pitching for Oroco Oil's account next week and the word is they're a shoo in now.'

'Eric is going to go apeshit!' Karen muttered.

'Provided it's not in green Lycra I don't care!' I shuddered.

Chapter Twenty Eight

Randy and the Men in Black.

On the Eurostar next morning I gave Karen a run down on the timetable I'd been sent and on the characters she was about to meet. After recounting the tale of Randy J. Feckenburger (the Third), the Freak, vodka, pineapple rings and all, she had a well formed view that she was about to spend the weekend in the company of at least one psychopath.

'He's OK once you get to know him.' I said, then recanted. 'Actually no he's not – he wanted to fire me, the Freak and anyone else he could think of. Eric would like him.'

Karen went through Randy's attributes ticking them off on her fingers.

'Let me sum up. He's a sexist, teetotal, alcoholic, Christian Evangelical, control freak who gets shitfaced and eats toilet fresheners. Well that's alright then. It's OK Denis you blagged this weekend for us - I'll come to the Finance thing with you – I can't wait to meet Randy J. Feckenburger.'

'The Third. And I did not blag the weekend! I just gently nudged Caroline.'

'The Third. Of course. And not blagging, nudging.'

'Good. Glad we've sorted that out.'

Something must have changed in the culture of Buy-O-Soft because, although the hotel was small it was very charming, right in the centre of Paris and must have been expensive. We checked in and after investigating both rooms decided that the one at the back was probably going to be quieter. I had a question in mind and twisted it this way and that before saying, 'Which side of the bed would you prefer?'

Karen gave me a seductive glance.

'We'll probably spend a lot of time in the middle so does it matter?'

How do you answer that? I probably went a beetrooty sort of shade and stuttered,

'Er, no... I, er, suppose not.'

Next we had to find our way to the conference centre. This was reasonably close by so we walked and walking through Paris hand in hand with Karen made me forget the woes of JDFT Media and Oroco Oil.

In the foyer of the centre which was a cavernous, brutalist modern building, the first person I caught sight of was Bob.

I prayed he wasn't going to say 'One big Bob greeting coming up!' or something equally toe curlingly embarrassing but he restricted himself to an enthusiastic,

'Denis hi! How you doing?'

'Very well Bob. Are you OK?'

'Yeah, as well as can be expected with Randy running things.'

'Oh, sorry, this is Karen Ellison, she's the presentation guru at JDFT. Karen this is Bob Scott from Buy-O-Soft. He's Customer Service Manager.'

'Pleased to meet you Karen. So is our Denis getting on OK - we miss him at Buy-O-Soft.'

I could see that Bob was trying to assess what relationship Karen was to me but I wasn't going to help him out. One question was in my mind though.

'Is the Freak here?'

Bob laughed.

'No we decided to spare Paris from the Freak.'

'You didn't allow him to come?'

'Well to be honest, Randy doesn't like him and the Freak doesn't have a passport. Something to do with his Mum not liking the idea of him meeting foreign people.'

Crowds of people were filtering past us as we stood chatting. Suddenly an object like a bull slammed me in the back, possibly dislocating my shoulder and moving several organs a few yards from where they were supposed to be. Even before turning round I knew whose greeting this was. There stood Randy J. Feckenburger (the Third) in all his glory.

'Hey buddy! Denis! How's it going? I hope you guys are looking after Buy-O-Soft well! I've gotta shoot – catch you later!'

Off he strode into the conference hall. Bob sighed and shook his head gently.

'I have to put up with this sort of stuff all the time! He tried to high five Mrs. Rhodes. And then he called her "Rhodesy baby"!'

'Jesus! How did that go down?'

'Guess! It was nearly as bad as the Freak calling her "Rhoda the Rhino"!'

'So that must be Randy J. Feckenburger?' Karen observed.

'The one and only.' I replied.

'Unfortunately of course that's not true Denis.' Bob said mournfully. 'He's Randy J. Feckenburger the Third. I dread to think what a family get together at the Feckenburgers is like! All that alpha male testosterone flying around. As you can probably imagine we're becoming very Americanized at Buy-O-Soft. I mean, I quite like their get up and go but he's started this early morning motivation circle where we all have to shout out our goals for the day!'

'Bloody hell! How does the Freak cope with that?'

'That's where he and Randy clashed a bit. The Freak had another of his out of body shout outs and his goal for the day was that Randy would be run over on Ealing Road. It got quite a cheer.'

'I'll bet it did.'

Karen was having hysterics at this. She finally got her breath back.

'It sounds as crazy as JDFT.'

Bob grinned ruefully.

'It says a lot when I tell you that Denis was probably the sanest person there. Ah well, once more unto the breach – looks like we're going in.'

Behind the stage in the hall was a huge screen with graphs of Buy-O-Soft business trends.

'Sorry – this could be very tedious,' I said to Karen.

'You can make up for it later,' she answered as we took our places next to the redoubtable Bob in the middle of the hall. As soon as I'd commented on the potential for boredom heading our way I realized I hadn't reckoned on Randy J. and his enthusiasm. He'd now taken to the stage and was addressing the crowd like the lead singer of a stadium band.

'HEY PAAAARRRRIIISSS FRAAANCE! C'MON!'

It was like that far away night in the Stockholm Suite of the Skypath Hotel but on a much grander scale. I was starting to feel the same horrible prickly sensation down my neck again and hoped to fuck that Randy wasn't about to call on members of the audience. But it seemed he'd learnt his lesson and stuck to the script this time.

'OK BUY-O-SOFT!' he exclaimed in case any of the gathering didn't know who they were.

'GIVE IT UP FOR CHARLIE JOHNSON AND STEVE SINCERE!'

'Steve Sincere?'

Karen got to the question just before I did. Bob rolled his eyes and whispered.

'Yeah I know – it makes "Maximilian Epworth" seem normal. Steve's one of the finance guys from Head Office. We have to send him monthly sales reports then he calls and gives us a bollocking if they're down or even flat.

'But... that's his real name?' Karen continued.

'As far as I know – mind you, if you can accept that someone in their wisdom called a child "Randy J. Feckenburger the Third" then "Steve Sincere" isn't too bad really...'

I focused on the stage again where what looked like a Blues Brothers tribute act had appeared. Two men, one stocky, one lanky but both dressed in sharp, dark blue suits and oddly, given that it was late afternoon indoors, wearing shades. The only things missing were the pork pie hats. They came on and stood stock still facing the crowd, as if assessing the audience for criminality. Bob squirmed in his seat and leaned over to me.

'The little bloke's Steve Sincere – haven't seen the other bloke, Charlie whatsisname before. They look like FBI though.'

And they certainly did. The one who wasn't Sincere kicked off.

'OK everybody settle down.'

This was addressed to a sepulchrally quiet auditorium. If we'd settled down any further pulses would have stopped.

'I'm Charlie Johnson and some of you will know me from the Annual Accounting and Fiscal Away Day which so many of you guys attended.'

'Fucking hell – that's one for next year's diary,' I muttered. Karen had sunk down in her seat and was, I think, dozing off. She gripped my hand and dug her nails in.

'What's that for?' I asked wincing with pain.

'Just in case you were thinking of inviting me - I'm busy all next year.'

The act was continuing.

'...and this is Steve Sincere – the guy you send all those reports to. Y'know Steve was just saying on the way here how he appreciates the work and effort you put into them and how awesome he feels when he looks at those reports!'

'I hope that's a lie,' whispered Bob. 'If not he's a sad bastard.'

Now Steve Sincere stepped forward to emphasize the pleasure he got from people he didn't know sending him columns of figures he surely didn't really care about.

'Y'know lots of people say to me, "hey Steve" y'know those reports you get. I know you love getting them and analyzing them and we love reaching out to you with those reports but sometimes we wonder if anyone else sees them?"'

Now, correct me if I'm wrong but personally if I send a report to someone, that's it. I don't give a rat's waistcoat who sees it. But Steve Sincere was made of different stuff.

'I can tell you folks right here and now,' he enthused, 'not only will I see the report but...' (pause for dramatic effect) 'Mike Jones will see it!' The other quasi FBI man Charlie Johnson strode across the stage.

'And not only will Mike Jones see it but John Serino will see it too!'

I knew the second bozo would have to outdo the first bozo.

'That's right,' Steve Sincere announced enthusiastically, 'and not only will John Serino see it but... Brad Hagstrom will see it!!'

I presume that in the heads of Charlie Johnson and Steve Sincere the whole crowd was now whipped to such a frenzy of excitement at the thought that Brad Hagstrom was going to read their reports they were standing on their seats whooping and cheering because Charlie Johnson nodded at the audience and gushed.

'Yeah I know? How exciting is that?? Yeah! RIIIGHTTT!! And not only will Brad Hagstrom see it but...'

The crowd sat silently, many of them looking at their watches. Some were tapping them to check they hadn't stopped.

'Do you think it'll stop when God's had a look at the bloody report?' Bob muttered in my ear.

'Probably not.'

I'd missed the name of the final unfortunate who would see this mind numbingly dull document, not that it mattered. The two guys were now pumping the air seemingly having joined Randy's stadium band and exhorting us all to have an 'awesome day' and to remember that we were 'working for the greatest company on earth'. Then they waved to the audience and exited.

'Charlie Johnson and Steve Sincere, ladies and gentlemen!' Randy announced. I think he was genuinely expecting applause but was greeted by a stony silence.

'It's gonna be difficult to follow that.' Karen murmured. 'Who's on next I wonder?'

'Pity we couldn't get the Freak up there to reveal his innermost thoughts,' I said.

'Can we just leave?' she hissed.

These words were music to my ears.

'Good idea, I can't take any more excitement – I'll tell Bob we'll see him later – there's dinner I think. How about a walk?'

I turned to my former boss.

'Bob we're going out for a while – let me know if we miss anything!'

Bob grunted.

'Lucky bastard - wish I could just get up and leave as well.'

He surveyed a sheet of paper in his hand.

'Oh great! We've got year on year sales comparisons by region coming up next.'

'Damn! I'm really gutted we're missing those but it can't be all fun and partying! See you later!'

Karen and I sneaked out and were on the Champs Elysees in five minutes.

'OK it's twenty past four. What's the plan?' she asked.

'How about a romantic walk by the Seine? Then drop in somewhere for a beer or whatever? I suppose we only have to be back by sevenish.'

'Sounds good – let's go!'

I stopped as did Karen. I'd spotted a flaw in our plan.

'Only one slight problem.'

'Which is, which way's the river? Am I right?'

'Right... the river...' I pondered.

'Unless I'm hugely mistaken the Seine is a river isn't it?'

'It was the last time I looked. Probably still is.'

'We'd better ask.'

'Yep... In French?'

'Ideally.'

There was a couple walking purposefully in our direction. They looked as if they knew what they were about so I hailed them.

'Excusez moi. Ou est le... er, la Seine?'

They stared at me blankly.

'They might be deaf,' Karen said helpfully.

'I think that's a very kind but the least likely explanation. You're too polite to say my French is crap. It doesn't help that I don't know the word for "river",' I explained.

A torrent of speech suddenly issued from our potential guides, none of it comprehensible to me. Karen however burst into an energetic dialogue with them or rather a trialogue since there were three of them and all were animatedly pointing in various directions while speaking in a guttural tongue accompanied by beacoup de laughing as the locals might say. I'd never thought finding directions to a river could be such fun and regretted my inability to join in. There then followed a fair amount of hand

waving and Karen's new buddies headed off in the opposite
direction.

'Well?' I asked.

'German,' she replied.

'Of course – if you're coming to Paris, German is the essential
language! What made me think they might speak French in the
country's capital? Crazy French!'

'OK sarky but I've found the way to the river!'

'Have you indeed? Well done! I didn't know you spoke
German – fluently too. You have hidden depths Ms. Ellison!'

Haven't I just! By the way the words for river are either un
fleuve, which runs to the sea, or une rivière, which feeds into
another river.'

'Fascinating. So are we going to walk by a fleuve or a
rivière?'

'Who knows? I'm rubbish at geography. And who cares –
we're in Paris!'

She put her arm through mine and we turned round and went
off down a broad avenue. We strolled through the romantic
surroundings of Paris and standing on a bridge with Notre
Dame as our backdrop I was about to say something loving,
deep and meaningful so she would never forget this moment.
But she beat me to it and said, 'We need to sort Martin out,'
which rather broke the mood. It didn't make sense to me and I
showed it.

'We? Martin? Sort out?'

'It's not a cryptic crossword clue! Yes. We have to do something about Martin and his self-destruction.'

'Christ, that would take years of therapy never mind our questionable skills.'

'I'm going to have a meeting about it.'

'What? You've been at JDFT too long. Who with?'

'Not sure yet - can you think of anyone who's clever and might come up with a good plan pretty quickly?'

'Yeah I can but in the meantime can we forget about Martin? We're in Paris and I love you!'

Karen stopped and stared at me as though I'd suggested we steal the Eiffel Tower.

'Do you? Huh!'

'What do you mean "huh"?'

'Nothing.'

'Didn't sound like nothing to me.'

'Well it was.'

'Do you mean it meant nothing as in, it meant nothing or do you mean it meant nothing as in, "I don't want to talk about it because it's all very difficult and I can't be arsed to explain?"'

She was staring intently at the parapet of the bridge. Interesting as that was, it didn't need quite so much staring at.

'I'm still a bit nervous about new relationships.'

'I'm not sure I like the use of the plural there…'

'I meant relationship. One. Singular.'

'OK - well there's no rush. Let's just see what happens - no pressure.'

'Thanks Denis.'

The lights were coming up and Paris was really putting in a sterling effort at being the most romantic city on the planet. We walked for a long time hand in hand, comfortable in each other's company. The weekend in Paris took our minds off the doom rich atmosphere at JDFT and it was almost with a bounce in my step that I romped into the office at the beginning of another exciting week.

Chapter Twenty Nine

Team Building

Our new recruit Dave Maxwell had arrived and I'd been delegated by Martin to take him round the company and introduce him to the more human elements before throwing him to the wolves. I avoided Canteen Pete's, remembering my own experience and carefully guided him past Nick the Bastard as well. He seemed bright enough, not too sensitive and would probably settle in fine. We found him a desk in the office and set him to work fixing a server that had collapsed under the strain of dealing with huge quantities of porn downloaded by Nick, Gary and their teams.

Leaving Dave to his unlovely task I went back to my own work. Among the emails offering stuff for sale and the latest news about who was going where on Friday after work, there was one from our esteemed chairman's PA. It was short and to the point.

```
From:        Chairman's Office
To:            All Staff
Subject:       Company meeting
tonight.
Importance:  Critical / career
threatening
```

All,

HR have brought it to my attention that they believe morale in the company is low and to counter this they have come up with another one of their 'initiatives.' There will be a company meeting this evening at 6.30 in the bar so they can outline their 'idea'. Your presence is compulsory. To encourage attendance, drinks will be half price (except for spirits, wines and the better selling beers). If you are thinking about not turning up bear in mind that the only thing I cannot send you by email is your P.45 (HR and IT have been tasked to work on this). See you all at 6.30 sharp. Do NOT be late.

Your Chairman

Eric

Karen, Martin and I got to the bar at 6.25. At 7.00 Eric sauntered in, attended by his PR henchman Nigel who had started out as a security guard in the early days of the company. Not only did his eyebrows meet in the middle but his eyes matched them. Gary our unlovely FD slouched across to us. He seemed subdued. Possibly concerned that Martin was going to sneeze again.

'You don't look well Gary,' Martin observed with just a shade too much glee in his voice.

'Had to take a few days off sick. Some fucker threw up over Waterloo Bridge the other night. I was on a boat below taking my Mum and Dad out for their wedding anniversary. Their wedding anniversary! I mean – disgusting - the youth of today. If I'd got my hands on them... Probably immigrants.'

More likely future archbishops I thought but this synchronicity of events startled me. Being startled had to wait as Eric sauntered up to the microphone and began speaking.

'Before I get on to the stuff about the away days etc I've a brief announcement about a new member of staff. I've, sorry *we've*, decided to bring in a renowned psycho-analyst to help us.'

I was momentarily impressed that our chairman was showing his touchy feely side and had thought of providing counselling for staff. Indicating a degree of amazement I raised my eyebrows at Martin who, assuming I wanted another beer, turned his back on Eric and shouted across the bar.

'Another three gnat's pisses here.'

Eric glared at Martin, visibly wrestled his hatred and continued.

'Dr Niccolò di Bernardo begins on the 15th March. He will analyze our clients and the users of their products so we can target their deep seated psychoses and fears thus making it impossible for them not to buy the products we advertise. I am putting him in charge of our creative output. All you creatives will listen firstly to what he has to say before putting fingers near the keyboards of your Macs.'

There was an odd silence as the meaning of this diktat filtered through the strata of drink and substance addled minds. A lone voice pierced the stillness.

'But we're creatives! We can't just cynically turn out commercials to manipulate the public into buying products!'

The chairman looked long and hard at the scruffily dressed creative, in much the same way that Robespierre might have cast an eye over an aristocrat.

'Really?' he sneered. 'Has it not struck you yet that if you were truly 'creative' you'd have an exhibition at the Tate Modern or MOMA, you'd be writing plays that provide deep insight into the human condition or composing thought provoking music and appearing on 'Front Row' every few months, not dishing up trite images and scrawling drivel about crap products? Now, the answer to the next question is "No." Any questions? Good. Meeting closed.'

Blodwyn, HR Director extraordinaire, coughed indiscreetly. Eric glared at her. Blodwyn glared back and after a few seconds of glarey eye wrestling, Eric remembered the whole reason his adoring staff were gathered here before him and winced.

'Ah, yes, I nearly forgot. The HR initiative. HR in their wisdom have decided that we should undertake a series of away days to motivate people. How you perform on these will be part of your appraisal for the end of year bonus. Details to follow from (looks at bit of paper), Jemima who apparently is this quarter's HR Manager following in the footsteps of er, whoever did it before. She will give each department head a piece of paper with details of your away day as they leave this meeting. You will be responsible for your own expenses for the away days and they must be taken as holiday.'

Martin muttered, 'Wanker', as Eric walked past.

Taking a lukewarm beer from him I tried to look on the bright side.

'Well at least there *are* appraisals.' I said, thinking back to being trapped in an airless room with the Freak.

Karen sighed.

'Don't get too excited. They identify the worst performing ten percent and fire them first so anyone coming afterwards is just glad to have a job and doesn't ask for a bonus!'

The bar was emptying. Martin went up to Jemima, who doled out a small crumpled bit of paper. Clearly they had gone to no expense to prepare for the motivating away day. Martin uncrumpled the scrap and muttered sarcastically, if inarticulately,

'Fucking Hell! Fucking typical! Fucking great! Fuck!'

He handed it to me. I stretched it out for the benefit of Karen who was peering over my shoulder. It read, "Friday 7th April 11:00 a.m. Long Wiston Safari Park. As this is a short term, twelve pounds per person deal with the Safari Park, it must be taken on the date and at the time shown."

'It'll be like a day with the media buyers,' Karen said.

'Probably less dangerous.' Martin commented dourly. 'A day out at a safari park in April. Any animal worth the name will be in its den. Do you think they got it on the cheap?'

There was only one thing left to do so we made a valiant attempt to drink the last of the worst lager I've ever tasted.

Chapter Thirty

Board meeting II.

I was casually flicking through my diary the next day when a little icon appeared at the bottom of the screen. It showed a devil dancing round and was Martin's marker for the day of a board meeting.

'Denis,' I heard him say in a wheedling tone and before he could go on I said, 'I know Martin; there's a board meeting tomorrow and you want me to go to give the report?'

'Clairvoyant!'

'Microsoft Outlook calendar in fact.'

'Is that OK?'

'Yeah, why not?'

I heard his chair creak as he slumped in relief.

As was now customary, Karen and I went out together for lunch. In the lift she said, 'Don't let Martin take advantage of you.'

I'd been thinking along the same lines and replied,

'I know - but it's OK. It's useful me going along for a couple of reasons. Firstly if Martin went he'd argue with Eric, making the whole thing worse. Secondly I can keep an ear to the ground and pick up what's going on - Gary's an idiot and never keeps his mouth shut. Oh, and I quite enjoy them - very entertaining -

it's like watching a cross between a crèche and stand up comedy. With real hatred thrown in.'

'I don't want you getting pissed off and leaving!'

'Where would I find anywhere more dysfunctional than this place? I'll pass all my career plans to you for approval.'

Neil was already in the Board Room, nervously reading through a screed of paper.

'Afternoon Neil - what's the matter?'

'Nothing. You'll hear shortly - Eric's had another concept - "character laundering" he calls it.'

'What does that mean?'

He smiled without enthusiasm.

'Here we go,' he whispered as Eric and Gary slid into the room.

Others followed them. Eric didn't waste any time nor was he modest about his 'concept.'

'A small group of us have been working on the company's image and as you know there were some who felt I could be a little abrasive. So we had a series of brainstorming sessions and after my success with East End charities we came up with the brilliant new concept of "character laundering". This involves the subject, in this case me, subjecting themselves...'

At this point Neil waved across the table to catch Eric's attention.

'I think we said we'd use the word "immersing" Eric.'

'Yes, very well. I'm reliably informed I should use the word "immersing" rather than "subjecting." Very well. "Immersing" themselves in good works. I'll report later on the success I've achieved. The idea is that if this can work for me we're going to offer it to clients. Tony Blair's signed up for it already. Doesn't matter what someone's done, we can rehabilitate them through our character laundering service. Shame Jimmy Savile died before we could introduce this!'

Neil went visibly pale.

'I think we have to be realistic and careful about the clients we take on for this Eric.' he said to the assembled and I think it's fair to say, very startled group.

'Cautious as ever Neil! Just as well some of us have the vision to take the company forward,' Eric asserted with his customary confidence or insensitivity, depending how you saw it.

'Anyway Caroline and I have agreed we're going ahead with this despite the concerns of the more short sighted members of the company… Caroline?'

Caroline had a finger in the air as though dismissing a batsman.

'We agreed nothing of the sort Eric!'

'I think you'll find we did. Now can we get on to the tedium of all your reports please.'

'Not until we've talked about this Eric!'

Eric fiddled with his phone but Caroline was not to be put off.

'Eric, leave your phone alone you don't understand how it works. We agreed that we'd pilot the concept with one subject and an easy one at that. What you called the 'low hanging fruit' I believe.'

'Well I've decided to roll it out in one go - might as well. It's a brilliant idea - it'll work.'

'No! That's an idiotic idea. We stick to the pilot project and that's final.'

Eric glared at her.

'Over my dead body!'

'If that's what it takes, so be it,' Caroline answered and for a split second I felt nervous for Eric's safety.

'Let's move on,' our irascible Chairman muttered.

Gary nodded vigorously. Caroline noticed and said, 'You're not on the back window of a car Gary; stop nodding.'

He shook his head.

'No Caroline. I mean yes…'

Eric dismissed Gary with a wave of the hand.

'Shut up Gary. Caroline, we'll talk about this later without this lot around. Now, I've had an idea for a campaign… and I don't think there will be any dissenting voices about this.'

Flicking his gaze like a lash round the room, he paused for dramatic effect.

'It's for Ariadne Insurance. The work so far on this campaign has been dire. We need to give it energy and vitality. Something to capture people's imaginations!'

Trevor protested.

'Our work's been praised by the client! They're really happy with what we've done for them Eric. You heard what they said last week.'

Eric sneered at the Creative Director.

'And what the fuck do clients know? Nothing. Doctors don't expect their patients to tell them how to do their job. They're boring little insurance drones. No creativity. The work so far isn't going to win any awards. What I'm proposing will raise their profile and ours.'

I could see Trevor was hurt and angry. He sighed, 'Fine. Go on then what's your idea?'

I had the impression that Eric was trying to smile to get us all on side with his Great Idea but with his thin lips and axe like face, the smile just made him more sinister.

'OK!' he announced, 'Imagine the Twin Towers in New York. It is September 11th 2001. We see the planes flying into them, the explosions, the destruction, the chaos. The voiceover says:

"They weren't insured! Are you?" Cut to a child's teddy bear on the ground covered in blood. Then the voice over says, "Ariadne Insurance keeping you safe in a world of terror." And fade out with all the terms and conditions bollocks.'

The silence was profound. It was the silence of a company entering a vacuum before imploding. Every mouth round the table was open. Eric was still smiling that weird, evil smile as he surveyed his audience.

'I know! Brilliant isn't it! I was speechless as well after I thought of it. A great chef once said he was a genius, a neighbour of the Gods and in that moment I knew precisely how he felt!'

To my right I heard someone move. Neil had stood up. First he pointed at Eric then he shouted at him.

'You sir, are a fucking moron of the first order. You are a heartless, self-centred cretin with the brain power of a sprout. You want to use the deaths of three thousand innocent people to sell insurance! Have you thought how their families will feel? Never mind our client and when the media get hold of this…! It's time someone did something about you. You're going to destroy this company singlehanded!'

Eric was dumbstruck. I think if Caroline had said this he might have answered her back but the fact that it was the quietest, probably most timid person in the room, shocked him into silence. Momentarily anyway. But with a hide as thick as Eric's it takes a lot to keep a bad man down.

'Thank you for your forthright views Mr. Cross. When I need a lawyer to help with creative work I'll call you. As for your massive overreaction I'm sure it's down to the stress of a job that's clearly far too difficult for you.'

There was a blur as Neil leapt onto the boardroom table, gripped Eric by his ridiculous green tie and pulled him up so their faces were level. The tie tightened round our Chairman's neck like a noose. With Eric literally hanging on his every word, Neil screamed into his terrified face.

'My cousin died on 9/11 you fucking scumbag! And he didn't die to give you material for some shit ad you miserable little creep!'

From a neutral onlooker's perspective it was interesting to note that the colour of Eric's face now matched his deep purple suit. He was probably only a minute or so from death by strangulation. Yet no one moved a muscle to help him. Finally Caroline slowly got up from her seat, came round the table and took Neil firmly by the arm. I thought for a moment she was going to help him throttle Eric but she just said quietly.

'Neil, I am sorry to hear about your cousin but killing Eric won't bring him back. I can assure you we will not be making an ad as tasteless and stupid as this.'

Neil let go his grip and climbed down from the table as the almost unconscious Eric slumped back into his chair. Caroline helped Eric loosen his tie. Recovering slightly from his near death experience, Eric started breathing again. The purple began to drain from his engorged face and he sipped a glass of water. Croaking, he addressed Neil.

'I will press charges. Not only are you fired Cross but you'll be done for attempted murder!'

Neil looked at him with contempt. Eric, returning to his normal vampire pale, glared back. Caroline, in a calm and reasonable tone said, 'I think you'll find that Mr. Cross may have just saved this company Eric, so he will not be fired. And I'm not sure why you imagined someone was trying to murder you. I didn't see anything. Did anyone else?'

Debbie looked at Caroline.

'Sorry Caroline, I was taking notes about New Business. Did I miss something?'

The rest of us round the table shook our heads and busied ourselves with notes and paper shuffling as if nothing had happened. Gary opened his mouth, unsure what was going on. His first instinct was to agree with anything Eric said but even he hesitated, before saying, 'I thought Neil... ow!' he jumped and looked at Caroline who sat to his left. His eyes were watering.

'Sorry Gary, did I catch your foot with my stiletto heel?' Caroline apologised to him then she turned to me.

'Denis please bring us up to speed on all the weird and wonderful happenings in the world of IT, if you wouldn't mind.'

'Yeah, of course,' I heard myself say, before delivering the report as if I'd just dreamt the events of the last few minutes. I can safely say it was the most surreal meeting I'd ever attended. You could feel power slipping from Eric and shifting towards Caroline. At one point, as I was updating my colleagues on the latest computer training, I glanced at Eric's face. It had become clear to him that no one in that room had shown even the slightest sign of helping him when his life hung in the balance.

He seemed to have aged twenty years. He looked diminished, scared even. The King was dead, long live the King.

Chapter Thirty One

Away Day

Martin was one of those people who, despite being paid a decent salary, insist on driving a rubbish car. They believe this gives them 'street cred' and suggests they are above mere commercial concerns and unaffected by money while the rest of the world think, quite rightly, that they are tight gits. Our trend setter redolent with street cred / tight git, depending on your viewpoint, led us down to the front of the agency where disfiguring the road was a Ford Escort that had seen its heyday some twenty years before. It sported an interesting colour scheme of blue and rust on one side, this then flowing, or segueing as I believe car designers put it, seamlessly into bright yellow and rust at the stern. It was facing the wrong way in the one way system.

'You're facing the wrong way in a one way system,' I pointed out helpfully.

'No I'm not.'

I carefully examined the car again.

'What do you mean you're not? That is the front is it not?' I queried, pointing at the portion with headlights, grille, bumpers and all the usual features traditionally found at the front of a car. He conceded the point.

'And by process of elimination that then is the rear,' I followed on, using logic and reason while pointing at the bit equipped with fog lights and other items typical of a car's nether regions.

'Exactly, exactly!' Martin replied.

'Therefore you are facing the wrong way in a one way system.' I almost added, 'I rest my case m'lud' but stopped at a smug expression and a flourish of the hand. Martin however wasn't to be defeated by such a simplistic argument.

'It depends which way I go.'

'You can only go one way.'

'Get in. I'll show you.'

Karen squeezed into the back seat and against my better judgment I took my place in the front passenger seat. The car smelt strongly of petrol, cheap plastic and whatever issued from the turtle shaped air freshener dangling on a little gold chain from the rear view mirror. Fitch started the engine and immediately I was hit by a gale from the air vents.

'Bit of a problem with a fuel pipe – have to keep the fresh air coming in.'

He revved the engine until all the plastic fittings vibrated at a certain pitch. My vision had become blurred as the seat beneath me shook. It was like being on the space shuttle in the moments before they release all the metal struts that keep it earthbound. Pedestrians crossed the street to avoid us as we approached terminal velocity. By way of explanation he shouted, 'If you don't do this she stalls! The knack is to get her up to about six thousand revs or so, release the handbrake and off she goes like a dream.'

We were still facing the wrong way but that seemed the least of our problems now that the engine was screaming and fragments of the cabin were starting to work their way loose. There was a massive bang as he dropped the clutch. It was like going into hyperspace. I was suddenly thrust forward towards the windscreen and our office building became a shrinking dot in the distance as the car accelerated in reverse towards the main road, veering left and right as Fitch plied the wheel.

'Here we go,' said Martin triumphantly as he rather skilfully controlled the thing. 'You're probably wondering why I'm reversing?'

In fact that was the last thing on our terrified minds. Karen was screaming while Dave said a prayer that involved lots of repetition of the words "holy", "mother", "Joseph", "God" and "Jesus".

'Well, it's your car. You drive as you see fit.' I said to Martin.

'It's just the gearbox is a bit temperamental. It won't always go into a forward gear directly. You have to warm it up in reverse slam it into first and it's fine.'

As he uttered these words of reassurance we had reversed out on to a busy roundabout causing a high degree of discomfort to our fellow road users. As we all stared through the rear window to decide where we'd go next Martin leapt on the brakes and swung the wheel hard round. The Escort slewed across the road like something out of a bad, rather slow car chase, its front tyres squealing and emitting blue smoke. When what was once more officially the front pointed roughly at the exit of the roundabout Martin engaged first gear by ramming the gear lever forward into the correct position. This type of driving might be unremarkable in say, Rome or round the Arc de Triomphe but the scene at the roundabout, thankfully behind us, was one of carnage. At least two cars and a white van had collided and their owners were in heated discussion, all pointing towards our rapidly disappearing vehicle. Karen sat in the rear less concerned with our brush with death and more acutely embarrassed at being seen in a distressed car driven by a lunatic. Martin either thought he was driving an automatic or had not fathomed the use of gears. We were still in first when he got onto the motorway and the wailing metallic anguish from somewhere up front suggested an engine close to if not beyond the outer limits of its operational parameters. Meanwhile the dashboard had lit up like a Christmas tree with various red and yellow lights pleading for him to stop the engineering torture. Several minutes elapsed before Martin dared to use third gear, second having given up the ghost years before. A sort of peace reigned. The heat gauge, which had been jammed in the 'Holy Fuck' area of the dial was now dropping back to the 'God Almighty' zone. I kept a cautious eye out for police cars chasing us. I can only guess that the victims of the roundabout mayhem had had no time or were too shocked to get our number. Thinking about it afterwards, the fact that the car sported different colours on each side may have played a part in our escape. After the thrills of the city our journey down the motorway, punctuated by the occasional moment of gear changing frivolity, was relaxation itself. Forty minutes later the safari park loomed on the horizon. From the front passenger seat I watched with a sinking feeling as we drove in through the faux bamboo gates. A spotty, callow youth with a splendid squint extracted £12 from each of us. I wanted to ask him if he'd been responsible for loading Noah's Ark resulting in only half the animals embarking but thought better of it. Martin revved the Escort to prepare it for launch through the high wire mesh and wood gates. As metallic noise reverberated around the flat grasslands in front of us, I could practically hear every animal in the county scurrying, loping, slithering, galloping or scampering to their burrow, sett, lair or other habitation. We lurched noisily forward past a notice that warned us, 'DON'T FEED THE ANIMALS THY CAN BE DANGEROUS!' the misspelling giving a quasi-religious tone to the warning. Another ungrammatical sign loomed, 'PLAY SPOT HOW MANY ZEBRA YOUS CAN SEE.' Easy - I looked round there were zero zebra. In the first field at which we arrived two goats grazed, setting a gentle pastoral scene. I have to admit that I'm no expert on goats, nor does a warm glow of anticipation fill me when I check the TV schedules and see there's a goat-rich programme featuring the loveable rascals and their fascinating antics, (in fact if I'm honest I can't remember seeing a programme solely devoted to goats at all but it's possible I missed it). Maybe these particular ones belonged to a rare species and avid goat spotters would not have been able to contain their excitement in their presence. Or perhaps somewhere in the world the goat is an exotic animal and people pay good money and look forward eagerly to a family outing to see them but here in England the goat is relatively common. Strictly speaking, goats do live in Africa among other places and if on safari I suppose there is a very high likelihood of coming across them, on the menu of a discerning lion for instance, so legally the safari park owners were within their rights to exhibit them but I have to admit it didn't make the pulse race. After warming up for a while with a demonstration of their ability to graze, digest and expel grass, the goats, presumably thinking there would be children and parents in the car, seized the opportunity to cause maximum embarrassment and began engaging in sudden, energetic sex. All four of us gazed out at the sight, unsure if it was prurient to do so but unwilling to miss any hint of interesting behaviour.

'Twelve quid a head to see goats shagging.' Martin muttered.

'I know – we could have just gone on the web and seen it for free,' said Dave, hastily adding a not convincing, 'probably.' We all stared at him for a moment and turned our attention back to the goats which, sensing our disappointment, had stopped their carnal activities and were chewing grass again, no doubt feeling that they had done their best but there was no pleasing some people. But at least they'd tried to enter into the spirit of entertaining their visitors. We drove a little further. A keeper opened a large wire gate in a fence. On the roadside a large sign in red words said, 'DANGER LIONS: DO NOT GET OUT OF YOUR CAR.' Some wag, careless for their own safety, had scrawled below it, 'TIGERS ON MOTORBIKES - FEEL FREE TO STRETCH YOUR LEGS.'

About fifty yards ahead over to our right I noticed what appeared to be three lightish brown rocks. One of the rocks yawned, licked a paw with a long pink tongue and fell back, exhausted from the effort. Lions! This was more like it. We stopped and looked. Martin turned off the engine and we watched a bit more. No more movement from the animals. Martin hit the horn button on the steering wheel. No sound. He started the engine again hoping to waken the brutes from their slumbers. The lions, as set in their ways as the inmates of an old people's home, were not going to have their afternoon nap disturbed by anyone. We watched some more. We'd got quite good at it by now. So utterly lifeless were the lions that even when we drove to within fifteen feet of them they didn't move a muscle. They were if anything more disappointing than the goats, not even bothering to engage in lewd activity for our amusement. We sat for a few minutes more staring at lions ignoring us. Ten minutes later, bored with this existential exercise Martin started the car and drove on. An air of gloom and disappointed expectations filled the interior. The next gate was opened. As we passed through I looked behind. The lions had woken up and were mauling each other, running across the grass, displaying the sort of behaviour we'd paid good money to see.

At first glance the new compound seemed to be a crow enclosure. Loads of them, hopping, taking off, flying, landing and generally displaying crow like characteristics.

'Well, a bit more interesting than the lions. And crows are very intelligent so…' I observed, realised I was fooling no one and gave up. We had a lacklustre conversation about quite interesting things we thought we'd seen crows do. Martin grunted and lit a cigarette. It might have been the sight of the flame that did it. Seconds later there was a thump at the rear of the car and as I looked out, a troop, if that's the word, of three baboons raced across the turf from the clump of trees in front of us towards our car. Things were looking up. Something hit the roof of the Escort with a loud thud. The vehicle rocked and an inquisitive face with a long black snout and a rather manic hairstyle peered upside down at me through the windscreen. I gave a small wave in polite acknowledgement. He scampered across the bonnet and leapt into the grass to one side and sat weighing us up. I saw the baboon assess the Escort with a couple of knowing glances. Something told me we were in the hands of a master. You know when you go to a doctor and their demeanour immediately makes you feel at ease, you can trust this guy to do a good job, well that's what it was like. The ape rubbed his chin in a thoughtful manner and leapt onto the bonnet. I thought for a moment he was going to present us with an estimate for work.

'They won't do any damage will they?' Martin asked nervously.

'Shouldn't think so. Probably just, well, curious,' said Karen trying to get further down in the back seat.

'Mind you…' she continued doubtfully as the large male ambled over, a look of mechanical intent on his face. Our wondering was quickly ended. The baboon that seemed to be leader flicked his eyebrows up in the way that monkeys do as if to say, 'Hey ho another day, another dollar, let's get going,' pulled up the radio aerial and with a deft flick snapped it off. Thus armed he set about dragging it across the bonnet. Possibly carving his initials, who knows? Martin was infuriated. Primate grimaced at primate through toughened glass as the baboon on the bonnet brandished the chunk of aerial, looking round to see what effect his assault was having. Martin flashed two fingers at him, quite why I don't know but what I thought was a futile gesture struck a chord and enraged the monkey. Within seconds both windscreen wipers were torn off and handed to another of the troop who carefully inspected them for quality then flung them dismissively into the ditch next to the road. Like a well drilled set of mechanics four of the gang began to remove anything that wasn't welded on. It surprised me and probably the baboons, how much of a Ford Escort Mk III is detachable. After the wipers they worked their way methodically round the car as if on a reverse assembly line. Seeing the leader heading our way again, Martin shook his fist at him only causing the animal to become more annoyed. Clearly there was bad chemistry between them. It's likely the baboon looked on Martin as an uppity second cousin taunting him with opposable thumbs and reflected that, but for a quirk of evolution, he should be the one sitting in a Ford Escort 1300L smoking Benson and Hedges filter tips while several humans trashed his car. The chromed guttering on the edge of the roof was next, coming off in a satisfyingly large chunk. This gave them pause for a moment so they had a bit of a discussion as to what it might be or could be used for. An odd metallic tearing noise alerted us to action at the rear and I saw a baboon race past with a Ford badge in its paw. I must say you couldn't fault their thoroughness and by the time they'd all regrouped in the grass with their collection of car accessories I couldn't imagine what was left to steal. Needless to say I'd underestimated the baboons and their seemingly infinite knowledge of the removable parts of a Ford Escort. I checked to see if one of them had a Haynes manual and was maybe directing the others.

'Hey look!' Dave shouted his voice full of admiration, 'that one's got a hubcap!' I wasn't convinced the car had anything as sophisticated as hubcaps but sure enough there was a baboon rolling a hubcap across the road behind us. The leader had other plans now. Not content with his booty, the large ape jumped onto the bonnet again and relieved himself on the windscreen on the driver's side just so that Martin understood this really was personal. A couple of the smaller ones followed suit. Fitch automatically flicked on his wipers then hit the steering wheel in despair as a whirring, clicking sound came from the motors and the two wiper stumps moved uselessly back and forward scoring the screen. It showed a great deal of cunning and foresight, not to mention bladder control, that the baboons had waited until the wipers were torn off before this final coup de grace.

Chapter Thirty Two

Saving Martin.

It can't be said that our away day helped bonding in the IT Department though I think the baboons learnt valuable lessons about teamwork and were tighter as a corporate unit. Our other big problem reared its head. Eric. Despite his diminished authority and questions being bandied about concerning his lack of judgment, he still held the power of professional life or death over Martin. They had resumed their ill tempered relationship following Martin's promotion and it wasn't getting any better. Presumably Eric felt resentful he'd been forced to promote Martin and Martin resented Eric patronizing him. All was not well.

'We need allies', Karen said.

'Good thinking. You've been here longer than me though; who are Martin's friends?'

She paused.

'Friends?'

'Yes, friends.'

There must have been a slightly half witted, maybe over-optimistic look on my little face shining with hope. Or naivety.

'He gets on OK with Trevor and Caroline. Debbie as well.

'Nick the Bastard? We have some leverage on him.' I suggested.

'Leverage? Do you mean we can blackmail him over the Chewbacca incident.'

'Exactly!'

'Why didn't you say it in English then? But I think you're looking at this the wrong way round.'

'Go on...'

'You're trying to find people who like Martin. Yes, there are a few. But think. How many people hate Eric?' she asked.

'Everyone?'

'Precisely. Even people who don't know him have an instinctive dislike of him.'

'Poor guy.'

'Don't go all soft and turning the other cheek at this point. Hatred is good, hatred is what we need.'

'Now I know why I love you – it's your gentle nurturing nature.'

'Thanks. I try to keep it well hidden.'

'Once we've recruited our team what do we do?'

'I have a plan.'

'Fuck. I thought you might. Does it involve me throwing a drink over Eric?'

'No.'

'Crushing him with a large metal safe or other bulky object?'

'No.'

'Or in any way causing him physical or mental harm?'

'Not directly...'

'I'm not getting the complete, fluffy, reassuring feeling I was hoping for.'

'Don't worry.'

'Let me be the judge of whether I should worry or not. What about Parky? Or Katriona? They're both smart cookies.'

Karen considered this.

'Katriona is completely radio and...'

'I have no idea what you're on about! Radio?'

'Radio Rental – mental. Haven't you heard that before!?'

'I've lived a sheltered life.'

'Huh...! Parky yes – he's a good guy. He'll do it as a challenge and he can research stuff for us. Caroline won't, because of her position. Debbie will because she hates Eric. Nick the Bastard we have by the balls.'

'Not a pretty thought.'

'That reminds me. Sue in Accounts! She does Eric's expenses – I bet she knows a few things.'

'I hate to ask but why did that remind you of her.'

'She gave Nick a blowjob in the lift. I think it was part of his bonus when things were a bit tight cash wise.'

'What? Instead of money this company offered staff sexual favours?'

'It was a few years back – we'd lost a big client or two.'

'Oh, I see...OK. Completely understandable.'

Considering the practicalities of this I couldn't help asking.

'Sorry - did you have the glass lifts then? What floor did she get in at? On second thoughts ignore those questions…'

Luckily I didn't have time to think about this much more as Karen was carrying on with our planning.

'That'll do for a start.' she concluded

So through various uses of blackmail and low cunning, we convened a meeting of people who we thought might be helpful or have some stake in Martin staying with JDFT media. Before we knew it Nick the Bastard, Debbie, Parky, Sue, Karen and I were in a meeting room. Kicking off the meeting, Karen gave a synopsis of the situation.

'Right!' she said assertively, 'Just to sum up; our boss, Martin, is within a hair's breadth of getting fired and we all know what that means. Eric will install his son in his place. Plus Martin's girlfriend is Olivia Lloyd who is our only, remote chance of getting Oroco Oil back.'

Parky, considered as ever, put his fingertips together and in his calm and soothing Welsh accent asked, 'On the Eric's son point - is this a bad thing and if so in what way?'

Nick the Bastard made a noise like an ill tempered warthog.

'He knows sod all about IT and he makes Saddam Hussein's sons look like fucking vicars mate!'

'Elegantly put Nick and as it was you that punched him I suppose you know best,' Debbie retorted caustically.

Parky, with his eye for detail, wasn't satisfied.

'But how has this falling out come about?'

Karen clarified for those who hadn't been following the Eric and Martin saga.

'Martin doesn't get on with Eric to the extent that he keeps calling Eric a dickhead in his presence. This doesn't go down well.'

'Eric is a dickhead - what's the problem?' Nick puzzled.

'Nick, just take it from us Eric isn't impressed.'

'That's pretty mild compared with some of the things I've been called,' he mused.

'And Martin's behaviour doesn't help. He goes off every lunchtime and gets shitfaced - Eric's noticed this as well.' Karen explained.

'More accurately Martin goes off at eleven in the morning and comes back around four.' Debbie added.

Parky tutted intolerantly.

'No self control. It'll end badly for him.'

I thought this was a bit rich coming from a man whose idea of self control was downing seven pints of Chimay and Green Chartreuse and puking with devastating accuracy over a tourist boat from sixty feet above. I felt I should intervene.

'Look, the hard facts are that Martin's girlfriend has, possibly for understandable reasons, left him. Let's focus on that.'

I went up to the flipchart at the front of the room and flipped its cover. There was a general snigger. I looked. Someone had drawn a set of male genitals on the first sheet.

'God, there are some puerile morons in this company!' I said, exasperated.

'Who are you calling a moron?" Nick the Bastard asked, indignantly.

'Did you do that?' I addressed the lewd one.

'Yeah - couldn't resist it. Actually - I thought Eric had booked the room next.'

I strove to control my annoyance and began writing on a sheet unsullied by genitalia.

'OK the options, as I see it, are;

A) Get Martin back with Olivia and hope she'll restore the account to us.

B) Improve Martin's relationship with Eric so it doesn't matter who he's going out with.

C) Find Martin a new girlfriend who is also the marketing director of a major company - I admit this one is a long shot.'

'Probably not as long a shot as B)', Debbie said thoughtfully.

Nick the Bastard spoke up.

'Why don't we pay Olivia to sleep with him again?'

'What?'

'I know loads of birds who'd do it for a few quid! There's a...'

'Nick!' Karen halted him in his tracks, 'I don't think Olivia's going to go back to Martin for "a few quid." She earns more than he does and... I don't really know where to start - there is no part of that suggestion that's going to work.'

'Just an idea,' said Nick reaching for a handful of the biscuits provided by Canteen Pete for the meeting. 'I'd fuck someone for money. In fact...'

'Yes, well....'

Parky tapped the table gently.

'I think I may have an idea.'

It was a relief that we might, just possibly, hear an intelligent, analytical contribution that wouldn't involve prostitution or other degradation.

'If I may?' he said, approaching the flipchart. 'Now we're all familiar with Maslow's hierarchy of needs?'

All except Debbie looked blank. Parky drew a triangle on the chart and went on for several minutes. I have to admit, I lost him pretty quickly but I think the gist of it was that human beings needed basic stuff like a roof over their heads then they could get on with more ambitious things or as Nick put it, 'So Parky what you're saying mate, if I got you right, is that you need to have warmth, and all that shit before you start thinking about shagging?'

Parky gave Nick an austere glance.

'Well, I suppose you could look at it like that. I prefer to see it as basic needs such as warmth and security lead to self-fulfilment...'

Debbie interrupted his lecture.

'Surely that's mutual fulfilment?'

Karen piped up, needlessly I felt.

'Not the way Martin makes love, according to Olivia.'

'Can we not discuss Mr. Fitch's sex life!' Parky protested before continuing. 'What we need is for Martin to embark on a charm offensive to achieve self fulfilment.'

It was when Parky used the words "Martin" and "charm offensive" in the same breath that I began to have my doubts. We were all subdued as we contemplated the Herculean nature of the task ahead. It was Nick the Bastard who broke the silence.

'Of course the real problem here is Eric. Kill Eric and it's sorted! Simple.' he beamed.

Karen raised her eyebrows, Debbie laughed and Parky scolded.

'I must say I think your moral judgment is clouded Nicholas and the sin of Cain is not one to be contemplated lightly.'

'But?' Nick went on.

Parky was struggling with an inner conflict. His face contorted in the way it had done just before he engulfed the tourist boat.

'Are you OK?' I asked, concerned for the person opposite him (me).

'I'm fine thank you Denis. I'm thinking that Nick's plan, with a bit of modification, might work.'

'What do you mean "modification"? Just kill Eric a little?'

'No. Who are Eric's friends?'

'He doesn't have friends in the normal sense of the word.' Debbie said.

'Gary, isn't he his right hand man?' I remembered.

'Exactly!'

'He's a tranny!'

This was Sue's first input to the meeting and a startling one it was too.

'Is he?' said Karen sceptically.

Parky looked perplexed, as well he might.

'What do you mean Sue?'

'He's a tranny - a transvestite yeah? Ralph in Press was telling us last week Gary has a satin evening gown that he wears at weekends.'

I remembered something from way back.

'Where did he hear that?' I asked.

'Well you see that's the connection innit? Apparently Ralph heard Martin, your boss, talking to Trev in the bar and Martin was saying something about Gary looks stunning in his satin evening gown! It's all round the company. What I say is good luck to him if he wants to dress in a satin gown. Can't see how he'd look stunning though - he's an ugly little bugger.'

Debbie tried to inject some sense back into the discussion.

'I'm not sure where this is getting us?'

But Sue was not to be sidetracked from her great brainwave.

'Well thinking about it - Martin seemed like, keen on the idea of Gary in a dress right? So maybe if he was to get off with

Gary, who's Eric's mate yeah? Well then he could be in with Eric yeah?'

'I think Gary's transvestite tendencies may have been exaggerated...' I said and was about to make a confession when I felt a sharp kick on my ankle. Karen's eyes were boring into me. First I thought she was being romantic, although in a psychotic killer type of way. Then I guessed the look was a warning not to let everyone know that I'd accidentally started the rumour of Gary's cross-dressing hobby.

'OK maybe not. Anyway have we decided anything?'

Parky was doodling on the pad beside him.

'So Sue, if I understand your plan, we're relying on Martin becoming attracted to Gary?'

'That's right!' she enthused.

'Has he ever shown any sign of homosexuality prior to this?'

Karen volunteered the information.

'No.'

'So we're hoping that not only will he change his life long sexual orientation but he'll also fall for a man for whom, if I'm correct in reading their body language, he seems to show a deep antipathy?'

Debbie was pushing her chair back and getting ready to leave.

'Seems like we'll be saying goodbye to Martin.'

Sue was crestfallen that her neat solution had crashed into the barrier of reality. None of us round the table could have guessed that our Martin and Eric problem was about to solve itself and in a spectacular and most unexpected way.

Chapter Thirty Three

How to Kill Your Chairman.

Next morning following our fruitless meeting and a couple of days after the team building / baboon encouraging / car wrecking exercise, I was crossing the road to the office. My mobile rang and I saw it was Dave. He'd been assigned to reclaim the remnants of the Escort from the baboons and was on a train back from deepest Berkshire. I asked him if he couldn't get the car to start. Most of his report consisted of words beginning with 'F' suggesting the recovery hadn't gone as smoothly as Martin assured him it would. He got to the point.

'I'm resigning.' he stated baldly.

'Why?' I asked. You've been here a couple of weeks and you're getting on fine!'

'They were waiting for me the fuckers.. the monkeys. They ambushed me. Pelted me with… well, y'know. One of them even threw a windscreen wiper. The guy with the squint at the Safari park let me have a shower there but I still smell of monkey shit.'

'Come to the office and we'll talk about it.' I coaxed him in what I thought was a placatory tone. 'Have another shower first though.'

'Monkey shit,' he whimpered, 'no one told me the job involved being humiliated by monkeys.'

I reassured him as best I could.

'I'm sure it wasn't personal Dave. Baboons are… playful creatures. They do that to make you smell like one of them. In fact it's a sign they liked you - saw you as one of the lads as it were.'

Perhaps this wasn't the most sensitive thing to say. He just whispered "monkey shit" again, assured me that it was personal as far as he was concerned and began blubbering.

'Listen Dave - call me when you get home - I'm sure… Hold on a sec… What's going on? Hear from you later. Bye.'

Hanging up on the sobbing Dave I'd noticed an intriguing scenario ahead of me outside our office. There was blue and white tape attached to cones round the front of the building and a large sign saying 'CRIME SCENE! DO NOT CROSS THE LINE!.' Three police vehicles were parked outside and my immediate thought was that someone had provided them with the number of Martin's car. One of the baboons perhaps. An officious policeman approached me. 'Are you thinking of entering this building sir?' he quizzed in an unpleasant way.

'As I work here I certainly am.' I assured him. 'Is that a problem?'

'Yes sir it is. This is now a crime scene.'

Resisting the urge to tell him it was probably always a crime scene I asked the obvious question.

'What crime's been committed then officer?'

The cop failed to answer this, seemingly easy, question.

'Well that's the problem; we're not sure.'

'OK, was it burglary or maybe vandalism?'

Though with people like Nick the Bastard around where do you draw the line? Is flinging a laptop across a room vandalism, if the said laptop belongs to the said flinger? These were murky legal waters. The policeman spoke and what he said surprised me.

'We think it's a murder.'

I thought for a moment about this.

'Is someone dead?'

'Yes sir.'

'Well, you're half way there!'

'It's not that simple…'

'What do you mean? Surely if someone's dead and it wasn't natural causes it was either accident or murder. Who is it?' I asked, suddenly concerned. He took out a notebook.

'A bloke called…' it was like waiting for someone to announce an Oscar winner, 'Eric West.'

'Eric!'

'You knew him?'

'Of course! I work here! So, why aren't you sure if it was murder?'

'He's been killed in several ways.'

I examined the policeman for signs of insanity or collusion, wondering if this was one of Martin's more hare-brained pranks.

'Right… I'm not sure what you mean.'

'The pathologist's not sure of the cause of death.'

'I see… actually, I don't.'

'Well we don't know what's made him dead.' The policeman furrowed his brow as he told me this.

'A question which has taxed philosophers for thousands of years.' I assured him.

'Are you taking the piss sir?'

'I don't honestly know,' I replied, 'but you have to admit it's a bit odd… What are we supposed to do? Go home?'

'Forensics should be finished with the building by lunchtime so I would come back then sir. You do need to be here on Thursday evening.'

'Do I?'

'Yes. The pathologist and one of my colleagues will be addressing the staff – to see if anyone can think of a reason for killing the deceased.'

'I'll be here OK - I wouldn't miss it for the world.'

In the circumstances I did the only sensible thing and shot off to the little Italian coffee place round the corner and called Karen to tell her the good news. She'd just got off the tube and was five minutes away.

'Eric's been murdered!' she exclaimed once I'd put a coffee in front of her. 'Was it Martin do you think?'

'No!' I said immediately, then thinking about this a little more, 'well I suppose it might have been. We left him in the Prince of Wales last night - but he was too pissed to murder anyone.'

'You never know - he might have sobered up and gone back later,' Karen was keen to press her case for Martin's guilt.

'We'll find out soon enough. By the way Dave was on the phone. He's not happy.'

'In what way?'

'In the way that he wants to resign. You know he went to get Martin's car? The baboons were waiting for him.'

'Ah...! You heard about the TV guys' away day?'

'No - haven't spoken to any of them yet. Where did they go?'

'Paintballing...'

'Oh well, help them release a bit of aggression.'

'It certainly did - the owners of the paintball place had to call the police. They in turn had to call firearms officers who needed backup from the Army. Nick the Bastard's been ordered to go on an anger management course.'

'Sounds like we got off lightly with baboons.'

'I'd hate to see baboons with paintball guns! Oh look, they're lifting the cordon.'

From the café we saw one of the policemen untie the tape from a lamppost. The metal shutter of the car park rose and a black van drove out.

'Must be taking Eric's body away.'

Forty minutes later we were allowed back in, though Eric's office and the sixth floor were still out of bounds. Not long after, an email popped up.

From: Caroline Miller

To: All Staff

Subject: Re: Eric West.

Importance: Must Read!!

Dear All,

There may be some of you who have not heard the news about Eric. If you haven't please don't cheer too loudly as you read this email… Eric was found dead last night in his office. Paramedics attended him but could find no trace of a heartbeat (this will come as no surprise to anyone who knew him well). Due to the rather strange circumstances of his demise, the Pathologist, a Dr. Osborne and a Detective Inspector Timmy Ruddick will address the entire company on Thursday at 6 pm in the bar. Drinks will be free (this should not be seen as an encouragement to celebrate Eric's death...). Please be there!

Caroline

On the eternally reliable principle that bribery works, by Thursday at six the bar was packed. All the different disciplines were in their separate silos like animals in the wild sticking together in case a lion or some such decided to take one of the weaker members of the herd. Surveying the throng, and I'd noticed this at other times, there were a lot of people in the bar whom I had never seen before in my life and suspect that quite a few staff alerted friends and possibly family, to the opportunity for free drink. A stern faced man stood at the front and cleared his throat a few times. When there was a degree of silence, he introduced himself as Detective Inspector Timmy Ruddick. He in turn announced that the pathologist would like to say a few words. Except there was no pathologist to say a few words. A voice from the middle of the crowd, called out, 'Hold on a minute just getting a drink!'

With a glass of red in hand, the pathologist took to the stage. Detective Inspector Timmy Ruddick was clearly not impressed and glared a bit. The doc seemed a cheery sort. He raised his glass in a toast and why not? With Eric gone everyone was in party mood.

'So', he started, 'a tricky one. In brief, your erstwhile chairman, Eric West, was shot, stabbed, poisoned, strangled with bare hands but also had a ligature applied round his neck. What is most bizarre is that all these injuries were inflicted at pretty much the same time. Frankly, in my twenty seven years experience I have never seen a case like it.'

There was a stunned silence as we took in this litany of violence visited on Eric. Even though he had no discernibly likeable traits in his personality, I felt a brief and tiny pang of compassion for him. A voice broke the muted atmosphere. It was Office Manager Mike.

'I was just wonderin' like… y'know, could it have been, like, an accident?' he asked.

'Fuckin' hell,' said Karen. 'If anyone was going to ask an idiotic question it would be him.'

The pathologist looked at Mike in the way a scientist might show interest in a species which, through its own complete ineptitude, was facing certain extinction.

'I think it's fairly safe to assume that we are not dealing with an accident here. But I never rule anything out until we've completed all our tests and the final results are in.'

I thought it was generous of him to leave at least a tiny chink of doubt about Mike's utter inanity. Of course this didn't stop our doughty colleague. With alarm I heard him say,

'It's just like, me 'n Denis over there nearly dropped a safe on him a few weeks back but he drove off just in time. An accident like but I was wondering if maybe 'e was one of these people like that geezer in Japan who's just really unlucky… Or it might be like a health 'n safety issue. That's my department.'

Caroline intervened.

'I think we'll take it as read Mike that this wasn't an accident.'

Mike nodded gravely and the pathologist continued.

'That's really all the information I can give you. All I can say is that the toxicity examination is producing some rather peculiar readings. Once we have more on that I'll be able to give you a clearer picture. In the meantime I would like to express my thanks for your attendance this evening. Oh, and my sympathy for your tragic loss.'

There was a baffled silence at this last remark.

'Now I'll hand you over to Detective Inspector Ruddick, your entertainment for the next few minutes!' he quipped, eliciting another glare from the irascible policeman who cleared his throat in an unpleasant manner before addressing us in a serious tone of voice.

'Ladies and gentlemen. As you can appreciate this is a very serious matter. One of the most heinous crimes I have ever seen and therefore I need your full co-operation so we can bring the wrongdoers to justice.'

Martin muttered, just a bit too loudly, 'It's only Eric. Get on with it for God's sake, I need a drink.'

DI Ruddick bridled and went a delicate shade of puce.

'Firstly I would like to know if there is anyone in this room who might have wanted to kill the unfortunate victim, Mr. West. If you could just raise your hand and my sergeant will take your name...'

The policeman was silent and with good reason. Two hundred hands were in the air.

'Bloody hell!' he exhaled and regrouped.

'Alright; is there anyone who might *not* have wanted to kill Mr. West?'

Caroline spoke up.

'I think I know someone who might not.'

A still shaken DI Ruddick asked, 'and who might that rare individual be madam?'

'Canteen Pete,' Caroline replied, 'Eric gave him a job shortly after Pete left... er, well when he was a bit down on his luck.'

At that moment Canteen Pete, affronted at being excluded, raised his hand.

'I'd just like to say I wouldn't have minded killing him.'

There was surprise on Caroline's face.

'Would you Pete? Why?'

'I found out he was shaggin' my missus while I was inside. I'd have done him in good and proper.'

DC Ruddick intervened.

'Are you taking the piss? No one says 'I'd have done him in good and proper.'

'I do,' said Pete, 'I watch the history channel.'

These seemed to be facts that were difficult to prove or disprove, so the hapless policeman took a different tack.

'OK. I might as well ask this question.'

Breathing deeply, he summoned up all his inner strength.

'Did anyone here kill Eric West? But I warn you if I see two hundred hands go up I will arrest you all.'

A familiar voice interrupted him.

'Unless it's like that Italian geezer a few years ago; I forget his name.'

Mike was back. DC Ruddick stared fiercely at him.

'What are you on about? Sir.'

'Politician bloke. Loads of people stabbed him. So like, no one knew who done it. For certain like. Name escapes me. He had leaves for a wig if that helps.'

Ruddick breathed in again, a man trying to control his emotions but not successfully.

'Are you referring to Julius Caesar sir?'

'Yeah! That's the geezer! See *you've* heard of him that's cos you're a cop. Don't think they ever got anyone for it. Mental it was; about twenty people jumped him....'

'Shut up! Just shut the fuck up!' Ruddick shouted.

Mike was offended.

'No need to be like that... Just trying to help you with your enquiries mate! No need to get narky.'

DC Ruddick spread his arms in a gesture that suggested despair.

'Sorry, it's been a very long day. Please, just answer this one simple question. Did anyone here murder Eric West?'

There was silence again but no raised hands.

'Very well. If we can't do it the easy way we'll have to take the long route! I will interview each member of staff over the next week, starting tomorrow morning at 11.00. This I will do in strict alphabetical order of surname; unless of course someone has information of vital importance they'd like to reveal to me after this meeting. I'll leave a mobile number. Any questions before I go?'

Mike raised his hand and Ruddick gave him a sharp glance.

'Except you sir. Very well. Thank you all for listening this evening and I will see you tomorrow,' sighed the policeman and he left the stage.

The next morning HR had compiled a list of staff and the good detective arrived to begin the process of interviewing us.

'Hmmm. Good luck to him with that!' said Karen as we surmised who could have done such a dastardly deed.

'Yeah, it'll take him a few days,' I commented.

'Never mind the length of time. Look who's first on the staff list.'

I took a quick peek at my phone list on the wall. There, at the very top, because we'd neglected to recruit anyone called Aardvark, was 'Abbott, Mike', our friendly and helpful Office Manager who had so impressed Detective Inspector Ruddick the previous day.

'Poor bastard.' Martin sympathized. 'Bad enough when you know Mike. I hope this cop's had psychological training.'

The interview room was a small dive across the corridor from our office. We heard the door open and close at exactly 10.54 a.m. (DI Ruddick entering). At 11.05 the door opened and closed again (Abbott, Mike, Office Manager entering). At 11.29, precisely, it opened and a voice shouting something about inner demons and unfair working conditions was heard followed by rapid footsteps, wailing and what could even have been gnashing of teeth. A crowd had assembled and was looking into the room where Mike sat alone. He explained why he was alone.

'I was only trying to give him some background like about historical shit 'n that; telling him about a geezer in Mitcham who had no lungs - used to see him in the Ship on Fridays. Can't remember his name. Something like Long… or Young. Anyway that cop bloke seemed to have a bit of a moment like. Must be pressure of work. I think he's taken a break to collect 'is thoughts.' he said calmly. Karen called us to the window looking out over the front of the building. Detective Inspector Ruddick, waving his fists at the traffic, was sprinting across the road towards Oxford Street, never to be seen again.

After the excitement of the morning, a visit to Canteen Pete's felt like a good idea. Karen was trying to dry a tray with her sleeve as Martin and I joined the queue.

'Stupid fucker!' said Martin laughing in a rather cruel fashion, 'look how Pete's mis-spelt the special today!'

I scanned the board and took Martin to task.

'He must be dyslexic, the poor sod.'

Martin blustered to cover his embarrassment.

'How was I to know that?' he said.

'How was you to know what?' Canteen Pete asked, emerging from his place of hiding behind the dishwasher.

'That you were dyslexic. Sorry Pete, I didn't realise,' Martin said in a sympathetic tone, 'it's just the special today says "Beans On Stoat".'

Pete stared at him blankly.

'What makes you think I'm dyslexic? Oh, bollocks! I see what you mean. My mistake! Should be an apostrophe in "beans". I'm not good with plurals to be honest…'

'No, no that's fine.' I sighed. 'Beans are not the problem. I think I'll just have a cheese sandwich Pete. As usual.'

'Holy fuck,' said Martin as we sat at our customary table like institutionalised patients, 'is stoat even edible?'

'It is now apparently,' Karen huffed as she examined her damp jacket cuff.

Several days later an enigmatic email appeared in our inboxes.

From: Caroline Miller
To: All Staff

Subject: <u>Re:</u> Police investigation into
the death of Eric West.
<u>Importance:</u> Must Read!!

Dear All,
Firstly I'm sure you will all join me in
wishing Detective Inspector Ruddick a
speedy recovery. His superiors say it may
be some time before he is able to resume
his duties. They have decided, in the
interest of the health and safety of their
staff, to close the case. This decision
was made when it also became clear that
Eric's close family expressed a wish that
they did not want to pursue the matter any
further as (and I quote) 'Once the will's
been read we're heading for the Bahamas to
grieve / celebrate in private and we would
request that the media don't intrude on
what is an intensely private time of joy.
It's what Eric would have wanted, had he
spoken to us in the last few years.'
The pathologist also thought it
noteworthy that the toxicology report
showed Eric is the only individual in the

334

West known to have died from fugu
poisoning.

Caroline.

'Fugu poisoning? What's fugu?' asked Karen, after perusing the email.

Martin chuckled, 'It's a fish – a delicacy in Japan where for some reason they like death served raw.'

'Must have been at a local Japanese restaurant and got food poisoning then?' I concluded.

'Dunno,' said Martin, 'I don't think there's a restaurant in London that does fugu… He must have got it from someone who brought it in illegally.'

We all looked at each other and came to the same, simultaneous conclusion.

'Canteen Pete!'

Martin chortled. 'Fucking hell! Good old Pete!'

I recalled what I'd seen behind his counter a few days before.

'Do you remember what it said on his board on Monday? "TODAY'S SPECIAL" "IT COULD BE YOUR LAST." I thought it was just one of Pete's philosophical jokes.'

'More a health warning!'

Chapter Thirty Four

Eric's Funeral

The best thing about Eric's funeral, apart from it being Eric's funeral, was that JDFT Media closed for the entire day. Once again Caroline had resorted to offering free alcohol to induce people to attend and as always it worked. We gathered as they say before the sight of God in a church in West London. Karen and I got there ten minutes before kick off and found a place a safe distance from the altar. The lingering smell of stale incense suggested it was a traditional Catholic church and various gory scenes of torture round the walls confirmed this.

'I thought Eric was Jewish?' I said to Martin who had slid in beside me with a loud, 'Budge up you fucker!'

Martin gave me the background to Eric's religious belief system.

'He pretended to be Jewish for a while – there was a Jewish charity he thought might help him bag a knighthood. He flirted with Islam as well during his 'multicultural' charm offensive. Bad luck he died during the Catholic phase.'

'Why do you say that?'

'Well they're pretty strict, so given all the evil things the bastard did during his life Eric is at this moment being spitted with a toasting fork up his arse. Shame there aren't webcams in Hell.'

'I'll talk to Dave about setting one up.'

'How is he by the way?'

'Not great. Every time I call him he just whimpers the words "monkey shit" and starts crying. But he's young, he'll get over it. Eventually.'

A group of people, elegantly dressed in black glided past us. They were led by a tall, blonde woman who was smiling and laughing with a much younger man.

'Eric's widow, Liz... The rest must be his family.' Martin mumbled.

'They seem to be taking it well - I guess it hasn't sunk in yet.'

'Yeah right', commented Karen. 'You get rid of Eric *and* you inherit his money! Win win I'd say.'

'Was he worth much?'

Martin did a quick mental calculation.

'Well, he started two companies before JDFT and sold them for about fifty million each so I'd say he's done OK.'

'And he took fifty quid off me in a bet!'

Martin and Karen laughed in a surprisingly malicious way.

'You don't get rich by not taking advantage of your staff.' Martin said.

Just as it approached eleven a few more of the motley crew arrived from JDFT. Nick the Bastard and Grimy Gary slipped into the seats behind, probably chatting about the latest Papal encyclical. I heard Nick whisper in an admiring tone.

'Did you? Really? You are a fucking operator Gary man!'

Karen tutted loudly.

'You're late!' she scolded them.

'Sorry - got dragged into a pub.' Nick whispered. Gary nodded.

'Tell you what - Parky can't half put away the drink! He had some weird mix… what was it Nick?'

'Not Chimay and Green Chartreuse?' I asked.

'Yeah - fucking hell!'

'Just hope he keeps it down.' I added.

At that moment a slow piece of organ music started up as Eric's coffin, carried by six people press-ganged from Finance, began his final journey up the aisle. The priest, sprinkling holy water on the lid, was followed by a small group of altar boys bearing a candle, a book and an incense burner.

'You'll hear a hiss in a minute and he'll come leaping out,' muttered Martin.

An aura of halitosis wafted over us as Nick the Bastard leant forward, his head between Karen and me, the reek slightly eased by a strong smell of spirits. As the procession came alongside us Nick announced in a voice that carried through the church.

'Here lads, Grimy Gary's just told me he shagged a nun once! Didn't ya Gary, you dirty old bastard! Says she was as tight as a cock ring! Good man!'

The priest flinched and flicked some of the holy water in our direction. Reaching the front of the church the Finance conscripts laid the coffin down on two trestles and scooted off to take their seats.

'Good morning everyone and welcome to St Xavier's on this occasion which, although sad to us personally, is also a chance to reflect on the joy that the life of Derek brought to us all.'

There was a cough. It was Eric's widow, Liz.

'It's "Eric" actually. Not that it matters but just for your information. Or legal reasons - we don't want any snags with the will...'

'Yes of course - I do apologise. As we bear witness to the joy that the life of our brother Eric gave us we remember the words of John.' "I am the resurrection and the life,' says the Lord. 'Those who believe in me, even though they die, will live, and everyone who lives and believes in me will never die."

The priest paused for a moment. I cannot imagine what was going through his mind as he contemplated the strange congregation before him.

'Eric's family has requested the short version of the funeral service so the order will be, Thanksgiving for the life of the departed...'

There was a cough from Liz. The holy chap glanced over at her. She shook her head.

'Right. No Thanksgiving for the life of the departed. OK...'

He consulted his order of service sheet.

'Prayer for those who mourn?' he ventured and was rewarded with another shake of the head.

Sighing, he went to the next item on the list.

'Prayers of Penitence?' this time shaking his head, anticipating their response.

'Bit late I think,' Liz said, again nixing the idea.

'Prayer for readiness to live in the light of eternity?'

Our reverend asked in hope like a bizarre game show host trying to chivvy a particularly difficult contestant. This time there was an ironic laugh from the grieving / joyful widow.

'Best not. He wasn't all that good at living in the light during his life.'

'Y'know,' whispered Nick the Bastard, 'it's only just struck me. Eric West is dead. I can't believe it!'

Of all the people to be touched by Eric's death Nick would have been close to last on the list.

'Fucking brilliant!' he added, denting his short lived credibility as mourner in chief.

'Hear hear,' Martin joined in. 'Did you find a decent pub Nick?' Martin asked getting down to the real business of the day. From up at the sharp end the reverend cleared his throat to silence the pub going contingent. His announcement gave me a strong feeling that the worst was still to come.

'I'd now like to offer this opportunity for anyone to come up and share their memories of Derek, er Eric, or their thoughts about his life.'

His family shook their heads, except for Liz who, surveying the congregation behind her, said, 'I believe one of Eric's colleagues, a Mr. Parkinson, would like to give a brief eulogy?'

'Fucking hell. I hope he's not going to take long...' Martin muttered.' Why Parky though?'

Karen leaned towards us.

'For the simple reason that he was arsed to do a bit of research and he's the only person in the company who had anything good to say about Eric.'

'Really?' I asked as Parky lurched past, gripping our pew for a moment to steady himself. The priest watched him approach and I could see he'd noticed that Parky's route to the altar was not in a straight line but he stood aside and left the floor to our fine upstanding colleague. Parky gazed at the assembled throng. Then, very graciously, he bowed his head towards Liz.

'I am sorry for your loss Mrs. West and I hope your family can shed their mourning as night sheds its darkness and ushers in a new dawn of hope and joy.'

Karen sniffled a little and I nudged her.

'That's so poetic and beautiful!' she said.

'He is Welsh after all. Although it may be alcohol induced poetry; let's just see.' I cautioned. I remembered Parky telling me about his lay preaching habit and I relaxed, thinking this was as easy for him as falling off an altar. He gazed benignly, if fuzzily, at the congregation.

'I knew Eric and as Chairman he fulfilled a function as it were. A function that, frankly, may have annoyed us at times but he was our Chairman and the only one we had so there you go. But here today, gathered before God for this wedding…'

The priest, now alerted to the fact that Parky was not as sober as the Church might ideally have wished and alarmed at the potential for mishap, interrupted and hissed at Parky, 'It's not a wedding!'

Parky turned to him and just a little aggressively said, 'What's it got to do with you? Just be quiet will you! As I said, at this wedding and wedding it is, for in a very real sense Eric has today gone to marry God to live with him forever.'

Behind us Nick whispered 'I thought Eric was against same sex unions.…'

Parky, expanding on his theme addressed this very point.

'By that I don't mean there's any, y'know, hanky-panky or lewdness going to be going on between God and Eric.'

Martin muttered, 'The mind boggles.'

Parky continued.

'I mean not like say between this fellow,' pointing behind him to the priest, 'and the fat choirboy over there. Oh yes! I saw you leering at him boyo! No, with the Lord's bountiful forgiveness Eric will be in bliss in Heaven as we speak, with God at his right hand and perhaps a nubile angel at his other as a secretary for, although there are many things you can say about Eric he was a bit of a letch eh? I mean he didn't choose his PAs for their brains now, if you know what I mean. Sorry Mrs. Eric but you probably knew that already so what's the harm? Anyway where was I? Oh yes…'

A strange sound was coming from somewhere in Parky's direction. It was his mobile which he pulled from a pocket and taking in the caller's id held up a hand in apology.

'Hold on a mo it's my Mam – I'd better answer it.' he explained.

'Hello Mam! How are you? No I'm not at work I'm at a funeral. Eric - that's right, the one I told you about. Did I say he was a miserable bastard? Oh well. No, it's going very nicely, everyone seems to be enjoying themselves. I know she sent me a text so I'll see you then. Yes, no, probably not. Yes, that's OK. Bye!'

'Where was I? he asked rhetorically.

'Eric and the fit angel,' Grimy Gary reminded him lasciviously.

'Oh yes. Anyway we can all hope he's ensconced there with fit angels for all eternity but in a very real sense Eric epitomised evil so looking at the situation realistically and as a believer in the fires of eternal damnation…'

By this time the priest, realizing that forgiveness and bliss had been ditched and damnation was now the theme of the day, saw where Parky's eulogy was heading and didn't like the sound of it one bit. He manouevred himself back to the lectern and began gently guiding Parky down the altar steps. There was a brief tussle, a spot of cassock grabbing (Parky on Priest) and hair pulling (Priest on Parky) but the reverend was fairly stocky so Parky gave up and traced a zig-zag path back to his pew. Our host for the day watched Parky sit down, a tangible sense of relief settled in the church as the reverend said a few more words and closed the gig. He ushered the six finance wizards to pick up their burden and carry our erstwhile boss to the burial ground round the side of the church. Fortunately the actual shovel-ready part of the proceedings was just for close family and we were free to go and do whatever we wished. As we trooped out, the reverend shook each of us by the hand and gave us a cheery, 'Hope to see you soon!'

'Not for a funeral of course!' Martin joked. The priest didn't smile.

'First time I've been in a Catholic church,' Martin ploughed on, 'very nice.'

'Incorrect on the first two counts,' the religious bod answered. 'It's not a Catholic church, we're just High Anglican.'

Martin wasn't going to let this go.

'Well, it's the same thing isn't it? I mean all the God believing part, the incense and the er....other stuff.'

Our amateur theology student had run out of steam. In a spirit of reconciliation he gestured to the priest.

'We're just off to the pub over the road if you'd like to join us.'

'I have a corpse to bury and a grieving family to comfort,' the priest said, a tad sharply.

'Do you? Oh, you mean Eric! I'd guess the family have got their dancing shoes ready.' Martin grinned.

'I have no idea what you mean!' a now angry holy bloke retorted. At that fortuitous moment Parky arrived from the depths of the church. He collared the religious dude.

'If I might have a word - about the service and such. If you don't mind.'

This sounded ominous - Karen, worrying perhaps that the whole hair pulling, cassock grabbing action was about to resume, tugged my sleeve. Without hesitating I pointed Martin in the right direction and we set off like a small, unholy train towards the pub which Nick the Bastard had recommended. Looking back I could see Parky and the priest deep in conversation, all acrimony seemingly forgotten. Peculiar how a shared hobby can do that, making bosom pals of sworn enemies I thought.

We were sitting round reminiscing about Eric, as you do, although this wasn't a warm fuzzy reminiscing about his life, more a trawling over Eric's many crimes against humanity. As we toasted his premature demise the pub door opened and in came Parky. This was a less gloomy Parky than the one we'd seen bounced off the altar after his eulogy. He had a spring in his step and a glint in his eye. I imagined this was down to more Chimay / Chartreuse consumption but there wasn't another pub between us and the church and unless he carried a barrel of the stuff with him he couldn't have been filling up on the sly.

'You seem very happy. I know that Eric's dead and that's brought joy into all our lives but…'

Parky whispered to me.

'I've just got some inside info that will help me in my career ambition.'

He nodded knowingly. I had no idea what he was on about.

'I have no idea what you're on about.' I said.

'Remember what I told you about my career plans in the Coach & Horses?'

'Parky I can barely remember anything about that evening. Except of course the tourist boat and…'

'Yes - y'know Denis I talked that over with my spiritual advisor and he and I now believe that was an evil spirit being expelled from my body.'

'Right - anyway - I'm sure the tourists thought something similar. What ambition?'

'To be Archbishop of Canterbury.'

'Ah yes.'

Something was emerging from the mists of that night. I stirred the beer soaked brain cells for memories of the evening.

'Yes - you did say, now I think about it. So, what's the inside info?'

'The C of E is short of money!'

'And…?'

I was about to ask him to explain in words of one syllable what this had to do with his career when Canteen Pete drifted into the pub. This was a rare event as, outside of his restaurant setting, CP was notoriously anti-social.

'Good to see you Pete,' I lied. Not that there was anything wrong with him as a human being but he had a tendency to speak very quietly, which in tandem with his adventurous cooking style, had led me down a few culinary avenues I'd prefer to have left unexplored. Fox burgers spring to mind.

'And you mate… and you,' Pete whispered hoarsely and gave a sigh suggesting he'd just heard that a giant meteorite was approaching us and we were in our final moments.

'I feel terrible.' he admitted. I assumed he'd been trying out some new dish and had overstepped the boundary of what's edible and what isn't. Although it hadn't stopped him before.

'Do you want me to get you something for indigestion from the landlord?'

He looked offended.

'It's nothing like that…. No…. listen, I've done something really bad. I've sinned terribly. Terribly…'

This of course got Parky's attention, sin being his department as it were.

'Really!' he enthused. 'You can trust me in absolute confidentiality Pete.'

'And me,' I added.

'And me,' said Martin, Karen, Nick the Bastard, Grimy Gary and Caroline in turn, all of whom had tuned in to Canteen Pete's gloomy, sinful voice.

Pete surveyed the eager faces with a hunted look in his eyes.

'You won't tell anyone else?' he asked anxiously.

Heads shook and dredging up another soul-deep sigh he said bluntly.

'It was me killed Eric...'

Martin glanced at me as if to say, "told you so!" Nick the Bastard said to Grimy Gary, 'you owe me a monkey.'

Caroline called to the barman, 'Bottle of champagne for this man!'

'Yeah,' Pete continued mournfully, 'I gave Eric the fugu that killed him.'

Martin looked puzzled.

'Where the hell did you get fugu Pete?' he asked our lethal version of Heston Blumenthal, 'I thought it was banned in this country.'

'Yeah it is. It's the EU innit? Health and safety gone mad if you ask me. Anyway there's a geezer I know in Rotherhithe imports it... some bloke from Tokyo I think flogs it to him.'

'And he sells it to restaurants?'

'Nah - he's very careful - he only uses it in gangland killings.'

'Thank God there's some morality left,' commented Caroline pouring Pete a glass of champagne. He stared deep into the bubbles before continuing in a guilty, sorrowful tone.

'I didn't know that though - I thought he cut it up, y'know prepared it like real fugu. I should have known. To be fair he's more of a jellied eel expert but I just, like, on a whim, decided to try this fugu stuff. Anyway y'see, Eric was working late and he called me on my mobile. Said he was hungry and fancied some fish so I thought - perfect - this'll be a treat for him. I brought it to his office. Then I got the call...'

Nick the Bastard was getting impatient and wanted to get to the climax of the story. 'What call?'

Pete considered this.

'From Kelvin.'

'Kelvin?'

'Yeah Kelvin's the bloke I told y'about in Rotherhithe. He called to warn me he'd buggered up the consignments. So some geezer who was supposed to be, y'know, like, poisoned as it were, was enjoying a nice bit of sushi while poor old Eric... well... Anyways I went back - must have been about twenty minutes after he started eating and he was just sitting staring like. Eric this is. But he does that anyway doesn't he? Stares at ya? Like weird...'

We all nodded.

'I asked him if he'd enjoyed it and I think his eyes moved slightly. Then I thought to myself, something's not right here Pete. I'd had something similar happen before when I first tried out my dog fritters on a couple of mates. But they were alright of course after the treatment like. So I eventually called Kelvin

349

back and he knew immediately. He said "Pete mate, to be fair I did tell you; fugu's a bit of a Marmite thing like you either love it or it kills you. Sorry mate, he's a goner."

'I didn't know what to do. I thought to myself; Pete mate, you've a reputation to keep up, y'know as a purveyor of gourmet meals, people might not be so keen to eat in your restaurant again if they hear about this. Then Kelvin had the brilliant idea of the multiple death thing so the cops wouldn't know what they were dealing with. He sent over one of his mates, a hit man by trade, bloke called Andy Lamb - I've still got his business card somewhere if anyone needs something like that - it says "Lamb - to the Slaughter", and he did the rest. Tricky job but I have to say he was very professional - very decent of him too - cleared up after him no fingerprints or nothing. Nice work! Anyway, thanks for listening to me - I had to tell someone.'

Then Pete perked up and beamed at us all.

'If it's any consolation, I think Eric really enjoyed the fugu. Up to a point of course… To be fair, he didn't leave a scrap so I sort of console myself with that. I mean, if something's gonna kill you, at least make it something you like. Eh?'

It could have been the mission statement for Pete's restaurant.

'You won't tell anyone?' he pleaded again.

Caroline spoke for all of us.

'On one condition.'

'Yeah, anything.'

'You don't try fugu in the canteen.'

'Or dog fritters.' I added.

'No danger! I've learnt my lesson. I'll stick to what I know - road kill and the like. No more exotic stuff for me!'

Parky was perched by me. Pete appealed to him for forgiveness.

'Parky mate, you bein' a man of the cloth and all that shit… do you think God will forgive me?'

'Eloquently put Pete,' Karen pronounced.

Parky mused for a moment, tuning in to the great hereafter I supposed but he seemed distracted.

'Oh yeah Pete, you'll be alright. Anyway Eric wasn't very popular. Don't worry.'

Even the less moral or religious elements in our group could see the flaw in this.

'Fuckin' 'ell Parky,' Grimy Gary remonstrated, 'I don't think the Bible says - "hey guys no killing unless of course the bloke's a complete fuckwit!'

Parky stared through Grimy Gary.

'Hmmm. Maybe not - but Pete probably didn't mean to kill him.'

Karen raised an eyebrow, Caroline cut through to what was important and called for more champagne.

'It's what Eric wouldn't have wanted,' she said, 'being a tight arse.'

I was still concerned about our research chum. Pete had gone to sit with Mike Abbott and Parky was sipping another Chimay muddled with Chartreuse.

'OK Parky what's up?' I questioned my Welsh friend.

'Nothing, nothing at all. In fact things are going very well indeed Denis! It's that priest bloke - he's got contacts in high places.' Parky said mysteriously.

'Has he?'

'Yeah - he had a word with someone he trained with and he's got me an invite to speak at the General Synod!'

This seemed to excite Parky but I was none the wiser.

'Is that good or bad?'

'Good. Yep - very good. It's where all the bishops and high clergy go to discuss major issues of faith.'

'Wow! So do you know what subject you're going to talk about?'

'Oh yes!'

'Are you going to share it with us.'

Parky leant over to me and confided.

'I'm going do a presentation on my gambling software. To see if I can help them with their cash flow crisis.'

'Holy fuck!' My mind was boggled to such an extent I almost felt sober.

Caroline was tapping a glass to attract our attention. She looked round the pub.

'Are Eric's family here yet?'

Nick the Bastard put his pint down for a moment.

'Last time I saw them they were taking selfies in front of his coffin. Said they'd be over later.'

Caroline continued.

'I'd just like to say a few words to reassure everyone that the future of JDFT is secure even without our esteemed Chairman. For the moment or at least until we can dupe some poor soul into taking the job, the board has agreed I will be acting Chairman. This I'm sure will come as bad news to some and good news to others, I hope. Earlier I was asked about the Christmas party and whether we would cancel it in respect for Eric. My own view is that it should go ahead as we've paid for the venue which I can now reveal is the Polish Club in Kensington.'

'Good old Greg - mine of information.' Martin whispered.

Chapter Thirty Five

The General Synod

JDFT Media without Eric was a far, far better place - more relaxed and less full of creepy evil. It didn't change Martin's work pattern one iota. Pre pub time one day Martin, browsing the web, broke the near silence in our office.

'Huh! Have you seen this? The Church of England has a twenty billion quid hole in its finances. You'd think if he could turn water into wine, JC could turn say photocopier paper into money for them.'

I remembered my conversation with Parky.

'Oddly enough I think they'll be OK.'

Martin raised an eyebrow so I gave him a précis of Parky's gambling pitch to the General Synod.

'Bloody hell! Great moral leadership - what'll he do next? Advise them on pimping nuns?'

'No, that's Grimy Gary's patch.' Karen joked.

'So when are the great and good of the church going to be subjected to this?' Martin asked.

'Next week from what Parky was saying. It's quite a thought - Parky standing up on his hind legs and flogging gambling software to the C of E. Provided he stays well away from the Chimay and Chartreuse cocktails he'll be OK.'

'They don't see any moral conflict with a church encouraging gambling then?'

'Well, I think the need for loot overcomes any scruples they might have. Nick the Bastard's made a fortune with Parky's software so it should work for them.'

'Let me get this straight,' Martin sought clarification, 'the Church of England is about to base its policy around something recommended by Nick the Bastard?'

'I just hope there aren't lifts at Lambeth Palace,' I commented.

Martin looked puzzled and I was about to enlighten him but we were disturbed by Karen's mobile blasting out a rap song. Martin scowled at her. She scowled at the Martin, then at the phone, then looked shifty.

'Oh hi! I'd um… yep - hold on a… Back in a sec…' she said exiting the office as if pursued by a cheetah at the top of its game.

Martin puffed out his cheeks.

'Well - very suspicious behaviour. She's not dealing drugs or something in aid of the Salvation Army is she?'

The door was open a fraction, Karen was waving at me and making a 'come here' sort of gesture. My presence seemed to be required so I got up.

'Where are you off to?' Martin asked as I headed out, excusing my exit with a lie.

'Email server seems slow - just going to check it.'

Karen was standing in the corridor gazing at her phone.

'Guess who that was?' she demanded.

I considered how many people might call Karen and thought this was going to be a long game.

'Do you really want me to guess?'

'No! Just listen! It was Olivia!' she said.

'Olivia?'

'Yes - Martin's ex.'

'Oh yes. What did she want?

'I think she might want to get back with him.'

'What? Why?'

'Good question. God knows.'

Thinking about their relationship and the reasons for our concern about it I commented.

'Surely it doesn't matter anyway.'

'What?'

By the tone of her voice Karen seemed to think it did.

'Well, Eric's dead so Martin's job's safe!'

'Yes but if we won Oroco Oil back all our jobs would be safe.'

I wasn't convinced. Not by a mile.

'After what she saw - y'know the Nick on Kelly action - she won't forget that in a hurry!'

Shuddering at the recollection Karen hastily continued, 'Anyway I've invited her to dinner at your flat - all you need to do is invite Martin and we can get them…'

'What? Sorry? Hold on - you've invited a stranger to dinner at my flat…'

'I know it's a bit of a bachelor pad but I'll help you tidy up.'

Subtext here was "it's a complete tip but we've nowhere better".

'Thanks! No, you're missing the point - it's not whether my flat's fit for human consumption, which it is. You can't just spring this on me! Inviting other people to someone else's flat is well… I don't know what it is but it isn't going to happen!'

'But she's agreed - please Denis - it's our chance to do something really good. For everyone else here. Can you see that?'

As with everything Karen related I found myself in a sort of fog of romantic indecision. Through it I could vaguely see she had a point but there seemed to be all kinds of danger strewn about as well. The first obstacle was an obvious one.

'How am I going to tell Martin we've inexplicably invited his ex to my flat for something to eat? He'll run a mile.'

'That's simple - you're not going to tell him.' Karen replied.

'Right… are we just going to hope he'll guess that he should randomly come to my flat on the right day or maybe he'll develop telepathic powers?'

'No! I mean you're going to invite him but you're not going to tell him about Olivia.'

'Have you gone completely mad? That is a terrible idea Karen! It's like… forced marriage or something.'

'No it's not - it's just putting people who want to be together, together.'

'We don't know they want to be together!'

'Olivia says she misses him.'

Thinking back over conversations with Martin during the last few weeks I pointed out a harsh but undeniable fact.

'He hasn't shown any sign of missing her!'

'Of course he hasn't but he does. Anyway that's what's happening.'

'We don't know what they like to eat!'

Karen was having none of my arguments.

'That's dead easy to find out. I'll ask Olivia if there's anything she doesn't eat and you can check with Martin when you invite him.'

'I'll order the fugu now.'

'You're not being very co-operative.'

'Can I just put it on the record that I don't think this is a good idea?'

'If you like. I'll just ignore that,' my implacable girlfriend answered.

'I can't cook.' I lied.

'Yes you can - besides, Olivia's not a fussy eater.'

'Oh thanks!'

I was starting to run out of obstacles to put in the path of the meal arranging bulldozer that was Karen. I scrabbled desperately for a get out and tried one final effort.

'The cat won't like it!'

'The cat?'

'Yes - Wilson the cat. He doesn't like strangers.'

'He's not your cat! He belongs to the flat downstairs.'

'I know but he sees my flat as his spiritual home.'

'You mean he scrounges food off you because his real owners are Vegan.'.

'There may be an element of that but we also have a bond. I put a cat flap in for him!'

'Olivia loves cats. And Wilson's a real sweetie.'

'Bollocks… And he's not a sweetie he's a furniture scratching little bastard. OK. OK,' I knew when I was beaten, 'when were you thinking of?'

'Next Friday?'

'Fine,' I sighed, 'that should be an evening of joy and merriment. I'll get extra supplies of booze in to help it along. What does Olivia drink?'

Karen bit her lip. Then she shuffled her foot in an evasive way, raising static on the carpet. I could tell there was something else she'd omitted to tell me.

'I was thinking…' she said, 'well in fact Olivia made it a condition that there's no drink on the premises. Y'know because it was one of the things that made her and Martin…'

The world darkened as I saw what my fate was to be on the following Friday. I sought clarification.

'Hold on a second… You mean I have to entertain Martin and his estranged girlfriend in what could be a fairly frosty atmosphere without the warm, welcoming assistance of easing fluid of any sort?'

'Precisely. Got it in one.'

'And before then, I have to entice Martin to this evening of enforced temperance and unpleasantness without telling him we're also going to spring his ex out from behind a sofa at some point in the evening and hope that, like two giant Pandas, they're going to get back to mating?'

'Once again you've nailed it. Apart from the giant Pandas bit - they're not good at getting together.'

'Jesus wept... I can't believe I'm agreeing to this.'

I felt older but no wiser and said, possibly grumpily,

'Right I'm going to Canteen Pete's. I hope he has some fugu left. I'll eat it willingly.'

'Don't be so defeatist,' Karen admonished me, 'it'll be a breeze!'

'You realize I'm only doing this for you,' I added, thinking that accruing some brownie points was the only bright spot in this murky maelstrom of madness.

I went off muttering the word "breeze" to myself and lovely as Karen was, I was under no illusion that she could be a handful when she got an idea into her head.

It was towards the end of the lunchtime service at Pete's and according to his specials board he only had "Foraged Mushrooms and Wild Nettle Risoottto" (sic) left.

'Cheese sandwich please Pete,' I requested, disconsolately pushing a tray along the steel runners of the counter.

'I'm glad someone appreciates my cheese sandwiches y'know Denis. I must have a chat with you some time about why you like them so much.'

Phrases such as "low risk" and "probably non-fatal", came to mind as I idly watched Pete plying his sandwich making trade. He looked up and pointed with a lethally sharp knife at a container lurking among the others under the heating lamps on his counter.

'If you're in the market for dessert I've got a nice bit of that whiskey bread and butter pudding left - very popular especially among the heavier drinkers in the company… it's got nearly a bottle of Johnny Walker Black in it.'

'Right. Thanks but I'll just have the cheese…. Sorry - what did you just say?'

Pete repeated his recipe for what was, in effect, a loaf of bread swimming in a bottle of whiskey with a few currants and some sugar thrown in for good measure.

'Pete - you are a genius!!'

'You haven't tried it yet!'

'No, but I've just realized how I can get round a drinking ban at my dinner party. Brilliant! OK - have you got a recipe for a very alcoholic starter?'

'Yeah - of course Prawns and Marie Rose sauce - the sauce is made with vodka and schnapps. Some people ditch the prawns and just have it neat.'

'How about a main course?'

'No danger there - people can barely walk after my beef marinated in brandy and cooked in a bottle of Calvados with dumplings. Then there's Shitfaced Lamb...'

'The beef's fine Pete. OK - can you write down a couple of those for me? You're a lifesaver! Oh, except for, y'know, Eric....sorry. Anyway that's all water under the bridge.'

I manouevred Martin into the Red Lion that evening. I say 'manouevred' but all I uttered was the word "Red" and he was out the door like Pavlov's alcoholic whippet.

'I was thinking Martin; how would you like to come to dinner at my place? I'm cooking something for Karen and one of her friends - you're very welcome. It'll be next Friday.'

Martin was trying to attract the attention of Melvyn who was totting up a tab behind the bar.

'Yeah thanks Denis. Actually that would be perfect - gets me out of a hole. Olivia's making noises about meeting up on Friday for a rather sinister sounding 'chat'. Any excuse to avoid that pain in the arse would be very welcome.'

It wasn't getting any better. In fact if some sort of supernatural being had manifested itself at that moment (unlikely I grant you) and asked when I'd like the world to end I'd have said any time around 6:30 on the following Friday would suit me fine.

'Yeah, there's just one thing… this mate of Karen's…'

Martin was staring at me in a searching way.

'What about her? You're not trying to set me up with her are you?' he grinned in a very leery fashion.

'No, no nothing like that!' (Well, exactly like that in fact), 'no, it's just she's… she's a recovering alcoholic. And Karen says we can't have any booze round the place while she's there.'

His face said it all. I tried to reassure him.

'I know, I know… but that's kind of just the way it is. Sorry.'

'I can always have a few before hand - shame though…but at least it keeps me away from Olivia.' Martin conceded.

When I visited Canteen Pete the following day, true to his word he'd come up with the goods. Taking me through each recipe he explained them in detail adding helpfully, 'Dead easy - you'll bc alright Denis mate - even an idiot could cook these.'

I let this pass. Pete continued, 'I can guarantee all your guests'll be as pissed as parrots! Just wondering - you could put some hash in the dumplings - they'll be completely off their faces?'

'I think the drink will be enough Pete.'

'Just an idea - the icing on the cake if you like. Oh, a word of caution, don't turn the oven up too hot for the beef - there's so much alcohol it can ignite - blow the fucking oven doors through your kitchen windows if you're not careful. Worth it though!'

Coming from the man who had fatally poisoned the Chairman, I thought it wise to heed this warning.

'Just one more possible catastrophe on a night littered with risk.' I moaned.

'By the way, Kelvin in Rotherhithe has some Malaysian skate coming in if you'd like something more exotic?' Pete informed me.

'Is it toxic?'

Pete considered this for a moment as if it might be a selling point.

'Not sure. I'll check with him if you want.'

'Don't worry Pete - I'll stick with what I sort of know.'

I left the Delia Smith of delirium and headed back to the office, scanning his tasty but lethal recipes as I went. Karen collared me on my return.

'Have you thought about what you're going to cook yet?'

I started like a guilty thing, convinced she could read my mind.

'Er… yeah. Prawn cocktail to start, followed by beef stew with dumplings and for dessert bread and butter pudding.'

She frowned and commented, 'a bit conventional don't you think?'

Little did she know. I stifled a laugh.

'Well, I thought comfort food would get them in a relaxed, kind of homely mood.'

She deliberated on this for a second.

'Good idea! Thanks for doing this Denis it'll be worth it.'

Somewhere a remnant of conscience reared its head and put up a protest. For a moment I thought of removing the alcohol element and just cooking it as normal food that wouldn't make our guests see double. But then the adventurous, Canteen Pete inspired bit came zipping back. Karen was winding up her thank you speech to me when my phone bleeped. It was a text from Parky of all people. Maybe a recipe involving Chimay and Green Chartreuse. I had to read it several times before showing it to Karen. It said and I quote;

"I'm a Bishop - not coming back - call me later."

'What the fuck does that mean?' I wondered aloud.

Karen interpreted for me

'I'd guess he's become a bishop and isn't coming back. And he wants you to call him later.'

'Thanks! But what? I mean…'

I called Parky immediately.

'Just got your text - have you been on the Chimay and Chartreuse again?'

'No! I've become a Bishop and I'm not coming back.'

'Yes I gathered that but how…'

'Can you let Caroline and Katriona know for me?'

'No! Call them yourself!'

'They might be a bit…. Y'know funny about it.'

'You bet they will be and I can't blame them. Tell me what's going on.'

Parky explained how the General Synod had embraced his gambling software idea. I got the feeling from what he said desperation played a large part.

'So they made you a Bishop; just like that?' I asked disbelievingly.

'It's only a nominal title - just so I can work with them as a member of their finance group. We've started up a business called "Gambling for God Inc." It'll provide much needed revenue for the Church.'

I wasn't sure if this was more or less surreal than spending a teetotal evening with Martin but it was close.

'So… there's no conflict with morality - I know religion's quite relaxed these days especially about killing people but they don't see any problem making money from gambling?'

My wimpish, moralistic misgivings were swept aside in a torrent of evangelical enthusiasm from the new Bishop.

'No - that's the beauty of it! Twenty percent goes to charities dealing with problem gamblers!'

'So you create the problem and contribute towards its solution? Who could criticize that?'

'I think you're not looking at the bigger picture Denis and if I may say, you're being very cynical!'

'Maybe so Parky but I'm still not telling Caroline or Katriona - you do your own dirty work!'

On which note I hung up, leaving the freshly installed bishop to get on with spreading the word to his flock of gambling devotees and turned my focus back to organizing a teetotal alcoholic soirée.

Chapter Thirty Six

The Dinner Party

After a few days of preparing for the dinner party my fears
had begun to wane. Surreptitiously embalming my guests in
alcohol was beginning to seem like a stroke of genius. I took a
half day's holiday on the Friday to prepare my flat for the
evening's festivities. Karen was due to pitch up at six thirty to
help with final preparations so fortunately she wasn't around to
witness me mix my various devil brews and prepare to spike
my guests. She was late which gave me more time to add just a
touch more vodka to the Marie Rose sauce.

Martin was scheduled to arrive at seven and Olivia at seven
thirty in a carefully orchestrated plan to separate them so there
would be no awkward, "What are you doing here?" "No, what
are *you* doing here?" moments on the doorstep. With Karen's
advice I'd created a relaxing playlist in the iPod - nothing too
romantic but sort of laidback-ish which meant having to junk
my Melodic Death Metal choices. She'd added some of her
own. I was laying the table, checking lighting levels and
heading back to the kitchen to remove the marinating beef from
the fridge when I heard the cat flap swing back and forth like a
bar room door in a Western. My deductive powers led me to
conclude "the cat's come in" so I called out, 'Wilson - what are
you doing?' Then I remembered I'd just seen him lying on the

bed, the favourite among his limited number of other, mainly sleep related, activities. So I then deduced that what had seemed to be an entrance was an exit. Odd he was leaving when there was food in the offing. I went into the kitchen to start preparing the ninety percent proof Marie Rose sauce. In theory the prawns were thawing in their packet on the chopping board. In practice the prawns were in various states of chewed-ness littering the worktop and the kitchen floor. Their packaging had been surgically opened with a perfect right-angled incision and the contents licked, chewed and swallowed. The surreptitious exit through the cat flap was just the final act in a cunningly planned and meticulously executed crime.

'Wilson you little fucker!' I shouted in desperation at the long escaped miscreant. It was twenty to seven so time was on the short side. I was starting to hyperventilate, while trying to remain calm and think this calamity through. Fortunately most of the prawns had still been too frozen for him to bolt, otherwise I would have been separated from my entire starter by the skin of a cat. In short I was staring at a major problem but not quite a disaster. I scoured history for similar events that might shed light on what I could do. One example shone through the prawn theft darkened evening. Clutching at this faint straw I asked myself,

'OK what did they do on Apollo 13?'

I know their problems weren't prawn related but I was pretty certain the advice had been something like, 'see what you've still got' and could be adapted to the present situation

Of course in many respects they had it easier; for a start, as far as I know, they didn't have a cat festering round in the capsule undermining their every effort. Nor did they have dinner guests arriving in under an hour. Returning to the kitchen armed with my brilliant idea (courtesy of NASA) of working out what was left of my sumptuous starter, I began a triage operation on the prawns, sorting them into categories;

1) untouched (fine),

2) a bit licked (probably alright - reserve these for Martin and Olivia who hadn't witnessed the cat incident - I didn't want to put Karen at risk either)

3) chewed but still identifiable as prawns (quick rinse under the tap should be OK).

4) thoroughly chewed but not swallowed (might do as a sort of garnish)

5) swallowed (tricky one - there might be whole prawns in the top part of the cat's digestive system. Should be reasonably OK and a shame to waste them). As I sorted the prawns into their edibility categories on the chopping board, there was a slight noise, the cat flap racketed back and forward and there was the crustacean thief large as life and completely unashamed. He stuck his head round the kitchen door and stared up at me as if

to say, 'Everything OK? Anything you need a hand with? The prawns are very good by the way.'

I glared back, scooped him up and took him into the front room, a safe distance from food. I sat Wilson down and said in the best master to pet voice or possibly vice versa.

'Wilson, may I have my prawns back?'

He stared at me licking his lips. I could tell the malicious little fucker was thinking something but what he was thinking I had no inkling. Probably related to more seafood thieving. Then he turned his head and did that thing that cats do, licking their backs, making it clear that the conversation is over. I felt outwitted. I was just glad I hadn't put the Marie Rose sauce on the prawns otherwise I'd be dealing with a dangerously drunk, criminal cat. A year of practice with Martin, Norman and Holden had stood me in good stead for dealing with drunk, unreasoning beings but it wasn't helping here. It was, say, ten minutes since he'd filched the bloody things, they'd been frozen so probably the ones in the last category were still thawing and might be in a presentable state if I could retrieve them. I discovered very quickly and am happy to pass on the information, that it's surprisingly difficult and indeed painful to get your fingers down a cat's throat. Wilson wasn't playing ball, obviously wanting to hang on to what he saw as his prawns. Then I remembered his vet who had tended to his neutering a couple of years before. I gave her a call. Needless to say I didn't tell her that I wanted to get semi-frozen prawns out of the animal and serve them to dinner guests. She might have thought this was a thawing technique too far.

'Hi Penny. I've got a question - it's about Wilson. I think he might have eaten something a bit off. How can I make him throw up?'

'You haven't tried putting your fingers down his throat?'

'That's the first thing I thought of.'

'Don't. He'll bite you.'

'Yes, right,' I replied, checking my fingers which were still bleeding and throbbing a lot. Penny's advice was short and to the point.

'Not much you can do - just keep an eye on him - if he's still ill tomorrow I'll check him out.'

'Just one more question. Say a human ate something that a cat had eaten and er… regurgitated - would it do them any harm?'

It was at this point that the ghost of Eric appeared. Not literally thankfully but it did occur to me that Canteen Pete's influence on my culinary skill was deeper than I'd imagined. Pete had asked his fugu dealer a similar question and the consequences were now history. As was Eric. I didn't want to be the first host of a dinner party since Lucretia Borgia to kill all the guests.

Penny replied, 'I don't even want to think about why you're asking that Denis but stomach acid would probably kill any nasties. Don't quote me on that though. Anyway if Wilson's still off colour tomorrow bring over and I'm sure we can put him right.'

I was about to ask if she could put him down when the buzzer went. It was Karen who had stopped on the way home for an emergency napkin purchase, napkins not being part of my normal bachelor existence. After checking her in I sprinted into the kitchen and swiftly bundled the prawns together.

'Hi - how's it going?' she asked.

'Fine - er… yeah great - all going according to plan.'

Wilson had the audacity to slink into the kitchen eliciting a volley of cooing and general thieving-bastard-cat directed attention. I was whisking the last of the Marie Rose sauce and was staggered to hear Karen say,

'Yes Wilson, you are a good boy and Denis will give you a lovely prawn as your reward!'

'What? I don't think that's a good idea - they're very high in cholesterol… and…'

But by this time she'd reached over, nabbed one of the (I think) good prawns and fed it to the son of a bitch. I swear the little bastard winked at me as he turned and went off into the front room with his "reward". My reflections on the lack of justice or at least revenge in the world, were interrupted by the door buzzer.

'OK that's Martin - let him in and give him an apple juice - it's in the fridge.' I called to Karen who had followed Wilson and was scratching him behind the ear. When she went out to man the entry system I added another shot of vodka to the sauce and a large quantity of brandy to the beef stew, which was about to go into the oven. Provided the cat hadn't got there first of course.

Martin came in, gave Karen a bunch of flowers and very graciously accepted an uncustomary and repulsive apple juice.

'Cheers!' he said raising his glass.

'Cheers!' I replied though it was probably my least heartfelt rendition of the word. I was dreading that thorny moment approximately twenty five minutes away, when Martin's ex, unbeknown to him, was going to enter the scene from stage left. I could only see this as setting us up for an evening of either bitter recrimination rising through a crescendo of abuse and ending in a shouting match or three hours of frosty silence, accompanied by questionable prawns and alcohol laced stew. Either way I could see no good coming of it. Karen came into the kitchen followed by the shyster Wilson who stretched the meaning of chutzpah beyond breaking point by scrounging yet another prawn. After this final indignity I made sure the prawn cocktails (and never was that name more appropriate) were safely stashed in the fridge. Grinding my teeth I carried on stoically preparing vegetables but in a slightly psychotic manner. Once the stew had been consigned to the oven and bearing in mind Canteen Pete's warning about its explosive potential, I went and joined our guest.

'Nice place,' Martin commented surveying the bare front room. 'Minimalist?'

'Burglary last year. I haven't replaced everything yet.' I said, taking in the table and the stereo on the floor, apart from which the room was empty. The door buzzer jolted me out of my interior design induced reverie. Jumping at the sound I gestured Karen to let our mystery guest in.

'Who's this friend of Karen's?' Martin asked as he examined a photograph on the bookshelf.

'What?'

'She's just arrived.'

'Has she?'

Martin straightened up and scrutinized me carefully.

'Yes. She's just buzzed at the door.'

'The door?' I said, probably making Martin wish my probation period had been extended to a few years.

'Yes. You told me a friend of Karen's was coming and I'd suspect she, like everyone else will use the door to come in.'

'That's right. To come in. Yes. The door.'

I checked to see if I was wearing a Yoda costume. Martin, with concern in his voice asked, 'Are you OK Denis? You seem a bit… distracted?'

'Lack of drink,' I answered, partly truthfully but it didn't really matter for at that moment the reason for my distractedness became apparent as Karen ushered Olivia into the room. Olivia was an attractive woman, who seemed genuinely pleased to see Martin. I wasn't convinced the feeling was mutual.

'Ah.' was his initial comment. 'Olivia - how are you?'

It was like a Victorian suitor meeting a prospective bride for the first time.

Olivia replied, 'Very well. And you?'

Now it had become a re-enactment of a scene from a Jane Austen novel.

'Not bad...'

God's teeth! If the whole affair was going to be as stiff as this, the evening promised to be a long one.

Karen pointed in my direction

'This is Denis.'

'Pleased to meet you Olivia. I've heard a lot about you.'

'All good I hope!'

'Well, no, none of it actually.'

Of course I only thought this and said,

'No - all good. No difficulty getting here then?' I queried, as if we lived in some remote corner of a mountain pass in the Himalayas rather than Clapham.

'No - got a taxi.'

'Taxi. Right... A taxi... Yes.'

We all meditated on taxis for a minute. Or more.

'Interesting,' I said hoping to at least dent if not break the ice, 'I've always wondered if the word "taxi" and "taxidermy" are related?'

Wilson scurried off the sofa at this and I heard the cat flap rattle again.

'Hmmm. Don't know.' said Martin.

Olivia and Karen shook their heads. Now that the fascinating etymology of the word "taxi" had been exhausted there was further silence as we all pondered why we were here. No further introductions were required so the unpleasantness could begin immediately. Karen stepped in.

'Martin - I was the one who had this idea.'

Possibly not the most helpful intervention.

'Hmm.' He said in a noncommittal way.

'Music!' I heard myself say and chose Karen's party playlist on the iPod. Seconds later 'Bad Romance' kicked off. Hardly a good omen. I skipped to the next track: 'Love's Unkind.' Brilliant. One more attempt to create a suitable background ambience resulted in the Dead Kennedys' 'Too Drunk To Fuck.'

At this rate I would have settled for Michael Bublé. I glared at Karen who had put together the final playlist. Jazz instrumentals seemed a safe choice and off they went. Sweating with stress induced by the recent tense silence I turned back to our guests. At this moment, in any normal situation, the next line (probably mine) would have been, 'Who'd like a drink? Red, white, beer, spirits?'

But the situation was not normal, far from it and instead all I had to offer was apple juice, orange juice, coke, or some ghastly concoction made of 'exotic' fruits.

Martin, thoroughly pissed off, asked for a coke while Olivia chose an apple juice.

I was glad to bugger off to the sanctuary of the kitchen. Within a minute Wilson was back rubbing round my legs and generally crawling to me after his earlier atrocious behaviour. Animal instinct must have told him he was more likely to get a kick in the butt than another prawn if he stayed around the kitchen so he slunk off to meet and greet our guests. By the time I brought the drinks into the front room he'd managed to schmooze Olivia who was chucking him under the chin and he was working his charm offensive on Martin. Even our hard bitten boss was making appreciative noises. My resentment towards the cat was still high but I had to admit the atmosphere had, like the prawns, defrosted a bit.

Martin, sitting on the sofa with Wilson on his lap, asked Olivia with only a tiny trace of malice, 'So are GNB as creative as we were? Getting on well with them?'

Olivia fiddled with her glass of apple juice.

'Yeah… fine.' she said curtly, seemingly fascinated by the contents of her glass.

The frost returned and there was a silence even Harold Pinter would have thought excessive. I went back into the kitchen to check the explosive beef and brandy combination. Karen came in behind me. I put the casserole dish back into the oven and beckoned her towards me and told her,

'I am going out in a minute to get a crate of wine and I'll pour it down their necks with a funnel if I have to! This is ridiculous - they're ruining the evening. Which we wouldn't even be having if it wasn't for your great idea!'

'OK I get your point - I agree!' she said bad temperedly.

Shrugging her shoulders Karen peeped round the corner of the door at our guests. I joined her. Martin was playing with my Homer Simpson Jelly Bean dispenser while Olivia was at the other end of the room examining a bookcase containing only tech manuals so I suspected she wasn't entirely relaxed and going with the flow.

'Fucking hell!' Karen hissed at me. 'Sorry - you were right. We should have got them shitfaced first.'

'Works every time.' I agreed. I thought this was the appropriate moment to let Karen in on my Secret Cirrhosis plan so I gave her chapter and verse on the menu.

'Brilliant! I knew I'd be able to trust you to rescue me from a mad idea. Thank you Denis for using your initiative and sparing us from the horror that is unfolding in the front room.'

In my head this was the sort of sentiment I was sure I was about to hear but as always reality has a nasty habit of kicking you in the nadgers just when you think all is going well.

'You did what?' was her first response.

'I got the recipes from Canteen Pete - really good of him - he printed them out for me - absolutely foolproof.'

'Just as well because that's the most stupid thing I've ever heard! Jesus Denis what were you thinking? I said specifically there was to be no alcohol.'

'Yes well I countermanded your order! Remember the old maxim 'Only obey orders that make sense!'

'You just made that up!'

I've no idea how she guessed that but as human beings do when caught in an untruth, the heat of the argument was ratcheted a few notches from "Simmering Enthusiastically" through "Ooh Look Out!" to "Boiling Over" with a possibility of it hitting "Evacuate the Building" levels. I shouted back - something I rarely do but getting the blame for the rapidly growing fiasco that was this Friday night was more than I could take. It was like blaming the cocktail maker on the Titanic for the iceberg.

'Oh yeah and in some parallel universe of your deluded mind do you think the evening's going brilliantly with Martin and Olivia sitting cuddling on the sofa? No they're at opposite ends of the fucking room trying to ignore each other! Fuck's sake Karen!'

But as fate or some other malevolent cosmic bastard influence would have it they weren't at opposite ends of the room but standing in the doorway of the kitchen watching Karen and I give an object lesson in what a good relationship should look like.

'Er...' I said hesitantly. 'The starter's ready.'

'Excellent!' Martin boomed with enforced bonhomie.

If I'd been truthful what I really should have told my guests was, "The prawns the cat licked and chewed earlier are now in bowls covered with a liquor-laced lethal dose of Marie Rose sauce."

Olivia went and sat at the table. Wilson, on hearing our argument, had skedaddled, giving the impression we were to call him when civilization had been restored.

'So how long have you had Wilson, Denis?' Olivia asked. A perfectly innocent question but given my fevered temper and insider knowledge of what they were eating made me a tad jumpy. I almost asked 'Why do you want to know that?' but thought better of it.

'He actually belongs to Debbie in the flat downstairs...' I started saying.

Karen jumped in.

'How do you know her name's Debbie?' she asked suspiciously.

After chewing carefully on a few prawns and managing to swallow them, I answered her insinuation.

'Well, we all know each other - there only are seven flats and...'

Martin laughed in a boisterous way.

'Do you mean biblically?'

'What?'

'Well when you said you knew this Debbie?'

There was a long, strained period of reflective quiet.

'Er... no I meant...'

Karen sulked but Olivia came to my rescue.

'Martin's only taking the piss; ignore him! By the way this Marie Rose sauce is fantastic - what have you added?'

'Nothing really - some Tabasco. A small glass of sherry.'

I thought a little truth could do no harm. Just to test the water as it were. Olivia might not be happy but it couldn't get any worse.

'It's great! I must say when Karen told me you two were trying to keep completely off drink this evening I didn't think she'd succeed! I said there was no need. In fact if I'm honest after the week I've had I was looking forward to a large red but...'

'Sorry? I... Karen - I just need a hand in the kitchen for a second. Could you....?'

She looked as sheepish as a Welsh hillside. Once we were both in the kitchen I closed the door.

'OK what's going on? What did Olivia mean about us keeping off drink this evening?'

'OK I'm sorry - I should have been truthful with you.'

'I thought that was a given - y'know being truthful?'

'You didn't tell me about putting shedloads of alcohol in the food!'

'Yes - but I wouldn't have had to if you hadn't deceived me! And Martin and Olivia! You always try to blame other people for your fuck ups!'

Karen was a serious shade of deep red reminding me of the wine we were missing. Either embarrassed or angry. Or both. I busied myself opening the oven door and checking the brandy with beef chaser. As I took the lid off the casserole dish I could see fumes of evaporating alcohol shimmering above it. Possibly adding a bit more than Pete had recommended wasn't the wisest thing to do but by this stage I didn't care. Putting it back in the oven I stood up. Karen tapped me on the shoulder.

'OK. I'm sorry.' she said. 'I was trying to kind of manage the evening - I knew Olivia and Martin would want to have wine and I thought it might not be a good idea if they got pissed so I used you and me as an excuse. Sorry.'

'You mean control the evening. You are such a control freak!'

'I know. Fuck it. So what's next?'

'Do you mean relationship or food wise?'

'Denis I'm sorry! I should have thought it through.'

'OK - just be truthful - I can see what you were trying to do.'

I took her hands and pulling her towards me we hugged. At that moment Olivia appeared with the now empty prawn cocktail dishes.

'Er… sorry.' she said when she saw us.

'No it's alright. Was that OK?'

'Yeah - really good! Martin and I were just saying we're glad to hear other people argue as well!'

'It doesn't always happen. Thankfully.' commented Karen.

Taking the main course into our guests I noticed a definite relaxing of the atmosphere. The fickle Wilson had returned and was wandering about in his role of genial host mingling with his guests. Once Canteen Pete's stew had started working its magic I thought it would be fine to bring up the subject of Oroco Oil again.

'So how *are* you getting on with GNB Olivia?'

There was a momentary grimace from our guest and I worried that I'd mistimed my question but she just shrugged.

'Not great… they don't have the same… well, research and they're not great at communication. Or creativity.'

'But apart from that it's all fine?' Karen joked.

Olivia shook her head ruefully.

'I have to be honest we've only now realised what a brilliant job you guys were doing for us - it was that pillock Julian Loughton.'

'Who's he?' I asked topping up her glass with some more delicious apple juice.

'Our MD. Off his own bat he decided to ask for a re-pitch for the account. We argued about it - several of us told him he was being an arse but… I think he was trying to show he was in charge - there's some sort of a power struggle going on with his boss in the US.'

'Bollocks,' commented Martin. 'If we hadn't had to pitch for it again Nick and Kelly wouldn't have….'

Karen held up a hand.

384

'We're eating!'

Martin laughed.

'Ah. Nick's buttocks, filling your every thought!'

I think he was exacting revenge for us setting him up. Olivia screwed her face up.

'Oh please!'

She started smiling as well then burst out laughing.

'That was priceless - I really had to control myself not to laugh when we saw that.

What's funny is that the same thing happened in our office last week. Not quite as graphic but two account execs were caught in the lift!'

I was about to ask what floor they'd got in at and how high was the building but thought better of it.

'Really! I thought it was just in advertising that people had inappropriate sex. You heard about the poor boardroom table.'

'Yes, Martin was telling me earlier.'

'The good news is it's taking its case for unfair dismissal to a lawyer.'

'I hope it wins - seems very unfair.'

'A health and safety issue according to our office manager.'

Olivia pointed at the beef and alcohol blend, 'This is really good - what's in it?' she asked, noticeably slurring her words.

'It's a recipe from a gourmet chef.' I answered, feelings the effects of the stew seeping through my veins like a mild version of fugu poisoning

'Which one?'

'Very obscure - specializes in fugu, stuff like that.'

A spasm of alarm passed across Martin's face.

'This is from Canteen Pete?'

'Yep.'

'Brave of you!'

I'd now had so much brandy and wine I almost told them about the prawn / Wilson incident but luckily was compos mentis enough to appreciate this might be a story too far. Karen was clearly on the same trajectory.

'So Olivia - what do we have to do to get your account back?' she said straight out.

'Get rid of Julian for a start.' Olivia growled as she helped herself to another portion.

'Sounds like a job for Canteen Pete and Kelvin from Rotherhithe. ' Martin muttered.

Karen got onto her high moral horse.

'Why do men always have to come up with a violent solution to everything?'

'Nothing violent about it.' I pointed out. 'According to Canteen Pete, Eric died peacefully after a tasty dish of fugu. Sorry Olivia - this guy Julian…?'

'He used to be OK. He and I have worked together for years - we twice moved jobs as a team. Then he became a complete prick.'

'Right.'

'So Julian and you were sort of inseparable...' Karen mused.

'Only as work colleagues!' she patted Martin's arm at this point and he gave her what can only be described as an affectionate, though slightly cross-eyed glance. Interesting I thought, there seemed to be still a lot of sparky, crackling electricity between them. With the help of our disguised booze intake I was getting into full relaxy mode and beginning to enjoy the evening. Even Wilson's villainy of earlier was getting the revisionist treatment. I got up to put the finishing touches to the whiskey bread and butter pudding. Nothing much to do except add a bit more whiskey and the turnaround from the highly toxic atmosphere earlier on was remarkable and very welcome. Of course we humans are not destined for long periods of happiness and so it proved. As I came back in with a jug of cream (laced with the remnants of the brandy) I heard Karen venture,

'Y'know I think I might have an idea!'

A million nameless fears leapt to the front of my mind at these ominous words. I stepped in firmly.

'No way! No more ideas, no more ruses; no more getting people (me) to give up drinking or throw beer over strangers! Much as I love you Karen your ideas are as lethal as Canteen Pete's cuisine! Please just sit down and try not to have any ideas,' I pleaded. Wilson anticipating more stormy domestic scenes, slunk off the sofa and made a beeline for the door. Olivia waved my concern away.

'Don't worry Denis! Let's hear it Karen! It can't do any harm.'

I may have made a whiny noise or sobbed at this moment but Karen was determined to unveil the master plan,

'So if you decided to change jobs Olivia, this guy might go with you?' she quizzed

At least it didn't seem to involve me in any lunatic action. So far so good…

'He might - the only time we've fallen out is over JDFT. Anyway it's irrelevant - I'm not thinking of moving.'

'But say someone, maybe an agency, headhunted you…'

I've completely underestimated the effect of all this liquor on Karen, I thought. Once again I felt it necessary to intervene.

'Er, Karen. You don't think you're operating way above your pay grade here. I mean you can't just offer our dinner guests board level positions - very hospitable but…'

'No. I know *I* can't! But I know someone who can. Olivia - come into the kitchen for a minute.'

Martin and I were left alone to ponder the machinations of the women in our lives.

'Er… he said. 'Any chance of some more brandy, I mean gravy?'

There was no food left on our plates so I found a couple of large wine glasses and tipped the contents of the sauce boat into them. The concoction was approximately thirty percent brandy, sixty percent red wine and the rest might just, on a bad day at

Canteen Pete's, have qualified as 'sauce.' Martin savoured his drink.

'Denis, I think you may have invented a fantastic new cocktail!' he announced.

The terrible twosome came back in and found us sipping from glasses filled with brown liquid. Olivia looked disgusted.

'Eeeugh. What in God's name are you two drinking?'

I explained. She demanded a glass. As did Karen. There was plenty left in the casserole dish so we toasted the success of their plan.

'That is surprisingly good!' Olivia commented admiringly.

'A light mud colour with a beefy bouquet.' Martin added.

I staggered off to the kitchen to find the pudding which would be our nightcap. With one eye closed to aid perspective I was decanting cream into a small jug. Karen came in.

'All OK?' she asked.

'Yep, fine.' I assured her. 'So what's your plan?'

'I'll tell you later. In bed.'

My antennae twitched and that's not a euphemism.

'You can't bribe me with sex so you can drag me into some mad bloody caper!' I warned.

'You have no role to play in this - just lie back and think of England,' she said nicking a bit of the pudding. 'Wow - there's a lot of whiskey in that! Excellent!'

I left the scene of culinary crime to check if Olivia liked cream and noticed that she had her arm round Martin and he was looking very pleased with himself. Panic stricken I returned to Karen.

'They're, well, sort of y'know getting intimate?'

'What? Kelly and Nick intimate?' she asked.

'No! Just sort of…. hugging.'

'Good! That was the idea of getting them here - remember?'

It's more difficult than you might think serving four people when you can see eight of everything but I managed to get the bread and butter pudding onto the table without mishap. Just as well because I think I'd have dropped it if Martin had made his announcement as I was working out which of the two doors to the front room I should go through.

'We're getting married!' he beamed at Karen and me.

'Who is?' I asked stunned.

'Olivia and me!'

'Who to?'

I really hadn't got up to speed yet but in fairness events were moving pretty swiftly.

'To each other!' Olivia explained carefully and slowly.

'Congratulations!' Karen declared unsteadily.

At this point I was extremely concerned about the amount of strong drink I'd poured into these two. Could I be cited for coercion in some future divorce?

'Excellent - I'm very happy for you. Both.'

Olivia raised her glass again.

'And here's to Oroco Oil working with JDFT Media again! My God this bread and butter pudding is a work of genius!'

Which was almost the last coherent thing she said all evening. As we watched them holding each other up and weaving down our path to their taxi Karen gave me a hug.

'Thanks for saving us from a complete disaster!'

'I have a feeling they'd have got together again sometime.' I said as I shut the door.

I still had no real idea what Karen and Olivia were up to but I didn't have to wait long to find out.

It was an eerily quiet morning some three weeks later, no one had destroyed any computers or deleted life sustaining information and I was idly checking a website of media industry news. A headline caught my eye:

"LOUGHTON OUT IN THE COLD"

The name rang a bell and then I recalled he was Olivia's Managing Director chum at Oroco Oil. Reading the article my eyes went out on stalks. The gist of the report was that Julian Loughton and Olivia Lloyd had both resigned from Oroco Oil after being headhunted by Caroline Miller at the agency JDFT Media. Lloyd had subsequently decided not to take up the offer and rejoined Oroco as M.D. leaving no role for Loughton. JDFT Media then withdrew their offer saying they'd wanted both or neither.

I'd gathered that Julian Loughton wasn't the loveliest of people but this seemed harsh not to say underhand. I felt guilty that this coup had been planned in our kitchen and collared Karen about it when she came back.

'Oh', she said in a blasé sort of way, 'he's loaded - he had a stack of share options in Oroco - he'll be fine! And he'll have a new job next week - another major oil company but I can't tell you which one.'

'How do you know that?'

'Because Olivia and I sent his CV to them the morning after your dinner party. I mocked up the letterhead of a recruitment agency.

I was staggered. No, in fact staggered doesn't even go near what I was feeling. I'd been not only sitting next to but also going out with the female equivalent of Machiavelli for the last few months.

'If you're planning to rig the election next year or plotting a coup you'd let me know wouldn't you?' I asked, not entirely sure I was joking.

'Look,' she continued, 'we wanted to get Oroco Oil back as a client?'

'Yes.'

'And we wanted Martin back with Olivia.'

'Yes. Though that was only so we could get Oroco Oil as a client again?'

'You think?'

I thought. I realised that between them, Karen and Olivia had in effect used a multi million pound account so Olivia could get her man, while shafting (in the nicest possible meaning of the word) her boss and taking his job. I'd reckoned I'd pulled a fast one getting Randy J. Feckenburger (the Third) to pay me redundancy after I'd already got another job but that was nothing compared to this. Karen smiled engagingly, as Machiavelli probably did as well.

'So we all got what we wanted! What's wrong with that?'

I spent the rest of the day totting up the score and trying to calm my squirming scruples.

A) Martin was getting married to Olivia. (Good; I suppose)

B) Oroco Oil was our account again and our jobs were as secure as they ever could be. (Very good. In fact excellent result.)

C) Some guy I'd never heard of had been removed from his job but had got another, apparently better paid one. (Fine. Still something I wasn't happy about there; maybe I have too delicate a conscience…)

My phone rang it was Nick the Bastard. He was like a breath of fresh foul-mouthed air after all these machinations.

'Faaacking hell Denis! I've lost another faaacking presentation I'm doing to those faaackers at ITV tomorrow. I'm in the faaacking shit if I've lost it - can you come down and have a look for me, mate?'

'Gladly Nick! See you in a minute!'

Chapter Thirty Seven

The End of the Affair.

One dark December afternoon, a couple of weeks after the dinner party, I'd just been down to Nick the Bastard's desk in response to a panicked call from the mad bugger. Somehow, yet again, he'd managed to lose all the information in a critical spreadsheet. I sorted his problem and he was effusive in his thanks, even offering me "a go on the girlfriend" if I fancied it. I declined his kind invitation. I got back to our office, Karen looked up, 'It's been a long day, fancy a drink?'

'Why not? I'll see if Martin's about.'

'No, just us. Let's go over to the Warwick.'

Snow was beginning to fall as we left and even the hard outlines of Oxford Street softened as we walked through the evening. I held her hand and looked at her face as we walked. She always had a look of seriousness bordering on intensity but tonight there was something else.

'Karen, I love you. You know that don't you?

She didn't answer. The snow made the world silent but it was her silence that caused a flash of fear to surge through me. Then she smiled up at me, her diamond eyes sparkling.

'I know. Come on it's bloody freezing.

Pushing the door open I held it so she slipped underneath my arm into the warmth of the Warwick. I went to the bar, she found a table and after being served I sat down beside her.

'Quiet for a Friday?' she commented

'The snow I suppose. OK so what's up?

'Nothing's up!'

'But you didn't want Martin or any of the others along so I suspect you have something to tell me and it's probably not good news.'

'Don't worry It's not about us! Well it is about us but no, really we're fine. Aren't we?'

'Yes Karen, as far as I know we are fine.'

'I love you.'

'Good! I love you too.'

There was a silence as I thought about all the protestations of love that had just been bandied about. There was still a nagging doubt though at the back, front and side of my mind as I drank my pint and glanced at Karen. She took an uncharacteristically large swig of wine.

'OK. I'd better tell you... I've got another job. With BHJ.'

'What? I didn't know you were going for another job!'

'Nor did I. They came after me!' she replied with a look of pride or indeed smugness.

'Wow!'

'It was after the Buy-O-Soft pitch – they really liked the whole presentation I put together.'

'And I guess they're going to be paying a whole lot better than JDFT?'

'Oh yes. You don't move jobs for less than a 30% increase. Fifty per cent in fact is the exact figure.

'Wow!" I was impressed.

'OK that's two wows in quick succession - you're only allowed three in an entire evening so be warned!'

She paused for a moment.

'Aren't you upset?'

'What? That you've just landed a better job at half as much money again?'

'We won't be working together any more. You know I thought about that a lot before I accepted.'

'I hadn't got that far – you think a lot quicker than I do.'

'I've had more time.'

'That's true. I'll miss working with you but provided we're OK I'll manage. Maybe it's healthier for us not to be together all day, every day.'

'Maybe.' she mused. I could tell she wasn't convinced. Nor was I.

'But?'

'No buts. Just stay away from Kelly in Accounts when I'm gone.'

'I'll do my best.' Then I hugged her and raised my pint 'Hey, I'm sorry! Here's to your new job – congratulations!'

'Thanks.' she said quietly.

'You're supposed to be all sparky and full of new job excitement - what's up?'

'It's just the thing is… well the thing is… y'see… the thing is.'

'OK - do you want to do this in charades - it probably wouldn't take as long? Start with the thing and what it is.'

'It's just…'

'You've said that already.'

'Shut up! I'm trying to say something difficult!'

A few workers from the other offices nearby were filing in, shaking snow from their coats. Looking out I watched the flakes filling the sky and swirling against the big window at the front of the pub.

'I don't want to go.' she whispered.

'Then don't. No one's forcing you.'

'But I can't turn this down.'

I thought some clarification was necessary.

'OK if we weren't together, would you be thinking this?'

'Probably not… No. I don't know. It's not just that. I like JDFT. The people. Martin. You.'

I thought about this for a moment.

'I like the way you separated those! No, Martin's a good guy. A few flaws but yeah. It's a good place. And now that Eric's gone the human factor has risen. A lot. Has that helped?'

'No. I'm more confused than ever.'

'Thought you might be. Another wine?'

'No need to be so critical I'm trying to make a difficult decision.'

'Very funny.'

Turning back Karen leant against me, slipping an arm round my waist and we kissed for several seconds, oblivious to the world.

'Wow!' I said, without thinking.

Karen glared at me.

'OK that's three! I'm taking you home for your punishment!

We stayed in bed late the next morning, finally emerging from our duvet to a London dressed in white and serene after more heavy snow. I thought how a JDFT without Karen would be a very different place. As I was musing on this, the phone rang. It was, of all people, Caroline.

'Good morning Denis, sorry afternoon I mean,' she enthused. 'Isn't the snow wonderful?'

'Yes, lovely. Uh oh. Are you in the office? Is there a computer problem?'

'Denis! I'm not a reincarnation of Eric! No I actually wanted to speak to Karen. I've heard a nasty rumour that she's thinking of leaving…'

'Who told you that?'

'Greg mentioned it yesterday.'

'But she's only just told me and no one else at JDFT knows.'

'Greg has eyes and ears in other companies as well. I presume she's there with you?'

'She is... how did you know she'd be here?'

'I have my sources...'

'Greg again by any chance?'

'Of course! Anyway may I speak with her?'

I handed over the phone and went off to make tea which seemed like the right thing to do. I tried listening in to the conversation but could just hear a muffled blur of sound from the bedroom. The phone went down followed by suspicious quiet. I pushed open the bedroom door with my foot. Karen was sitting up in the bed, knees pulled up and her head on them.

'What's up?' I asked putting a cup down on the table beside her.

'Bad news...'

'What sort of bad news? Eric's returned as a zombie?'

'No... I'm not leaving JDFT.'

'What?'

'You could be a bit more pleased!'

'I go out to make tea and you change your career plans! I'm... wow!'

'Watch it!'

'So what happened?'

'Caroline's just offered me the same money as BHJ to stay!'

'Bloody hell! Fantastic! I know she values you but well... brilliant!'

'Whatever you do, don't try copywriting.' Karen advised.

'I thought that was quite articulate considering. If you think about it that kind of seals it all.'

She stopped sipping tea, put her cup down on the side and leant against me.

'What do you mean?'

'Well, Olivia and Martin are back. We're together and you've blagged a massive salary rise...'

'I did not blag that - it was down to hard work!'

'Anyway Oroco Oil are back in the fold so all's well.'

As I watched snowflakes touch the window then drift on towards the ground, Wilson made a dramatic and sudden entry through the cat flap. Entering the bedroom he was licking his chops and looking back at the door. The shifty git glanced at us as though to say, "If anyone asks, I've been here all the time."

Then he jumped up onto the bed and stared at both of us in turn.

'That little bastard's been stealing again.' I commented.

'I wonder how Parky's doing?' Karen said while scratching the thieving miscreant behind his ear. I hadn't thought of our former colleague for a while.

'Yeah! It's a shame. You work with people, get to know them, then they just drift off and you never see or hear of them again. I bet those tourists are thinking exactly the same thing at this moment,' I reminisced thoughtfully.

Karen leant her head on me and said, 'Cheer up - how about lunch at the Crown?'

'Brilliant idea! I can see why Caroline values you so much!'

I hugged her until she started making what might have been asphyxiation noises.

Epilogue

It was probably a year later, possibly October but definitely
before the pubs opened because Martin was at his desk. I was
telling him about a supplier who had delivered the wrong
hardware but I could tell he wasn't really engaged; the big give
away being the BBC news website reflected in his glasses.
Suddenly like a hunting dog that's noticed some very tasty
game, he rose from his usual slouch and became intently
focused on the screen.

'No! I don't believe it!'

He began laughing manically which caused Karen and me
some concern for his tentative grip on sanity.

'What? What's happened?'

'You are not going to fucking believe this! Listen to this!'

He turned the sound up. A BBC reporter with a Scottish
accent was on air.

"After a rollercoaster year for the Church of England, today's
announcement that the new Archbishop of Canterbury is to be a
young man from the valleys of Wales who made his name in
software before taking holy orders, adds to the sense of a
church renewing itself and embracing the modern world.
Speaking at a Lambeth Palace press conference, Bishop
Parkinson says his appointment is both "amazing and exciting"
and something he never expected although apparently he did

put a large bet on it some time ago. The nomination has been approved by the Queen, the Supreme Governor of the Church of England, Lambeth Palace confirms. A surprise choice for the job perhaps, having only been a Bishop for a few months, Archbishop Parkinson is, in a very real sense, a gamble for the Establishment.'

'He can say that again!' I asserted in disbelief.

Martin glanced at me; I looked at Karen. She stared at Martin.

'You didn't have anything to do with this as well did you?' I checked with her.

'No - I know my limitations...'

'Holy shit!' I muttered.

'Exactly!' commented Martin. 'Prince of Wales seems to be an appropriate place for a celebration!'

'Chimay and Green Chartreuse all round!' I said as I sat still rooted to my chair, unable to believe what we'd just heard. I picked up a laptop which bore all the hall marks of Nick the Bastard's handiwork. Somehow he'd managed to detach the built in keyboard, the screen was torn and there were strange marks on it which looked as though they could be dried bodily fluids. Dropping it into a nearby bin I emailed an order for a new one to our supplier and stood up to get my coat. At that moment the phone rang. A voice I recognized from somewhere in my past whispered, 'Can you listen?'

Interesting philosophical question I thought. And looking at Karen there was only one possible answer. I put the phone down on the mystery caller.

'Who was that?' Karen asked nosily.

'Wrong number. Now, who mentioned "the Prince of Wales"?'

THE END

This edition of first published in Great Britain and the United States of America in 2014 as a Kindle download and paperback published by CreateSpace.

copyright © 2014 Mial Pagan

Mial Pagan has asserted his rights to be identified as the author of this work.

This is a work of fiction. Names, characters, places and incidents are either products of the author's imagination or are used fictitiously. Any resemblance to actual events, locales, persons or cats, living or dead, is entirely coincidental.

Acknowledgements:

Many thanks to James Butler for a great cover design.

To the exquisitely named "Australian Beers" website for the (slightly adapted) title of the novel.
http://www.australianbeers.com/culture/bastard.htm

To all the creative, talented ones in the advertising and software industries who made it fun.

6413277R10224

Printed in Great Britain
by Amazon.co.uk, Ltd.,
Marston Gate.